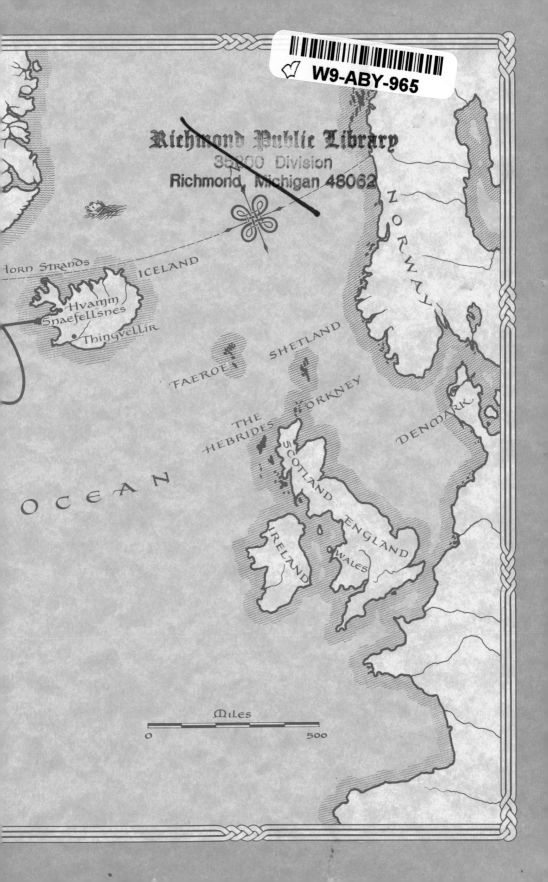

NORWAY

Horn Strands

ICELAND

Hvamm
Snaefellsnes
Thingvellir

SHETLAND

FAEROES

ORKNEY

DENMARK

THE
HEBRIDES

SCOTLAND

OCEAN

ENGLAND

IRELAND

WALES

MILES

0   500

A VIKING'S DAUGHTER

John Andrews

Doubleday

NEW YORK   LONDON   TORONTO   SYDNEY   AUCKLAND

PUBLISHED BY DOUBLEDAY

a division of
Bantam Doubleday Dell Publishing Group, Inc.
666 Fifth Avenue, New York, New York 10103

DOUBLEDAY and the portrayal of an anchor with a dolphin
are trademarks of Doubleday, a division of Bantam Doubleday Dell
Publishing Group, Inc.

Library of Congress Cataloging-in-Publication Data

Andrews, John, 1941–
    A Viking's daughter / John Andrews. —1st ed.
        p.   cm.
    ISBN 0-385-24971-3
    1. Vikings—Fiction.   I. Title.
PS3551.N4277V55   1989   88-31536
813'.54—dc19   CIP

TO CAROL,

AND FOR KRISTIN,

WHEN SHE IS A LITTLE OLDER.

Acknowledgments

I thank Marijane Meaker and the members of the Ashawagh Hall Writers' Workshop, without whose advice and support I could not have finished this book. I would also like to acknowledge my debt to the many who have written about the Vikings and the Vinland adventure.

Author's Note

This book is based on the lives of real people who lived and strove on the far shores of the North Atlantic a thousand years ago. We know something about them from two Icelandic sagas that describe the exploration of Western lands by Norse people, beginning with Erik the Red's discovery of Greenland about A.D. 985 and culminating with the attempt by Thorfinn Karlsefni and his wife Gudrid to found a colony in Vinland (North America) some years—perhaps decades—later.

We also know, from Helge Ingstad's discovery in 1960 of a Norse settlement in northern Newfoundland, that they really did reach North America. I am fortunate enough to have visited the site, at the end of a three-hundred-mile dirt road, in 1972, when the archaeological digs were covered by rough sheds and the signs informing visitors of what they were seeing were still written with marking pen on brown paper bags. More recently, the Canadian government has established a historic site there, with reconstructions of the settlers' houses.

I also had the good fortune, many years later, to visit Iceland and walk beneath the dark cliff of Thingvellir in a driving rain. It was not hard to visualize the Lawspeaker calling out in a loud voice the third of the law that it was his duty each year to recite.

The conflict between Christianity and the old Norse religion is a major theme of the story. Many viewpoints are represented, few motivated entirely by considerations of theology, but all had to contend with the inexorable northward sweep of the new Faith: the conversion of Denmark in 965, of Poland in 966, the baptism of Prince Vladimir of Russia in 988. King Olaf Tryggvason introduced Christianity to Norway in the closing years of the first millennium, after unsuccessful attempts by Hakon the Good and Harald Greycloak in earlier decades. Closer to the scene of our story, Iceland was converted in 1000 in dramatic fashion when the chieftains left it to the Lawspeaker to decide, and he lay under his cloak for a day and a night thinking the matter through. Even before the conversion of a whole people, whether peacefully, as in Iceland, or by force, as happened elsewhere, individuals would take the Faith onto themselves. Thus, we hear of Aud the Deep-Minded, a Christian when all around her were pagan, planting crosses on the hills and ordering her own burial between the high and the low tide so that she might not have to lie in unconsecrated ground.

I have borrowed many people and incidents from the Sagas: Erik the Red and his family; Gudrid and her father; Thorfinn Karlsefni; and lesser actors like Arnora, Orm and Halldis, Einar, the Sibyl of Herjolfsnes, and the Skraeling woman at the door in Vinland. This is, however, a work of fiction—a novel, not a history. Where the Sagas give information about someone's personality, I have usually followed their lead. In other cases, Thorstein Eriksson, for example, I felt free to imagine characters to go with the names handed down to us by the skalds.

These names themselves were sometimes a problem: too many of them begin with Thor for any reader to follow without a chart. I therefore changed the name of Gudrid's father from Thorbjorn to Bjorn and of her second husband from Thorfinn to Torfin. Freydis' husband Thorvard was dealt with by simply referring to him as Freydis' husband. Thorkel of Herjolfsnes became Durkel. The one remaining, Thorstein, I left alone.

One of the most fascinating things about the Sagas is that, although they are ostensibly about what the men did, they go out of their way to tell us a great deal about the women. The more one reads about the life of the Norse people, the more one realizes what a strong role the women played, not unlike the pioneer days in the American West.

For one of these women, Gudrid Thorbjornsdottir, I have long felt an enchantment akin to love. She has told me her story, and she thanks you, the reader, for listening.

Sag Harbor, New York
July 1988

A Viking's Daughter

From the Saga of Erik the Red

There was a warrior king called Olaf the White, who married Aud the Deep-Minded, the daughter of Ketil Flat-Nose, and they had a son. Olaf was killed in battle in Ireland. Aud and her son went to the Hebrides. They formed an alliance with Earl Sigurd the Powerful, and conquered Caithness, Sutherland, Ross, Moray, and most of Argyll. Then the Scots rose and killed her son.

Aud was in Caithness then. She ordered a ship to be built, by stealth, in the woods, and she sailed to Iceland with twenty freeborn men. She claimed a great section of the Dales between two rivers; her home she made at Hvamm. She was a Christian, and had crosses erected on the hills . . .

One of Aud's men was named Vifil. Vifil married and had two sons. His younger son had a beautiful daughter named Gudrid, a most accomplished woman . . .

1.

In the midst of Corn-Cutting Month a raven flew over the hall of Bjorn Vifilsson. The house stood against the sky, high up the slope of a long, open valley that reached down to the sea. The bird paused in its flight, uttered a cut-short cry, then continued on up the dale.

A woman was deep in thought as she tended the herbs in her little plot on the sun-facing side of the house. Now, with difficulty, she rose to catch sight of the raven, hoping it was no evil omen for the child stirring within her.

The season was late. The sheep were already down from the high places, little dots of white in the golden pastures. Her hand went to her belly. The baby made a sudden movement in response to her touch.

The suddenness of the pain shocked her. She fell to her knees. She tried to cheer herself with thoughts of spells she might weave, though she was yet a novice in the sisterhood of those who would be wise in the ways of spirits and of men. This brought to mind Arnora, her sister, who had taught her the little she knew.

The pain left her then, but she knew her time was near, and she stumbled along the wall to the door and so entered the house.

"Mistress?" She heard a voice in the gloom, lit only by a peat fire and an open-wick lamp set in the wall. A few glimmers made their way in through two small windows set high, near the peak, at the gable ends. She recognized the voice as one of the servant girls'.

"Where is the over-sitting-woman?" she asked, anxiety high in her voice.

"She's been sent for." The girl seemed not to know how insufficient this answer was.

The woman sank to her haunches as another pain came on. The girls, three of them, eased her back onto a pallet of straw. One ran out to watch for the midwife and hurry her on.

To distract her mind she looked about the house, familiar now through two years and more of marriage: the wooden platforms running the length of each wall, on which people ate, slept, and got children; the earthen space between the platforms, where the hearth fires were laid; the double row of posts supporting the roof; the high seats on the dais. Her husband had gone to great lengths to build himself a dwelling that would be worthy of comment.

The pains came again and again, and she struggled to maintain control. She wanted a practiced hand at her side. What did these slave girls know about birthing?

At length the door opened. "Welcome, Light-Mother," a relieved voice whispered. The midwife spoke in soothing low tones and beckoned the girls to bring cups of water and cold, wet cloths. Her hands probed the woman's belly, seeking to know all that might be known that would help her as the birth came on.

Suddenly the pains seized her more tightly, stretched to bursting, and they were no longer moving. Fear caught her breath and broke the barrier she had built up so carefully against the swelling agony. Even the fingers probing between her legs betrayed worry. A wave of pain only a little worse than the others came before she was ready for it, and all control was lost. The woman screamed. It was as if her gut were being torn apart by some clawed beast. Again and again the beast ripped at her, and again and again she screamed. But the pain only became more like the claws of a beast, and though it pierced through to her backbone, it did not move.

Time passed, interminable time. The girls weaved back and forth on minor errands, while the midwife's face hung in the glow of the lamp like the moon.

Slowly, like the being that had formed in her womb and was now struggling to free itself, an idea formed in the woman's mind. "The baby resists. She will not be born." The women were all around her, the midwife no longer trying to hide her fear. The door opened and someone came and went. The bright flash betrayed that it was again morning, as the slivers of light from the peak windows had not.

Fear possessed her now, for she well knew that many women did not live through a birthing. Even more did she fear for her child, and she was overwhelmed with love for this little one she had never seen and who was causing her such pain. She would not see the child born dead.

"You must cut it out," she said to the midwife. "It can wait no longer."

The reply was a whisper. "I have known for some time that this would be necessary. It is not a thing that I would do unbidden. It will be done quickly."

"I want to see the baby."

"That would be much the worse for you. I beg you let me shorten your suffering."

"No. I want to see the baby before I die. I want to remember her in the spirit world."

The midwife breathed out slowly. "As you wish." Even now the girls were tying the woman's arms and legs to holes in the platform.

"There is one more thing," said the woman. "My chest, in the bed closet. Open it and bring it here."

Her right hand, yet unbound, searched through the small jewelled box. She lifted out an amulet, a strange milky stone that had the shape of a hammer in it, encircled by a snake. The stone was set in a pendant of gold and suspended on a golden chain.

"Place this around the child's neck, if it is a girl," she said. "If it is a boy, see my sister gets it. And see that no man touches it—evil will strike him if he does. Remember that, and make sure my husband knows it."

"Dear foster daughter," the midwife said, tears running down her face, "I will do as you ask. But why?"

7

"It will protect the girl. My sister must come now. It was hers . . ." The lamp sputtered and went out.

Another pain washed over, and the woman allowed her arm to be bound. The midwife raised the knife, like a shadow in the glow of the fire, and in one quick motion she slit the belly from the breast to below the navel. The bound body jerked in a spasm but gave forth no sound. Then she slit the sac, and the woman felt blood and what remained of the water gushing out. The midwife's hands went deftly in, trying to make the pain as little as possible but knowing it to be great nevertheless.

Then the woman—a mother now—heard the cry, and she opened her eyes to see the little face still tied to the cord. My daughter, she thought, and she smiled. It was her last thought, as the midwife used her knife once again. One of the slave girls retched into the fire.

Seven days later Bjorn Vifilsson, sitting in his high seat, lifted the baby girl up over his head. His sister-in-law Arnora sat opposite. Bjorn had taken great care to see that the amulet was tucked inside the baby's inner wrap before he took her into his hands. Arnora had confirmed the dire prediction concerning the fate of any man who touched it. All the household were seated round, and guests from nearby farms, in places appropriate to their rank.

Bjorn spoke the words that signified his acceptance of the baby into his household. All were aware that the choice was his to make, that he could have had the child exposed to die, and none could have gainsaid him. "You shall be called Gudrid," he said, and he sprinkled water onto her forehead in a ceremony as old as the gods. "Odinn, watch her. Thor, protect her. And Freyja, see her grow well to womanhood."

Gudrid let out a piercing cry and would not stop, and Bjorn gratefully handed her to Arnora. Gudrid wailed louder. Arnora carried her out into the afternoon light and up the hill to her mother's burial place. Gudrid stopped crying, abruptly, and save for the twitter of a lark, all became strangely quiet.

Arnora pulled the amulet from under the baby's wrap and held it out over the mother's grave. The little bird hopped about on one leg, then fluttered away. After a while she slid the stone back, next to the baby's skin, turned away from the dead, and walked back to the house and the living.

2.

Far to the west, over a driftless sea, the mist parted. The air that had been fixed above the water stirred itself, puffs gathering to gusts, foam sparkles rousing waves over dim submerged whales. Then in a rush toward the land, it sent surf crashing, calling black cliffs down to boulders, seal-burdened. Cantilevered upward, snaking through shimmering grass, hurtling ravines, the wind eddied among houses and barns, bearing away beast-breath. Starting again, it parted the red-dyed heath, rising to seek the shadow of a dark bird.

"The girl's spooked o' the raven." Sigunna had been watching from the low fence built of turf. Now she swept Gudrid onto her broad lap, holding the sparrowlike body close to her breast.

"She should be." The other woman's voice startled; the girl had not seen her approach. "Come."

Gudrid turned to Arnora, held by her she-hawk eyes, and she stirred herself to obey, though her left hand clung to Sigunna's breast brooch. "Hold me, Unni," she said, and Sigunna drew her close for an instant and then released her.

Arnora took Gudrid roughly by the hand. "The sun is in the northwest already, and I've been waiting for you at the herb plot. You're eight years old, and you still haven't learned the leaf stems and the roots that grow there. You spend your time with this woman, making cheese, and playing foolish games with the little boys. They'll rule you some day if you won't learn, and you the head man's daughter, kin to Queen Aud. I wouldn't waste my time with you if it weren't for that."

In the morning Sigunna brought porridge to Gudrid and to Hakon, Runolf's son, and Mord, the son of Floki. Taking the bowl, she mouthed the warm spoonfuls as once she had mouthed Unni's breasts. Then, flinging aside her nightshift, she threw on her dayclothes, her red-brown shift of fine linen and her blue cape, bordered with a rich pattern weave. She jumped to the platform and ran out the door, hair gathered behind, the color of straw. She ran across the courtyard, stirring dogs to barking, and up the hillside, through yellow poppy fields. Higher and higher she climbed, so that the farm seemed a child's toy below her, higher than Hakon ever had gone, Hakon, whose eyes were bright as Mord's were empty and dark.

For the first time in her life she saw the immensity of the world, the blue of the sea meeting the sky, the black and white of rock and ice rising steeply behind her. A desire was kindled in her, a need for power to ward off the portents that sprang forth from every thing.

She ran down the hill to break the spell, until again in the courtyard she knew that she was under a greater restraint, as her father passed by, helmet-headed, mast-tall.

The frenzy left her then, and she was a little girl again, going to Unni for comfort and love. Sigunna's own child had been stillborn, and she'd come to Bjorn's hall to take Gudrid up as foster suckling. It was only to have been for a time, but Sigunna had stayed.

It would be easy for Gudrid to surrender her will, as she had seen the old thrall Fionna let go her final breath. She saw herself drifting through her years, like sea wrack swept by the tide, and it seemed she must give herself over to the rhythms of the world, of tides and storms, of the moon's phases, of sungoing and sunreturn, and of the lunar current that would one day flow within her own body, making it quick for new life.

Then again she would face the center of herself, feeling the anguish of her smallness, the craving to hold the staff in her hand, the yearning to see. A voice unspoken bade her resist the winds of the world that swept all life to dusk and dust. She would go to Arnora and show her resolve.

"Mother's Sister, you've never been kind to me, but you've taught me many things. This came from you too." She pulled the amulet from her clothing and held it out. The woman touched it. "Teach me more. I'm not as stupid as you say I am, and you know it. You knew that my mother would die and that I'd get this charm."

"You've spoken up well, girl. I can tell you now. Your amulet has a secret, a secret you must discover if you are to have your heart's desire." She stood, a fixed expression on her face. "I will teach you. But don't smile too broadly. You will suffer for your understanding."

Gudrid did not hear the end of this speech. She jumped up and, almost dancing, swirled around Arnora like a blown leaf.

3.

At first they saw neither the man nor his horse coming over the rise just beyond the courtyard. Then the horse whinnied. Gudrid looked up, and Arnora turned around sharply. Gudrid felt her teacher's stiffening, and fear grabbed her also, forcing her breath out. The man was alone, but he was dressed for battle. His head was covered by a round metal helmet. A finely wrought guardplate covered all of his face but his beard and the deep sockets of his eyes. His heavy leather jerkin was covered with chain mail.

Then she sensed something familiar about the curly beard and the hair that fell down below the lip of the helmet, darker than that of most men, something she recognized in his stocky frame and big-boned arms and hands that propelled her from Arnora's side to the ground beside the horse and made her reach up toward the saddle, to the one man who could make her smile.

"Orm! Orm!" she cried out in delight.

Orm. The girl's thoughts ran back to the dark hollows of earliest memory, back to a time when fear had held her and he had released her from it. The source of the fear was Floki, Mord's father. Floki looked more like her father than any other man. Perhaps that was why, when he'd stopped to hug her in the bright sunlight, she'd been glad for his notice, closing her eyes and pretending it was Bjorn who loved her. It meant little to her that sometimes in the fog he'd run his hands up under the wool of her shift.

Then had come the strange kisses, his tongue like a fish in her mouth, and later he'd taken her into the byre. In the stall on the far end, spread with fresh straw, he'd undressed her, spreading his big hands over her small body, and he'd called her Freyja-Sma, his little goddess.

She didn't understand at first, didn't know to protest, but then Floki's attentions became more frequent, more insistent, and once he'd slapped her when she cried. "Don't tell Sigunna," he'd ordered. "I'll kill her if you do."

Summer bore on. Floki's fingers became more curious. Afterward it would hurt to go to the privy.

Autumn brought shivering cold along with more shame; but Floki was not ashamed, nor did the cold deter him. He undressed himself then as well as her, flexing his muscles and telling her to lick his nipples, and he lay down on his back with her on top of him, pressing her legs together so that their soft skin enfolded his hardness. He moved her on it until she felt the wetness on her thighs, and smelled the salt-sweet smell that she remembered from winter nights when everyone, even the lately wed, slept close together.

She'd desperately wanted Floki to stop. Even though the pain was less than before, it hurt more inside.

Orm had appeared like a god out of the sky, terrible in his anger. Floki had at first been too surprised to speak, but then he grasped his sword and swung it in frenzy, not caring where it might strike as long as one stroke reached Orm. Orm drove at him with his knife, forcing Floki to the ground and pinning him with the blade against his throat.

She hadn't understood then, but did now, how Orm had risked his life to save hers, though he knew Floki to be Bjorn's best swordsman.

Orm had to let Floki go, but Floki never touched Gudrid after that.

Orm reached down now and pulled Gudrid up and held her. Removing his helmet, he kissed her on the forehead and tickled her face with his beard. She reached for the helmet and began to knock her fist against it, harder and harder until she hurt her knuckles and made a wry face. Bjorn's men had by this time recognized him. A thrall took the horse's reins, and Sigunna ran out to retrieve Gudrid.

Full of excitement, Gudrid pulled away from her and raced into the hall, not far behind Orm, so that the heavy wooden door almost closed on her as she darted in.

Bjorn happened to be at home, seated on a stool next to the fire, gnawing on a joint of meat he'd demanded of a maidservant, though it was nowhere near time for dinner. The glimmer of the lamp shone against the oiled hardwood paneling behind him. He rose to greet Orm, towering over the visitor by more than a foot, while the latter blinked to accustom his eyes to the smoky dimness.

"I came fast as I could," said Orm, leaning on a dais post and gulping air between words. "Erik's banished. They're after him through the islands."

"Thor's balls! I've let him down." Bjorn pitched the joint into the fire, sending sparks flying and a pungent cloud of smoke swirling into the room. He sank back onto his stool and held his head in his hands. "I've been to every Althing since I was a boy. I had to pick this year to stay home!"

Orm stepped closer to Bjorn and would have put his hand on the taller man's shoulder. He was a free man, with a good farm, and he'd married well enough, but he was by no means Bjorn's equal. Nevertheless, he tried to speak reassuringly.

"Erik told you not to go. He said he'd enough friends there, and you had trouble here."

"Everyone knows how many of my sheep have died. I'll be a poor man if I can't rebuild my flocks. But a friend who needs my help is more important than sheep!"

Bjorn rose and rushed out of the house, nearly knocking Gudrid over and brushing aside Sigunna, who had come inside to take the girl in tow.

He was shouting now. "Asgrim! Floki! Knut! Runolf!"

These were not the names of thralls; they were men who sat around him at table morning and evening. Even Gudrid could sense that something important was going on when he shouted this way to men of rank.

Three of the four came running. One cuffed a thrall. "Get Floki! In the high field. Run!"

Bjorn shouted louder. "Get every man who can swing a sword into this courtyard with his best horse, armed and ready to go!"

Gudrid stood in a corner of the yard, watching the rush of men and horses. Young women stood about, preening, smiling, craning their necks and waving to the warriors. Older ones hung their heads. A thrall brought Bjorn's helmet and leather battle jerkin and helped him put on his coat of mail. Another brought his horse. Bjorn stood impatiently, eager to go, shifting from one foot to the other and shouting orders.

Mord did a little war dance with his toy axe, waving it about in a way he must have thought resembled the heroics of a champion but that to Gudrid were no more than the antics of a fool. She would have left him alone, but he insisted on prancing in front of her. She lunged at him and grappled for the axe, and she was sure she could have taken it, had Floki not dragged his boy away.

Orm came over. He picked Gudrid up and hugged her, and the girl smiled and felt again the warm feeling that no other man had ever called up in her.

He spoke, however, to Sigunna.

"It's bad this time. Every man from here to the Dales is in it." He shook his head. "Erik's not got the men."

Sigunna broke in. "This man Erik. Is he the one they call 'the Red'?"

"Aye, the Redbeard, that's the one. The red's for the color of his hair, but might's well be for blood. Bjorn's got to help him, but Erik'll be lucky to get out of Iceland before they catch him."

Bjorn called to Orm. "How is it in Arnarstapi? Will your kin be safe there?"

"My neighbors don't care about Erik. But the Froda men down coast are all on him, and they've got the berserk there. We're all moved up to Stapafell. The men'll meet us on the Haukadale track."

"What's a ber . . . ?" Before Gudrid could finish her question, Orm was off to attend to his horse. She followed him with frightened eyes.

Bjorn turned away also, intending to hasten a crew of thralls who were throwing provisions onto the backs of some packhorses. Arnora stood directly in his path.

"You'll leave us to the mercy of whoever comes by, then."

Bjorn's helmet tilted at the angle his head always took when he was angered. "You're safe enough here. You've got a strong house with a stout door, and I'm leaving you seven armed men."

"Old men. They haven't fought in years."

"We'll be back before anyone knows we're gone," Bjorn said with finality. He pushed past her.

Gudrid could see that Arnora was right. There was no protection here worth speaking of, and wasn't Froda within a day's ride? Hadn't Orm taken his kinfolk to a hole in a cliff for protection?

She tried to speak. "Father . . ." Bjorn looked to his daughter, but she could not continue. Though his eyes were dark in shadow behind the nosepiece of his helmet, she remembered the many times he had looked at her, and she remembered the strangeness of his eyes, always the same, whether in the dim light of a lamp or the bright light of a summer afternoon. It was a look of pain, that much she knew, but more was in it than that. It was a look that said, "Stay away, as far away as you can manage, living in the same house as we must."

Bjorn removed his helmet and set one knee on the ground to look her in the eye. "My honor demands I defend Erik with every man I have." His face twisted to a knot. He spoke under his breath, so that Gudrid could not be sure he wished her to hear him. "You should know this more than anyone. Every time I look at you, I see the woman's curse."

Curse? she thought. No one, not even Arnora, had ever said anything like this. She barely knew what a curse was, but she did know it came unseen and did no one any good. Did she look cursed, that Bjorn could see it in her face? She'd always been told she was a pretty girl. She wanted to ask Bjorn what he meant, but by the time her mind framed the question, he had stood and was gone.

Orm came over to say farewell. His hand spanned her shoulders, drawing her to him. She would not let him see her cry.

The tumult went up again and did not subside until the men were ready to go. The procession, twelve, fifteen men, left the courtyard, led by Bjorn, who seemed as if he could pluck the sun from the sky. Gudrid would remember the sight of his blue cape fluttering in the wind as he led the others away from the farm, down the hill toward the sea. And she noticed that at the last moment Runolf and Floki lifted their small sons up to their saddles and kept them there as they rode away. A hush fell over the women left in the courtyard and the only sounds were the rushing of the wind and the barking of a dog on the hillside.

Now began the time of waiting, the quiet time, the fearful time with mostly women about, thralls, and old men. Sigunna was especially uneasy, and she spoke her fear.

"What'll we do if them's come from Froda or one of the other places up coast? They're all up against Erik, it's sure."

"It's no surprise," another woman interjected. "Erik brought this on himself. Who does he think he is? His father just came from Norway, and now he gets about the best farm in Haukadale by marriage to a woman whom luck gave no brothers! You'd think he'd have the sense not to start trouble until he'd got some friends, but a man like him seems to prefer enemies. I wish Bjorn hadn't felt so obligated. I know something's going to happen this time."

"Hush that kind of talk," a third said. "We can't do anything about it. There's no point in making folk more uneasy than they need to be."

Gudrid pulled Arnora aside. "Has someone cursed me?"

"I heard your father too." Arnora sat down to face Gudrid, lowering herself to the girl's level in an unaccustomed way. "I know most of the sibyls of Snaefellsnes and Haukadale. I don't know anything about this curse."

Night passed, with the door bolted shut and everyone, except the thralls, sleeping in the main hall, the few men with their weapons, long unused, at the ready beside them. Then day came, and lookouts were posted on the hills, and night again, so that a week went by in this way without incident. Several nights Gudrid awoke in terror, but Sigunna would rise from her sleeping place and go over to the little box bed and pull her close. Gudrid would gaze blankly past the embers into the shadows until sleep returned.

Enough time had now passed that all began to look for the return of Bjorn and the other men of the estate. The women had resumed their incessant spinning, and the three looms again clanked in an alcove at the far end of the hall. We're short of yarn, one said, her manner suggesting that Gudrid might design to take up a spindle, but she would have none of it. Pouting, she hurried the length of the great room, which was empty of people this time of day, and ran outside.

She was about to go to Arnora in the herb garden when she heard the shouts, far away and muted in the wind. Then she saw the lookouts running down the hill. "Bjorn's coming," someone shouted. Even at a distance Gudrid could see enough of the men's faces to know it was not Bjorn. Their words became more distinct as they approached.

"Run! Run!"

Arnora jumped up quickly and shouted to Gudrid. "Come with me! Now!"

Gudrid saw Sigunna at the door and she dragged Arnora to a stop, holding out her other hand. "Unni! Come with us!"

Arnora would not wait. She jerked Gudrid along with a strength that seemed beyond her spare frame. Gudrid tore away from her grasp and looked back to Sigunna.

The cause of the lookouts' fear could be seen now, their helmets coming into view as they gained the crest of the little rise that separated the farm from the concavity of the valley. They came on a run, axes raised, and their voices were beating out a rhythmic chant.

"Horfa-Hefna! Horfa-Hefna! See! Revenge! See! Revenge!"

Arnora reached the end of the row of barns and called back. Gudrid waited for Sigunna to catch up with her. She pulled on the heavier woman's hand, trying to move her even a little faster.

They clambered up the hillside. Arnora ran ahead, the folds of her garments in her hands. Gudrid followed her example. Sigunna was not so deft. Her foot caught her woolen overgarment. The brooches came loose from the shoulder straps, and the green rectangles, front and back, began to slip away. Sigunna clutched at them, as if the preservation of her dignity were more important than the saving of her life. Arnora was halfway to the slope of strewn boulders at the bottom of a cliff when one of the attackers saw them and started up.

"Run faster, Unni," Gudrid pleaded, but Sigunna was gasping loudly. "Get away, Gudrid. Go." Her face was pleading, and she pushed the girl's hand as she stopped to catch her breath. Arnora had made the edge of the talus and was shouting down.

For a moment Gudrid stood desperately still, looking up and then back. Sigunna remained motionless, only her face and her hands communicating her plea that Gudrid should leave her. The man was racing toward them, his shouts carried up by the wind.

They reached the grassy slope beyond the rockslide just as the axeman came to the near side. Sigunna was struggling over the rocks, barely a third of the way across. The man leaped out onto the slope and bounded from boulder to boulder. Gudrid started back, then hesitated. She looked to the seeress to do something.

"Let's go!" said Arnora. She pulled Gudrid up with her. Gudrid could not take her eyes away from Sigunna. By now the man had reached her. The axe glinted as it made its arc, and when it came up again, it was dripping red.

Blind fear now forced her up the slope toward the copse of birch trees that hung in a little valley. Surf roiled white far below in the sunlight. She followed Arnora into the trees, far back, almost to the end where the cliff rose again. Arnora's head moved back and forth, looking for something; then she found it. She raised some branches, pushed Gudrid into the hole they covered, and followed her in, pulling the branches back over them. Gudrid smelled the newly dug earth, though from the top she had seen no sign of disturbance. She remembered what Arnora had told her once, almost as an offhand remark: "One of the powers of the seeress is that of foresight." If she lived, it was something she would never forget.

The man's heels crunched leaves and branches as he searched. Once he gave out a low curse of frustration, but mostly they could hear only his feet, trampling back and forth, up and down, far and near. She could hear his breathing as he stopped almost directly over their hiding place. She began to wonder what doubtful tactic they might try if he should step into the hole.

He moved away then, and after a time it seemed he had given up and gone. She would have stood up, her body was cramped and sore, but Arnora pressed her down and held her hand over the girl's mouth. It was well she did, because the man returned, and at one point both of them were within axe's reach. Her disgust at the warlike ways of men was forgotten now. If only I were a man, she thought, then I could jump out of this burrow and slice his head off with one swipe of my sword. Revenge! Could anything else matter now? To avenge Sigunna would be as sweet and as quenching as the watered mead she sometimes got to drink during an ale-feast.

The man went away a second time. The light coming through the trees began to dwindle as the sun went lower. The rock wall that formed the north side of the valley of birches threw its shadow over them, and Gudrid began to shiver uncontrollably. Arnora pulled her closer but would not let her move until the late-summer twilight was at its dimmest.

They pressed their heads up slowly through the branches. Gudrid was soon able to walk normally, but Arnora took some time unbending herself. They looked around in the gathering dusk, making certain that the man had not tricked them into thinking he was gone. But they were alone, and when they had assured themselves of this, they started down. At the edge of the birch grove they could see the farm. Smoke still rose from the burned-out roofs of the buildings, and nothing was moving. For the first time, Arnora spoke. "You'll have to see Sigunna, the sooner, the better." For once, Arnora's speech was soft, and Gudrid reached for her hand. Together they started across the talus until they reached the body.

The axe had cleft the head to below the ears, and the brains were scattered over nearby rocks. "Her face is down," Arnora breathed. "The gods be thanked for that." Gudrid sensed Arnora's unaccustomed gentleness, and she clung to the offered hand. A hard, dry feeling came over her. She gazed on Sigunna's remains and promised herself that she would never forget. She was only an eight-year-old girl, and she had no inkling how she would repay this crime. But one way or another, she told herself, she would, even if only when she was old and wise, and could put a spell on the man's children and grandchildren. She looked down on the farm, and in the wind she heard women keening. She did not want to join them. She was grateful when Arnora remained above, to wait for the waning moon.

4.

Bjorn returned the next day, his voice and that of his men recognized well before their ghostly figures loomed out of the fog. The women counted horses and men until Orm at the last took Gudrid up and it was known all had returned. Now Bjorn stood, circled by his henchmen, surveying the wreckage of his house, his flared nostrils noting the smell of burned flesh. Arnora pushed her way into the circle and laid into him.

"I told you when you left what would happen, and now it has. You call yourself a man, in your shiny helmet, but where were you when we needed you? If it hadn't been for me, your own daughter would lie bloody there in front of you, just like these others."

Bjorn surveyed the carnage. A group of women, one nursing a baby, sat in the angle of the turf fence, whimpering grief. Four of the seven men who were meant to protect them lay dead, skulls creased or guts opened out in honorable fashion. Three had been left to lie after receiving their mortal wounds, but one had been mutilated beyond recognition. His clothing was torn away, the bloody tunic reduced to strips of rags, the breeches slit from the hip to the knee. His face was bisected by a deep sword cut, and his penis leered lopsidedly from a swatch of broken skin. Two thralls also were killed, but the rest apparently had escaped. "Thralls know better than anyone where to hide," someone said, to a hint of nervous laughter.

Bjorn, followed by his retinue, went into what remained of his house, the door ajar, the walls still standing, but little else amid the sticks of charcoal that once had been roofbeams. His finely carved tables were smashed. His cushioned benches and stools, once covered in fine drapery, were charred and shattered beyond reclaim. Under some blackened skins lay Bjorn's dais posts, unsinged by the flame. Loyalty and presence of mind had led Bjorn's men to put them down and cover them before the end. Among the fallen timbers were the roasted bodies of the remaining men. No one said a word as they came back out into the open.

Bjorn went over to the clump of women and pulled one away. "Tell us what happened."

It took her a long time before she was able to speak. "We bolted the door shut. These four slowed them down to give us time. They called to us to come out, but we wouldn't. Then they set the roof on fire and shouted again for the women and children to come out, that we wouldn't be harmed. We went, but the men had to stay. They made no sound when the roof caved in on them."

"And what did they do to you?" Bjorn's question came in a strange voice.

"Nothing. They just left us here after they set all the roofs on fire."

Back in the circle of horses, the men began to murmur. No voice stood out, but the talk had settled on a single word—Froda.

Then they looked around the barns and byres. Dead cows lay in their stalls, udders still full of milk. Some were hacked, some burned. Roofless walls gaped at the sky.

Bjorn accosted Arnora. "Was it the Froda men who did this?"

She turned to him, hands on hips. "Do you think I had time for proper introductions? Do you suppose I had the presence of mind to take their hands in mine, to welcome them as guests and assure myself as to their pedigree? How in the name of Hel should I know?"

Arnora's invocation of the goddess of the underworld, half woman, half corpse, brought again to Gudrid's mind a picture of Sigunna's murder. She saw the man clearly, raising his axe, and remembered things she had not seen even as it happened. If there were any way she could help to fix the blame, she would. "Father," she said, "I can describe one of them as closely as if he were standing here."

"Then do it, daughter."

"He was as tall as you are, and his hair flowed down behind his helmet. The helmet was dull, like lead. His trousers were sleek and gray, like seal fur."

"Doesn't tell us much," one of the men said in disgust. Bjorn looked his way, and he fell silent.

"And," she continued, "he wore a bearskin shirt without any chain mail."

"The berserk!" The same man said this. "Then it was the Froda men!"

She looked toward Orm, who was standing in the background, his eyes scanning the flank of the mountain in the direction of his home.

"Bury the dead in the sacred plot," Bjorn ordered, "and be quick about it. We'll ride for Froda as soon as you've finished."

She walked to the far end of the courtyard, where Hakon and Mord were sitting. Hakon had on his favorite tunic, the one on which Sigunna had embroidered a bright red-and-green border, the same one in which he'd left a week before. Mord hadn't had anything to change into either. For all that, Hakon smelled clean; Mord smelled of the privy.

She would have gone with the men assigned to Sigunna's burial, but Bjorn forbade it. In her heart she was not sorry; she was afraid she might disgrace herself. Her desire for the death of the killer had not slackened, and there was nothing these boys could say that would help with that. The silence was oppressive. "Did you see any fighting?" she asked them.

"We beat 'em into the ground," said Mord. "Killed half of 'em, the Froda men and the others. At least the Froda men knew how to fight. My father even let me kill one of 'em that still had some life left." Mord ran his fingers over the blade of his axe. Small though it was, it seemed sharp enough, and it did have the stain of blood on its edge.

Hakon looked at Mord with disgust. "You were with me in a farmer's house the whole time. You hacked a dead man up after the fight was over."

"Did Erik get away?" Gudrid asked. She did not know why she bothered to ask. Certainly the fate of the man who was the cause of Sigunna's death was no concern of hers.

"It seems that way from what our fathers said," Hakon answered.

She looked toward the women and pictured Sigunna sitting among them. If she hadn't pulled her along to follow Arnora, she might still be there. In fact, it seemed now, had Gudrid and Arnora gone into the house with the others, there would have been no need for them to hide in the birch grove. But this line of thought was broken as one of the women continued to tell Bjorn what happened.

"After the roof was burned down completely and we women were together in a circle, surrounded, the berserk came back. He would have killed us all if the others hadn't held him off. As it was, he unstrapped his fury on old Bork there." She pointed to the dismembered man.

Arnora stood straight and tall, but said nothing. She had saved the women by leading the berserk away from the fight. Neither the women nor the men appeared to have understood this.

By now Mord had gone, and the fog had come in so thick she could glimpse only the shadows of the buildings, so that she could imagine them whole and the killings only a dream. Hakon moved close beside her. She felt his hand on her shoulder.

"It's a sad day for you, Gudrid," he said. "And for me too. You're not the only one who loved Unni."

She looked him in the eye. "You're a boy," she said. "What would you know about love?" But his eyes were wet, and she saw that the sleeves of his tunic were wet too, and not from the fog. She pulled him close to her and held him in the privacy of the mist, feeling his body, long and thin like a girl's.

Little could be salvaged for the journey other than the clothing the women wore on their backs. Several horses had broken away during the melee, and these were rounded up for the women. Arnora wore breeches for riding; she was an accomplished horsewoman. She held her horse firmly, her knees tight against its ribs. Gudrid rode astride behind Orm, grasping his chain mail, her shift and woolen wrap hiked up to her knees. Leather creaked as the horses shifted in place. The smell of flatulence swirled up with that of urine in the still air. Then shouts, and the troop began to move.

"What's a berserk?" she asked Orm.

For a long time Orm said nothing, so that she was not sure he heard her. Then he spoke. "The strongest and strangest of warriors. They're not many in Iceland, because they like to fight for kings and we've got no king. They whip up frenzy in fighting, and they're not stood still with fear. A chieftain's son from the East Firths went to Denmark and brought this one back. But they couldn't do with him, so they paid him to leave. He came here."

"What do your neighbors think of him?"

"We try to stay clear in Arnarstapi. Even Froda men can't keep him from anything he's a mind for. But he helped them win some fights they'd'a lost."

Gudrid's mind was not well arranged, and she asked questions just as they came to her. "Do the Froda men always kill women when they go out to settle a score?"

"No. Only the berserk. He kills what's in his way. He'd've killed you. He hates your father."

"Why?"

"Bjorn tried to run him out of Snaefellsnes."

"I haven't heard any of this."

"You were a babe then. But Hrolf swore he'd get even. Man's name's Hrolf."

"There were others with him. Do they hate my father too?"

"No. But they had no choice. They owe some Haukadale men. We fought them on the way."

"And who won?"

"We did. Killed four."

They rode in silence the rest of the way to Stapafell. The dark ridges of Snaefellsjokul contrasted with the brilliant white of the snow, the crowning glacier fringed by an archipelago of snowfields. The lower slopes varied from the rich green of thriving grass to the gray-green of lichen-covered lava. In the distance a black cliff loomed, clothed in a kirtle of loose scree. The cave where Orm's kin were hiding stood high up the precipice, with only a narrow ledge going up, narrow enough that horses must be led single file.

They found nearly twenty people in the cave. Gudrid expected to find them living like animals, but they seemed to have set up house-keeping in a civilized way. A makeshift hearth fire burned just far enough inside to keep it out of the rain but not so far that the smoke would fill the cave. Cooking utensils were set neatly alongside—pots of iron and soapstone, wooden bowls for boiling with heated stones, wooden serving bowls, ladles, knives, saucepans, frying pans, spits, spoons, skin bags, and water buckets. A few low tables and benches had been brought up. Joints of meat hung from rock protrusions, and tubs of fresh butter were flanked by others containing sour-cream butter, soft cheese made from sour milk, and the tastiest of all, the cheesy curds called skyr. Sleeping conditions would be less luxurious. Piled in the rear of the cave were rolled skin bags of the type men used on shipboard.

Orm jumped from the horse and ran to embrace his wife. "Halldis! Halldis!"

Halldis let drop a string of strange beads with a cross on the end, and one of Bjorn's party said to another in a tone of surprise, "She's a Christian, by Thor!"

She looked to be strong, with a face neither thin nor fat, and long blond braids that came down to her hips. This was an unusual hairstyle. Most women let their hair hang loosely from a knot at the nape of the neck. She smiled at Orm and was reluctant to let him go.

Then Orm helped Gudrid down, and Arnora led her into the cave. Bjorn was going to waste no time. In less than an hour he was away again, into the mist, his band augmented by others from Arnarstapi.

Gudrid peered through the fog, hoping to see something of the fighting that must by now be taking place below. She imagined Bjorn and Orm facing the berserk of Froda and cutting him down as quickly and as mercilessly as he had cut down her Unni. But nothing was to be seen. Only the drip, drip of the condensed moisture from the cave mouth could be heard and felt.

Halldis held her beads and spoke strange Christian prayers in a soft voice. Gudrid moved closer and strained her ears to hear, but the prayers were in an unfamiliar language not at all like the Norse. Arnora emerged from the cave and, seeing Gudrid so close to Halldis, took her hand and led her away along the ledge.

Gudrid sensed a certain competitive spirit in Arnora that she had not shown before. Unlike many who followed the witch's profession, she usually dressed much like other women, garments held in place by ordinary breast brooches, keys and sewing things and scissors dangling from her collarbone brooch. But now in Halldis' presence she brought out a little of the paraphernalia of her trade—leather bags hanging from her side, a necklace of bright stones and walrus teeth, and mittens of catskin.

The seeress knelt and pulled out a small hide bag closed at the top by a drawstring. She motioned to Gudrid to kneel beside her. Opening the bag carefully, she took out three small, thin pieces of wood.

On each was scratched three or four lines, joined together to make a crude figure. What they were meant to depict escaped Gudrid.

"These symbols are the first of the runes, the most powerful except one. They were taken up by Odinn when he hung nine days on the World Tree."

"I know that story," said Gudrid. "Unni told it to me. She said that Odinn also gave one of his eyes so that he could drink from the well of wisdom." She thought how gladly she would give up an eye of her own to have Unni back.

"This is true," said Arnora. "Odinn of all the gods is the one we women most honor, those of us who are after knowledge. This is the verse about Odinn and the runes:

> *"I know I hung*
> *On the windswept tree*
> *For nine days and nine nights.*
> *I was struck with a spear*
> *And given to Odinn, a sacrifice,*
> *Myself to myself.*
> *They helped me not*
> *By meat or drink.*
> *I gazed downward*
> *And took up the runes.*
> *Screaming I took them."*

Arnora continued her instruction. "Look at these runes. Each is the favorite of one of the gods." She separated one from the rest. "This is a seeress greeting the rising moon." Gudrid could see the straight body, the beckoning arms, both on one side. "It is the rune of Frey. Frey and his sister Freyja are of the Vanir, a very old race of gods from far away. They give the world bountiful harvests and children and peace." Gudrid remembered Frey's image, beside the hammer of Thor, at the burying ground. The god held a plant in his hand, and the carver had taken advantage of a branch in the wood to form his powerfully erect penis. Arnora picked up two more pieces, and showed Gudrid the runes of Odinn and Thor.

"What do you do with the runes?" Gudrid asked.

"Men use them to inscribe their deeds, but for us it is different. We are after power, not glory."

Gudrid was puzzled, and she knew she looked it.

"The world is full of patterns," Arnora continued. "They look very different but are really all the same. The shapes of clouds. The windings of offal. The fall of runes. The fates of men. With practice, you'll be able to see how these are the same and use one thing to tell about another. Sometimes we can even change the patterns, bend them to our will."

Then she began to fish around in her bag of runes, finally coming up with one, much like the others, that had no marking on it. Gudrid reached out to turn it over, to see what was on the other side. She half expected Arnora to stop her, but the teacher made no move to do so. Arnora's face broke into a full smile when the other side of the rune-piece showed nothing either.

"The missing symbol is the most powerful of all runes. It's the only one that even Odinn could not take up. It is the rune of Mother Earth and is heavy as the earth itself. No one knows its shape, unless somewhere a seeress has discovered it."

"If I were to learn the shape of this rune," said Gudrid, "what would it mean?"

Arnora smiled and let out a little laugh. "You could rule the world. But don't get excited. Many wise women have spent lifetimes in search of it, and none has succeeded."

Now Arnora pulled the other rune-sticks from the bag and laid them in a small pile on the ledge, between herself and Gudrid. She spoke some words softly, as strange as Halldis' Latin. Then quickly she picked up a handful and let them fall, taking care that the light breeze should not carry any of them away. She regarded the result of this effort with a scowl, scooped another handful, and let them drop on top of the first. From the look on the woman's face, Gudrid could tell that this try had been no more successful than the first. Arnora grabbed at the runes and dropped them again, and then again and again, with a rising sense of frustration. Gudrid wanted to help, but what could she do, with her limited knowledge?

Then she thought of her amulet and, pulling it out, dropped it on top of the runes. This moved Arnora. She stood and gazed out over the ledge, into the mist.

"You amaze me," she said at last, turning to Gudrid. "I don't know why I didn't think of that myself. The runes have spoken. You must cast them. Just be careful not to lose any."

Gudrid hesitated, only staring at the pile of wood shards that formed a nest for her stone.

"Cast the runes," Arnora prodded, and slowly, hesitantly, Gudrid gathered a few of the sticks into her hand. She held them for a moment and then, feeling the other's gaze, lowered her hand almost to the ground and dropped them.

Arnora relaxed a little, and now they both noticed that the sky was brightening. "Cast the runes again, Gudrid! Quickly!"

Gudrid picked up another group of sticks and held them, a little higher this time under Arnora's guiding hand. A breeze caused the ones on the ground to shift slightly.

"Cast the runes!"

Gudrid hesitated.

"Cast the runes!"

She dropped them. The sun burst through the clouds, and now the plain below was open to view, all the way to the sea. Arnora pointed to a small group of houses in the distance, adjacent to a little cove.

"Arnarstapi," she said. Then she pointed off to the east, to a loose sprinkling of dwellings, near where the golden grass came up against a river of black lava. "That's where Froda begins." Halfway between was the smallest movement, as of insects in the grass. It had a rhythm, a coming together and then a parting, and again a coming together.

"They're fighting now," someone said, and a feeling of apprehension came over the group.

Arnora knelt again and hissed to Gudrid. "Cast the runes again, quickly."

Gudrid was slow to kneel by the pile, and Arnora pushed her down. "Cast the runes!"

Gudrid picked up a pile, slowly, dumbly, and let them drop.

"Not like that! Again!" Gudrid cast them.

"Again! Again!"

The specks on the plain separated, though some did not move at all, and then one group raced over to the houses on the right, the other standing in a clump over the ones that did not move. Smoke began to appear on the roofs and then flames, and the other band began to move to the left. Reaching the houses by the lava field, they played out a similar pageant. Then both small armies regrouped and converged again toward the middle.

"This has gone far enough," said Arnora. Placing the amulet in Gudrid's hand, she picked up first one group of runes and then another, dropping them in sequence, rhythmically, more confidently than before, until the two groups of men met in the middle and stopped.

"They'll be talking peace," she said. "Their anger is spent. If the rune of Frey covers the rune of Odinn . . ."

She dropped the last set of symbols, and they fell as she had hoped. She stood up in satisfaction and turned to stare down at the motionless group of men. No sound came up from the plain, except for the rising breeze, and Gudrid became aware that all this time she had been hearing the soft voice of Halldis praying to her Christian gods.

The horses crunched up the narrow path to the soft swearing of men. They came around the last bend in the rock and all could see the reason both for the swearing and the softness. Four bodies were laid across horses, sideways, inert. And the foremost of them all was Orm! Gudrid ran to him, before belief, past hope.

"No!"

She stroked his face. She gave Arnora a hard stare.

Then she heard a groan and saw that Orm was moving his head. By this time Halldis and some of the men were getting him down and laying him on the ground in front of the cave.

"Terrible wound to the thigh. He's lost a lot of blood." Bjorn stood over them. "You've got a strong man there, Halldis, and a good one. His sword saved us from worse trouble. Any other man would be dead of a wound like this."

The other three in fact were dead. Each was attended by a woman crying grief. Bjorn ordered some of his men to take skin bags down to get clean water to wash Orm's wound. "If we can keep the rot from setting in, he'll live. He'll walk with a limp maybe, but he'll be sound otherwise."

Arnora came over to Bjorn and Halldis. Both women spoke at once, and both said the same thing.

"How much longer must this go on?"

"We've made a settlement," said Bjorn. "A hundred marks of silver for each dead man of rank, fifty for a yeoman, ten for a thrall. Half the amount for a wound to the bone. The houses and cattle on each side we let cancel. Their four dead were expensive, a hundred apiece. We had seven at home worth fifty, and three more in this last fight, two thralls and twenty-five for Orm here. So I'm a hundred forty-five to the good." He lowered his voice. "I can use the money. Everyone thinks I'm wealthy, but the truth is, I couldn't have paid even fifty marks if the reckoning had gone against me."

Bjorn stood to full height and paced along the ledge. He was eager to be going. Gudrid looked at him and wondered what was going on in his mind. He could have avoided this last raid, she thought, but then he would have been thirty marks in debt. Money had little to do with it, something told her, as she felt the disappointment welling up in her own heart. The arithmetic made it clear that the berserk was still alive. Gudrid would pay closer attention than ever to Arnora's lessons. She might even find, some day, the missing rune of world rule. And from herbs and runes and the darker secrets that lay ahead, she would weave the net that would catch the berserk in her power.

5.

"Patterns. You must learn to recognize patterns." Arnora was always finding ways to teach Gudrid, sometimes without her knowing it. They were by a little stream, where they'd come to get water for a birthing. "See the pebbles in the path of the flow, how the water eddies around them. Find numbers. The world is made out of numbers."

Arnora fell silent, and Gudrid knew she was expected to respond.

"I see three stones in the water here. Two of them are dark, like the black rock of the mountain. The other is shiny and white."

"Can you read their meaning?"

Gudrid needed time to think. Then, "Our cousin will be in labor two days, but then the child will be born, alive and healthy."

Arnora smiled. The girl was a good pupil and now knew most of what could be taught of the arts of divination. She cast runes as well as Arnora herself, and she'd had much practice at cloud reading and smoke reading and reading the patterns of streams. Birds in flight, sequences of thunder and lightning, spiders' webs, all provided information to one who knew what to look for. She was ready to begin the three major arts of future-telling: reading the stars, interpreting dreams, and calling up the dead. There was so much to teach, and so little time, however fast she could learn. Arnora understood this as once again she stumbled and Gudrid caught her.

Three years had passed since Bjorn settled the blood feud. He'd put his farm back in shape by the labor of his household, and with the last of his hard silver he'd bought new furnishings and restocked his herds.

Today was a day to look for portents, as the sun played in the mist, hiding behind broken clouds and sending day-sprites to dance among the hill flowers. They'd come to a place high above Bjorn's farmstead. From here they could look out to sea and up the slopes of the mountain and down onto the track that led away from the farm.

"What was my mother like?"

Perhaps it was the unaccustomed brightness of the day, but this was the first time Gudrid was able to ask this question.

Arnora looked away in silence.

"She was very beautiful. I remember when we were both young. She looked just like you. How I wished that I could be so . . ."

She went on, but Gudrid no longer heard. She was thinking of what her father had said about the curse.

Is that it? she thought. Was it my mother? Did she curse him?

She asked Arnora. Arnora didn't know, but doubted it. "Your mother was not a good pupil. I don't think she could have cursed much of anything. I tried to teach her." Arnora shook her head and, in doing so, caught sight of something.

"Look there!" she whispered. "Men!"

Gudrid looked in the direction she pointed. She could tell they were in no danger, seeing the group numbered only four horses and their riders, and one of them was considerably smaller than the rest. She sat down in the short, flowery grass.

By the time the horses reached the farm, the sun had circled around toward the west, though it would be several hours before it slid briefly under the northern horizon. Arnora gathered her shawl around her and pointed her feet downward. "We'll see who our visitors are," she said, as much to herself as to Gudrid.

They found Bjorn on his high seat in full state. Even seated he seemed ready to spring to action, as taut as the blade of a sword in its scabbard. His best drinking horn was in his hand, and a large, red-bearded man was seated in the chair of honor opposite. On the dais sat a boy, rangy and thin, with flowing blond hair. The boy looked at Gudrid, and she looked back. He was about thirteen or fourteen years old, on the edge of manhood, and his expression told her that he felt vastly superior to the child she still was, for all her eleven summers. He said nothing to her, but she knew at once she didn't like him. Well formed though he was, something on his lips was more a sneer than a smile.

The man's physical presence and Bjorn's attitude toward him showed that he was important. One could not have divined this from his clothing. He wore a plain tunic of undyed wool, with only a pale yellow band at the hem for decoration. His sleeves served, inadequately, to absorb the flux of bodily humors from his mouth and from his nose, which was running copiously through his mustache. He smelled like a rutting fox.

The boy, by contrast, was dressed spectacularly. His immaculate bleached tunic was bordered in many colors at the collar, hem, and sleeves, and down the front an embroidered interlace of mythical creatures was done in silver threads. His trousers were full at the thighs and gathered below the knee, which many considered the best style, and they were dyed a rich color midway between red and brown.

"Erik," she heard her father say, "this is my sister-in-law, Arnora. Arnora, Erik Thorvaldsson of Haukadale."

32

So this was Erik! Time had mellowed the memory of Sigunna, but now the hot anger rose again, as fresh as it had been the day the berserk came. This man was the cause of it all. She was tall enough now to be on a level with the seated man and old enough to feel her bitterness flow to its natural end, but she could do nothing about it, so she stood straight, expressionless.

Arnora stepped forward and allowed Erik to take her hands in his. "I know Thjodhild well," she said. "You are fortunate to have so good a woman. I regret that it has not been my good fortune to make your acquaintance till now."

A cloud passed over Erik's face. "You know I've been three years in exile."

"And your wife," Arnora continued, still avoiding the tender subject that Erik seemed so willing to bring up. "Has she not come with you?"

"No. Thjodhild isn't one for life ahorse, and to bring a cart—why, I'd be traveling all summer long!" Erik laughed a laugh that came from very deep inside and that Gudrid would never forget.

Turning to the boy, Arnora continued. "Can this be young Leif? He's grown! It won't be long till he's a man. A comely one too. I'd like to be a young girl like Gudrid here." Gudrid wanted to slink away, but she stood her ground.

Leif Eriksson, she thought. Something's in that name. She looked into the fire that lit his face for some clues, but they eluded her.

"It's said you're a seeress," Erik said to Arnora. "It may be you could make yourself young again. Then you could chase after my boy." He smiled through his beard.

Arnora laughed. "If that's my reputation, it goes far beyond the truth. I poke around in birds' innards, and once in a while I do see something. But I'm no form-changer."

"That's good," said Erik. "I wouldn't want my boy to sleep under the same roof with one of those."

All this time Gudrid was watching Erik. Now she felt some uncertainty creeping in. Erik didn't kill Sigunna, after all; the berserk did. Were it not for Sigunna, she might have liked Erik, just as she'd liked Orm the first time he came. She found herself wanting to approach him, to feel his bushy beard. Then the anger came back, and she had to bite her tongue.

Bjorn broke in. "Tell us more about this Green Land, as you call it."

"It is a green land. The slopes that line the fjords are heavy with grass, and the waters are full of seals and fish."

"And the people?" Bjorn asked.

"That's the best part," said Erik. "There aren't any. That's why I'm here. You saved my life, Bjorn, when I was outlawed and my enemies were hunting me. I couldn't have gotten away without you. While I was gone, you looked after the interests of my sons."

Bjorn fidgeted a little at this, as if not knowing what to say.

"I know you didn't intend me to notice it, but I'm not blind. You're the best friend a man could have. But let's get to the point. I'm going to lead a colony out to Greenland, and I want you to come with me. If you agree, you'll have the first choice of land for your farm—except for the stretch along Eriksfjord that I took for myself."

Bjorn did not speak. Gudrid understood Erik's offer well enough: what an honor it bestowed even beyond the value of the land. Her father was lost for words. That, at least, was unusual. And then there was this boy, who only sat and stared at her. She did her best to be dignified and not stare back, but she couldn't keep from looking out the corner of her eye at the boy's smooth face and long limbs and flowing golden hair.

She was sure her father would accept the offer. He was, after all, Erik's best friend. The move would reduce one worry. The curse. Even if it followed them to Greenland, she could hope that its strength would be diminished.

Nevertheless, the thought of going saddened her. She loved the land beneath the snowy mountain. She heard the talk in the evenings, from visitors having it second- or thirdhand, about Erik's land, and from what they said it wasn't very green at all, but mostly mountains of ice floating in a cold, gray sea. The thought that her father would take her there made her freeze, to think of such a cold place and her father's cold heart . . .

Erik and the boy and the two attendants stayed a fortnight, and Arnora was given the task of seeing that the young ones were kept out of the way of their elders. Leif was disdainful of this arrangement and took it out on Gudrid with his sharp tongue. His vanity was heightened by the cut of his clothing, which he'd taken pains to attribute to his mother's, and not his father's, affection. Gudrid's initial dislike was strengthened as the days wore on. Even so, she couldn't take her eyes away from him for very long. She was struck by his appearance, looking much the way her father was said to have looked in his youth, and the thought came to her that were she older, she might have loved him in spite of everything. Older girls were often very foolish. She wondered whether she'd be that way when her time came.

It was on the day before Erik was to leave that Arnora had her vision. Leif had heard about the amulet, and he began to taunt Gudrid. "Little Girl Hide-Behind-a-Stone," he called her, which made her so angry that she pulled the amulet from her clothing and held it out to him. She knew how strictly she'd been forbidden ever to bring the stone where man or boy might touch it, and she could sense that Leif was afraid. She was exulting in her power to chase this upstart boy who until now had maintained such a mien of condescension. Arnora, more than anyone, knew what the consequences could be if she failed to act, so she hurried to catch Gudrid. The girl raced away from her, and she tripped on a hummock.

Leif and Gudrid turned to see what happened, and they saw Arnora pick herself up, walk slowly forward toward Leif, and place her hands on his shoulders.

"Don't touch the boy," she said to Gudrid. "The spirits are protecting him with a power even stronger than your stone. This boy will be a man soon, and he'll sail the Western Sea, farther than his father. His name will be remembered for a long time."

Then she collapsed in a heap, and for a moment it seemed she'd roll down the steep hill, but her limp body came up on a tuft and hung there. Gudrid ran to her. Her breathing was shallow, but at least she was still alive. Leif stood over them.

"So you see, there it is. You have not liked me ever since our coming here. But you cannot deny what your own kin tell you. I will grow to be a man—I am nearly that now—and I will have a ship, and I will do greater deeds than even my father has done. You are just a girl. When you are grown, you will become the toy of a man not of your choosing and you will keep his house and bear his babies. Is that why you hate me?"

Gudrid hadn't hated him; she saved that emotion for the berserk. But her dislike for him grew stronger, and she had to do something. She held her amulet out in front of her and chased him down the slope. It won't be like that, she thought, yet in the deepest part of her she knew it would be. Wasn't it this way with all the women of her father's estate? "Unless . . ." something inside her whispered. "Unless . . ." She cried aloud to him in a piercing voice, "There'll be a day when you'll kiss my feet and admit that you're my slave, and you'll beg me for the smallest drop of mercy." She didn't believe a word of it herself, and Leif just laughed.

The upshot of it was that Erik and Leif and the henchmen left the following day, while Gudrid's backside was reddened with a birch rod. She ached for days. Nevertheless, she felt she had the better of it. They were gone, off to Greenland, and Bjorn had decided not to go. The visions of cold and darkness and terrible aloneness that had haunted her dreams ever since Erik's coming slowly receded.

Arnora returned from Haukadale after going there with Erik and Leif. She told Gudrid that her prediction concerning their cousin had been mostly right; the child was healthy, but the labor had gone three days, not two. The next morning the courtyard stirred as Bjorn came up from the ship cove. He rode a sleek gray stallion, said to be the largest in Snaefellsnes, with a coat like seal fur. Its mane was braided and its tail was tied in a knot. The saddle was of finely tooled leather, and the bridle was trimmed with colored stones. Some henchmen were with him, and they had a man they'd bought from a trader.

Bjorn's height seemed magnified at a time like this, when the morning sun shone brightly and cast long shadows. He set his horse as straight and as firmly as a house timber that had been set into the damp earth, and his face was set also, the straight nose and straight mouth and closely trimmed beard adding to his air of unmovability.

The newly purchased thrall slumped dejectedly in his bonds, seeming almost about to fall from the poor horse on which he had been thrown. His dark hair and beard had not been groomed for a long time, and though Gudrid did not fully understand the hopelessness in the man's heart, she could feel that he was very sad.

The next day, as they were emerging from the sauna, Gudrid and Arnora came upon the man, still hobbled, led on a rope by another thrall. His odor was rancid, not at all the honest, cheesy smell of freeborn men. Arnora raised her hand, and the two slaves stopped. Neither had any look of questioning on his face.

Arnora told Gudrid to bring out her stone, and then she invited the hobbled man to take it into his hands. Gudrid was surprised and frightened. Had it been anyone but Arnora, she would have cried alarm. The man felt the stone, and though the look of sadness never left him, amazement shone in his eyes, so deep that even a child could perceive it. Then he was led away, and Gudrid gave it no more thought.

Some days later she heard that Bjorn had ordered the man to be trained to handle horses. He still wore his hobble, somewhat loosened, and this made him awkward and clumsy. While watching the training from beside a byre, Arnora explained to Gudrid that a new thrall would sometimes attempt to run, even in Iceland, where there was no place to hide. Suddenly Arnora ran out among the horses. They shifted uneasily, bumping one another. The thrall tried to run, but tripped over his hobble. The frightened animals began to rear and kick, and Gudrid was afraid she might be trodden under their feet. The fallen man attempted to rise, but a hoof caught him on the forehead, above the eye, and he fell back onto earth red with his own blood. A servant girl rushed out of the house to pull Gudrid inside. She would never see the man again.

That evening, when a thunderstorm was approaching across the valley, Arnora took Gudrid up to the copse of birch trees, the one in which they had hidden from the berserk. Though Thunder was as rare an event in Iceland as rain was common, she didn't know why her mother's sister brought her there. She could only hold her hand and watch the lightning sky. Arnora said nothing, but tightened her grip on Gudrid's hand and watched with her.

The experience with the thrall confused Gudrid. Her most vivid memory was the man looking around like one of the little birds that hopped near the barns, looking for seeds. As she tried to remember the rest of it, the thoughts came jumbled, like newly shorn wool. But even then she knew it was Arnora's doing.

The squall line reached the trees, and large drops of rain began to fall, followed by hailstones that stung her arms and head. She tried to pull away, to take refuge deeper within the grove, but Arnora held her. The clouds bore directly overhead, and she looked up at their ropy undersides and held her shawl close.

Arnora turned to face Gudrid. She had around her neck the full array of beads, shells, and bones of animals that marked her as one who talked to the spirits. Her hair flew back in the wind, sloughing off rain, and her face took on the shape of a long, screaming wail. Her hands flew above and around Gudrid like birds. She moved out into the open, letting the full force of the storm work on her. Her body moved strangely, angularly, and her face showed the same voiceless writhings. She dropped her sodden garments to the ground. The effect was frightening. Everyone lived close together, but children were taught to respect others' private acts as much as possible. Gudrid drew back farther into the birches, so that she could barely see Arnora, and it was then that the seeress beat her breasts and let forth a single cry that froze Gudrid in her place. The cry was like the cry of some strange beast, and it chilled and darkened her heart.

Gudrid knew enough to recognize this for what it was, a kind of farewell. Even so, at the moment she could only think of herself. "Can you see my fate?" she shouted into the wind. She could ask no more, could only wait, shivering, for Arnora to speak. But Arnora became quiet and stood calmly, waiting for Gudrid to come out of the wood into the wind and rain. They were there then together, woman and girl, until the rain lessened. Arnora picked up the wet skins from the ground and wrapped herself in them once more.

"You used your mother's stone as a plaything to frighten a boy. You've seen it do its work upon a thrall. You should beware of its power. It could turn against you." Then the face softened, and the seeress sighed. "It's time you understood something of what has happened to you." She stroked Gudrid's face with her hand, gloved in catskin, and she told her much about her mother's early years. Gudrid felt a longing for her mother such as she had never before felt. But she knew she must not weep, and in the presence of Arnora's contorted face she strove desperately and, in the main, succeeded.

The rain slowed to a sprinkle, and she smelled the freshness in the air that comes after a lightning storm. The wind rustled the leaves of the birches, a wind that had become gentle after its ride up the cliff. Arnora reached inside Gudrid's woolen shift and pulled out the stone.

"Your mother gave you this so that its power would protect you. Look at it closely. It was once mine. I found it on the shore after a storm just like this. I gave it to your mother because I knew she would need it more than I did. She should have made use of it. There's just one more thing. The secret of the stone. I could tell you what it is, but it would lose its power. Find the answer for yourself. Then you'll have your heart's desire. You know this. See that you don't forget it."

In spite of her fear, Gudrid had to ask one question. "What will happen if I can't find the answer?"

Arnora's face was more stern than it ever had been. "The fate you fear most will overtake you."

Then, as abruptly as she had first led Gudrid up the hill to the birch grove, Arnora turned and began to walk back to the farm. Gudrid could do nothing but follow, though there were many more questions she wanted to ask.

She would never get to ask them. Arnora was dying. Gudrid remembered the hints, even before Erik's visit, the stumbling and the incoherent speech. At first she'd thought it part of her instruction in sorcery, going beyond passive divination to controlling the winds of the world. Arnora had managed to hide her sickness, even from Gudrid, almost until the end.

It took time, but Arnora finally did die. Gudrid held her grief inside. She was old enough now not to shame her father as the shrouded body was carried through a drizzle along the slope of the hill to the sacred plot, beneath Frey's phallic image and the stone-carved hammer of Thor. Beyond grief she felt alone, separated from what little warmth Arnora had been able to give her and from her teaching.

When the funeral was over, Gudrid did her best to put all the memories into neat places in her mind. Arnora. Sigunna. Even Erik and his strangely affecting son. By the time they reached Bjorn's house, the sun appeared for the first time in nearly a month, and a rainbow arched over the lower valley. The rainbow and all that went before would be fixed in her mind through the years as she passed over the threshold of womanhood.

6.

After the funeral, Gudrid stayed close to Orm. He and Halldis had come to pay their respects, but they would have to go soon.

"Take me home with you," she begged, and she could see that both he and Halldis, who was childless, smiled at the suggestion. There was, however, an impediment.

"I'd more than else take you along," Orm said.

"And so would I," Halldis sighed, in a voice as soft as Unni's had ever been.

"Then ask him!" Gudrid begged. "Bjorn might do it, you know. It's a common way for a man to honor a friend of lower rank." Then, embarrassed, she covered her mouth.

"But," Orm said, "I'm too far below your father. I'm only a small farmer. He'd take insult if I asked."

"You have a big farm!" Gudrid countered. "With cousins to herd your sheep and mow the hay. And thralls."

"Two thralls, just. No, Gudrid, he'd never."

She looked up at him longingly. She was aware of the effect she could have on this man, who was her image of a father. The look never worked on Bjorn. She reached up her arms to Orm, so that despite his lame leg he had to pick her up. She kissed him on the cheek several times and hugged him. Against this, there was nothing he could do.

"Aye, your way, child. But it won't do, and it might put me on bad footing with him."

Gudrid waited, sitting on the turf fence with Halldis. She watched the sheep coming down from the summer pastures, and she looked out to sea. She held Halldis' hand. She bit her nails.

Then Orm emerged with Bjorn, and Orm was smiling. She ran to him, and now it was he who was all eagerness, gathering her in and holding her, and calling her foster daughter in Bjorn's presence. Halldis put her hand on the girl's shoulder. Even Bjorn seemed pleased. The day that had begun in sadness turned to joy.

And so, at the start of Gudrid's twelfth year of life, Orm took her home with him. There, through the seasons of the lambs and of high heaps of hay and of dim fires within winter's darkness, he never neglected to lift her high on his shoulders and carry her around the home field on legs that were strong though unsteady, until with more years Halldis thought it unseemly.

Gudrid came to love Halldis also, she with her soft voice and her tales of lands to the south. Her father had been a merchant, a man as smitten with a daughter as Orm ever was, and he'd shown her the world. Halldis spoke to Gudrid of her faith in the quiet of the evening. Her father had been baptized out of expediency—it eased transactions in the warm countries—but Halldis truly believed. She told tales of the god Jesus and his mother, the Virgin. The cross of Jesus seemed much like the World Tree of Odinn, and Gudrid wondered why even gods had to suffer.

Halldis told how the new religion was sweeping northward, how even the people of Denmark had turned to Christ when their king, Harald Bluetooth, was baptized. It happened when Halldis was a girl. Norway was still pagan. Two kings in Norway, Hakon the Good and Harald Greycloak, had tried to convert the people, but had not been strong enough to do it. In Halldis' opinion, however, it was just a matter of time.

Orm's house was in keeping with his modest status. With walls built entirely of turf, it was smaller by half than Bjorn's. The finished wood panels that lined Bjorn's walls were here seen only behind the dais; rough planks displaced them beyond. Bjorn's carved and cushioned benches contrasted with Orm's bare boards. Orm's single box bed of rough-hewn timber fell short of Bjorn's ornate bed closet, the smaller but just as fine bed that had been Gudrid's, and several enclosed sleeping boards for his chief men and their wives. Orm's kin all slept on the floor, the same as Bjorn's lesser householders and thralls, and as now would Gudrid. The lack of things she'd taken for granted would take some getting used to. Still, she'd live in a cave if she had to, if only Orm were there, and Halldis.

Those years were happy ones. Gudrid's body was growing full, and she couldn't contain the excitement she felt when a boy looked her way. Sometimes she would pretend to ignore the look and imagine the yearning that he was feeling. Other times, she would smile and encourage the attention until it would come to the notice of Halldis or Orm and they would scold her. She put Arnora's lessons into the back of her mind. But she kept the amulet in spite of Halldis' disappointment.

One day, in her fourteenth year, she was standing in the doorway that led off an angle in the rear of Orm's house toward the dairy, intent on a young man hewing a rough timber with an adze. As she watched the rhythm of his arms and shoulders, she fingered the amulet that had always been part of her life and that she never removed except to bathe in the warm pools fed by the water and the fire of the mountain. She watched him for a long time, and was amazed that he didn't stop to rest, even to wipe away the little rivers of sweat that ran down his arms and made them shine. A shifting of her footing made a sound. The youth turned to look, and seeing her there, he snatched up his tunic and put it on.

She pulled back into the room, and as she did so, she heard her foster father's voice growing louder as he returned from one of the fields.

"Ho, Einar, the quarter beam! You're like your father with the cutter!"

"Har, Orm, it's you who should be proud. I see in your house what's worth more than all the gold in Iceland."

Gudrid knew he was talking about her, and at once she sensed in every pore of her skin how much a woman she had become. She knew the tingling of flesh, of which some of her foster cousins, girls a year or two older, spoke when away from their elders. She peered back out the doorway in time to see Orm come up to Einar.

"That's how I'd have it, Einar, and I could be done with cattle and sheep and have a shipload of thralls to do for me. As it is I have two just, and so I—" Then he stopped, and she heard the little chuckle he always gave out when he caught someone's drift.

"Who *is* that beautiful young woman I saw just now in the doorway?" Einar asked.

"Gudrid, my foster daughter. She's been upslope Stapafell with Clovis the bondsman."

"She must have many suitors."

"Some have looked at her here. She won't be easy to get. She has a will, and her father's not one to take the first pig offered. But it's no harm for you to meet her, and if you're here the night, it can't be anything else."

Her face felt warm as Einar entered the house, and she felt her flushed cheeks betraying her excitement. She allowed him to take her hands in his, in the unfamiliar way of grown men and women, and she imagined all the women of faraway fjords whose hands he had taken. His face was square and manly, with deeply set eyes. His beard was short and trimmed. His tunic was embroidered with silk threads of many colors, in patterns like those on her father's and her foster father's dais posts. How unlike the Arnarstapi boys, who knew nothing of the world.

"I saw your father other summers," she said, "when he brought his ship around to trade. He spoke of you often, and I wondered why he never brought you up here." She felt herself blushing again and began to jabber about flowers growing through holes in the ice on the mountainslope.

That evening some other men came up from the ship, and Orm ordered a minor feast to be prepared for them. A joint of beef spat grease into the fire. A large codfish broiled on a slab of stone. Halldis and Gudrid and the young bondswoman hurried about, bringing out pots of skyr and soft cheese, heating stones to drop into a broth, and pulling the last of the barley bread and oatcakes from the baking pit beneath the hearth. The aroma whetted everyone's appetite, the men gaping unabashedly at the crackling and bubbling food. After they had settled in, Orm chuckled. "Einar, you say I've hid Gudrid up here. Blame your father. He kept you at the ship. Too much work for a boy. By the way, where is he?"

The servant girl came to the dais with horns of ale. Einar drank a long draught, then replied. "I'm sorry to say he's not well. The sea's soaked into his bones, I think, and I convinced him it would be better to stay home this year. That was the easy part. The hard part was getting him to let me take the ship."

"You made it this far," Orm replied. Soon the food was ready, and Einar was telling tales of the summer's trading voyage, to Ireland, first, and then the Shetlands and Faeroes, and finally to Iceland. "Dublin," he said, "is a fine town, with stout wooden houses and horses and wagons filling the streets and green grass by the river where the washerwomen work. And the girls . . ." His eye caught Gudrid's and he continued on another tack. "I've been to Hedeby, trading in gold and silk, rubies and ivory from the farthest east. I've been where it's so hot we could roast a pig on the planking of our ship. Yet the people who live in those places don't seem to mind it at all."

"It's hard to believe," said Halldis, smiling in her own memories, "but it's true. People not only live in such places, they actually like the heat, and wonder how we can live where it's so cold!"

Orm laughed. "If I can see ice from my doorstep, then I'm happy."

Later, Gudrid lay in her bedding, gazing out over the embers. She smiled herself to sleep, remembering that Einar had asked her to show him the country around and that Orm had given his consent with no more than a moment's hesitation. "I'll trust the father's son," he said, though she couldn't tell whether he said this more in admonition or in confidence.

The next morning Einar was up and out early, and now she waited for him in the lee of the dairy. In contrast to the leisure that Bjorn had allowed her, Halldis expected help with chores. Gudrid learned the essentials of dairying, making butter, cheese, and skyr, and she spent many an hour at loom and spindle. She had come to appreciate how much of a spoiled child the women of Bjorn's household thought her and how much here she savored Halldis' approval.

Today her foster mother let her go. Soon Einar appeared, though Gudrid felt she'd been waiting forever. He was carrying a skin satchel of bread and smoked fish. They walked up the sloping hayfield to the end, then up a short-grass slope that gradually steepened. They stopped to drink from a rivulet that sprang from the hillside. Then they climbed again, stride matched by stride, both of them turning around occasionally to let the scene renew their energy. When they reached a level spot they sat down. Einar opened the food sack and passed some to her.

"You are very beautiful," he said.

Those were words she liked to hear. Only she didn't know how to respond. She'd known what to say when Orm riffled her hair and how to smile or withhold a smile when a local boy said something to her, but this was a man who sailed in a ship, and she could only say, "Thank you." She looked out over the fjord. Even at this height they could hear the birds' cries, and several whales in a group had spouted and were preparing to sound. The freshening breeze was churning up whitecaps. Closer by, tiny pink wildflowers still held their heads up, though they would be gone soon. Her fingers, fumbling over the folds of her woolen outer garment, found the amulet beneath, and for a while she felt it through the cloth.

"I could be more dangerous than you might imagine," she said, and noting his questioning look, she told him the story of her birth. "My mother's sister said I must learn the secret of this amulet if I am to have my heart's desire." With this, she pulled it out, at the same time holding out her other hand to make sure he didn't touch it. Then she laid it aside.

"You are my heart's desire," he said. "I wish I were yours." He sighed. "There's probably someone here who has a hold on your heart."

"Oh," she laughed. "There's Hakon." She noted with satisfaction his alarm at her mention of another man's name. "We played together when we were children. I don't see much of him anymore, except when we visit my father, and he's been promised a girl from the East Firths. Anyway, he's too young for me."

Einar seemed somewhat relieved at this news, but now it was he who did not know how to continue. After a while, he pointed out toward the sea. "There's my ship—I mean, my father's ship. Soon we'll have to push her off the beach and be gone. I wish I could stay here with you."

In the distance lay a merchant's knorr. Gudrid had always loved these honest working ships. Their hulls were built in the same way as those of warriors' ships, with overlapping strakes running from stempost to sternpost, but they were broad of beam, not long and narrow, as different from the fierce longships as women's bodies are from those of men.

The tingling of flesh that she had felt before was kindled into flame now, so that she wanted him to hold her. She could feel the strength of his body in his hands. He kissed her. She felt strange in his embrace, his mouth pressing against hers, but she could only press herself closer. How different this was from anything she'd known before, from her foster father's hug, his kiss on the cheek.

She held Einar even more tightly and kissed him again and again. She wanted him all the more, for all her imagining of how it would be to love a man, imagining abetted by her foster cousins, and she pulled him down until they were lying together on the ground. She pressed toward his hands as they searched out the gentle curves of her body. A thrill went through her to know how sweet he found her. She remembered him as he was, when he was cutting the ship part outside the dairy.

His man-smell excited her too, neither the scentlessness of a boy nor the reek of a gaffer, but the ripe, oily, muscular smell of a hot-blooded young man.

Her arms went inside his tunic, mapping the contours she'd watched from the doorway. His hands moved gently over her breasts, brushing the swelling nipples to her gasps of pleasure. She was his now, she knew this, it was past her power to pull back, however much Halldis had taught her about a woman's honor.

His hand stroked her small mound of fur, then dipped to the soft valley within. The warmth radiated through her loins, outward to engulf her, until the pang of a dark memory stabbed her, of Floki's probing fingers . . .

It was different now. Einar was as fine a piece of young manhood as she was ever likely to find, and her body was ripe and ready for him.

The memory caused her to shiver uncontrollably, and Einar, taking it for passion, pressed closer. This was more than Gudrid could

46

bear, and she cried out, unmistakably hurt now. Einar looked at her uncomprehendingly.

Gudrid sat in dumb shock. Would these memories rise to haunt her for the rest of her life? She wanted to hold him, to explain, but she could never do that. No one knew but Floki and Orm, and if she could help it, no one ever would.

Her mind became jumbled and confused, and clutching her amulet, she ran down the hill, Einar behind her. She reached the house a moment before him, just in time to run into Orm, who was emerging from the doorway. The three of them stood for a moment, speechless. She tried to smile that she was all right, but she saw the questioning look in Orm's eyes, and the desire and the pain were both overshadowed by a feeling that she had betrayed him. The feeling deepened when Orm turned abruptly and reentered the house. Einar would have followed him in, but Gudrid fixed him with her gaze.

"A slave's son has lowered me in my foster father's eyes."

Einar flashed anger. "It's true my father had to earn his freedom. But he's done quite a lot with it, and I've given him every reason to be proud of me. I wouldn't trade him for your father under any circumstances."

Gudrid's anger flared also, though she knew she'd wronged him. Einar didn't give her a chance to speak.

"I've heard what the poets say about love," he said, "but I never believed them. It seems to me now they know what they're talking about."

"What are you saying?" Gudrid asked, knowing she was being drawn in.

"No one should trust the words of a woman, for their hearts are turned on a potter's wheel."

"What's that supposed to mean?" She let more of her temper show.

"Your heart has turned away from me, and it would be foolish for me to hope it might turn back, for who's to say it might not turn away again?"

"Never quarrel with a fool," she said—she also knew some poetry. "A wise man will often turn aside rancor, but a fool will fight without cause or reason."

"It seems to me," he replied, "that you ought to look to yourself when you say that." He stomped off.

The next day he came up again from the ship, greeted Gudrid perfunctorily, and asked the whereabouts of Orm.

"In the back hayfield," she said evenly, then spun away. Something made her turn back to watch him though, something in the tone of his voice or in the touch of his step on the ground. After he left, she went to her foster father.

"What did Einar say to you?" she asked.

Orm smiled. "He'll be going tomorrow."

Gudrid's heart fell to the ground. She knew how much she wanted him now, in spite of what had happened. But he'd confirmed what had only been gossip before. His father had been a slave, and so her father would never tolerate him as a son-in-law. And even if her father had nothing against him and even if his heart warmed again to her, it wouldn't matter. Her marriage would be decided two, three years from now, most likely to a man she'd never met.

Put him out of your mind, she said to herself, but then she'd remember the day she'd first seen him and she'd want him again. She never thought she'd feel this way. When she was younger she'd laughed at the older girls and wondered how they could be so foolish. It wasn't foolish, she knew now, and anyway, in one important respect she'd be different. She'd chosen Einar, though she hadn't really known it until now, and she'd have him, no matter what.

She slipped out along Orm's turf fence, the one that separated the back field from the wild heather. She ran up the hill to the still pool, ringed by rocks. It was not the first time she had done this.

She would look at herself quickly and, in this first flash, would recognize the exquisite form emerging from a child's face. If only she could leave it at that, but she never could. The second glance was never the same, and by the third or fourth the nose had become bulbous, the eyes dull, the face distended. The hair, which at that first look was like the trails of shooting stars, became a soggy mixture of haystalks and seaweed.

Still, Einar's testimony seemed to validate the first impression, and for this, if for nothing else, she was grateful.

When Einar returned the next day, she appeared in the doorway in her shift and smiled. At first, he brushed past her, moving directly to Orm to finish some piece of business. When he was on his way out, she smiled again, and although he feigned indifference, she noticed his second glance toward her.

She followed him down to his ship. He hadn't heard her soft footfalls behind him, but when he reached the pile of cargo, his men's faces told him to turn around.

She stood fifty paces behind him and smiled. At first, he also stood, neither of them moving to shorten the distance between them. Gudrid let her shawl fall to the ground. She knew the others must think she was a nymphet or a whore, but she didn't care. She'd gather Einar in now, or she never would.

Einar dropped the satchel he was carrying and walked to her.

"The potter's wheel turns again," he said. She felt the bite of the remark but stood still, saying nothing.

"You were right, Gudrid," he said. "I am a slave's son. I could never have you for my wife, and if I can't have you with honor, I won't have you at all." He looked at Gudrid's sad mouth. "Try to understand. Suppose I took you away with me today. I could never come back here to trade."

Gudrid felt hot again. "So that's it!" she shouted to his face. "All you care about is trade!" She stood on her toes and thrust her breasts forward. "I'm worth more than all your stupid gold!"

Einar took her by the shoulders, and she began to squirm in his hands. He moved them down to the small of her back and pulled her close and kissed her. Then she broke away and ran up the hill toward a little dale where they would be out of sight of the others. When she reached it, she stopped and waited for him. She would be ready this time.

They embraced, and she felt herself soften into him. His kiss was the promise of the love of his body. She felt his eagerness coming back, the press of his thigh. He entered her mouth. She drew him in, their tongues playing like eels in a pool. She yielded to his hands. "Take me," she whispered.

Then the wind came up again, strong enough to chill her moist body, and the mist became a hard drizzle. Sometimes the weather of Iceland enforced prudence as no parent could. Einar could do nothing but accept, for now, this vexing obstruction the gods had set between them.

"I'll take you for my wife if I can," he said, "and I'll love you and hold you dear as long as I live. It may be we'll have a little girl just like you to throw into the air and catch, and a son to sail with me. We'll have to get your father's approval, you know, and that won't be easy. Let's see what your foster father thinks. If we can convince him, he can convince Bjorn."

That evening, over a mutton stew, Einar presented his proposal to Orm. "I'll protect her as I would myself," he said, "and every summer we'll come back to see you. As for Bjorn, though he won't think much of my birth, nevertheless the marriage would be good for him. I hear his fortunes have declined lately, and my father and I certainly do not lack for money or possessions."

Orm ladled himself another bowl of stew. "You're a good man, Einar. You know how bare this house'll be if you take her. But I'd be for you anyway. You'd be good to her." He fell silent. Then, "It can't be. You're a slave's son. You're no less a man for that, but to Bjorn you're not good enough. Remember, his father was a nobleman in the Hebrides. He came here with Queen Aud. You know this already. Forget this business and let's have a good dinner."

That night, as Gudrid lay awake, she knew more than ever how much she needed Einar. She wouldn't let him go. Next morning, after breakfast, she caught him alone between a byre and the bog-iron smithy.

"Take me with you to Orkney," she begged. "I want to be your true wife always."

Einar smiled. He moved toward Gudrid as though to kiss her. Then he stopped. "Gudrid, you don't know how much I ache to have you. But I can't. I've already told you why. If I did, I could never come back to Iceland, and our best trading is here. You'd never see your foster father again either. I can't take you away. I also can't think of sailing without you." He shook his head. "We'll just have to bide our time."

Gudrid's mood changed again. She was angry with Orm for not being willing to sponsor the marriage before her father. She was angry with Einar for being more concerned with his trade than with her. She was angry with herself for falling in love in the first place and then for not being able to do anything about it. She thought of Halldis' Holy Virgin. She, least of all, deserved to be the target of Gudrid's spite, but there it was. She turned away from Einar and sulked off toward the dairy.

"The potter's wheel turns exceeding fast," she heard him say to her back.

Einar decided to spend two or three more days in Arnarstapi, but Gudrid found herself avoiding him and wishing he would go. That evening he expressed a wish to capture some birds for the voyage home.

"The cliffs are loaded with puffins and fulmars," Orm said. "We have nets. Sounds like a good time."

Gudrid gave thanks for a day by herself, but then Orm said, "Gudrid can stand at the top and haul up the birds."

So there they were, at the cliff's edge, with the ropes, the nets, and a satchel of food. Orm pointed out to Einar the route that could be taken down the cliff to where the birds congregated, how best to catch them unawares, how to throw the net, and how to secure the birds once they were caught.

Gudrid peered over the cliff, and she thought of the danger to a man in going down the ledges. She was afraid for Einar, in spite of everything, and she was especially afraid for Orm. Though he'd never touched her amulet, he had brought himself within the thickness of a fingernail from it every time he'd hugged her. She felt in a way that in yearning for Einar she'd already killed Orm in her heart. Now, in her mind, she saw Orm's body at cliff bottom. Orm gave no hint that he was afraid.

"Don't go," she pleaded. Orm looked at her with surprise.

"No worry, Gudrid. I've been before. I have to go first. A landsman can show something to a sailor."

She wanted to fling herself at his feet, to prevent him from going, but in spite of her fear, her sense of decorum won out. She gave him a long hug and let him kiss her cheek.

Orm started down. A series of ledges interconnected by cracks and projections stretched away to either side and to the sea far below. He approached the first nesting area, silently inched his way along the ledge, and flung the net. He caught two birds. He wrung their necks, left them on the ledge, and prepared to go for more. Einar had just started down and was on the second or third ledge when she heard Orm's cry.

Her mind reeled, and it felt as if she, too, must be carried over the cliff and into the sea. The air was as quiet as death. She knelt and crawled slowly to the cliff edge, knowing all the while what she would see.

The waves washed forward and back, and in the surf something was moving. A ray of hope went through her mind, that Orm might have lived through such a fall. But no, it was not possible.

Then she could see he was hanging by his hands from a ledge.

"Can you see him?" called Einar.

"Yes, just keep going as you are. He's five or six levels below you."

Einar moved downward from ledge to ledge, finally seeing Orm. "Gudrid, shake the rope down here!"

She did as she was told, but without conviction. Einar took the end of the rope and crossed over what looked like a sheer face of rock. "Find something to snub the rope around," he yelled up as he tied the end of the rope tightly around Orm's wrists. Then, like one of the birds themselves, he shot up from ledge to ledge to the top of the cliff and raced for the rope.

"Get behind me and pull," he ordered.

They pulled, and the rope began to move. Twice Einar called out to Orm, and she heard his call back. For the first time, she let herself hope.

"We'll set you down on the first ledge," Einar shouted, "and I'll help you from there. We can't pull you over the edge."

At last Orm rested on the top ledge, a broad one, and Einar dropped down to him. From their gestures and snatches of voice she could tell that Orm was all right, and soon both were at the top of the cliff. Orm rubbed his wrists. He looked up at Gudrid and smiled.

That Orm had been saved was beyond belief. She ran to him and held him as though a great wind might come up and blow him away. Then, out of the corner of her eye, she saw Einar standing, and her feeling for him surged back anew.

She threw herself into his arms and once again let herself be engulfed by his kiss. This time she knew she was his forever. After a while Orm coughed.

Gudrid sat down on the grass beside Orm. "Einar has saved your life now, Foster Father. I know little enough about honor and the ways of men, but it would seem to me that honor must bind you to plead our case to my father."

Orm looked at her for a long time with an expression that she had never seen on his face before. She knew he was begging her to release him from this obligation, but she held firm and said nothing. Finally, in a soft voice, he agreed that what she said was so. With sadness on his face, he coiled the rope and picked up the few birds they had caught. Gudrid held Einar's hand as they walked back to the farm.

The farewell had to come. Einar's ship was anchored in the bay, and all his men were on board except for five in the ship's boat, which was beached on shore. Einar stood before Gudrid and held her for the last time. Again she felt his lips on hers, a feeling she would have to remember all winter. She tried to fix in her mind the sights and sounds of the moment, the smell of the salt spray and the sweet-bitter smell of the oil on his beard. She sensed the boy in the man, and she knew his pain in parting was as strong as hers was. She tried to hug him the comforting way Orm had hugged her when she came to him with a hurt. She whispered a reassurance that Orm's plea would move Bjorn. He held out two large brooches of solid gold and watched as she put them on. Then he climbed into the boat and took an oar. The men on the ship were already unfurling the sail. By the time Einar reached the ship, the anchor was up. Gudrid ran up the hill to watch as the ship began to move. Einar stood at the steering oar waving, and she waved back. Then she could no longer see Einar or any of the others, just the dark ship with its great striped sail. The ship became smaller and smaller, and she stood, desperately trying to keep track of the sail, until it, too, was lost among the seabirds on the horizon.

7.

The days became shorter and shorter, and summer slid into autumn. She'd hoped that Orm would by now have had some need to go to Bjorn, but no such chance presented itself. Orm, still reluctant to sponsor Einar's proposal, could not be induced by anything she might say into making the trip specifically for that purpose.

After Einar left, Gudrid went up to the shieling, the little turf hut by the summer pastures, to help tend the sheep and watch the stupid ptarmigan—plump, succulent birds whose only defence was their change in color to match the season. The lengthening nights before bright fires and watching the sheep and the stars from out on the hills helped her to forget him, if only for a little while.

The part of her mind not taken up with Einar was occupied by her foster mother. Ever since she came to Arnarstapi, Halldis had told her small stories from the lore of her faith, so that Gudrid became more curious about it and asked to know more of its deeper mysteries. Of these, however, Halldis would not say anything, because she'd promised to keep her religion to herself. Gudrid kept up her questioning, and little by little Halldis relented. In some ways it seemed this new religion was very much like the old, especially in that suffering seemed ordained from the earth's creation to be the common lot of humankind. But for Gudrid, the message of love and forgiveness that Halldis related carried the new faith far above the old belief, with its ethic of violence.

Still, she felt uneasy. She would never give up the amulet, not even if all the world became Christian, not even if priests came and threatened her with everlasting fire. Nor would she give up Arnora's teaching, though with each passing year she remembered less of it. She wished she could take from the new belief the things that lifted her spirit and leave off the ones that repelled her, but it seemed that Christianity was a religion one had to swallow whole or not at all.

At last the days shortened enough that the sun peered over the horizon for barely seven hours, and cast a twilight glow for only an hour or two more. It was time to go to Bjorn's hall for the harvest feast. Gudrid both loved and dreaded Bjorn's feasts. She loved them because of the pure spectacle of dishes piled high with meat and fish, bread puddings and special sweet cakes with fruits from the southlands, and because of the multitude of guests, most of whom she saw only once or twice a year. She feared them because she feared her father for the power he held over her to grant or withhold her happiness.

As always, Orm and Halldis and Gudrid were invited, and it was expected that at least one thrall would accompany a party of guests. So four dark shapes, with Clovis in the lead, rode off down the track with only a crescent moon to give them light.

"Thanks to Thor for this clear night," Orm called out. Halldis crossed herself and mumbled a short prayer for him. Orm continued, "And to Frigg for a good and true wife." He kicked his horse forward and slapped Halldis on the behind, which caused her horse to lurch sideways. Halldis clutched at the saddle, muttered something incomprehensible, and laughed.

The glow appeared in the southeast, over the water. The mountain and the sea gradually took on form. By the time the sun had risen, they'd reached the high track over the lava flow.

They came within a short distance of Bjorn's estate in the dusk of late afternoon, and not wishing to spend a night outdoors, they picked their way toward the house. A thrall ran up, recognized who they were, and called for another to help. Orm led Halldis and Gudrid into the hall, as another thrall opened the door.

Bjorn met them there. His tallness, especially in relation to Orm, surprised anew one who had not seen him in months. He was dressed in his best—his long tunic embroidered with silver threads and the puffed-out breeches that he didn't like but wore on special occasions for their style. Silhouetted against the rich backdrop of his dais and its furniture, he suggested the great man he was striving to become, in a way she'd never noted when she lived under his eye.

For Orm, he had the warm welcome reserved for a loyal supporter of long standing; for Halldis, the polite greeting due the wife of an honored guest. With Gudrid he was awkward, one hand seeming to reach out, in spite of the barrier that existed between them, the other formal and self-conscious. Gudrid smiled as best she could, took his hand briefly, and then followed Orm and Halldis as they made their way between the rows of roofposts to a place nearer the fire, where tables were being brought out. Orm sat down alongside Halldis and took up ale in a large mug carved from soapstone, with an ornate iron handle.

"Thanks to the gods for the gifts of the earth, and a fortunate year to all who shelter under your roof." Orm raised his tankard in the traditional toast of a guest to his host. "And to you, Bjorn Vifilsson. You gave me what the gods begrudged." He glanced toward Gudrid.

Gudrid sensed Orm's discomfort with formal speechmaking. Bjorn smiled thinly and replied simply, "Thank you, Orm. You've been a worthy friend and a good foster father to the girl, better than I ever was." He stopped abruptly and then said simply, "Enjoy your meal. We'll see more of each other tomorrow." He turned and hurried off.

The next day saw the arrival of the other guests, most from Haukadale and Snaefellsnes, a few from farther away. The feeling of good cheer rose as the day wore on, the ale made its rounds, and the house filled up. The women showed off their finery, the fine linens and woolens—dyed red and red-brown, violet and green—held in place by breast brooches of gold and silver, many inlaid with emeralds and rubies. The younger women let their long hair flow naturally; the matrons held theirs back with colorful head scarves. Gudrid could not help thinking of Einar as she fastened the gold brooches he'd given her, but she tried to put him out of her mind and trust to fate and to Orm's power of persuasion.

Bjorn moved through the enlarging throng, greeting newly arrived guests and having a word here and there with those he had greeted before. Thralls moved up and down the long house, carrying jugs of ale. When Bjorn reached Orm, he stopped and took him aside.

"I'd like you and Halldis to have the high seats tonight. Gudrid's old enough to sit beside me."

She understood Orm's look of surprise: Bjorn usually let some visiting man of wealth or reputation have the seat on the dais opposite his own. "It's an honor to us," Orm said. He was straining for something more to say, but had to let it go.

Now it was time for the feasting, and the guests took their places along the side platforms. Orm and Halldis settled into their seats. Gudrid felt uneasy sitting next to her father, with a thrall of her own to serve her small pieces of meat as she required them or to bring bread and mead almost before she knew she wanted any. She managed to catch Orm's eye and forced a smile. Orm smiled in return, more relaxed. He was obviously enjoying the evening, and she began to worry that he had forgotten his promise.

She tried to imagine what she should say to her father. He spoke of the weather, of the harvest, and, then, of the days when Erik the Red came visiting.

"Erik asked me to go with him to Greenland. I would have a large estate there if I'd gone. But . . ."

"I remember that," she said, "and I remember Erik's red beard. What kind of a man is Erik? I've heard stories."

"He's a man worth having for a friend. It's too bad you were so little when he was here."

"It wasn't that long ago!" Then, "From what I've heard, I wouldn't want to have him for an enemy."

But she could say no more, nor could Bjorn, for sounds came from the door, long after any guest should decently have arrived, and then three men came in and strode to the center of the hall. One was tall and dressed in furs from shoulders to knees. His hair and beard were almost white, and his face was red with the cold of the night. The second was short and stout and dressed in leather. He still had his helmet on. The third was small in both height and girth, but he wore a finely wrought sword whose hilt sparkled with jewels. Bjorn stood and, recognizing them, stepped down from the dais to greet them.

He called them by name in a booming voice. He flung his hand at a thrall to summon drink. "I thought you'd be on your way east by now."

"We were," said the short man with the sword. "But our chieftain is dead. We've been on the road seven days, from Hvamm to Snaefellsjokul. Everyone's agreed who's the man to take his place." Then the man assumed a more deferential posture.

"Hail, chieftain," he said.

At first, Bjorn was silent, as was everyone in the hall. Then he asked, "What about the chieftain's son?"

"He is simple," said one of the messengers.

"Nay," said Bjorn. "I grant you he isn't known for his wit, but simple he is not."

"There'll be a question of gold," one of the other messengers broke in, in a smoother tone of voice. "To ease his disappointment. But this will be no problem for you."

It wasn't often that Gudrid was able to read subtlety in her father's expression, but the frown and the furrow of his brow indicated an obstacle. She knew how he lusted to be counted among the thirty-nine chieftains of Iceland. The office could be inherited, or it could be purchased for money, assuming there was one who wished to sell. Above all, one needed a following, and this did not come automatically, for the free men of Iceland had the right to shift their allegiance from one chieftain to another.

Bjorn had no chieftains in his family, and until now, he'd had no chance to buy the office, but he had gone to great effort to promote himself against the day when the opportunity might offer itself. Now, it seemed, his perseverance had paid off. Had it? Were her father's finances so shaky as to keep him from his purpose? But no, now Bjorn's expression brightened, as though he had located in his mind some long-lost chest of coin.

He stretched out his hands toward the men before him and pulled them up onto the dais. A great cheer burst out all around, and everyone pressed forward to congratulate Bjorn. Gudrid did her best to retain a semblance of dignity on her seat as arms and bodies and smoke from the fire swirled around her. After a while the tide ebbed, and Bjorn returned to his chair.

"It's a great day for you, Father," Gudrid said.

"And for you too, I hope, daughter."

The feast continued, and the guests ate prodigiously. The rivers of ale and mead continued in flood, until the raucous laughter and clamor of voices began to subside. Even Gudrid began to feel at ease, having had enough mead—for the first time unwatered—to soften her anxiety. The fire flickered, and some of the guests slid into reclining positions to rest or to nap.

The guests revived when the thralls brought out trays of sweets and cups of mead mixed with raw honey. These had their effect, and soon the sounds died down to soft murmurs of isolated talk here and there, and she looked expectantly toward Orm. He took the cue, and crossing over to Bjorn, took his arm and, after a word, led him toward the end of the hall.

For a long time their shadowy forms hovered almost out of the range of the firelight, now still, now gesturing. She tried to guess from the gestures how the talk was going. Then Bjorn left the hall. Orm stood motionless in the shadow for a moment, then walked slowly back toward where Halldis and she were sitting. As he approached, the fire lit his face, and it was obvious the talk had not gone well.

She looked into Orm's eyes. Here was a greater sadness than would come from a simple refusal. Halldis sensed it too, and she wrapped her arm around him. The look on his face should have been saved for something like a death. Why here, why now?

"Gudrid, Gudrid, I can't talk. I never saw anger like this, even in him. He says if I'd marry you to a slave's boy . . . and have him live off a trader's gold . . . he's sorry he let me have you. Halldis and I have to go now. We have to leave you here."

Gudrid grasped Orm and fought to keep from shaking. They embraced, and then, knowing nothing could be done, Orm and Halldis accepted their cloaks from a thrall and stepped through the door. Gudrid stared into the dark end of the hall. Then she climbed into her bed, not having the energy to change into her nightclothes.

Her mind ran over a small prayer to the Virgin that Halldis had taught her, until she noticed that her left hand was clutching the amulet. The hall remained quiet except for the occasional pop of something in the fire. She sank to her mattress and no longer struggled against the silent tears.

8.

She could do nothing but wait out the winter. Memories danced on the flames of the hearth only to spend themselves among the dim roofbeams. She saw herself again in Halldis' dairy, listening to her singing the conjuring songs. Halldis liked the old songs, even though she was a Christian, because they seemed so sweet to her, so different from the Christian chants made for men's voices. Gudrid liked them too, especially the one that had the refrain "Dance here, dance there; frolic here, frolic there."

Did spirits dance? Did they play like children? Gudrid had been a child once, not very long ago, but something she'd learned barred any return to childhood. All men were thralls, and all women, regardless of birth, bound by the thin cord of custom, a cord as slender and yet as strong as the cord the great god Tyr used to bind the wolf Fenrir. And custom would bind the living as long as the wolf was bound, until Ragnarok, the end of the world.

Perhaps the spirits danced because they were no longer bound by this cord. She felt for the amulet. Was this its secret? It gave no hint. She shuddered. Even if she discovered the secret, how would she know she'd found it? She caught herself about to curse the stone, to curse her mother even. She cast aside the reverie and went outside.

She missed Orm, missed the fatherly smile that bound her to him, more than custom ever could. But she had to admit, even to herself, that she missed Einar more. Now she had only Hakon, who, though he'd grown these past years, was still more a boy than a man, and Mord, who seemed to have become even more spiteful than she'd remembered.

The Yule came and went, Gudrid sitting through the feast in a corner of the house, sulking and renewing her father's displeasure. When spring came, she climbed the hillside and scanned the horizon for ships. Three passed by, but none made for the land. Gudrid spoke to Hakon of her disappointment until the look on his face told her something she'd never guessed before. He had a small, secret hope that if he could only grow a bit and thicken around the shoulders, she might one day be his. Nevertheless, she persuaded him to run to Arnarstapi and back quickly, before his absence would be noticed. He found no sign of Einar there. He went three times without any word, but the fourth time, shortly after midsummer, he reported with a half-hidden smile that Einar was seen trading along the Snaefellsnes coast east of Arnarstapi, as far as Froda, and then had sailed away.

I can't believe it, she said to herself. She spent the day in the birch grove where she'd hid with Arnora from the berserk. She stood at the edge, watching the surf pound the cliff below until the fog obscured it.

Let him rot with Hel and her dwarves, for all I care, she thought. She chanted a mild spell Arnora had taught her, one that was said to cause uncontrollable itching, and she wondered whether it would work at such a distance. He's lucky Arnora never got around to teaching me anything stronger, she mused.

But Einar still had a hold on her. She thought of Halldis and sank to her knees. "Holy Virgin," she prayed, "bring Einar back and I'll throw my amulet into the sea. Show me you've got more power than it has."

A week passed, then two more, and she decided the Virgin wasn't interested. A feeling of finality came over her like the hush that comes over the crowd returning from a burial. She walked slowly from the house, down the ravine that led to the sea. The wind had blown away the morning fog, but high, thin clouds still patched the sky, and it was cold, like autumn. She held her clothing close against her body.

The beach was narrow and rocky. She'd been cautioned not to come down to the shore alone, because of danger from the sea and from the men or ghosts it might bring. Today she didn't care.

She came to a place where two fingers of rock pointed seaward, nearly enclosing a small body of water. A seal was swimming near the center of the pool, and she wondered whether it would find its way out the narrow opening. The seal seemed to call to her, to join him in play. In Arnarstapi Clovis had taught her how to swim in the little warm pool where the water bubbled high on the mountainside behind Orm's farm. The water was too cold here though. Nevertheless, she stood on a rock at the water's edge, pondering.

She sat down slowly and pulled off her boots, the ones Orm had made for her. Then she stood up and unpinned her brooches and let her woolen wrap fall. She slipped off her shift and stood at the edge. The breeze marked her out: her legs, her breasts, her hair. Then the wind found the stone that hung from her neck. She saw Arnora's face in the wind. It came to her again that she still might throw the stone away, into the sea, and thus perhaps escape her fear of it, fear she seldom acknowledged but that often seemed stronger than its protection. She knew she could never do that, though she did not know whether the reason was love or fear. She placed the amulet on the ground carefully, and now she was naked, as she was not before. The wind tightened her skin, and in spite of her mood, the feeling was exhilarating. She smiled, glanced over her shoulder, and dived.

The cold was like the sting of bees all over her body, but she reached out her arms in the strong strokes that Clovis had taught her and kicked her legs. The feeling of exhilaration did not leave; it grew stronger as she headed for the far side. She glided through the water like the seal, feeling the rush of water, and triumphantly slapped the far rock. Then she headed back, her body sensing the numbness creeping in over her skin, and images of Arnora flitted through her mind, Arnora the seeress with catskin mittens. She remembered how she'd often pleaded to be told the stone's secret, but each time Arnora had resisted firmly: "To tell you the secret would be to destroy the power of the stone. You must find it out for yourself."

The cold sank deep into her limbs, and she began to falter. Orm entered her mind, and she saw herself as she was when she first went to Arnarstapi, cuddling in his lap, listening to his stories. Vikings from Norway came a hundred years before, he'd said, to take up the land. Being so far away from Europe, they mostly had only each other on which to turn their fighting instincts. And so they were struggling to find a way to bring law into the land. She'd loved to hear about the Althing, the yearly conclave on the plain of Thingvellir, where free men met to attend to the law. Though this assembly could sentence the guilty to fines or to banishment, its judgments could only be enforced by the sword of the aggrieved. Justice was cold and uncertain, as cold as she was now, slipping deeper into the water, and as uncertain as the rocks ahead of her, toward which she strived.

Her arms grew stiff. Her legs could hardly kick. But she forced herself on and at last came close enough almost to be able to touch the rock from which she started. Something on the rock reared up, as if to fend her off. She touched the rock but slipped, and then a hand pulled her out onto the flat surface.

She lay exhausted, wanting to say thank you to the hands that covered her with linen and wool, but she could not. Then she heard a voice, and this snapped her into full awareness.

"Hakon, it's you!"

"Gudrid, Gudrid, I was afraid you were going to drown! What made you do that anyway? I was just about to jump in after you." Gudrid's eyes focused on Hakon's bare chest, and she saw that against it he was holding her amulet.

She jumped up and snatched it away. She could say nothing in her fear for him. Nor for a moment did it occur to her that she was standing naked before this boy, who was displaying more than casual interest in her new-woman body. She threw on her clothes and began to jump and stamp her feet, partly to banish the cold and partly to chase away the fear of what her negligence might bring on him.

She managed to rid herself of the cold, though not the fear, and Hakon stood with her, saying very little, listening to the cries of the birds that swooped and soared over the water. Then a subtle change came into the air. The sky had become considerably more cloudy, with only a few splashes of sunlight on the water, and the wind was rising. Whitecaps foamed, even in the little cove, and the seal was gone. Except for the wind, everything became very silent. A gust, stronger than any of the others, sent a chill of apprehension through her. Something Arnora had said came back to her now: "Tune your feelings to the wind, and you will hear what others cannot." The vague fear deepened to definite foreboding. Something was wrong. They had to get home fast.

Before she had time to act on this impulse, some figures came running along the shoreline, and she knew they meant to cut off her escape and Hakon's where the rocks joined the beach. They were young men, most without beards, but they were carrying spears and axes. Gudrid shouted to Hakon, at the same time jumping from rock to rock. Hakon followed.

They reached the beach just before the intruders got there, and they began to run uphill toward the farmstead. Hakon was the faster runner; he would get ahead a little, then stop to urge Gudrid on. Hakon hesitated, knowing he could do little to help her. She could see in the swaying motion of his body his fear of being shown a coward. Gudrid ran as fast as she could, but she stumbled on the hem of her shift. Then her foot found a hole and her ankle turned. She heard the shouts of her pursuers getting louder and closer, and once felt a hand graze her back. Each step on the ankle was pain. She willed her body up the hill and managed to get a little ahead. Hakon shouted encouragement. But the pain grew worse, and her run was reduced to a hop, limp, hop, and she was caught. Several of the pursuers stopped to take hold of her, while others kept on toward Hakon.

Hakon turned away and ran up the hill. At one point, it seemed he, too, would be caught, but he was too swift and the hill was too high, and one by one the others dropped off. Hakon paused at the top of the hill at a point where he could see the distant farm, and looked back. Gudrid saw him hesitating, and again she could feel the conflict between cowardice and bravery, prudence and foolhardiness, swirling about within him. He called back, "You'll have Bjorn Vifilsson to deal with if you don't let her go right now. I know who you are." He called out several names, then turned and was out of sight over the rise.

Gudrid paid attention to only one of the names, the first Hakon called. That was Ymir Hrolfsson, son of the berserk of Froda. It was he who held her now in his rough hands, while the others simpered around him, waiting to see what he would do. She trembled like a ptarmigan caught by a fox.

One of the younger boys mumbled Bjorn's name, but Ymir silenced him with a glance. Then, with both of his hands, he picked Gudrid up and half carried, half dragged her down the steep slope to the edge of the water. He pulled her shift down over her arms to her waist, so that she was pinioned. He stood in front of her, leering and

64

curling his lip, and squeezed her breasts. She tried suddenly to break away, but Ymir caught her almost before she was able to move, and two of the others came forward and held her also. She continued to struggle until someone slapped her in the face.

She screamed again and again with all the power her voice could call up. Ymir laughed. "Howl away," he said. "Maybe the boy'll hear you." She could remember nothing of what Arnora had taught her; she was as helpless as any untutored girl. The amulet hung heavy on her chest.

Ymir grasped it, breaking the chain, and held it in his hand. Gudrid took some comfort that Ymir had taken the amulet, for now its effect would fall on him, but since it had been taken from her, she no longer felt under its protection.

Ymir threw the amulet to the ground and once again approached her. He tore loose what remained of her clothing, while two of the larger boys held her arms behind her. The others began to masturbate furiously. She hurt, but the fear was stronger than the pain. She kicked out at Ymir until two more boys grabbed her legs and lifted her from the ground. Their fingers gripped her thighs, prying them apart. She heard voices all around her, but they seemed strangely muffled, as by surf, so that she could not understand what they were saying. She tried to listen for her father and the others coming to rescue her, but the hill was empty except for a dumb sheep looking down.

Ymir let his trousers fall, and he displayed satisfaction that she could not move her eyes from his swelling penis. She'd seen boys before, pissing in the hills, and she'd seen rams rutting the ewes. But her idea of the male organ's size had been formed more by the feel of what her own body might accept than by what she'd seen in field and byre. Her mind slowed. One thought slipped by: He's a freak. Now Ymir pressed it toward her thighs. Veins bulged out the side of it. She struggled to avoid it, her lunges damped to quivers by strong hands. It didn't go. It would never go; it was too big. What remained of her mind seized this thought in desperate hope. Then even that hope slipped away. She felt like a butterfly about to have her wings picked off, and she knew it was not the sex need that drove Ymir and the others but something dark and hideous. Anger forced its way out and burst past the fear, and getting one arm loose, she grasped for the knife at a boy's side, within her reach. One of them wrenched her arm back again, and a new shock of pain hit her. She felt her head drop loosely back. She smelled the rank man-odor. Through a corner of her eye she saw Ymir pull back his loins to thrust again.

Then a thin sound came, muffled by the wind, of shouts from high up the hillside. She glimpsed movement and a glint of helmets. Ymir's erection fell. She heard a murmur of fear from those who held her, and Ymir's face lost its look of pleasure. After the others had dropped her, he kicked her flat onto her back and spit onto her face. She saw him draw his foot back from beside her head but could do nothing to ward it off. She choked on a mouthful of pain but could not move as he prepared to kick her again. Then one of the others shouted to Ymir, and he turned and ran. Gudrid did not watch them go; she could only stare numbly at the blood dripping onto the stones.

9.

She watched Bjorn come toward her with the others. She lifted her head and saw the circle of faces surrounding her, faces from the farm, Runolf and Asgrim, Knut and Floki, armed with swords and helmets. Hakon came running down the hill. He'd done his best to warn them in time, and he had been in time—just. Behind him was Mord.

Bjorn stood over her, making no move to help her. He spoke without feeling. "You were warned, daughter, not to come down here by yourself. You are no simple child. You might have known something like this might happen. You did know! You wanted it to happen. Just as *she* did." He looked at her. "Get up."

She sat up, gathering her shawl around her, and Hakon, seeing her struggle to preserve her dignity, gave her the rest of her clothing and the cord from his own tunic. She fumbled with it, trying at first to tie it around her waist, and when that didn't work out, around her shoulders. Finally she stood up, ignoring the men's stares, and slipped her dirtied linen over her head.

"I will go now," she said.

The procession made its way up the slope. It was very much like something she'd heard of, where a woman accused of adultery was taken to the drowning pool.

When they reached the house, Bjorn dismissed the others.

"You've let a man rape you."

"What do you mean let? How could I have stopped him?" And then, "Father, he didn't— I mean . . ."

"He raped you. Ymir Hrolfsson of Froda."

The name rolled off Bjorn's tongue with a sickening sweetness. He seemed to savor it like mutton broth. The downward curve of his mouth turned upward, but there was no hint of softness in it.

"Why are you smiling?" she asked.

He exhaled slowly, silently. "This is a chance I've waited seven years for. The truce I made at Froda—do you know how it's torn me?" She smelled yesterday's meat in his breath. "I didn't want to settle. They burned my farm. I could have beaten them that day, but they had allies. They'd have been back. I had no choice. Now things are different. The rape of a chieftain's daughter is worse than a killing. They'll find far fewer friends in Snaefellsnes or the Dales."

Her eyes crawled up from his beard to the top of his nose. "Father, I have to tell you something. He didn't— He hurt me; they all did. He tried, but Hakon . . . you . . ."

Bjorn's expression darkened. "He did, he didn't—it's all the same. What the world will know is that you were raped, and I'll have my vengeance. Anyway, I've already called for midwives."

"Midwives? Father, I've just told you—"

"You were half unconscious. I doubt you know what went on."

"Father, I can tell you—"

"Silence, child! I've sent for two midwives from farms upcountry. I can trust them."

He ordered her confined to bed. Her whole body ached, the sockets of her arms, the skin of her thighs, her ankle, but most of all her jaw. Several teeth were loose, and blood still seeped into the cloth she chewed. The only part that didn't hurt was the one that Ymir had most tried to injure.

Waiting for the midwives, she was an object for display, and people coming and going would look her way, some furtively, some openly. She felt the shame of it, of remembering herself on the ground, legs aspraddle, and all those men around her, gawking. The looks of most who came by drove home that it was her fault, that she'd soiled herself. No one came to console her.

Except for Hakon, who needed consoling himself. At least he'd come over and talked with her, and then stood in front of her bed, in order at least partially to obscure the view of others. He held her hand when no one could see, and she his. She understood that his sadness wasn't entirely for her, but until Mord came by, she didn't discern the source of his other grief.

"Coward," Mord said in a half whisper. "This wouldn't have happened if you'd stood by her." Hakon seemed to shrink at this remark.

"No, it wouldn't," Gudrid said. "He'd be dead, and so would I. I'd wonder what you'd have done if you'd been there, except I don't have to guess. You'd have run so fast you'd be halfway to the East Firths by now."

Mord sneered. "You think you know so much. I guess you know a lot more about men now. I wonder if you'll have Ymir's baby?"

"Nothing happened!" Hakon's face flushed. "We were in time"— his voice dropped—"just."

Mord shot a finger toward Gudrid's belly. "She was bleeding at the twat."

"You're a liar!" Hakon said, screaming softly that others might not hear. He hesitated, not sure of his ground. "Anyway," he continued, "it may be it was her time of month."

"She had no rag on that I could see."

Hakon seized Mord around the neck, and so entangled, they rebounded off several roofposts, shouting oaths as they did so. A man nearby tore them apart. "Go outside and fight," he said, and they hurried out. They returned later, both with cut and bruised faces, so that Gudrid didn't know who had gotten the worse of it.

She was left to worry over what the midwives would say. Her father's talk did nothing to ease her anxiety. Then, when they did arrive late in the day, they decided to wait until morning to examine her. The light would be better, they said.

The night passed slowly. Many times she recalled the scene by the water and consulted her aches and sores. She discovered that in searching for the hymen, she'd pierced it through with her finger. This woke her, and she felt a moment's relief that this at least had been only a dream. Then, again, someone shook her, and she awoke to the bustle of morning.

The midwives took her outside, between two byres. Everyone but the midwives was sent away, and thus isolated, she had to endure their poking, grunting, and whispered conferences out of earshot.

"Remember you are women too," she begged them, but they said nothing in response. She tried to look them in the eye, but they shifted theirs away.

Finally they called for Bjorn.

"Your daughter is no maiden," they said, one after the other, in ritual voices.

Gudrid received an explanation for the midwives' perjury, though it was from a source she did not want to believe.

"Two women went home with heavy purses," Mord said to her through a mouth twisted with mirth. He would have said more, but fell silent when Bjorn entered the house. To her surprise, Orm was following him.

Was this real? Or was Orm dead too, and this his ghost? She ran to him, expecting him to gather her in as he always had. He, however, greeted her formally, and then the two men walked to the far end of the house, talking softly, not wishing to be heard. She went outside and sat on the turf fence.

Hours later Orm emerged.

"You understand, aye? I'm not your foster father anymore. But Bjorn asked me to help him. It's not easy work he's set for me, you know."

"Work? What work?"

"I have to go to Froda."

"By yourself? The berserk will kill you."

"Nay, child. But I'm the only one of Bjorn's men he'd not slay, and only for I'm a Stapi man. That's why I'm to go, just to give his terms to settle this." Orm paused, thinking. "He could ask a heavy weight of gold for what's been done to you."

Her sore face warmed. "Gold! Is that all?" She thought of the midwives and calculated a fat return on Bjorn's investment in them.

Orm remained without expression. "Bjorn won't take blood-price."

She said nothing, but her face was a question.

"He won't take gold, but he's terms. Hrolf's to tie Ymir hand to foot and roll him over cliffside."

"He won't do that."

"Aye. But I have to go still. Your father will trust me again when I come back."

"Will you be back soon?"

"I'm going home first. Bjorn needs time, so I'll look after my fields awhile. Then I'll be to Froda. After that . . ."

He hugged her now, until his horse, led by a thrall, whinnied behind him, and he mounted and rode away.

In the days that followed, men began to appear at Bjorn's gate until the house seemed full to overflowing. Weapons and armor hung everywhere. Gudrid began to notice a change in the attitude of people around her. Mostly it was because of the newcomers. Rather than look on her as something ruined, they began to treat her as a noble victim, crying for revenge. That she wanted revenge was something she made no effort to hide, but this was a fraud, a fraud she could not even protest.

Gudrid's feelings toward her father had always been ambiguous. She'd always been in awe of him and still was. He was a brave man, never at a loss. His aloofness toward her, which she had taken for granted when she was small and knew of nothing beyond the farm, she now had come to resent.

Despite this, she'd never hated him. He'd never wronged her before. Now he was using her for his own purpose, in some ways as cruelly as Ymir had, and more cruelly in that he had the force of law and custom behind him.

But this rage of his was hers too. She wanted the berserk dead— and his son too, if that were possible. She almost would be willing to be regarded a wasted woman if that were what it took to bring satisfaction. She imagined the berserk lying on the ground, spurting blood, with Orm's sword in his gut. She envisioned Ymir's severed head. She smiled. Some of Arnora's teaching came back to her, and she set about preparing charms and herbal remedies for the men to take with them. Even Mord approved of her behavior for once.

A week passed, filled with preparations for war. One afternoon she found herself with Hakon on the hillside, watching some men practicing at swords.

"The Froda men will be getting ready too," he said.

"They won't be able to match Bjorn," she replied.

"Don't be so sure. There are many who owe them a favor."

"Bjorn's a chieftain. They won't go against him."

"Iceland has other chieftains. Gizur the White and Valgard the Gray have kin in Froda. Most of your father's friends are in the north. Swords are in demand just now."

"Well, then, he'll wait for them. He's not a fool."

"He's a man of honor. You don't think he's doing this for you, do you?"

"For me? As Freya lives, no!" She reached out her hand to him. "Would he really go to Froda outnumbered?"

"He has to. He's a chieftain. He'd lose his following otherwise."

Gudrid closed herself off in thought: Orm will be with them. He won't hold back, limp or no. What chance will he have?

She watched the fog come in over the ocean until the farm was covered with it. Her love for Orm began to soften the sharp edges of her anger. Yes, she wanted Hrolf and Ymir to die, as slowly and as painfully as possible. Would she see Orm die for it? Halldis a widow? No.

Then Hakon shifted beside her. He'd been thinking, too.

"Mord was right about me. I was afraid. I wanted to help you, but there were so many of them. They would have killed us both."

Gudrid understood what was in her friend's heart. Something needed to be said.

"I believe you, Hakon. If you hadn't shouted my father's name, they would have been quicker about what they did. And if you hadn't run back to the farm, Bjorn wouldn't have known where to find me."

"If it happens again, I'll stand by your side. I promise." She could not misjudge his sincerity. It came to her then that this blood feud might be averted.

"Would you say what happened before chieftains and jurymen at the Althing?"

He held her and pressed his cheek against hers almost as though she were his mother. "Yes, Gudrid! I would! I would!"

She pursued the point. "Even with Ymir standing next to you?"

Hakon hesitated a moment, but forced out his answer. It came more softly than she would have wished. "Yes."

She nevertheless was satisfied. That evening she approached her father.

"Why can't you come to terms with Ymir's father? He'd have to acknowledge himself in the wrong and offer payment."

"You don't place much value on yourself." He looked at her questioningly. "What's come over you? Until now you've been pleased with the way things were going."

"What value have you placed on me, except as an excuse for more killings?"

"You want revenge as much as I do."

"It's not for me that I wanted revenge."

"You or that woman who nursed you. It doesn't matter. You'll get what you want now. There'll be a lot of dead men before this is over."

"Orm . . ."

"Probably. Me, too, maybe, though I doubt that would trouble you."

"There is another way. You could bring a lawsuit at the Althing."

"I could. And gain a few marks in gold."

"And exile the berserk and his son!"

"Only to see them back in three years. To harry me again and provoke laughter behind my back. There's not much honor a chieftain can gain at Thingvellir. The law is for cowards."

"You're no coward, Father, but you know what you're doing to me. It's your honor you care about, not mine."

"Your honor is my honor, whether you like it or not. That's why I have to do what I'm doing. It's why I've always done what I've done. You're little more than a child. You don't understand blood. You don't understand honor."

"Blood and honor, they are the same. They both mean death and people left all alone."

"That may be. But a man isn't a man without honor. Without honor he becomes a slave. Look at you, what they did to you. If you could only see your face. They would have killed you. I've seen the berserk's whole family. Outlanders, but they fit right in at Froda. Dirty. Lazy. Cowards.

"Make no mistake, child. Ymir's father expects me to strike. If I don't, he'll laugh at me publicly, and then he'll rub my face in the mire by striking himself. In a cowardly way, like the last time, but you can be sure he'll strike. No, I must hit him first." Bjorn scratched his thigh. "I hope Orm is moving his family up to Stapafell."

"I'm sure he'll see to it after he's run your errand."

"Good. Then it's settled."

She felt nailed to a post by her father's talk. She searched her mind for another argument, though he was beyond reason. Orm's life was at stake, and many others too. She could do no more than beg.

"Please, Father." She knelt before him.

"I don't understand you. Maybe you aren't my daughter after all."

He caught himself while saying this, as though to take it back, but he let it go and then would say nothing more. Gudrid said nothing either and left it to Bjorn to speak.

"The next Althing's not till next summer, as you well know. It'll be a long winter for me to wallow in my anger. What witnesses do you have? None of those who did this will admit to it."

"You forget Hakon."

"Yes, Hakon. Runolf—" Bjorn's expression took on a worried look, as if to say, "That boy's father has something to deal with." He did pause, however, seeming to consider, so that she thought he might have changed his mind. Then he said, "No good. It's still two against many. There's only one way. My kinsmen and henchmen are ready. We'll ride over to Arnarstapi tomorrow morning as soon as it's light. We'll attack as soon as Orm returns with Hrolf's refusal."

What she said next came neither from bravado nor from fear. The words formed themselves.

"Then, Father, I have to tell you that I'll do something you'll say is dishonorable. I'll say I lied about what happened. That I really encouraged Ymir, so that he thought I was willing, and then blamed him because I was afraid of you. That will make you a murderer yourself, subject to action at the Althing. You'll be the one to pay, with money you haven't got. Maybe you'll be exiled yourself."

Bjorn froze. Then he erupted. "Shut your mouth and keep it shut! If I ever hear that kind of talk from you again, I'll see you regret it!"

His face was red as a war shield. His voice spawned fear. He walked slowly away, almost the length of the house, then strode back quickly as though about to strike her. She flinched, but she held her ground. She looked straight at him and did her best to set her jaw the way she'd seen him set his.

Then she reached inside her shift and pulled out the amulet, thrusting it toward him, seeking bare flesh. Now it was his turn to flinch; but then he cupped his hands below it, daring her to drop it. They both stood still, listening to each other breathe, until sounds came from outside. Gudrid slowly pulled back the stone and replaced it out of sight. They looked toward the door, but no one entered.

Bjorn broke the silence. "The young man—Einar. I could change my mind about him. He's in no position to care too much whether you've been . . . violated."

Her blood rushed to her head, to hear him speak the word. "To Hel with Einar," she screamed. "You think I'd take him now?" Her gorge tightened in a jumble of words that blocked each other's way out.

"Orm, then," he said, composed, soothing. "You love him. You'd like to go back to Arnarstapi. Leave off this foolish business and you can go after I wipe Froda up."

This was tempting, she was nearly persuaded, but logic brought her up short. Would Orm still be alive after all of this? Would it ever end? Even if he was, and it did, would Arnarstapi ever be safe for her?

"No," she said.

He looked at her, his eyes shiny and dark like wet stones.

"You're a strong-willed little woman," he said at last, "and I do see my blood in your face. All right. I'll wait for the Althing. But remember, if the judgment doesn't go the way I want . . . that stinking maggot-gut boneless bag of skin . . . I'll spill more blood than you can imagine. Now get out of my sight, and the less I see of you between now and then, the better."

10.

Winter blew cold that year. It blew even colder whenever, in spite of her every attempt to avoid him, she would meet her father unexpectedly and once again feel his black frown. The Yule feast was a meager one, and the guests did not fill the hall as in past years. Orm and Halldis stayed at Stapafell with their household relatives. Others were away in Norway or the Hebrides, and still others had gone to Greenland.

Among those who remained, there was much talk of Greenland. Twenty-eight ships filled with colonists had departed the year after Erik's return from exile, and by now—if traders were to be believed —the farms were thriving. Bjorn sometimes wondered aloud whether he should have gone with Erik, but he always came down on the side of satisfaction that he'd stayed where he was.

Her jaw healed slowly, until a missing back tooth was the only reminder of it.

Spring came, then midsummer, the time when the light never left the land, even when the twilight sun slipped briefly under the northern horizon. Now it was time for the Althing, the great gathering that, in addition to its main purpose of deciding the law in Iceland, was the principal social event of the year.

Gudrid, however, did not look forward to it. Her feelings remained at odds, still wanting revenge but indignant that to gain it her father would forfeit her standing in society and her chance for an advantageous marriage.

She'd set this in motion herself, she had to remind herself. She'd have to take it as it was, like wool cut from the hindquarters with the dung still on it. The day before they were to leave, she took Hakon aside.

"Remember what you promised. This lawsuit my father's bringing, it's instead of the blood feud. I had a hard time convincing him, and only on the strength of what you would say. You will tell what you saw, won't you?"

Hakon's face bore a look of fear. "I want to," he said weakly.

Gudrid stared in apprehension. "Hakon, what's the matter?"

"Onund."

"Onund?"

"Onund. Onund of Froda. I saw him in Arnarstapi."

"Oh. Did he say anything to you?"

Hakon was shaking. "He said beware the blood eagle."

She wanted to ease his fear, but this was no night terror to be swept away with a kiss. It was real enough. She'd often wondered what she'd do if she were a man and had to consider the possibility of such a fate, to have the lungs ripped out through broken back ribs and feel them stretched out behind like the wings of a bird. Then she remembered her mother, and she decided that one had to live one's life as best one could. Hakon would have to testify.

"Are you afraid?"

"Yes."

"But you're not alone here. Your father and mine and my father's men will protect you, and in a few years you'll be able to stand in the line and protect yourself. In the meantime, you've made me a promise, and I expect you to keep it."

She looked at him firmly, and he seemed to understand that she meant what she said. He nodded to her and walked away slowly.

The ride to Thingvellir took four days, most of which were spent getting the twenty horses out of mudholes and over streams. Runolf had taught Gudrid the finer points of riding, but her gentle old mare was dead, and she still felt uneasy on the new horse. They had to take the more difficult path, because it was the only way to get past Froda. One of the ways to win a lawsuit was to prevent one's opponent from reaching Thingvellir.

She'd never forget her last glimpse of home, the mountain Snaefellsjokul. The cone of white glistened in the distance, the day uncommonly clear. She'd never seen it like that before, from afar, but only up close, so that its wholeness remained unperceived. So it is, she thought, that one can live with something all of one's life, and never understand it.

They'd had plenty of time to discuss the lawsuit. It had been necessary last summer to catch Orm before he reached Froda. Orm's mission, which had been to offer haughty terms that had no chance of being accepted, was now to give proper notice of the lawsuit and to name witnesses. All through the proceedings, from this first announcement to the trial itself, they would have to adhere strictly to the proper verbal formulations and court procedures. Even one slip would mean that the suit was lost. Orm must have done his part perfectly, because by all reports Hrolf Marsson was making thorough preparations to defend himself.

When they reached the base of the peninsula, they turned south, across the boggy plain of Myrar, and up between the mountains of Skorradale. They had a long ride over lava soil, with only a track to follow that hurt the horses' hooves, and then beneath a dull sky they came in sight of the dark cliff.

She'd heard descriptions of this feature that defined Thingvellir, but none of them had prepared her for it. Superlatives could not do justice to it, because superlatives were beside the point. Compared with the mountain behind it, it was not high. Compared with the glaciers, it was not long. The sloping plain below ran bleakly down to the lake. The lake was large, but still it was small when compared with the sea.

Thingvellir awed her nevertheless. The earth, torn in two here, was healed imperfectly, leaving this great ragged scar that towered above and stretched far into the distance. She looked at the cliff more closely. Its dark brown rock seemed eternal, impregnable, yet clearly it had been beaten into the indented, undulating texture. It bore Thor's hammer marks.

Then came to her mind the great buildings, the temples of Rome and of Mikklagard, called by the southerners Constantinople. They were not large when compared with mountains or rivers either. Yet they were great because they embodied intelligence. This was Iceland's great building, and it was built not by men but by the gods.

Facing the cliff and separated from it by a declivity wide enough for several horsemen to ride abreast was a much lower ridge. At one point this secondary ridge rose to a little summit, so that a man standing at its highest point could feel almost able to touch the side of the cliff and at the same time be seen by all who congregated on the slope below.

"The Law Rock," Runolf said to Hakon. "The man on top is the Lawspeaker, Thorgeir of Ljosavatn."

The Lawspeaker was the most respected man in Iceland. Though he did not himself decide anything at Thingvellir, he could have tremendous influence over the way things were decided by the chieftains and by men the chieftains appointed. He needed a good memory. The one task he had to perform flawlessly was to stand on top of the Law Rock and recite all the laws of Iceland. These were numerous enough that only a third of the Law could be recited each year. For this reason the Lawspeaker was appointed for a three-year term, which could be renewed. Thorgeir was in his third term.

Until now it had never really come home to Gudrid what it meant for her father to be called a chieftain. She'd seen men come to his farm on important business, but she'd never paid much attention to them, even before she ran afoul of Ymir; after that, she'd done her best to stay out of sight when strangers came calling.

Now Bjorn rode ahead of the group, sitting upright in his saddle as several groups of people noticed who he was and came over to greet him.

"Hail! Hail, Bjorn! A word with you!" This was to be repeated many times in the next few days.

Nevertheless, she had to remind herself that there were thirty-eight other chieftains and that all it took to keep a blood feud going was for a roughly equal number of chieftains to be ranged on either side. They had the Althing as a safety device, so that a bloodletting could be stopped if it got out of hand, but often considerable carnage was necessary before these men began to consider that it had done so.

Bjorn led them down to the plain. It was full of people and animals. Every family of decent rank had a plot of ground and one or more booths, little roofless houses, which henchmen and thralls were busy covering with tent cloth. Women dressed in their finest were passing from booth to booth to renew acquaintance with those they had not seen since the previous summer. The fine woolen cloth that they wrapped themselves in, dyed in various hues, demonstrated their industry and skill at distaff and loom. Their breast brooches, whether of gold, silver, or base metal, bespoke their wealth and their rank. The men, too, were dressed in their finest—straight-fitted tunics appliquéd with patterns in red and green and gold, and trousers that could be either straight-legged or the new style that was loose in the thigh and gathered below the knee. Over everything they wore great shaggy cloaks of sheepskin, which would keep out the rain and the raw wind. The fingers of the more wealthy were clustered with rings; Gudrid noticed that Bjorn's fingers were bare. Her father did wear his favorite sword; he'd never sell that, she knew. The smoke of fires blended with the smell of horses. Children squealed and goats bleated.

She leaped from her horse and hurried through the encampment. Several times she saw a man or a boy from Froda, but they appeared not to notice her, and she passed them by without expression. Then, at the end of a row of booths, she saw Orm carrying a hamper of barley in each hand, and she ran to catch up with him, calling "Foster Father, Foster Father!"

Orm turned around, set the hampers on the ground, and stretched out his arms.

"Gudrid, Gudrid," he said as he embraced her. "Are you all right?" He looked at her and smiled. "A hard winter it was without my daughter." The feel of Orm's hands around her shoulders showed that his love for her was the same as ever. Now Halldis appeared through the doorway of Orm's booth, and Gudrid ran to embrace her. Clovis stood shyly in the background.

Then Orm spoke. "Where's Bjorn?"

"I think he's on his way to the Law Rock, to give notice of our action against Ymir and Hrolf."

"Does he know Hrolf's changed chieftains?"

"No, I don't think so. What difference does it make?"

Orm slapped his forehead. "You know so little of the law! He'll go the wrong quarter!"

79

"What do you mean?"

Orm jumped up and began a limping run toward the Law Rock. Gudrid kept up with him easily and could have run ahead, but she didn't know what urgent message Orm had for her father. His remark about the quarter reminded her that four separate courts met at Thingvellir, one governing each of the four coasts of the island. Suit had to be brought in the proper court, or it was invalid. And the proper court was not necessarily the one in whose jurisdiction the crime was committed, but the one in whose quarter lived the chieftain to whom the accused owed allegiance.

She understood now. She broke ahead of Orm and raced toward the Law Rock. People were gathered around it, some talking in groups, some on errands. She pushed past them and through a group of six lowing cows being led to the slaughter. Ahead she saw Bjorn standing on the Law Rock. He was conversing with the Lawspeaker. She couldn't tell whether he'd finished speaking or hadn't spoken yet. She pressed through the clotted throng at the Law Rock's base, and now her father began in a loud voice.

"I give notice of an action against Hrolf Marsson and his minor son Ymir in that the boy did sexually violate Gudrid, my daughter, and that the father did harbor the son and so did make the crime his own. I demand that Hrolf be outlawed on account of this, that no one hail him or help him or hide him. I claim half his goods, the other half to go among the men of his quarter as prescribed by law.

"Now, therefore, I refer this action to the proper quarter court, which is the . . ."

Gudrid leaped up onto the Law Rock. She threw her head back and let out a loud wail. The Lawspeaker looked at her as though she were possessed. He looked questioningly toward Bjorn, who by now had come down and had begun to shake her.

Then Orm managed to press through the crowd, and he was able to give Bjorn a full explanation.

"I refer this action," Bjorn continued, "to the proper court, which is the South Quarter!" Gudrid saw Hrolf in the crowd, and she enjoyed his frustration.

Bjorn finished the charge according to form. "I give notice of this action. I give proper notice before witnesses at the Law Rock. I give notice of this action, to be heard at this meeting, for full outlawry against Hrolf Marsson."

The Lawspeaker told those within hearing that the charge appeared to be properly brought and would be heard by the South Court the following day.

Hrolf had gained one point. The jurymen who would decide the case were chosen by the chieftains of the quarter whose court it was. Bjorn was of the West Quarter, and had the trial remained there, he would have had a hand in this selection. Now he could only try his influence from afar, and Hrolf surely had at least one South Quarter chieftain in his pocket. Bjorn tore off to see what he could still do, and Gudrid saw nothing more of him that day. He rose early, so she didn't see him the next morning either.

The South Court was held near the shore of the lake. It seemed an appropriate place for something as serious as the law. The water stretched out before them, calm or ruffled or whipped to froth, depending on the day. Up the hill the whole cliff stretched out, with the Law Rock near the center. Mountains, half covered with snow, ringed around them, the highest towering above and behind the cliff. The morning was clear, the first without fog or drizzle since Bjorn's arrival. Pitched on a low rise was a single awning beneath which nine finely carved chairs had been set. They were for the chieftains of the South Quarter. These men, dressed in fine silk, stood talking with their advisers and with other men of high station who had taken the lull in the proceedings as an opportunity to discuss some issue that affected their fortunes. Hrolf's coup was plain to everyone. Bjorn would have been sitting in one of those chairs if the case had remained in the West Court, and as he was both plaintiff and chieftain, the case could hardly have gone against him.

In front of the chieftains' seats were three benches long enough to accommodate twelve men each. These were for the jury, thirty-six men of good standing chosen by the chieftains to decide the cases brought before them. At the moment, the benches were empty.

Ymir and his father stood off to one side talking with others who supported them. They did not appear to notice Bjorn.

Bjorn strode forward and addressed one of the southern chieftains by name, and the greeting was returned with apparent cordiality.

Gudrid kept looking up the hill for Hakon and Runolf, his father. At last, she saw their figures at the edge of the camp.

The chieftains seated themselves. The man in the center seat raised his hand, and all about were silent. The jurymen, as bedecked and bejewelled as they could afford, stood with faces ruddy in the wind, most with long hair and beards. At the eldest chieftain's signal, they sat down.

Bjorn as plaintiff was the first witness. He spoke of Hakon's frantic cry of alarm, of how they found Gudrid, and of Ymir and his gang running away. His accusation was short and sharp, his long finger pointing out Hrolf and Ymir on the opposite side of the awning.

Hrolf Marsson's turn was next. He and Ymir were of the same mold, but he was larger, still the father to the son. His eyes were deep and his mouth was large, and beneath the embroidered tunic and the court manners crouched the berserk's scream. He walked to the center of the awning, his hard glance fading to a placid look of humble respect as he turned to face the jury and the chieftains.

"Respected sirs," he began, "I must speak of certain things. I cannot avoid this, though I assure you that the honor of this court is uppermost in my mind. Nor do I have anything against this girl, whose injury, real or imagined, is the cause of this proceeding. But when a man of high reputation uses his daughter to defame another man, then the truth must be told." He glanced around. For the jury he had an obsequious smile; for Ymir, the grin of a crafty conspirator; for Bjorn, a sneer of contempt. "I am certain that what Gudrid has done came more from ignorance than from cunning and is the result of a lack of upbringing in the proper behavior of a young woman. Highborn wench! Even slave girls are better bred. Do you know that before her twelfth year was finished, she'd shown her body to all the boys of Arnarstapi *and* Froda, and lain with half of them? That she tried to get my son to lie with her in my hayfield? This is what she has against my son—that he wouldn't have her! I don't know whether she ever suffered an injury or not, but if she did, my son had nothing to do with it."

Now, facing the jury directly, he made his challenge. "Show me one witness, other than the girl herself, who will say that what I have said is false or that what she says is true."

Hrolf stepped aside to join Ymir, who was smiling the same sickening smile she remembered. She tried to catch Hakon's eye, but he, too, was watching Ymir. Ymir looked toward Hakon and made a slight gesture with his elbows, seeming to imitate a bird flying, but he did it subtly. Neither the jury nor the chieftains appeared to notice.

While she was considering the meaning of this, she sensed another presence at her elbow. She looked up, and it was Einar! The shock of seeing him nearly knocked her into a heap. No words could pass their lips because the herald was calling for the next witness.

Hakon moved tentatively toward the front bench. One of the jurymen, selected by the others as foreman, leaned forward. He looked into the boy's face and seemed to sense the caged fear. He held his hands forward, facing the sky, in a gesture of reassurance. "Tell us what happened," he said to Hakon.

Hakon hesitated. He was looking over toward Ymir. Ymir made the flapping gesture again. Hakon shuddered visibly. The blood eagle, Gudrid thought; this is Ymir's way of reminding him. Nothing could be done, she knew. To anyone else, it would be nothing more than a nervous tic. Einar tried to get Gudrid's attention again, but she nudged him aside.

Hakon began. "Gudrid and I were down at the beach, right below the farm, when Ymir came with his friends. They chased us up the hill and . . . and . . ."

Einar took hold of Gudrid's shoulder and whispered into her ear. "I've bought five of the chieftains. The jury's stacked. Hrolf has no idea what he's in for. As long as you and Hakon tell the same story, they'll outlaw Hrolf. Bjorn's so pleased with this he's decided he likes me after all. He says if things go well here, I can have you." His eyes were all anticipation.

"Continue," the foreman said to Hakon.

"I ran for help. Before I went over the top of the hill, I saw . . ."

"Go on."

Hakon opened his mouth, but words did not come out. He was trying desperately to speak. "Gudrid . . . Gudrid turned and ran the other way, and she fell down the cliff and cut her face." He buried his head in his hands, fighting to hold back tears before these important men.

The foreman continued the questioning. "Hakon, you must tell the truth now. It's very important to test what has been said here already. Have you ever seen the girl there, Gudrid Bjornsdottir outside her own house unclothed?"

Hakon hesitated. When he replied, it was in a voice so soft Gudrid could hardly hear. "Yes . . . yes. But it wasn't— You must not think . . ." Tears streaming down his face, he turned and ran along the lakeshore. Gudrid would have followed him, but Orm stopped her.

Ymir strutted into the immediate presence of the court.

"I have nothing to add to Hakon's words. It is as he said. Do you have any questions to ask of me?" He sneaked a glance back at Gudrid.

The calm exterior she'd maintained up to now nearly failed her. Even to herself she'd denied emotions that desperately wanted to come out. If only she knew a spell that could kill. She was sure she'd be unable to speak, let alone convince anyone. The foreman called her name three times before she heard him.

She walked forward to the jurymen's seats, stopped, and looked around. Ymir's smile only made her hate him more. Orm and Bjorn both stood still, expressionless. Einar leaned forward from his place to the side. All around them stood a crowd, their clothing a dazzle of color and swirled embroidery: henchmen, onlookers, favor seekers, litigants awaiting their turns.

The foreman asked for quiet. Everything that had lurked in the corners of her mind now came to the fore all at once, demanding to be heard. Einar was only the latest surprise. She would not look his way. She reminded herself that he had come back to Snaefellsnes without even attempting to come for her. Could she ever forgive such neglect? But then he caught her eye, and she had to look at him, and in spite of everything a part of her still wanted him.

The foreman was speaking to her, but it was as if she couldn't understand what he was saying. Her mind was tuned to the wind, so that she had to force herself to listen, to catch the tag end of his question.

". . . after Hakon ran up the hill and left you?"

Everyone waited for her answer. She saw the people in front of her, but in the distance she saw blood and fire. In spite of Einar's bribes, after what Hakon had said the judgment would probably go against them, regardless of what she said. If they lost the case, Bjorn's wrath would be set loose once again. Yet these lies had to be answered, didn't they? The jurymen waited, patiently at first, then restlessly. Finally one said, "You must speak, Gudrid."

She felt within the folds of her robe for the amulet that was supposed to protect her. She remembered as through a fog the words of her mother's sister, and she knew that even more than revenge, her heart desired peace. But of the amulet she knew nothing more than she had the day Arnora passed into the spirit world, which is to say nothing at all, and a wave of despair passed over her. Then it came to her that only one thing could be said, and she said it.

"I have nothing to say. Many falsehoods have been spoken today, but better lies than blood. I hold no fault against Ymir, and I beg my father take back his lawsuit."

The jury rose and went far enough aside to be out of earshot. A few spoke quietly, the others listened, and in a short time all were nodding their heads. Then they returned to their seats. The foreman rose and turned to face the chieftains. "We find no judgment against Hrolf Marsson or his son, and we enjoin Bjorn Vifilsson against any further action, to inflict no brain wound, internal wound, or marrow wound by his own hand, his kinsmen's, or his thralls'."

11.

Bjorn returned to Snaefellsnes on worse terms with his daughter than ever. She'd frustrated all his efforts at Thingvellir, and she'd made sure he'd have few supporters in any renewed attempt at violence. She'd even rebuffed Einar, which Bjorn found puzzling. Gudrid never explained. A man as prideful as Bjorn might have expected this reaction in his daughter, she thought. In a way, she could even understand her father's feelings, though she could not understand his forgetfulness concerning what he'd done to her. In spite of all this, something held Bjorn back, which made his anger less profound than she would have expected.

He began to act strangely too. He would brood about the house, then rush out to survey his barns and byres, count his cattle and sheep.

One afternoon she entered the house quietly and saw him at her bed, her open jewel box in front of him, fingering the gold brooches that Einar had given her.

He looked up, and for the first time in her life she saw embarrassment on his face. He said nothing, but put the brooches back and slowly closed the lid. He wanted to ask her for them, but pride prevented this. He could simply take them, but a curious combination of honor and pride prevented that also. Men are strange beasts, Gudrid thought, and she mused on how her father thought it honorable to steal her reputation but not her gold.

"Is it obvious to everyone," he said in almost a plaintive voice, "that I have no money?"

So it was true. Suddenly it all came together. Bjorn's many conferences at Thingvellir with the kin of the dead chieftain whose title he had purchased, his behavior since coming home, and now this. He hadn't yet paid for his chieftainship! Or not all of it, at any rate.

The amulet burned on Gudrid's chest. It was becoming more and more a burden, less and less a thing to be relied on. Why didn't she do the obvious, then, and get rid of it? Was it out of love for her mother beyond the grave? Was it fear? Maybe the amulet was attracting evil forces eager to test its strength, just as Gunnar of Hlidarend, because he was the strongest man in Iceland, attracted opponents, even though he did all he could to end disputes peacefully. It could be said that Gunnar was killed by his own arms. Would the amulet do the same to her?

She felt some kind of warning, that something might happen if she acted improperly. But what? Should she offer Bjorn the brooches unasked? She felt a sudden urge to do so, that to refuse now would bring on the result she least desired. The amulet's secret! She still did not know it, but she recalled Arnora's warning: "The fate you fear most will befall you."

She couldn't make the offer now. If he wants to be a chieftain, she thought, let him find his own gold to pay for it, or let him take mine. I won't give it freely.

Bjorn seemed to know her thoughts. He looked at her, then placed the box on the bed and left the house.

The next day he called his household together.

"I have to tell you something," he said, "that I suppose you already know, even though I've done my best to hide it."

He had everyone's attention, standing in front of the fire, rubbing his beard with his left hand, his right against a dais post. The others were ringed around, some seated on the sleeping platforms, some standing, a few on benches. It was a scene to remember, the men in their working clothes and boots leaning forward, the women sitting quietly.

"I don't have the money to buy the chieftainship. They've been very generous in waiting for the sum I agreed to and in letting me take the office right away, on the strength of my word. But the story of my poverty has gotten out. Even an Orkney trader knows about it.

"And so I'm not going to see the pained smiles of my friends or listen to the ridicule of my enemies. I'm not going to watch more sheep die or suffer another bad harvest. I'm going to see whether Erik's friendship is worth what it's reputed to be. I'm going to Greenland."

The announcement sent a shock through the assembled householders. Gudrid's mind went to a time past when Erik and his boy visited. She'd been so happy to see them go. Would she have to deal with Leif again? He'd have grown; he'd be a man now. No, it just wasn't possible. It was beyond thinking. It couldn't be.

Then she felt anger that her father, on top of all the other wrongs he'd done her, was now heaping this one over the rest. She'd have to do something, anything she could, to prevent it. Perhaps her father might listen to reason. She'd give him the brooches after all. She'd stay with Orm.

He didn't want the brooches now. He'd made his announcement and didn't intend to go back on it. And Orm had already agreed to come with them.

The violent squall of her emotions gave one last blow and then

spent itself and left her in quiet, if not contentment. At least she'd
have Orm and Halldis with her again, and with that perhaps she
could put up with her father and maybe even Greenland. Her heart
was wrenched loose from her mind, and it would take her a while to
put things together again.

She sat on the slope of the mountain. She tried to forget
Ymir and the scene at the Althing. Bjorn could gnash his teeth, but
after the judgment he couldn't garner enough support to take action.
She deemed it wise, however, to keep to herself the thought that
she'd worked her own will.

She surveyed a long stretch of coast from her own high seat. The
day was bright, and for the first time since that terrible day of the
summer past, she felt like a little girl again. Seabirds rose from the
cliffs, and in the distant waters of the fjord a whale spouted. The
glacier sparkled in the sunlight. The grass was golden on the hill that
rose to a cliff cut off by the sea. Something caught her eye. It seemed
a lone figure was standing there. It was hard to be sure, though, so far
away.

Now it moved back and forth, then stopped again. Suddenly she
ran down the slope, out through the hayfields with their thriving
grass, over stone fences, across the track, and up the hill to the cliff's
edge. The figure grew until she recognized who it was. It was Hakon.
He spoke no word, nor did he move. He only looked at her for the
longest and yet the briefest of moments. Then he flung himself out
into space. Slowly she walked, then crawled to the edge, and forced
her gaze downward. His body was washing back and forth in the
waves like a doll's.

12.

She stayed at the sacred plot, oblivious of the rain, passing
from Sigunna's grave to Arnora's, to the newly dug place where
Hakon rested uneasily. It still seemed unreal to her, Hakon dead,

though she'd touched his body and kissed him on the lips. She wiped her tears with her muddy hair.

She did not hear Halldis approach, until the hand on her shoulder startled her. Halldis' long braids hung in the space between them as she stooped over.

"It will not do to cry, Gudrid," she said. "You can't blame yourself for Hakon. He'd have come to his end sooner or later. He wasn't made to be a Norseman."

"One of the few," Gudrid said quietly. "I shouldn't have made him testify."

"If you hadn't, then what? The blood feud would have started all over again."

"Maybe. Why couldn't it have been Mord?"

"You cannot think that way," Halldis said.

"Why not? Men do."

"You know how men think?"

"I know how they rule. They control our thoughts and feelings, and we don't even know it. Hakon would have been different—he was different! That's why . . ."

"One has to take things as they are, I'm afraid."

Gudrid drew in a long breath. "Things weren't always as they are."

"What do you mean?"

Gudrid took one of Halldis' braids between her thumb and forefinger and looked at it. "Let me tell you something. Women once ruled men. The men were stronger, and they had spears and arrows, but the women all knew how to cast spells. They could make men sick, kill them if they had to. They could sprout teeth in their vaginas. Everyone worshipped the Great Goddess Mother Earth.

"Then one time when the men were out hunting, they decided to kill all the women. They'd do it quickly when the chief hunter gave a cry. They'd not spare any, not even the girls, none who were old enough to have had any training in witchcraft."

"I've never heard this before," said Halldis. "Who told you this?"

"Arnora."

"I find it hard to believe. What did the men do for sex after that?"

"They had to wait for the little girls, the ones young enough to be spared, to grow up."

Halldis laughed. "I find that very hard to believe. Did the plan work?"

"Yes. The girl-children grew up not knowing what the men had done to their mothers and sisters, and ignorant of the powers that should have been theirs. The plan had only one flaw. When they returned from the hunt, the men avoided their own kin, because they weren't sure they could kill their own wives and daughters. A man named Odd loved his daughter Ellida more than anything. He had to see her. That's when the sign was given. Odd looked his daughter in the eye and knew he couldn't kill her. He took her into the forest and hid her in a cave. After that, he brought her food and warm clothing, creeping out of his hut at night, month after month, year after year. Ellida was only thirteen when this happened, so she was only half wise. Even so, a few of the little girls came to her in the forest, and she taught them secretly. All our witchcraft has come from those girls."

"If what you say is true, witches must have much less power than they once had. Yet it seems to me the power of Satan is stronger than ever."

"Why do you talk as though anything dark and hidden must be evil? The power of the seeress is a good thing. It gave me this after all." She displayed the amulet.

"You cling to it, don't you."

"Why not? If I can discover its secret, I'll have the thing I want most." She startled herself with a thought. "I think I do know it! It kills men, we know that. The secret is, there is one man it won't kill, and that's the one who's worthy of me. All I have to do is touch all my suitors, and the one who survives is the one I will marry!"

Halldis shook her head. "Hakon touched it, and so did Ymir. Whatever Hakon lacked, do you think that Ymir is a better man? No, the priests are right: witchcraft is evil—and so is your stone. Gudrid, I wish you'd give it up."

"Your priests are all men! That's why they slander us."

"You've seen something in the Faith," Halldis replied gently, "more than you've been willing to let on."

Gudrid took Halldis' hand. "Does it make any difference, your religion or ours? We have gods and you have gods. Odinn, Thor, Frey. Father, Son, Holy Ghost."

"The Three are One," said Halldis.

"Three cockerels in one stew," said Gudrid. "I think I understand."

Halldis sighed. "My God has always been. Your gods came out of mist and fire, from the milk of the cow Audhumla and the bones of the frost giant Ymir."

"Don't speak that name!" said Gudrid, heat in her voice. Then, more quietly, "Though it was aptly given."

"My God is real," said Halldis. "The Norse gods are tales told in the winter."

"Mother Earth is real!" said Gudrid. "The Norse took her away and replaced her with a cow. I thought the Virgin might be Mother Earth come back to us. Why not? If God can become man, can't the Goddess become woman?"

"What I've told you has disappointed you, I see," said Halldis.

Gudrid slid closer to her foster mother. "No. Nothing you've said has ever disappointed me."

"Then listen. The Virgin is a virgin as far as man is concerned, but she has God's seed in her. He came to her and he loved her. Her thighs knew the joy of love."

Gudrid looked straight at Halldis.

"She became a mother. And being a mother, she knew how different a woman's life is from a man's. God has made us so. A man is the same from childhood to old age. He is the same before he has his first woman as after he has had many. But a woman's first love cuts her life in two. She becomes another person then, when something begins to grow in her that she carries in darkness. She is a mother. She is a mother if her child lives or if it dies, or even if all her children die. This is the strength of woman, which no man can know . . ."

The little sobs began to come from Halldis' throat even before her speech was half through. Gudrid held her, knowing for the first time how painful Halldis found her barrenness. This explained much of Halldis' behavior toward her, at once soft and giving but at the same time distant, in a way she'd not been able to understand.

She loved Halldis better than she ever had before, but Halldis' humble acceptance of things only kindled in Gudrid a renewed urge to strive and to know.

Bjorn sold his farm, agreeing to be out by midsummer. He returned the chieftaincy to its heir. Then he bought a ship. Halldis and Orm moved in, bringing with them as many of their possessions as three horses could carry.

Soon it was Sun Month, Shieling Month, time to go. Bjorn and his household shuttled between the farm and the ship, moving out the last of their goods. Cousins and nephews who'd decided to go to Greenland camped nearby in tents, with a few thralls who, like Gudrid, had no choice in the matter.

The ship was an old broad-beamed trader's knorr, scarred but sound. She sat on the beach as the low tide turned to flood, while men scurried to load her. First came the heavy items for the hold— house timbers, ironware, and rope. Nestled among these things, like a baby in the womb, was the ship's boat, almost a copy of the ship but scarcely a quarter as long. Next came sea chests and wooden casks of salt fish, pork, and sailor's bread. Several crates of chickens went up the ramp. Then sheep and goats and four heifers, pushed, pulled, or carried, and penned near the bow. Bjorn's dais posts were tied to the mast. A young man embraced his mother and sister, stood back for one last look, then hugged them again.

The company numbered more than forty, mostly young and recently married. The women walked aboard easily, scissors and sewing things dangling on chains. The men tramped on, laughing loudly and making ribald jokes, swords clanking at their sides. Bjorn boarded with Floki, who held the hand of his new wife, a very young beauty with dark eyes and a mouth that was always parted slightly, made to drink honey and to yield it up. Mord's eyes bulged in envy of his father.

Gudrid walked silently onto the ship, with Halldis and Orm. Seeing Bjorn with the newly married Floki sparked a startling thought: Why hadn't Bjorn taken a wife? All these years, when any other man in his position would have married again to have a son, Bjorn had satisfied himself with a succession of slave concubines. It was unthinkable that a man would not want a male heir. It was another mystery.

They were ready to go now. Well-wishers gathered around the bow of the ship, which just touched the shore at high tide. Bjorn raised his hand one last time, and the men on shore pushed them off. The sail was raised, the anchor lifted. The day was fair, the breeze from the south over the port beam. Small whitecaps churned in the expanse of open water. A gust caught the sail, causing it to snap loudly. The steering oar cut the foam of the stern wake like a knife in dark ale. Snaefellsjokul glinted in the distance. Gudrid was leaving the home of her youth forever.

She wanted nothing more than to jump off and swim ashore, though she knew it would be impossible. She could only stare at the receding coast and let dull regret work its way through her. After a while the feeling lightened a little, and she was able to turn her back to the land.

She'd never been at sea before, and she gazed back and forth over the craft, as light in its element as it was heavy at the beach. The aft quarter of the ship was planked over; the rest was open. A tent extended from the mast fore and aft. The animals nattered and bellowed in the bow, while men leaped over household goods amidships, setting the angle of the sail. The breeze freshened as the lower slopes of Snaefellsjokul sank below the horizon, leaving only the icy summit in view.

The mountain is falling away from me, she thought sadly, but she comforted herself with the thought that at least she was putting distance between herself and the woman who had cursed her. She'd nearly forgotten her father's words the day he went to help Erik, but they came back to her now: "My honor demands I defend Erik with every man I have. You should know this more than anyone. Every time I look at you, I see the woman's curse."

Then another thought came, and it was as if shapeless lava had congealed beneath her ribs. Bjorn's need to support Erik was linked, in his mind, to the woman's curse. Why hadn't she seen this before? Only one woman was tied to Erik this strongly. His wife, Thjodhild. Far from leaving the curse behind, she was getting in the way of yet more trouble. This was why Bjorn had resisted going to Greenland until he'd had no other choice. She stared dully as she contemplated this and as she wondered what Bjorn had done to earn Thjodhild's enmity.

A girl named Unn sat down next to Gudrid. She was betrothed to a man who now was on the swaying mast, loosening part of the sail. Gudrid forced a smile.

"The land is good, they say. You and Kol will have a fine farmstead and raise a family to be proud of." She felt a flash of envy. This girl was not much older than she was, and already she had a life prepared for her.

"You speak encouraging words," Unn replied. "But I have to tell you my father would not let us be married in Iceland. He was afraid we both might not survive the voyage."

"As long as you're a maid, he has control of you," Gudrid said knowingly. "A widow has rights. She can manage her own affairs."

Gudrid dropped into a reverie, becoming so lost in thought that she did not notice the thickening clouds on the horizon or the continuing freshening of the wind. Unn did, and she nudged Gudrid's arm. Apprehension showed on Bjorn's face. He shouted some orders, and the men began to reef the sail. This was new business for most of them. Before long two of the reef points had parted.

A gray line of clouds eclipsed the sun. The waves grew darker. The ship's timbers worked more and more heavily as the waves passed under, and while a stoutly built ship should be able to handle this kind of a sea, they could not know what the night had in store for them. Sail was again shortened.

The afternoon light grew progressively fainter. Flashes of lightning sought out the wave tops. Gudrid pulled Unn's shivering body close to hers.

Night was a long time coming. Had the sky been clear, a twilight glow would have remained, even at midnight, but in the gloom of the storm all they could feel was the heaving of the ship, all they could hear were the wind, the waves, the creaking of wood, and the muffled shouts of men. The darkness enclosed them. The ship seemed to gather speed, as though it could sail to the end of the earth before daybreak. The gray morning retained its early dimness, the clouds trailing loose rags in the water. Bjorn and his mates did their best to head the ship into the waves, but beyond that, they were at the mercy of the storm.

Then, slowly, the force of the wind began to diminish, though the waves tossed the ship as violently as before. Gudrid and Unn allowed themselves some sleep, together in a heap.

When Gudrid awoke the ship was sailing before a light breeze. Bodies in various stages of seasickness or stupor, male and female, were strewn about the ship. The animals lay listlessly against their stanchions. Some women went out to do what they could for the sick. Gudrid sought out Halldis and Orm, who were lying against the ship's boat.

"Foster Father," she said, touching him gently. He opened his eyes. The sallow lids didn't look right to her, though his smile for her was the same as ever. Then Halldis—something more than seasickness hung about her. Her face was as yellow as her hair. Gudrid brought some salt pork, hard bread, and water, and they seemed to revive. Then she went to look after others, and in the hope of a brightening day, her anxiety began to dissolve.

But hope was not to be for long. Another storm came over the horizon, and when it had spent itself, another, day after day, until not even Bjorn could say where they were on the broad, black sea. Once a loom of land appeared in the mist, and someone said it was Iceland and they should all go home. Bjorn said it was the land of the fairies, that it would be death to go ashore. An east wind blew them back out to sea before anyone could argue.

The cold, salt wet soaked linen and wool. Lines grew reluctant in their blocks. Ice gathered on stays.

Then the dying began. Kin and thralls found lifeless were bound up with cords and rolled over the side. At each burial Bjorn invoked the gods for the farewell of the one who was gone and the safekeeping of those who remained. Seven such ceremonies took place in as many days, but it seemed like many, many more. Halldis prayed to Christ and the Virgin to have mercy on pagan souls.

One morning, after it seemed the worst was over, Gudrid was unable to wake Orm. At first, she could only stare dumbly at his jaundiced face and hands. Then she buried her face in his breast. She would have cried out, but she felt her voice stopped up by demons, the ones that carried away damned souls. She looked up and saw that Halldis, too, was dead beside him. By now, raw grief had spent itself. It was as if she'd had the spirit sucked out of her. Bjorn and several others rushed to her side and saw the cause of her anguish. He began to shake her.

"Holy Virgin!" she cried out. She could think only of the many times Orm had held her, with just two thin layers of cloth between him and her stone. "You sent Halldis to me. Why wouldn't I listen to her?" She pulled out the amulet, flinging aside the chain, and rushed to the side of the ship. "Christ Redeemer!" She raised her hand to throw it into the sea.

Bjorn stopped her arm at the top of its arc.

"Why do you call on the Christian gods?" he asked, incredulous.

Gudrid stared at him, still shivering. "Halldis tried to teach me. I wouldn't listen. I can have nothing more to do with pagan things."

Bjorn stood in silence for a moment. Then he said to her, "You're more a fool than I thought. This charm has protected you all your life, and you'd throw it away. Well, I wouldn't stop you, except for one thing. If its magic can save you, it can save the ship too. Therefore you will wear it until we reach Erik's house in Greenland. If you throw it overboard, you will follow it in haste. That you can be sure of."

Once again it was Gudrid's turn to look at the set jaw that seemed to be a family characteristic. Retrieving the chain, she tied it together as best she could and slipped it back over her head.

She'd intended to watch as the bodies of Orm and Halldis were sent to the deep, but she couldn't. When it was over, she emerged from the tent and tried to keep busy. She sensed a subtle change in the weather, and for the first time in a week, no storm clouds showed themselves. Early the next day someone shouted, "Ice!" and in the clearing mist the land unfolded. Reflected sunlight nearly blinded them. The men stood toward the ship's prow; the women gathered amidships to gaze at the new land. In the distance, far inland, loomed a dark shape. It could only be the mountain called Blue Shirt. They were on course.

"All I see are ice and snow and rock!" one summed it up. "Not a patch of green anywhere!"

Bjorn responded to the mood. "This isn't where we're going!" he shouted. "We have to sail around the other side. That's where we'll find Erik and his fields!"

So they coasted southward, the chill wind off the icecap mixing with the freezing spray. Whenever they could, they'd huddle in their skin sleeping bags, men and women alike. Gudrid and Unn drew the folds up over their heads.

"My father's a good captain," Gudrid said to comfort herself as much as Unn, and she gave thanks that whatever else he was, at least he was that. She kept to herself, though, the thought that it was a long time since he'd been to sea.

The monotonous East Greenland coast passed slowly by, headland alternating with fjord, rock with glacier. No sign of human life could be seen. A whale spouted close to the ship; then it was gone. They saw no others.

On the sixth day they entered a fjord, and soon a huge glacier appeared on the starboard side. It continued far into the distance, a blinding whiteness. Then the sky darkened and the wind shifted to the northeast. A pelting rain poured down, and they could no longer see land on either side. Lookouts kept a sharp eye for rocks. They sailed that way for three hours, until a cliff loomed out of the spray, dead ahead. No orders were needed, beyond Bjorn's first shout. Men leaped to haul the sail to as great an angle as the rigging would allow. Others pulled on the steering oar. Gradually the bow moved away from the rocks, and the the cliff slid by. A cloud of birds screamed over the mast.

Then a rift opened in the cliffs of ice and rock on the other side of the channel. The blast of wind from the gap heeled the ship to port, so that water began to splash aboard. Turned again, the ship raced downwind through a broadening strait. The rain slackened, and they could see open ocean. They were through! A loud cheer rose from every throat, and they hardly could remember now that they were cold and wet and as yet had no idea of what their new home would be like.

They sailed along the coast on a broad reach, north of west, as the blow slacked off. Bjorn looked landward, as one prominent headland grew larger and larger. Then the lookout shouted, "A farm!"

97

They all saw it, the huddle of buildings near the shore. As they closed in, they sensed something amiss. Here was not the usual bustle of a farmstead but only a few cows grazing on what looked like a poor field. As the ship drifted to the edge of the land and touched bottom, a man appeared from behind a heavy sod building.

"Is this Brattahlid?" Bjorn shouted the name of Erik's farm, and shouted again as his voice was lost in the wind. The man peered out from a hooded garment made from some kind of animal skin, with deep-set eyes over an unkempt beard. Heavy lines ran over his face. Years had passed since Erik's visit. Could this be him?

The man shouted back, but all they could hear was the tone of his voice, not the words. The tone was of welcome, however. Anguish and foreboding lessened their grip. Gudrid allowed herself to wonder what kind of hospitality Greenland might have to offer.

13.

The man called himself Durkel, and from the look of him there wasn't much to eat in this part of the world. In response to Bjorn's questions, he confirmed that many of his animals had died and most of the rest were sick. The men who'd gone seal hunting were back empty-handed. They'd run out of imported grain, and the small crop of lyme grass was growing thin, its pitiful kernels even smaller than usual; it would not last beyond the Yule.

They'd landed at Herjolfsnes, the first piece of land in Greenland that could support domestic animals. A narrow fjord could hide a ship from rough weather, and behind it rose sheer rock, mounting in jagged ridges from the water to the highest snowbound crags.

Durkel's house was built on nearly the same plan as Orm's, but the walls were much thicker, thicker than a man was tall. Though stone of a quality for building abounded in Greenland, it was used only as facing and to strengthen the wall. Most of the thickness was turf, to keep out the winter cold. Driftwood burned on the fire. This seemed a shocking waste to the Icelanders until they learned that it was plentiful on this shore and that peat was scarce. The crackling of the burning wood and the glow of the lamp were a welcome change from the cold, wet existence aboard ship.

In spite of the famine, Durkel opened his larder to the visitors, and he invited the people of the neighboring farmsteads to join in the welcome. The first man to settle this point of land, Herjolf Bardsson, had recently died, but his son Bjarni came to share the meal. He was strangely reticent, so that Gudrid had to begin by telling him her story, but something about him gave the feeling that he also might have something to say.

"Why did your father settle on the headland, and not up in the fjord?" she asked him.

"We're traders, our family. Living on the first landfall in Greenland gives us a chance to make a good bargain with other traders, especially if they haven't been here before." He laughed. "I suppose I shouldn't be telling you that."

He would have ended there, but she had more questions.

"How often do you get away from Greenland?"

"I don't. Not anymore."

"What do you mean 'anymore'?" Her question was bolder than some would think proper for a young woman.

"Since I saw the land."

"Land? What land? Tell me, please, I'm interested."

"On our last voyage, we saw some land, south and west of here. But instead of it making me famous, I'm a laughingstock because I didn't go ashore." He looked down in his beard, his bemused expression incongruous in a man as big as a bear.

A noise at the door brought them up short.

"The Little Sibyl!" someone whispered.

The door opened on the dark outside. Durkel led her in. She was a small, light-boned woman, with straight white hair that fell to her knees and a face that was almost blue. Bjarni could have carried her under his arm. Yet as the seeress looked around the dim room, her eyes seemed to press into the minds of each of those present. Gudrid felt their power. She became conscious of the will behind the shrunken visage. This was an accomplished seeress, a *volva,* so far gone in her art that she could no longer live as most mortals lived—on the common run of victuals and such love as they could find—but only on unseen sources, from which she derived her power. Arnora had been well on the way to acceptance as one of these herself when death interrupted her progress.

Durkel led the Little Sibyl to his own high seat, on which he had placed a cushion stuffed with hens' feathers. She sat on it with the ease and dignity of one accustomed to such courtesy. She wore an overvest of blue fur fastened with straps over her shoulders and decorated with shells and stones. Glass beads of many colors draped her neck, and she had on a hood lined with cat's fur. Her mittens were also lined with catskin, and she wore a belt fashioned from smooth pieces of wood. From this hung a large skin bag. Her shoes were of untanned leather with the hair out.

A special meal was brought out for her, which consisted of a porridge made from the first milk of a goat after it had given birth and a stew made from the hearts of every kind of animal that lived in the region. She took from her bag a spoon of brass and a knife with an ivory handle and a broken point. Everyone watched her eat the food, slowly, solemnly, but with observable relish. Between mouthfuls, she would give her elbow a jerk as though chasing away a too familiar lamb or kid, and she had a dewlap that would undulate each time she swallowed. When she finished the meal, she raised her arms and fluttered her fingers. Then her whole body began to shake, slowly at first and then more violently, until finally she emitted a loud hiss and then fell silent.

Now Durkel spoke. "Is everything satisfactory to you, honored guest? Will the spirits come?"

"That is not for me to say at the moment. I will have to sleep the night, and then I will let you know."

Durkel acted as if he had not expected this to span more than one evening, but he did not protest, and he showed the seeress to his own bed. He and his wife spent the night on the floor with the rest of the household and the guests, jammed close together. Gudrid lay beside her father, and spent most of the night watching the smoke curl up to the ceiling.

The next night the Little Sibyl was again placed on Durkel's high seat. She looked about her and made little pecking movements with her head, like a chicken. Durkel asked her whether she required anything further.

"I need some woman who knows the conjuring songs. My own voice is dry and is not pleasing to the spirits."

Durkel looked around, but no one spoke up.

"I cannot talk to the spirits if no one will call them," said the seeress.

The day before, Gudrid had stood in wonder at this apparition, but now she felt more fear than awe. She would have remained silent, but the witch's stare forced her to speak. "My mother's sister taught me the conjuring songs. And my foster mother used to sing them sometimes. I can remember them as if I were sitting at her hearth. But I can't sing them now." How could she bring back such memories?

The seeress raised her eyebrows. She spoke to Durkel. "It is up to you to provide me with what I need."

Durkel went over to Bjorn and said a few words. Then the two of them came to Gudrid. She knew what they were going to say. Their host needed something only she could give. She could not deny him.

Softly she began the melody that Halldis had loved the most. The fear left her as swiftly as it had come, and she was back in Arnarstapi smelling the warmth of her foster mother's hearth and feeling the light of her smile. When she finished the song, everything was quiet, even the fire.

"You have sung well, Gudrid," said the prophetess. "Better than you could know. Many spirits are here; some I have not seen in a long, long time. Now I know many things that were hidden from me before.

"This famine will not last much longer. Before the winter closes in, there will be seals offshore. The coughing sickness that has been among us will go away, and we will live in health for many years.

"And Gudrid, in thanks for your song, the spirits have revealed a bright future for you. You will marry well, as well as you might in Greenland."

Everyone was thankful for the good news about the famine. They crowded around Gudrid to get a better look at this woman who was to have such good fortune. Gudrid at first could hardly contain her excitement, but later she wasn't so happy with the prophecy, when she saw how it seemed to point to a marriage with Leif. Though it was five years and more since she'd seen him, she still remembered his sneer, his taunts.

Afterward the sibyl came to Gudrid.

"I knew your mother's sister before I came to Greenland. I taught her many things."

Gudrid showed her surprise.

"You know a little." The sibyl's eyelids fluttered. "Don't fool yourself: much more you don't know."

"This is true," Gudrid agreed. "And so?"

"You think you might be a Christian because of things your foster mother told you. That religion may have fit her, but it won't fit you. I know what you did with your mother's sister, casting the runes on Stapafell."

Is there anything this woman doesn't know? Gudrid wondered.

"Anyway," the seeress went on, "Greenland has no priest of Christ to pour his water on you. And that's a very pagan stone you have around your neck."

Gudrid's hand went to her breast. What could she say? The sibyl went on.

"I have an answer for you. You stay here, and I will teach you. You'd like to be rid of your father, I know." The sibyl paused, until Gudrid began to feel uncomfortable in the silence.

The arrangement was tempting. The knowledge she'd gained from Arnora was so meager, and she'd not remembered half of it. This woman seemed so wise, so . . . deep. Gudrid was set to leap at the offer. But the sibyl spoke again before she could answer.

"My offer has a price. Your amulet. Give it to me."

How could she? She hung on to the little charm. The memory passed over her, like the raven's shadow, that she'd almost thrown away the only thing left of her mother, a gift from death to life. The sibyl tantalized, but should Gudrid jump away from her father into this woman's clutch, trade one master for another?

"It is not to be given up" was all she could say. She faced the seeress.

"It would be well for you to reconsider," the sibyl replied, in a low voice but one that was not used to contradiction. Gudrid stood silent, making no move to give up the stone. After a while the sibyl said, "One would expect Aud's kin to have more wit than you have shown. The spirits have revealed one more thing. Your marriage will not be a happy one, and you will curse the day you first took man to your bed." She looked at Gudrid with eyes that sucked air from the room. Then she was gone.

Bjorn was impatient to get to Eriksfjord. Autumn was drawing on, and in Greenland one did not travel far in winter. He made his desire to leave known to Durkel, who made no effort to hide his relief. The wind, however, had renewed its force, so they had to wait. Bjorn paced Durkel's house, muttering and clapping fist to palm. Gudrid felt equally nervous, wanting nothing more than to get as far away from the sibyl as possible. Clouds passed, and spaces of blue sky, and then one day all the sky was blue. Bjorn thanked Durkel, and they were off.

The fair weather held, a day and a night and another day, and they were in Eriksfjord, mountains dropping to the sea. The wind was before them now, coming down the fjord from the icecap. Bjorn ordered sail down and oars out: they could make more headway by rowing than by the frequent tacking the narrow channel would require. At intervals, if they looked up from their effort, they would see a little farm clinging to the land. After six or seven hours of rowing, the sun dropped over the cliff to port. The men rested fitfully. They had to be ready, should the watchmen see a shoreline looming; the fjord was too deep here for an anchorage.

The morning dawned beautifully, the sun rising over the head of the fjord, birds circling overhead, a school of porpoises splashing close by. The breeze was southerly, nearly behind them, a good omen. They raised sail and continued on.

Habitations became more numerous, especially to the west, where the meadows were greenest. People stood on hillside and shore gazing out toward the ship. Bjorn hung a white shield over the landward side to indicate peaceful intent, and he took care to have the women in view.

"That's Brattahlid!" the man next to Bjorn shouted, and all on board strained to see Erik's farm, the great house of the colony. "Erik does not forget his friends," Bjorn had said, and everyone hoped that this was true. Sail was lowered, and the ship's momentum carried it to ground between two others, directly below the cluster of buildings on the sloping pasture.

Gudrid knew which one was Erik the moment she saw him. He was just as she remembered him, a tall man (though not as tall as her father), with muscular arms, red hair and a thick red beard, a broad face, a hawk nose, and narrow eyes. He'd developed a modest paunch, which betrayed that his fighting days were probably over and that he'd been enjoying the perquisites of head man of the colony. Even so, his presence was as powerful as it had been years before.

A gangplank was put from the ship to the shore as stone anchors were dropped astern to keep the ship from swinging. The crowd on shore gave way as Erik came through and bounded up—quickly, for so big a man—and grasped Bjorn's hand. Erik's broad smile displayed sincere pleasure at seeing this man who had stood by him when he had been most in need of help.

Bjorn called for Gudrid. She made her way forward, clambering over casks and chests. When she reached Bjorn and Erik, she stood up with what she hoped had the appearance of dignity.

"Ai, Gudrid, your beauty has bettered its promise! The last time I saw you, you were just a little maid. I threw you up in the air. I bounced you on my knee!" Erik laughed a deep, satisfied laugh, and that, too, was just as she remembered. She hadn't been *that* small, and he hadn't done those things, but she let it go. Gudrid felt his eyes on her, filling in with his imagination what was only suggested by the undulations of her garments. She sensed how easily he did this, as he would essay any woman of more than moderate beauty whom he met within his domain.

A younger man bounded up the platform. Clearly he was close kin to Erik: he had the same red hair and beard. Even his man-smell resembled Erik's—sour, like cheese gone bad. He was certainly not Leif; in no way could the blond, fair-faced youth have undergone so drastic a metamorphosis. This man's body was taut and firm, and he indicated his presence by jumping from the gunwale down to the space between Gudrid and Erik. As his eyes played over her, she searched his face for some hint of understanding. None revealed itself.

"This is my son Thorstein," said Erik. "And this is Bjorn's daughter, Gudrid. A lady of high birth. Don't get ideas in that thick head of yours." He gave his son a jab in the ribs, which had no visible effect on Thorstein but struck Erik as funny. Gudrid was again treated to the round laughter that seemed to emanate from every joint of Erik's body.

"A poor host I am indeed!" Erik said after his mirth subsided. He jabbed Thorstein again and said, "Get up to the house and see whether your mother has anything roasting on the spit besides snores and farts." Erik slapped Gudrid on the behind. Then, sensing Bjorn's raised eyebrows, he leaped up onto the gangplank and reached down to help Gudrid up. Bjorn followed, and the three of them walked up the hill in Thorstein's wake.

14.

Erik's house was thick and squat like Durkel's, but larger, as befitted the colony's founder. It had a great room about the size of Orm's and several smaller rooms linked to the main house by a covered passageway. These were used variously as an overflow sleeping room, a workroom, a storeroom, and a dairy. Other buildings spread out from it—barns, byres, the sauna. Farthest off was the smithy, segregated for fear of fire.

Bjorn hesitated slightly as he approached the house, pausing to examine a bullock cart under repair. He eyed the workmanship knowingly, seeing the five broad sections of wood come together to form the wheel, with each section joined to the hub by two short spokes. Then he watched as Erik's home boar grunted its way across the sidehill toward them, and he commented approvingly on its fatness. He looked up to examine the angle of the sun with respect to the mountain across the fjord.

Gudrid shared her father's reluctance. It only confirmed what she surmised already—that within was the woman who had cursed them.

She was convinced of this, now more than ever, even though Bjorn refused to speak of it.

Bjorn finally straightened himself, smoothed his tunic, and entered behind Erik. Gudrid followed the men in.

The music of flowing water greeted their ears. A stone-covered stream ran underneath the wall, emerging in a little basin near the hearth. At the far end of the house two men were playing the table game. They were hunched over a pegboard seven holes square, twelve pegs playing against one, the one aiming to jump the twelve before he was himself driven into a corner. Closer by, the smell of roasting meat excited a surge of hunger in Gudrid's gut. Her nose pulled her eyes toward the fire. A woman stood there. A set of keys dangled from her right breast brooch, setting off the deep green of her outer wrap. Her hair was caught back in a green head scarf.

"Thjodhild, Bjorn Vifilsson's here!" called Erik. "He has his daughter with him!"

Gudrid looked at Thjodhild more closely. She was a handsome woman, though her hair was beginning to gray and her eyes lacked the softness of youth. Gudrid looked closely for signs of coolness between Thjodhild and Bjorn. Bjorn's hand closed the distance to Thjodhild's unsteadily; Thjodhild seemed more assured. Other than this, allowing for Bjorn's nature and what she surmised of Thjodhild, they gave no other evidence of feeling.

"Welcome to our house," Thjodhild said. She looked Bjorn over, casting only a glance toward Gudrid.

Bjorn responded. "First, I must ask your leave for my household to camp on your shore until it is decided where we are to go."

"It's done already," Erik replied. "I knew you'd come sooner or later. I saved you a good stretch of land on Stokaness, across the fjord."

They sat in the chairs on the dais, a formality not often observed at the morning meal, but the occasion seemed to demand it. Thjodhild came over to Gudrid's side and said in a low voice, "Our circumstances are a bit rustic compared with what you're used to, but I hope you'll learn to like it here."

Thjodhild's voice seemed gracious and genuine, and Gudrid was nearly moved to forget what, after all, had been only a single remark of her father's long ago; but something in Thjodhild's smile made her shiver, even though a thrall had just added peat to the fire, and an overlayer of fresh driftwood was beginning to blaze. She looked toward Bjorn, but his straight face did not yield any clue.

Now the smell of the roast began to overwhelm even Bjorn's reserve. A thrall came in with a knife and began to hack the meat into small pieces. Another brought bread and skyr. "Seal's flesh, from the fjord," Thjodhild said. Gudrid remembered watching the seals that came inshore below her father's farm and wondered whether she'd ever learn to like seal meat. Thorstein drew a pitcher of ale from a cask in the corner.

"You'll find there isn't much drink in Greenland. What we have we save for the feasts. Most days we make do with water." He wiped his hands on the front of his tunic and drew up a bench beside her, straddling it so that his knees almost touched her thigh.

"The land here is good enough if you like ice and rock and a little thin grass." He turned his palm in deprecation. "The best part's up coast, in Vestribygd, the Western Settlement. It's smaller than here, the Eastern, but it's better. Grazing's better. Hunting's better."

"Thorstein has half of a farm there. He traded away good land here," said Thjodhild. "Now he has to talk it up." Thjodhild fell silent for a moment, though in some strange way she held her turn to speak. "Leif—"

"We're talking about Thorstein," Erik cut in, spilling ale in his agitation. "He's a good man. He knows what to do with a sword, and he never puts up a front like his brother."

Gudrid glanced sideways toward Thorstein and saw his unabashed grin. Bjorn nodded. Gudrid clasped her hands tightly. Something was to be feared in this.

Thjodhild spoke. "Erik never did have a good word for Leif. But Leif got a ship and sailed for Norway. He's never relied on anyone but himself."

"When do you expect him back?" Gudrid asked. Etiquette demanded she say something, and she might as well try to get some information.

Thorstein spat into the fire. "Maybe never. He's probably holed up with some wench in the Hebrides."

Erik looked toward Bjorn. "You're going to be busy building your house. I'll send you some sheep to round out your flock. Meantime, Gudrid can stay with us."

She hadn't expected this. Little as she loved her father, staying with him was far preferable to sleeping with this family.

Bjorn laid aside the rib he'd been gnawing on. He thanked Erik warmly, then went out to the rest of the household at the shore. Erik joined him, beckoning Thorstein to follow. He complied, looking reluctantly back toward Gudrid.

A slave girl entered and began cleaning away the scraps. Her black hair and olive face revealed her southern origin, and as she stood to go, the buds of breasts showed themselves under her coarse gown.

"What is your name?" Gudrid asked.

The girl's face wrinkled, straining to comprehend the unfamiliar Norse. Then, with a little bow, she replied, "Nika." She turned and left quickly through the narrow door.

Another woman entered just after Nika left. She straightened up and walked between the rows of house pillars toward the fire, where Gudrid and Thjodhild were standing. She was a handspan taller than Gudrid and looked to be several years older than Gudrid's sixteen winters. She had a full head of flowing red hair, a soft mouth, and a firm chin. She had a nose as prominent as Erik's, moderated only enough to fit a woman's face. Gudrid turned in her direction, expecting an introduction, but Thjodhild said nothing.

"I might expect to be introduced to our guest in a civilized house," the woman said to Thjodhild. "Here I have to do it myself. I'm Erik's daughter, Freydis. His bastard, I may as well add, before *she* does, though in this case to be a bastard has to be counted a blessing."

Gudrid was taken aback by the timbre of her voice as well as by its tone, for it was not her harsh words alone that penetrated so deeply. A woman's voice, to be sure, but it was a voice such as she had never before heard. She looked into Freydis' face and was engulfed immediately in her deep green eyes.

"I have been welcomed to Brattahlid," Gudrid said to Freydis, "and I am grateful for your welcome too." Freydis' eyes caught hers again, and in their depth they were like a restless green sea. Freydis' lips parted and she exhaled deeply; then she smiled and extended her hand to Gudrid.

"I'll show her around," she said to Thjodhild. "You might get the girl to bring her things up here if she's going to stay."

"I hope you will," she continued to Gudrid. "I may be a bastard, but I can also be a friend."

"I'll be grateful for any such I may find in this land." Gudrid felt, more than ever, the need to reserve judgment.

They left together. Freydis showed her the rest of Erik's farm, pausing at the sauna.

"We need this," she said. "Especially in winter. You won't be prepared for the winter here, but you'll get used to it. These houses must seem like hovels to you, but they're built to keep out the cold. Even their small size helps. We're forced to keep close together and keep each other warm. It'll help to have you here." She took Gudrid's arm and pointed across the fjord.

"There's good pasture over there. My father's a lout in many ways, but at least he knows how to take care of a friend. That's one thing I got from his seed. Remember that."

Gudrid searched for a suitable response to this direct manner of speech. "Where're the sheep?" was all she could come up with.

"By the shieling. It's not far. Come on!"

Freydis strode up the path. Gudrid followed, step for step.

The increasing altitude brought out the cold beauty of the place— snow-covered mountains, sheer cliffs, a few icebergs still on the fjord. Beneath their feet the tiny Greenland wildflowers showed pink and white and yellow. Gudrid could come even with Freydis, but she had no energy to spare.

By the time they reached the top, a bank of fog was sweeping up the fjord. In the opposite direction a flock of sheep were baahing randomly, a bell tinkling in their midst. A boy tended them. A little stone house stood against the hillside.

Freydis moved closer. She touched Gudrid's face.

"The shieling," Freydis said, pointing to the house. "We could make a fire."

Freydis stood squarely in front of Gudrid. The smell of her body was strong, though not unwholesome. Gudrid felt uneasy, very much alone. She sought an excuse to move on.

"Let's run down the mountain!" she said, and with that, she jumped up on the high side of the trail, slipped past Freydis, and, pulling her garments above her ankles, sped away. At first, she heard Freydis' footsteps close behind her, but then they fell back. The next time she looked up, Freydis was a speck on the trail far above her.

Her anxiety quickened. The mountainside, which moments before had been so beautiful, now bristled with danger. She ran faster.

She did not know what she was afraid of, or whom. Freydis? Thjodhild? The sibyl? Wisps of fog floated past her. Soon she'd be in the thick of it. She heard something ahead of her, like a man's voice. A troll maybe? She wished now that Freydis were nearer. She stopped and peered into the mist. For a long time everything was quiet; then she heard the sound again. She froze. A hand touched her from behind, and it was beyond her power to hold back the scream.

It was Freydis.

Doing her best to calm herself, Gudrid straightened up and asked, "Did you hear something? Do you know what it was?"

"I wasn't close enough," said Freydis. "I don't doubt that something was there. We'd better be careful. Come, I know another way down."

Freydis led the way along a narrow, frightening path that snaked down a sheer cliff. Sometimes they could see through a break in the fog—Brattahlid like a clump of sod, the ships like piglets at the shore. Then the mist would close, and Gudrid could only put one foot ahead of the other, grasping for handholds where they were to be found.

They came out at a little cove, just over a low hill from Brattahlid. Gudrid was not ashamed to express her relief when Erik's roof came into view.

They reached the house late in the afternoon. Gudrid excused herself and ran down to the shore, where Bjorn was overseeing the tasks of camp setting and organization.

She had intended to tell her father about her close escape, but as she approached him, she became less and less sure that what she had heard was real and more and more aware that he had problems of his own just now. Three men were engaged in an argument, and unfortunately they were the three who ranked highest, next to Bjorn himself. Floki stood, hands on hips, with Mord behind him. There was Asgrim, stolid and slow to anger, but formidable when provoked. And Knut, the smart one, the one others looked to most often in Bjorn's absence. Bjorn was just managing to smooth over the dispute.

His face had not lost its tenseness over the task of arbitration he'd just completed; when he noticed her, it tightened further.

"Daughter," he said, "I trust you will honor Erik as his guest and show him respect. He's been very generous, more than I had any right to expect."

Coming so abruptly, with nothing to have incited it, the speech carried import beyond the bare meaning of the words. The feeling of apprehension came back, the same that she'd felt sitting in Erik's house, Erik and her father exchanging a nod and the cast of an eye.

"I will," she replied. She wished to say more, but Bjorn stopped her with his hand. The feeling was strange, as though he wished to tell her something. Then the hand dropped, and she knew she was dismissed from his presence.

"No! I won't go!" Her words surprised her, even as they came out of her mouth. She'd let him put her off several times before. "I won't go until you tell me what's going on between you and that woman."

"Nothing's going on," he said evenly. He knew who she was talking about. He turned away, and she could do nothing more than go to the shore and kick pebbles into the water.

15.

Summer was nearly over in Greenland. The long days were fading with the wildflowers into the autumn of chilly days, racing clouds, and increasing darkness.

Bjorn's long house and his barns were progressing rapidly. Things would be crowded at Stokaness come winter, with people enough for three farms huddled in one house, but at least they would be warm.

Gudrid remained at Brattahlid, at Erik's invitation and Bjorn's insistence. Thorstein hung over her, but said little. The few words that did come from him were like the snorts of a young bull, drooling before some brown-cheeked heifer. She took care not to encourage him. She was sure that Erik and Bjorn were negotiating her marriage.

"He's been following me everywhere I go," she said to Bjorn the next time he came over to visit Erik.

"As he well might. You're not hard for a young man to look at, you know."

She decided to come to the point.

"You want me to marry him, don't you?"

"Erik and I have discussed the matter."

It was in the open now. She was being forced into a corner, like the lone man in the table game. Unlike that playing piece, however, she could not jump, could not capture, could not retaliate in any way against the many who pressed her in. She did not want Thorstein forced on her. She did not want any man that way, even though she knew this was the common lot of woman.

"Does Erik know about Ymir?"

"I've told Erik all about it," Bjorn answered. He looked in her eye. "The truth of the matter."

"And Thorstein?"

"You see how he dotes on you. Do you think he'd care whether or not you are a virgin?"

The subject was closed. She searched for another opening, another way to buy more time.

"Erik has another son," she said.

Bjorn's tone was one of conscious control. "Leif isn't here. He may never return."

"I think he will. I think he may not need his father's approval. He's the firstborn son, and he may take a liking to me. Erik won't live forever. Leif may not be pleased that you've married me off to his younger brother."

"There'll be no question of you marrying Leif," said Bjorn.

"Why not?" She nearly choked as she said this, knowing how little she'd liked Leif the last time they'd met. The irony was not lost upon Gudrid, that most young women would envy her predicament.

"I have no more to say about Leif. Shut him from your mind."

"Well, you can't force me to marry Thorstein!" She stamped her foot and shook her head, knowing she looked like a frustrated child.

"I can, and if I have to, I will." He took a deep breath, then exhaled slowly. "Why do you resist the idea? Take a good look at him. You think you'll find better? He could swing Thor's hammer with those arms of his."

"That's all you can say for him, if you ask me."

"He's just like Erik, only younger. What's wrong with that?"

"Why do you compel me? Because you can? How is that different from what Ymir tried to do?"

Bjorn remained silent, but his expression was not that of a man who'd been convinced by argument.

"Give me time," Gudrid pleaded. "Give me time. Surely Thorstein would prefer a willing bride."

"Your state of mind," said Bjorn, "is Thorstein's least concern. If he weren't Erik's son, I wouldn't demand this, but he is. If time is all you ask, you may have some. Not too much though. Try to be a little warmer toward him. There's talk going around already that you were begotten on an iceberg."

As the days progressed, Leif and his whereabouts became more and more the center of conversation in Erik's house.

"I say he's stuck the winter in Norway," Erik said.

"He was to visit Olaf Tryggvason. Maybe he's gone into the King's service," said Thjodhild.

"Let Thor take care of him. We have work to do here," said Thorstein, still annoyed that Gudrid had slipped away from him yet again that morning. He rose from the stool where he had been consuming a barleycake and walked out the door.

Later that day Erik took her aside. His inflection went a step beyond annoyance. "My son wants you for wife. Bjorn's in line with it. Thorstein's a strong young man, with my hair and beard but not my belly. Most girls would jump into his bed if they could get the chance. He's got half of the biggest farm in Vestribygd, and he'll have more when Hel drags me down. Leif won't get everything, if that's what you're worried about. You asked Bjorn to put it off. Why?"

She felt as if she'd been caught naked with no place to hide. She had to compose an answer quickly. "It's not what I have against Thorstein. My father brought me against my will to this strange place. My foster father is dead. I'm grateful for your hospitality, which has been more generous than my father or I had any right to expect, but can't you see how hard it is now for me to think of marriage?"

"The marriage can wait then, until the spring, but let the betrothal be now."

"My father promised that I should have a little time yet." She felt very uncomfortable and longed to race for the door, but Thorstein was out there, and she didn't want to face him. She wished more than ever that Halldis were here, to advise her. Erik left, seeming to have consented to her plea for the moment. She went to the far end of the house and absentmindedly picked up her distaff and spindle. She became so lulled by the rhythm of the spinning that she didn't notice Thjodhild until she had come close enough to touch. Gudrid, startled, jumped back a little. Then, seeing who it was, she forced a smile.

"I can understand why you aren't looking to marry Thorstein," she said.

Gudrid made no effort to hide her surprise. "*You* say that, his mother?"

"I am that," she said. "Many observed my big belly, saw me push the brat out. There's no way to deny it, the way men can." She sucked in a breath of air. "He's not the man Leif is."

Gudrid began to see Thjodhild in a new light. At loggerheads with her husband (perhaps in matters other than which son to favor), uprooted from her kin, she hid something behind her unexpressive eyes. She tugged at her clothing until Gudrid feared she might rip her wool wrap apart from the brooches that held it.

"What does Erik have against Leif?"

"He's independent. He doesn't sniff Erik's ass like a dog that wants a pat on the head." She smiled. "Don't worry. Leif will be back soon. I think he'll be interested in you when he learns you're here. You met him once, didn't you? He had only good words about you."

This surprised her, if that's what Leif really said. If, more likely, Thjodhild was making this up, how was she to deal with her? It didn't matter, Gudrid decided. She needed any help she could get, from whatever source, however unlikely.

"I've asked for time. If you can do anything for me, I'll be grateful."

"I'll help you all I can," Thjodhild replied. "It may be you can help me too. You know something of the spirit world, don't you?"

Gudrid told her about Arnora and described what she knew of sorcery. She was surprised that Thjodhild seemed to know less than she did. Thjodhild was especially inquisitive about her encounter with the Sibyl of Herjolfsnes. After that the conversation trailed off in a strange way, Thjodhild moving alternately closer and farther away until finally, having worked her way to the door, she slipped out, as if hoping Gudrid wouldn't notice.

The east wind coming down from the icecap presaged winter. A thin layer of skim ice had formed around the rocky edges of the fjord, to be carried off by the tide. People moving about the farm remarked on the cold, in the manner of those who know that worse is on the way. Freydis emerged from the door of Erik's house.

"Gudrid! Gudrid!" she called. That voice. Gudrid had no choice but to come up the hill to meet her.

They walked together along the shoreline. She'd go that way with Freydis, though she would not walk the cliffs again. Gudrid held her heavy wool shawl close; she marveled that Freydis went without, not seeming to feel the wind or the cold. Soon they were farther from Brattahlid than they had been since their frightful fell climb barely two weeks before. Freydis put her hand on Gudrid's shoulder.

"I know what you're afraid of. The seeress of Herjolfsnes is in some ways the most powerful woman in Greenland. I've always thought it best to stay clear of her myself." She pulled a long knife from her woolens. "I can use this if I have to."

This did little to reassure Gudrid. What good would a knife be against whatever it was that the sibyl might send. Freydis, however, smiled, put the knife away, and dropped her arm to Gudrid's waist.

"Just a little farther," she said. "Around that hill we'll be out of the wind."

Gudrid obeyed. Freydis kept up a chatter, which Gudrid, preoccupied, hardly followed, until, just as they passed behind the hill, they came to a little cleft.

"I want to show you something," Freydis said.

Freydis went into the dell, at the bottom of which small willows clumped in a thicket. A few outliers were struggling for foothold up the slopes. After an interval she emerged, carrying something long and thin. It was a rustic bow carved from driftwood, and some arrows.

"Hang your stone on that branch," Freydis told her. Gudrid complied, amazed that she felt no reluctance about it. Freydis strung the bow with some gut she'd brought with her, then stood off from the tree, perhaps a ship's length distant.

The first arrow missed its mark, making thwacking noises as it passed among the trees beyond. Freydis scowled, but she immediately drew back the second arrow. That and the third pierced the branch, cracking it, and the fourth found wood also, so that the branch hung limply, and the amulet swung on its chain, suspended from Freydis' arrows.

Gudrid's eyes grew big. "Who taught you that?"

"I did myself. The same as with everything else. No one pays a bastard girl much attention, even one of Erik's."

Gudrid was mystified. "I've never seen you hunt or even speak of it."

"No one knows about this—except you now, and I trust you not to tell. It never hurts to have a secret or two. Isn't that what the sibyls are about?"

"Yes. But why this?"

"At first I only wanted to see if I could do it. Then I thought it might stand this bastard in good stead." Freydis' voice changed suddenly, her stance, her mood. "It's not so bad being a bastard and a woman, except I'm two years older than Leif. Did you know that? No? You're being kind. Leif will rule this place when Erik dies, because I'm a bastard and a woman. It's not so bad, except for being so ugly."

Gudrid started. She looked at Freydis, scanned her face, limned her body under thick wool. The red hair quickened in the breeze. She had a big nose; perhaps that's what irked her, but it set off her other features. It could be said she had the face of a queen. The green eyes swallowed Gudrid up.

What were these feelings? How could she know them, a tangled heap of affections she'd had before, but one at a time? She recognized something of the admiration and awe she'd felt for Arnora and maybe some of her love for Halldis too. There was softness in it, the promise of safe harbor, what Sigunna had once been, and then Orm. A stronger note was a yearning, a physical need, like what she'd once felt for Einar, and this frightened her. Her mind raced back to the reflecting pool on the mountain where she'd gone to look at herself. Now a new wind was riffling the water, so that even the third or fourth glance did not suffice to reveal the darkness of her true self.

"It is I who feel ugly sometimes," Gudrid said.

Freydis' face seemed about to burst open. Emotion was pressing for release like steam from a dormant volcano. It did not seem a practiced expression.

"Gudrid," she said, "you're the most beautiful creature that ever set foot upon a shore."

For a moment the need she felt threatened to possess Gudrid. She saw in Freydis everything she lacked, the refuge of one who could advise her, the easy warmth of a friend, and then there was this yearning, which she could not extinguish any more than she could stamp out a hearth fire with her bare feet.

Only with great effort could she force all this down, below the threshold of consciousness, so that she was again aware of the stony hills, the willows, Freydis' arrows, her amulet swinging in the breeze.

Freydis retrieved the stone, handing it back to Gudrid as if it were a gift. She touched Gudrid's face, the way she had the day they'd walked the fells together. This was too much for Gudrid; now she was beyond control of herself. She ran fiercely up the hill, into the wild space beyond, until her racing heart would not let her run anymore.

Much later she returned to Brattahlid. Freydis only smiled, giving no hint that anything unintended had passed between them.

16.

They heard a voice from the top of the rise behind Erik's house, first muffled, then louder. "A ship! Sailing up the fjord!" Everyone rushed up to get a better look.

"It's Leif's sail," Erik said, more than a trace of disappointment in his voice.

The striped sail showed a full belly in a following wind. As the craft came nearer, the sweep of its lines, from the waterline up to the stempost, became more distinct, more insistent. Then it turned toward shore, and the sail began to come down.

"What's that behind the ship?"

"It looks like the afterboat! Ship's low in the water too. Near awash on both sides! They can't have sailed that way from Norway!"

Others made similar comments. Everyone's curiosity was aroused to see what cargo could have induced them to trim the ship so dangerously.

"He's got a lot of people with him," Erik said, as much to himself as to anyone else.

Some of the men jumped into chest-deep water and hauled the afterboat to shore.

"What's in the boat?" Thorstein asked. "It looks like some kind of berries."

"It's grapes." The voice came from above. A man leaned over the side. He was dressed in a silk tunic with an ermine collar. A medallion, suspended from his neck, spun slowly in the breeze. Gudrid knew at once that this was Leif. He looked exactly as she imagined the boy would look, grown to manhood: a thin beard on an even thinner face, deep-set eyes, golden hair that hung to his shoulders, a long straight nose, and a cold, firm mouth.

Erik inspected the boat. "Where'd the grapes come from?"

"From a new land to the south and west. We were blown off course."

Erik climbed the ladder that had been thrown over the side of the ship. "Odinn's eye! Look at that lumber! Straight and true, and as long as the ship!"

"We got that in Vinland too."

"Where?"

"The new land. We will have wine this winter!"

Leif and Erik climbed down from the ship. Leif beckoned to two men standing amidships. They at once came to the fore and climbed down the ladder.

Thjodhild reached the shore and rushed to Leif. He embraced her and then stood back. "Mother, it is good to be on the same shore with you again!"

The two men were standing by, nervously waiting for Leif to address them. Each wore a silver cross on a chain around his neck. One, tall and thin, was finely dressed, with thick hair and a full beard. The other, shorter, wore plainer clothing and had no hair on the top of his head. Aside from these things, they looked little different from other men.

"Who are these scarecrows?" Erik demanded.

Leif stiffened. "They are priests of Holy Church, sent by order of King Olaf Tryggvason. The King is baptized a Christian and has decreed his realm to be Christian also. I carry his order to bring the Faith to Greenland."

"We'll see about that!" Erik roared. "I rule here, and I hold with our own gods."

"The gods do not exist," Leif answered. "They are illusions of Satan's design."

"Thor lives. Odinn lives. This Christ is no god. He's for slaves, not for free men."

"The power of God is far greater than the power of all your gods. King Olaf has decreed it. Will you resist the lord of all Norway?"

"He has subdued all the Viking chiefs?" Erik asked.

"They are in total submission. Olaf is supreme."

"I don't believe it," said Erik. "I won't abandon Thor, and neither will anyone who wants my friendship."

Leif made a study of ignoring his father's outburst. He started up toward the house. Halfway there, he noticed Gudrid. He turned to his mother. "Who is that young woman?" he asked.

Thjodhild made the introduction.

Gudrid faced Leif. Slowly their hands rose to touch in the traditional gesture of greeting. She wondered what was going through Leif's head, behind the half smile.

"And Bjorn is in Greenland, then?"

"Yes. Your father gave him land on the other side of the fjord."

Leif smiled more broadly now. "Greenland is indeed fortunate. More fortunate still will be the man who wins you."

Gudrid felt she should say something now, but was at a loss for the correct words. The feelings she remembered came back in a rush, running counter to what she had heard of him and with what she now saw before her. He was a worldly-wise man from all appearances, far more enterprising than his brother. The wavy blond hair, the steel-blue eyes, the turn of his mouth—in these he had fulfilled all of his youthful promise. And yet there was something about him that struck her as askew, out of place. The feeling, however, was fleeting, and she could find no reason not to walk beside him as the group made its way up to the house.

"Tell me about King Olaf," she asked.

"A remarkable man. His physical strength and agility are legend. He throws two spears at the same time, one from each hand, on a dead run, and then catches one in midair that has been thrown at him. He leaps over the side of his ship and walks the oars as his men are rowing."

They reached the door and entered. Erik sent a thrall to bring some ale. Leif looked around, then sat down on a stool beside the high seat.

"The place looks the same as when I left." He settled in, draping an arm over the side of Erik's seat. "It's good to be home."

Thorstein had come to rest on the other side of Erik's seat, so Gudrid, in order not to play favorites, sat on the opposite platform.

"Tell us about the land you saw." Her curiosity was genuine.

"We were blown south in a storm. Then the fog came, so thick you could not see the mast from the stern. One day the fog lifted, and we saw land. A beautiful land with great trees. We made camp at the head of a fjord, in a harbor protected by a long, sandy island. Tyrkir here found the grapes." Leif nudged the swarthy southerner who had cared for him as a boy and whom he had taken on every journey ever since. "We cut wood and picked grapes. When we had loaded as much as prudence would allow we left and went north."

It was obvious that Leif set great store by this Tyrkir, who, though a slave, had fostered him. The short, stocky man reminded Gudrid of Orm and could hardly have been less like his master in appearance. Nevertheless, Leif smiled at him as he did at no one else. That might have turned Gudrid's mind against him, but she saw that he had a smile for everyone, not just Leif.

"We saw another shore, also lined with trees, which went on for several days' sail. Then we left that land and headed out over open water. When the polestar came to the right height for Greenland, we struck another coast. From there, it was an easy matter to reach the settled coast of Greenland directly opposite."

"Do you think these are the same lands that Bjarni saw?" Gudrid asked.

"Bjarni!" Erik snorted. "He didn't even go ashore. Who could believe that? Here's grapes and wood, excellent wood! Who can doubt it now? A good sail for a son of Erik!" Erik, almost in spite of himself, had clapped his hand onto Leif's shoulder. Leif ignored the gesture.

Thjodhild came in abruptly. "The priests! The priests! A wonder of God that you should bring them here." She went to Leif and embraced him. "Sira Geir has so much to tell. The other holds back. No matter. I'm to be baptized!"

Erik looked at her in disbelief. Thjodhild rushed on.

"I've waited a long time for this day. These priests of Christ have the power of God with them. They'll send the sibyls to the hills, and their devils with them."

Erik's face was redder than his beard.

"Frey's stiff prick they will! No wife of mine will be a Christian! Clown of a god let himself be tortured to death! A real god suffers by his own hand, like Odinn, if he suffers at all. That's a sacrifice!"

"Well, Erik," said Thjodhild, "you'd better get used to the idea. I'm signed with the cross already, and I will be baptized." She looked toward Leif.

Leif smiled. "A convert already, and we haven't been in Greenland a day! My priests will preach the Faith to all. Anyone who hinders them will earn the wrath of King Olaf. Even now he is preparing to receive the homage of the chieftains in Iceland."

"You're crafty, Leif," Erik said. "Iceland will never go under. You know it and I know it, but we both know there's no way to prove it until a ship comes from there."

"Surely my father is not suggesting that I would lie! No, it is as I have said."

Erik maintained his taut stance. "We'll discuss this later. Who are all those people on your ship? You didn't come all the way from Norway with a crew like that!"

"You didn't recognize the trader? His ship went aground in the small islands, the skerries opposite Herjolfsnes. Had we not seen them, they would have perished. I picked them up and brought them here. By the laws that sailors recognize, I am entitled to all their goods. I could only take on a small portion of what is there. As soon as we unload, we'll go back for the rest."

"A lucky turn of fortune for you, son," Thjodhild said. "First Vinland, with timber and wine, and then a ship full of trade goods!"

"Leif the Lucky!" Erik snorted, then let go a fart that he must have been saving for the right moment. Scowling, he stomped out of his own house.

The entry of Christianity to Greenland both excited and worried Gudrid. Though she had partly accepted her foster mother's teachings about the new religion, there was much in it that she did not understand. This did not matter to her: its message was more important than its mysteries.

She could see, though, how two competing religions would tear people apart. Halldis and Orm had lived together and loved, Christian and pagan under one roof. They were the exception. Thjodhild and Erik would be the rule. As for Erik, Christianity represented a direct threat to his authority. Could anyone not have noticed Leif's studied insolence?

And what of Thjodhild? She'd never mentioned the Faith in Gudrid's hearing, yet here she was, jumping into it, in defiance of her husband.

As if in response to her thought, Thjodhild sat down beside her. "I really am going to be baptized soon. What about you, Gudrid?"

"Religion has always confused me," Gudrid temporized. "Maybe it's that my foster father and foster mother saw things differently."

"But you think the Christian faith is better."

She had to think about this. She clung to the amulet, she held the sibyl in awe, she even feared a curse from someone like Thjodhild. What powers did the new faith have? A god who let himself be killed, a ritual in which he was eaten every day by ordinary people. Still, when looked at from a certain angle, there was a joy in it that the old religion did not have, a feeling of love and hope. Gudrid was not sure which religion was better. Nevertheless, she could give only one answer here.

"Yes. I do."

"Good," said Thjodhild. "This bears directly on your marriage. Now that you've seen Leif, no doubt you're even more reluctant to marry Thorstein. Leif's grown well, hasn't he? A far more suitable match for you, don't you think?" Gudrid hesitated to say anything; she could feel Thjodhild reading her face.

Thjodhild continued. "Thorstein's got Erik and Bjorn behind him. We just have to find a way to slow them down." She stopped to let this sink in. "Now, if you were baptized a Christian, that would prevent you from marrying Thorstein. A Christian can have nothing to do with a heathen. That's not my whim. The priests have said it is the law of the Church. There's no way Erik will let himself be baptized, and Thorstein follows his father in all things. So you'll be safe. As for me, Erik better satisfy any lust he may have for me soon. After I am baptized, I will no longer have anything to do with a heathen man either, even though he is my husband."

Gudrid rose to go, but Thjodhild held up her hand. "There's one more thing. You can't become a Christian with that amulet draped on your body. Give it to me now so that I can take it to one of the priests. He'll know what to do with it."

Gudrid sensed the cunning in Thjodhild's words, but she could think of no subtle counter. She could only beg for time crudely, as she had done with Bjorn. Everyone wanted something of her. Every move she made only trapped her more inescapably. She could run down the shoreline, but in the barren land of her strained imagination, she had no place to hide.

17.

Bjorn came at last to bring her home. She could see how proud her father was of the way things were going. The walls of the long house were already up to eye level. Women were busily cutting sod, and men were bringing it to the house and laying it between the inner and outer courses of stone. Other men were assembling the roof timbers from the posts they'd brought with them. Outbuildings were going up too, their timbers coming mostly from driftwood Erik gave them. The animals had grown fat in the meadow. The only trees were in one stand of scrubby birch, no taller than a man, in a protected corner. Bjorn gave strict orders to leave them alone, but not before several had been cut.

The boat emerged from the noon glare. Leif was at the steering oar, four thralls rowing. He leaped the last short space between the boat and the land, and strode up the slope toward Gudrid.

He wanted to see Bjorn. She took him in, then retired a discreet distance and took up her spindle.

"The best news I found on coming home was that you had decided to come out to Greenland," Leif said. "We need substantial men like you. I'm not saying that the farmers who came with Erik are not good men. By and large, they are. But most of them are not from the best families. They came because they were not doing well in Iceland. You are different. You come from a noble line. You are versed in saga lore. You understand the way of the world.

"Olaf is a powerful king. All the legends about him are true. He will brook no resistance to his will. That is why I brought the King's priests to Greenland. You can see that I am a worldly man. It is of no consequence to me whether I offer sacrifice to Christ or to Thor. What matters is that King Olaf has taken me for his liege man, and I am sworn to uphold him. I knew the priests would upset my father, but I also thought that, given time, he would see reason. His anger seems only to grow as days go by.

"We are no match for the combined might of Norway or even for a small part of that might, should King Olaf choose to throw it against us. We are far enough from him that he will leave us alone if we do him honor, but not so far that we can escape his wrath if we defy him."

"What would you have me do?" Bjorn asked.

"Accept baptism. Join with me and others from among the best men in Greenland. We will go to Erik and tell him that he must set aside Odinn and Thor and take up the cross."

"And if he refuses?"

"Then he must give up the high seat of Brattahlid." Leif raised his palm. "I don't think it will come to that. He doesn't love the old gods that much. He's just stubborn. If many of us press the Faith on him, he will relent."

Leif's back had been to Gudrid during this speech, but she could see Bjorn. She was amazed that Leif, for all his supposed craftiness, had not seen the strange look on her father's face. There was more between these men than met the eye.

"You say Erik is angry," said Bjorn. "I say you have no idea how angry he is. I swear by Odinn that I have never been asked to agree to anything as treacherous as what you have suggested. You heap dung on my honor! How can you come skulking over to involve me in a plot against my chief? I don't know why Erik doesn't cut your head from your body and heave both rotten parts into the fjord! You can strut before me in your indifference to religion, but the wrath of the gods is still to be feared!"

Leif left the house and walked down the hill as Gudrid laid aside her spindle. Bjorn watched him go. Then he turned to his daughter.

"Now you see why Erik favors Thorstein. Ingrate! Leif stands to inherit most of what Erik has, but he can't wait for that. If money were more important than honor, Leif would be the man to side with. He will win in the end. Greed makes beasts out of men. I know you don't always see the reason for what I do, but maybe now you can see a little better."

"Is that why you want me to marry Thorstein?"

"He's not my ideal choice of a husband for you, but he is Erik's son."

"Leif is also Erik's son."

Bjorn turned away a little, as though to think. "Has Leif made his love known to you in any way?"

"No. Not that I've given him any reason to. To me he's the same snotty braggart he was when he came with Erik to Snaefellsnes."

The corners of Bjorn's mouth turned up slightly, but his head remained fixed. "You don't want to marry Leif, then."

"No."

"Good."

"But that doesn't mean I want to marry Thorstein. Why do I have to marry a son of Erik at all? Are there no other men in Greenland?"

"I accepted Erik as my chief the day I accepted this land. I'm bound to support him in anything he desires."

"Even in the marriage of your daughter?"

"In anything that is honorable. Unless you can show me some dishonor in Thorstein, I must command it."

"You promised me time."

"I did. Time has gone by. Try to see Thorstein's merit. He's strong. He's brave. He's loyal."

"And he's stupid."

"You've been talking to Freydis. Don't trust her."

"Freydis has offered me her friendship. I need a friend."

Gudrid waited tensely for Bjorn to say more, but he remained silent. She listened to his breath, which went in and out with a slight wheeze.

His face looked a little less hard than usual. The amulet pressed against her breast. Here was the chance she'd waited for, a way to keep it and also to use the cross as a barrier between her and Thorstein. The lie must be put over.

"Halldis baptized me. On the ship, before she died. I am a Christian."

Bjorn stared straight ahead, then caught himself, almost as if about to lose his balance, and sat down on a stool. "It's coming. I know that. I just didn't think it would come here as fast as it did. This new religion is a refuge for cowards. No one who would call himself a man would have anything to do with it. No woman who desires such a man should touch it either."

"King Olaf Tryggvason was baptized. Do you say that he is not a worthy man?"

"If it's true, then King Olaf is a crafty tyrant, which is what Leif is going to be here. He wants to make slaves of us all, so he brings us the religion of slaves."

"There are many Christian warriors in the southlands, and great kings," Gudrid countered. "They fight and sometimes win. The king of the Franks, for example, the one called Charlemagne."

"He lived two hundred years ago," Bjorn snorted.

"He fought the Saxons and forced them to become Christians."

Bjorn's worried scowl told of more than theological differences. "It isn't possible to be both a Christian and a warrior. If what you say is true, then this religion isn't what you think it is. Not even the Christians believe in it. At least with Odinn and Thor you know where you stand."

"Nevertheless," she said, "I am a Christian. If Thorstein wants to marry me, he will have to be baptized. This I know he will not do."

Bjorn again struggled to maintain his self-control, saw that he was losing the struggle, and walked out of the house.

Some weeks before, Leif had removed the offending priests from Erik's farm and set them ashore at farms belonging to his supporters. Sira Geir went to Solarfjoll down Eriksfjord, and Brother Ulf was sent to Vatnahverfi, on the far side of Einarsfjord, the next fjord south. Sira Geir was the taller, more formidable of the two. He was very jealous of his priest's title and on more than one occasion had let drop that he soon expected it to be replaced by that of bishop. The title "Sira" was an innovation. Geir had heard it used by a Norman priest at King Olaf's court, and liked the Frankish sound of it. The King frowned on the idea of lowly priests puffing themselves up. The missionaries he'd sent to Iceland used no honorifics; they depended on their tongues and, when necessary, their swords to win respect. Nevertheless, as soon as the mountains of Norway had slipped below the horizon, Geir had taken the title unto himself, with

Leif's approval. Ulf, though he had taken Holy Orders, out of humility held onto the lesser designation "Brother."

Gudrid preferred Brother Ulf, from the little she'd been able to speak with him, but it was to Sira Geir that Leif took her and his mother on a bright autumn morning. Gudrid was reluctant to go, but Leif and Thjodhild both insisted, and for once neither Erik nor Bjorn was on hand to prevent it.

Sira Geir came down to meet them. The veins showed through the sides of his face. Leif explained that his mother was to be baptized, but that Gudrid said she was already baptized.

"Who baptized you, child?" he asked.

Gudrid liked him less each time he opened his mouth. "My foster mother, Halldis. On the ship. Before she died."

"Since when is woman granted the power to baptize?"

"Halldis taught me that anyone can baptize when death is imminent and no priest can be obtained."

"This is true. However, this exception is granted only when the unbaptized person is in danger of death, not the person doing the baptizing."

"Well, I won't be baptized by you," she said, not bothering to hide the truculence in her voice. "Brother Ulf may see things differently."

"Ulf is not here. If he were, he would say the same."

Gudrid expected that Sira Geir was probably right in this. She stepped back from him. "There will be another day."

"Unless the devil takes you in the meantime." The priest said this in a tone that had more of hope in it than of warning. He proceeded to baptize Thjodhild, after which Leif took them back to Brattahlid.

As they stepped from the boat, Thjodhild took Gudrid aside.

"Leif visited your father. What did Bjorn say to him?"

"He was angry. Hasn't Leif told you about the meeting?"

"Yes. Did Bjorn say anything about me?"

"No."

For a moment Thjodhild said nothing. Then, "Erik is angry too. Angry over Leif. Angry over me. And yet he must see that in the end he will give in and be baptized himself. It's the only way."

Gudrid had to call her on this. "You said he would never allow himself to be baptized! You said that when you told me how to hold Thorstein off."

Thjodhild turned her head abruptly. "Oh, it will take time. Longer than will be necessary for you and your father to come to terms with Leif. Yet, sooner or later, Erik must see his only course."

"I never said I wanted to marry Leif."

Thjodhild looked into Gudrid's eyes. "What? Are my sons not good enough for you?"

"That's not what I said."

"Tell me how else I can take it."

By this time Freydis had come down to the landing to meet them. "Don't be so hard on her, Foster Mother. It makes for too much bile." Her voice dripped irony.

"Any Greenland girl would long since have been married at her age."

Freydis ignored the reply, though it applied as much to her as to Gudrid. She placed her body so that she could face Gudrid while turning her back to Thjodhild.

"Just remember what I said. Thjodhild wants you to marry Leif just as much as Erik wants you to marry Thorstein. You're the jewel. Don't be in any hurry to give the stone away. If you must marry, marry a man you can control. You won't be able to control either of them. Thorstein's too pigheaded. Leif is too shrewd."

Gudrid could understand why Erik wanted her to marry Thorstein. Thorstein's lust for her was plain, and she was too highborn to be given to him in any way other than marriage. Thjodhild's concern was harder to understand. Leif so far had shown no interest in her at all. Why should his mother be so insistent? Couldn't Leif get his own women?

Erik and Thorstein were on the shore watching some thralls cleaning fish when Gudrid and Bjorn came down to their boat.

"A good catch, I see," Bjorn said.

"Aye, and there's no better fisherman than my red-bearded son," Erik said in a loud voice, as though he were trying to be heard over the spirits of the fish.

Erik put his face close to Gudrid's, so that she could hear and smell his breathing. "I trust Thorstein. You can do the same."

"I am a Christian woman," said Gudrid. "I cannot marry a pagan."

"Is that all you hold against me?" said Thorstein.

She had thoughts, but nothing that could be said openly.

"Yes," she said.

"You'd marry me, then, if I were a Christian?"

These last words of his were followed by a fish, the headless, bloody end of which slapped him on the face and smeared him with gore. On the other end of the fish was Erik.

"We'll have no talk of Christ while I'm around! You and I, we'll stick with Thor!"

Thorstein scraped the fish guts from his face and beard with his fingers. "Gudrid, I ask it again: will you have me if I get baptized?"

She was trapped. There was only one possible answer.

As she was rowed out across the fjord in her father's boat, Gudrid wondered whether she had been tricked by Erik or by Thjodhild, or whether she had tricked herself.

18.

Winter drew near. As the days grew shorter, ice began to accumulate along the edges of the fjord. With the summer birds gone —the raucous loons, the knife-voiced shearwaters, the agile terns— the air became strangely quiet, and when the wind was right, one might even hear a voice or the clank of an iron pot across the water. The hay had long since been cut and gathered into the barns, and such grain as there was—the wild lyme grass, on which the barest attempt at cultivation was imposed—had been harvested and stored. The animals were looked over carefully with an eye to the number that could be fed and housed over winter, and the surplus, the poorest, were slaughtered.

This was the time, too, to haul ships out of the water and roof them over to prevent damage from snow and ice. Ships were cared for even in Norway, but here there were no forests from which to rebuild them, and so they were treated as treasures.

As the preparations for winter were completed, eyes turned skyward, looking for the first great snowfall that would tie together all the people of each farm. For weeks they waited. Then one day it came. At first, it fell slow and fine; then it merged into a blank whiteness. Now one needed to take great care out of doors, not because of the cold, which had not yet approached its peak, but because of the danger of becoming lost in the featureless sameness.

In the end, the cold did come, unbelievable, numbing cold, the low sun frozen and far away during the short span of day. More and more, the people retreated indoors, until at last the only outside activity was a hurried coming and going in the protected passageways between the outbuildings and trips to the privy.

One preparation was new. Under the sloping roof of a byre Leif's foster father, Tyrkir, watched the wine fermenting in wooden vats. He'd had to borrow all the containers he could, of whatever kind, from as far away as the mouth of Einarsfjord. Erik, as was his custom, invited guests from nearby farms to his Yule feast. Others farther off he honored at more clement times of the year. Leif, perhaps as a peace offering to his father and perhaps just to celebrate his success, had promised as much wine as they all could drink.

Bjorn sent his daughter over early. She buried her fears in work, of which there was plenty for everyone, from thrall to guest, to lady of the house. Meat for the spit, fish for the smokehouse, skyr for the tub —all required preparation. The outbuildings nearest the house, the dairy and a small barn, would serve as extra rooms—the dairy as a sort of retreat for anyone in need of fresh air, the barn as extra sleeping quarters.

Gudrid visited Tyrkir in the byre.

"Leif says you come from the banks of the Rhine. You're no stranger to grapes and wine, then. I can't wait to taste it. It's a wonder folk haven't drunk it up already."

"He made everyone swear not to touch a drop until the Yule," Tyrkir replied. "That's made my job a lot easier." He winked.

"By whom did they swear?" This was an opportunity to assess the priests' progress.

"Some by Christ. Some by Thor. The wine will be the same for both."

"You were with Leif. Tell me about the land you saw."

Tyrkir smiled, wrinkling his eyes. "Trees as tall as the longest ships, meadows rich in grass, wild grapes and berries. Warm summer breezes that made me want to be young again, nuzzling sweet girls in the gardens of Cologne . . ."

"It sounds like a better land than this one."

"It is. But don't let yourself say that in front of Erik. He's afraid Leif will take us all there." He looked up from his work to face Gudrid. "Forgive me, lady, if I seem bold, but I'm grateful for the notice you've given me. There aren't many who'll talk to me as you do."

"Your speech betrays your education."

"I was a student once. Then I thought it would be a brave thing to go to war, in service to a Frankish lord."

Gudrid remained silent, but she looked at him in a way that made his whole frame relax.

"I may be able to do you a favor some day. Leif is my master after all, and he remembers how I looked after him when he was small."

It came to her then. "You were with Erik and Leif many years ago, when they visited my father in Snaefellsnes."

"Aye," said Tyrkir.

"I would hardly have recognized you. You didn't seem like a thrall then."

"I loved Leif. He was like my own son, the son I would never have. I was so happy, I would have rather been a thrall and Leif in my charge than a free man anywhere else."

"And now?"

"Leif has changed. Take care you don't cross him."

The guests began to arrive in twos and threes and occasional groups of five or six. With the fjord iced in, sledges could cross, pulled by horses breathing mist from flared nostrils. Each time that it seemed no more people could possibly fit into Erik's house, more arrived, and somehow they were accommodated.

The feast was to last for three days, and the first evening was at hand. Erik stood up on his high seat and gradually the guests noticed this indication of his desire to be heard, and grew silent.

"Thor has upheld me. Every summer I've given sacrifice and scanned the fjord for Bjorn's ship. I've finally filled your belly, old god, my best cows, my best ewes. Oh, Thor, I knew you'd keep faith with me. He's here at last, the best and bravest friend a man ever had, Bjorn Vifilsson."

Everyone shouted approval. Bjorn acknowledged the recognition, but his wave of the hand was perfunctory, shaky even, not at all the same as when he was pursuing a chieftaincy in Iceland.

The door opened and three or four men clothed in fur and with frost on their breath carried in one of the makeshift casks that Tyrkir had fashioned from a wooden bucket and a tight-fitting wooden-and-leather cover. Setting it down, they knocked it open. Drinking vessels were dipped—horns, soapstone mugs, Frisian glass—and soon it was empty. Other casks were brought in until all had had one drink and were working on a second. Bjorn brought Gudrid a mug of wine and sat down beside her.

Leif and Thjodhild were moving through the crowd of people, greeting and talking with various ones. Then Thjodhild spotted Bjorn and Gudrid, and she made her way over, towing Leif along like a stone anchor dragging along the bottom. As they drew nearer, Gudrid could hear Thjodhild.

"And I must have my church, do you hear? The power of the Sacrament will not be nearly so potent out of doors as in a church. I don't care how you arrange it with Erik. Just get it done."

Leif was trying to shut her up. "It will be done when it is done. I will not speak more of it tonight."

Thjodhild greeted Bjorn and Gudrid. Leif nodded. Gudrid replied with pretended warmth, Bjorn correctly but without feeling.

"You've hardly touched your wine, Bjorn," Thjodhild said. "Drink up. We want to see a smile on your face."

"I will smile when there is something to smile about."

"And Gudrid," she continued. "Don't let your good looks get the better of you. Summer doesn't last forever. All flowers fade sooner or later."

"Beauty is of little use without wit," Gudrid replied.

"Don't be a fool," Thjodhild whispered to her. "When you find a good man like Leif, take him. Your father will come around if you demand it. How could he refuse you a son of Erik?" Leif had to have heard this, but he looked off in another direction until his mother finished. Thjodhild turned to Bjorn and smiled. Gudrid had not noticed before that she was missing a tooth.

The food was brought in—small loaves of coarse lyme-grass bread, tubs of skyr, and great hunks of beef and mutton. The guests began to slice off pieces of meat.

Freydis came over to Gudrid with a chunk of mutton and set it down on a low table. She whispered into the ear of a large man with a puffy, rotund face, then patted him on his ample behind. He scurried off toward the wine tubs.

"I'm going to be married," she said to Gudrid.

Gudrid turned toward her sharply, unable to conceal her surprise. "Aren't you the one who told me, 'Avoid marriage at all costs'?"

Freydis leaned toward Gudrid's ear. "Maybe you didn't hear all of what I said. Remember? 'If you must marry, marry a man you can control.' My betrothed has at least this virtue." She leaned closer. "He also has a ship and a big farm."

Tyrkir and the other thralls continued to roll in casks of wine as fast as the revellers could empty them. Steaming slabs of meat came to the center of the house in a continuous stream; a rising pile of bones around the hearth bore silent witness to those that had gone before. The smell of peat from the fire mixed with exhalations and sweat. Faces became flushed, red as the wine itself.

Erik stood up again. "Clear off the dais! We have some entertainment! Ketil Einarsson thinks he can beat Thorstein at the mock-sword game. We'll see, if they're not already too drunk to stand up."

Ketil pushed his way forward. "I could drink all the wine in Tyrkir's vats and still be sober enough to thrash the likes of Thorstein Lame-Legs."

Thorstein stood up and laughed. "Ketil Son-of-a-Wild-Goat will feel the weight of my blows."

Gudrid had not seen this game before. She looked inquiringly toward Freydis. Freydis drained her cup, sent her man for more, and replied.

"They use leather-covered swords and small wooden shields. The first one to force the other to move his left foot is the winner. Mostly they beat each other's shields to splinters while looking for a chance to go for the win."

Thorstein and the other man handed their tunics over to Erik and took their swords and shields. At a signal, they started to swing at each other, the crashes of leather on wood rebounding through the house. Gudrid watched the movements of Thorstein's body, the surge of muscle as he slashed downward on Ketil's upraised shield. Ketil's sword crashed down on Thorstein's shield, breaking off a sizable piece and sending it flying through the crowd.

The move brought a cheer from the spectators, but Ketil had let his guard down. Thorstein's sword came sweeping in from the side; to avoid it, Ketil had to arch his body backward. This threw him off balance, and with a final thrust Thorstein pushed him off his spot.

His body shining with sweat, Thorstein accepted a horn full of wine from someone in the crowd and drank it down. Then he clasped Ketil's hand. "Good fight. You almost had me." The people began to drift back to their eating and drinking.

Gudrid supposed that Tyrkir must soon be running out of wine, but the casks kept coming. The drink was showing itself now not only on the revellers' faces, but also in their gait. Some were holding onto the roofposts; others leaned against the walls. The din of voices softened to a buzz, and Gudrid knew that she herself had drunk more than she'd intended.

Thorstein walked over toward Gudrid, his tunic soaked with the sweat that still poured from his body. He made a place for himself next to Gudrid by shoving aside a sleeping woman.

They sat in silence. Thorstein looked at her, wanting her. Freydis continued to sit on Gudrid's other side, her breath moist and warm on Gudrid's cheek.

Then Thorstein leaped up. In spite of the load of wine he was carrying, he bounded nimbly to Erik's dais seat and hooted for attention.

"Listen, everyone! This is about Gudrid Bjornsdottir and the son of Erik Redbeard! She says she's a Christian lady. She says she won't have a man who leans on Thor. You all know this. Well, Thor be damned! I'll take bloody Christ, like my brother and his Norwegians."

Erik perceived the import of this about halfway through and shouted, "No, by Thor, no!"

Thorstein shouted, "Yes, by Christ, yes! I'll have her now!" He jumped back over to Gudrid and picked her up, his hands grasping her waist, and raised her over his head, seemingly without strain. He carried her down the middle of the house. In a daze she saw the wooden pillars go by. Once her head fell back and she saw Freydis, a look of surprise on her face; then all was a blur again. The revellers began to shout, "Gudrid! Thorstein! Gudrid! Thorstein!"

Then, over the shouting, she heard a louder voice, her father's. He shouted again. "Stop! Desist! Silence, by my honor and by Thor!"

The shouting subsided. Thorstein turned and set Gudrid down as effortlessly as he had picked her up. Everyone was looking toward Bjorn, but he was no longer shouting. His mouth was moving, as though he were trying to say more, but no words came out. Slowly, at first, like an iceberg peeling off the front of a glacier, he began to sag, his knees bending a little. Then he fell freely, slumping down, his hip hitting the floor first, then his shoulder, then his face. Gudrid ran to him, bent over his motionless form, and felt his shallow breathing. Thorstein came up.

"Please," Gudrid said. "Make a bed for my father."

Thorstein picked Bjorn up and carried him through the crowd to the far end of the house, where it was a little cooler and the air a little better. Erik bent over him.

"He's alive," Erik said, "but that's all. Better we let him sleep. The morning will tell what's to be with him."

Amid the pain and shock at what had happened to her seemingly invincible father, she felt a twinge of gratification over this just retribution to one who had wronged her.

Everyone was subdued now, and the fatigue that had been kept at bay by the excitement and the wine now stormed in. The guests rolled out their bedding wherever they could find room. Gudrid asked Thorstein and Erik to make her a place next to her father, and soon her tired body, too, had made its demand and she was asleep.

She awoke abruptly. She sat up and looked around the house. Bjorn breathed raggedly beside her. The fire still glowed, mostly embers now, with an occasional tongue of flame licking up from the remainder of the peat. People were scattered about the room, crammed in wherever they could find space, the men using their tunics as pillows, the women's outer garments folded carefully next to them.

She knew something was amiss, and not just with her father. She was conscious as never before of the power that lay within her to perceive something without knowing how she had become aware of it. She took in scenes whole, the sight of them, the hearing, the smell, without knowing where one sense began and the other left off. Perhaps this is what had drawn her to Arnora, had made her want to learn sorcery. But now she saw one thing at least that had set her intuition in motion. Erik's bed was empty.

She slipped on her boots, stood up and put on her outer robe, fastening the brooches hurriedly. Then she made her way quietly to the other end of the house and the door. She knew she wouldn't find her own fur cloak among the many that lay piled there, but any one would do. As silently as she could, she pushed the door open and went out into the night.

The cold hit her face and nearly forced her back inside, but she stood still, looking up at the stars. Then she ran to the barn, opened the door, and quickly slipped in. Several men and women were asleep near a small fire. The smoke curled up to the roof. One of them stirred as the cold air drifted across the room. She looked around in the dim light but could see nothing wrong.

Then the dairy. She pushed open the heavy door. A dim glow from a small pile of smoldering peat was the only light, so dim that Gudrid had to struggle to see.

"Who's there?" she heard. A man's voice. Then she heard another sound, a young girl's voice, pleading, "Please, Master Erik, I am cold. Please."

She could see now. It was the young slave girl Nika, naked, and there was Erik in the middle, on the floor, covered with a fur robe.

"Who's there?" Erik called again. Then, recognizing Gudrid, "What are you doing here? Go back to the house."

"What are *you* doing, Erik, and why is that girl standing there freezing to death?"

"She's my thrall. I want her. She can come here with me and be warm, or stand over there and let her teeth chatter."

"She's too young," Gudrid said. "I doubt she's twelve years old." Gudrid walked over to Nika and threw her fox robe over the girl. "Come. Come with me. We're going back to the house now."

"You will not," said Erik. "I'm master here."

"It looks as if I'm to be your daughter-in-law." Until now, this hadn't quite sunk in. If it had to be, she might as well use it to the advantage of this poor girl. "If you want to argue with me, you'll have to use force. What do you think this will look like? You want the one son who loves you to think you were trying to get in ahead of him?"

Gudrid led Nika past Erik, who was still sitting on the ground in his fur. As she made her way past, she said, almost as an afterthought, "No reason for me to be cold." She snatched the fur covering from a surprised and naked Erik. Quickly she dashed for the door, pushing Nika in front of her, and then they were outside, running back to the house. Gudrid picked up two more robes from the pile by the door, gave them to Nika, and led her back to her place by Bjorn.

She laid down the furs. Soon she was lying next to Nika, warming her with her own heat. Nika was very cold; it was a long time before any warmth returned. After a while Nika lost some of her stiffness, and sleep came over her. Gudrid nestled in among the fox furs, the now warm body snuggled close to hers. She looked again over the forms in the dim red light of the embers before dawn, felt as she so often did for the stone against her breast, wondering whether she would ever discover its secret. She gave her mind over to brooding on her fate and then, reluctantly, released herself to it.

19.

"Gu . . . Gu . . . Gu . . . ," she heard her father say, then try again, "Gudit!" Things had changed between them.

She pitied his slurred and labored speech, his need to be supported by a thrall. The feeling was new; how recently had she hated him for taking her away from Orm, for taking her to this derelict land, for drawing Orm and Halldis on to their deaths. Although it was a woman's fate to be wed to a stranger, she'd hated him for that too. For Thorstein himself she had neither desire nor antipathy, only emptiness.

She had known the strength of her feelings the night her father was stricken, as he lay there, breathing heavily, and as she lay next to him, trying to give warmth to Nika's body. If she'd had a knife within reach, she knew she could have killed him.

Now, seeing him pass the long winter at Stokaness, she felt the pain he felt, that showed on his face as he tried to speak, the pain that did not end, as it did in even the cruelest torture. Beyond compassion, however, was admiration for the way he held on to his duty, keeping charge of the planning for two new farmsteads, in spite of the need to rely almost completely on gestures.

"Gudit. Gudit. Gudrid." It seemed important to him, to be able to say her name correctly. How little it had mattered before. "Cah . . . cah . . . can . . . you . . . fo . . . for . . . give . . . an ode man?"

She looked at him. Stooped over a staff, robbed of his stature, he did seem suddenly old. The face was still the same, frozen as from inside; only now a veneer of decrepitude had replaced the former hardness. It reminded her of the squash plants that Clovis had tried to raise in Arnarstapi. They had been his most spectacular failure. The vegetables had gone from green to rotten without ever being ripe.

Like Clovis' tubers, he would soon be in the earth.

Gudrid had not been able to ask him before, when he could have answered articulately, but now she must, even if all she could get were a grunt of acknowledgment.

"Why did Thjodhild curse me?"

Bjorn looked into his daughter's face. The look was one she'd never seen on him before, a look of recognition, a look that almost had understanding in it. For a long time he made no sound, though trying to speak.

"Nah . . . nah . . . not . . . you . . . Your   mo . . . mo . . . mother."

She would have argued with him. Didn't he remember the day he'd said, "Every time I look at you, I see the woman's curse?" Now it was no use, to get more than a struggled word or two from him. But he had made no effort to deny what Gudrid had more than suspected: Thjodhild was the source of the curse.

The half-dead man remained before her, his plea as yet unanswered. She looked at him, and then she looked into her own heart. It was not easy; the pain was still there, as strong as ever. Every time she thought of Orm, and she thought of him often, she longed to rush to him, to let him gather her into his arms. Halldis she thought of less often; she'd appreciated her foster mother so little in life that now the memory hurt too much. Her father's bright eyes burned with pain.

"Yes, Father, I forgive you." She would have taken his hand, but this was more than she could bring herself to do.

The sun rose higher in the sky each day, though the only time Gudrid saw it was when she went to one of the outbuildings to oversee the care of the animals or to decide on the day's rations to be brought in from the storehouse or when she went to the privy.

Then one day she received a shock as she walked outside. It was warm! Not summertime warm, for it was not much above freezing, but warm compared with what had gone before. The animals in the byre sensed it too, stirring in their pens as they had not since the cold descended before the Yule. Cormorants flew about and rested on the ice.

The warm southwesterly breeze continued for many days, until one day huge chunks of ice began to break away from the mass that lined the shore. The seals returned, and she could see their heads in the water and their smooth forms basking on the ice floes.

She had had plenty of time that winter to ruminate on what

marriage to Thorstein would mean to her. He was not a man she could love, nor could she even have the satisfaction of hating him. He was what he was, an animal with the strength of a man and the unsubtle mind of a boy. He would take her away with him, and she would live among strangers. She would lie in his bed and be his newest toy. How long would it be until he tired of her? Then she would pace about the house, with a thrall or two to wait on her perhaps, until boredom overtook her and she grew fat and slow.

On the other hand there was Leif. Her feelings for him had not changed, though she had to admit that at least a life with him would be interesting. Of course, it mattered little now. He'd never asked her, though his mother had given her to understand that she could arrange it.

Why did her thoughts run this way? She didn't want Leif, any more than she wanted Thorstein. What did she want? She remembered Einar and mused on the life she might have had with him. Even Hakon would have loved her, and perhaps he could have learned to be brave enough to live in the world he was born to.

Her mind sailed through the shoals of wishful thinking until it found deeper water beyond. Her father would never let her marry Leif. He'd said as much several times. Somehow she was sure he would maintain his resolve, in spite of his affliction. And in this a way might still be found to escape both Leif and Thorstein. If she could induce Leif to ask for her hand, she could count on Bjorn to oppose him. If she then declared her love for Leif, a stalemate would ensue, with Erik, Bjorn, and Thorstein ranged against Leif. She calculated that Leif would not be the loser in such a confrontation, but neither would he be strong enough to carry her away in the face of such heavy opposition. True, what she had in mind required that she ask Thjodhild's help, and if things didn't go according to plan, she might end up in Leif's bed after all. But desperate as she was, desperate measures were called for. She enlisted Asgrim to take her to Thjodhild's house.

"Madam," she said, as Erik's wife opened the door. "The time has come for us to speak."

Thjodhild said nothing. Did that not confirm that she was responsible for the curse? Gudrid quivered with fear as she had before the sibyl and as she once had shaken in front of Arnora in the storm.

"You have spoken to me of Leif." A light came into the woman's eyes. "You've urged me to marry him. Yet he has never asked me."

"You've given him little encouragement, daughter-in-law."

How those words smarted. It was true that she'd snubbed Leif on every occasion she could, limited only by the most basic kind of civility. What man with any pride at all would have asked for her under such circumstances?

"Thjodhild," she said, "suppose I encouraged him now?"

The woman's face warmed like a newly lit fire.

"Do you mean what you say, Gudrid? You would not play with me?"

Gudrid forced out the words. "I would have him come to me."

She watched the boat approach, its bow carving runes in the water. As it neared the shore, she saw that the man at the steering oar was Leif. He was dressed in his finest—silks brought to Norway from jewelled Mikklagard, an ermine cape made from Greenland pelts, and a gem-encrusted sword given to him by King Olaf himself.

He walked up the slope to Gudrid. "Good day, noble lady. I would have a word with you, if you will do me the honor."

"Of course," she said. "I saw you coming. Let us go inside."

They entered Bjorn's long house. She could not help thinking how good a house it was. Whatever else she had thought about her father, she had to admit that he had been thorough and competent in everything he did. The walls were straight and true, and made Erik's house look little better than a byre.

Bjorn awaited them, stony-faced. He did, however, observe every courtesy, even gesturing Leif to join him at the high seat. Gudrid sat opposite. A thrall brought cups of fresh-fermented mead, then stood by to see whether anything more was required.

Leif and Gudrid talked of doings at Brattahlid and Stokaness, then ranged to the world beyond, Iceland, Norway, and news of the success in battle of the Emperor Basil II of Mikklagard, against the Arabs. "Another Olaf Tryggvason, by all reports," was Leif's opin-

ion. "With God's help he will destroy the false religion of Moham-
med."

Bjorn sat silent in his chair. Gudrid complimented Leif on his taste
in clothing, running on at some length out of nervousness. Finally,
even Leif could stand no more of this flattery and came to the business at hand.

"I have been to many lands, from Norway to the unknown mists
to the west. I have acquired a goodly amount of wealth in my travels,
and the goodwill of many in Norway, in Iceland, and in the Hebrides. One day I will be jarl of all Greenland. You are a beautiful,
strong woman of good family and are not without substance of your
own. I think that you would be a good match for me. Your life will
be one of ease, with thralls to wait upon you from morning till night.
I know that my brother has spoken up for you, but perhaps it is not
too late to forge a better match. I would have you for my wife."

Gudrid looked into Leif's blue eyes as he was making this proposal, but his were averted ever so slightly, enough that she could be
sure that this was not his own idea. His manner was casual, as though
he'd come to a merchant to buy a new silk shirt. No doubt he meant
to treat her as he'd treat the shirt, to cast it off as soon as the embroidery began to fray. This didn't concern her very much; she didn't
intend actually to marry him. So far, in fact, things had gone just as
she had planned. The rest depended on her father. She looked to
Bjorn. He was trying to gather the energy to speak. In the meantime,
she would have to fill the silence.

"I am grateful for your compliments," she said. "This is all very
sudden. Have you never spoken to my father before about this?"

Leif crossed over and sat down beside her. In a whisper he said,
"You know what happened the last time I spoke with him, though I
swear I have done nothing to earn his anger."

She felt his fingers indenting the skin of her shoulder, and she
wondered what it would be like to have him all over her. Her mind
raced back to the time on the hillside in Snaefellsnes when she'd
chased him with her amulet and cried out so bravely, "There'll be a
day when you'll kiss my feet and admit that you're my slave," and
he'd laughed at her. Did he remember? He would make her his slave,
now, in marriage, and this would be worse than Thorstein's rough

attention. She knew that now, now that it loomed as a real possibility. What had she hoped to accomplish by this stupid ploy?

Thinking these thoughts, she hadn't noticed Bjorn rise from his chair, his one hand gripping the armrest, the other pointing straight at Leif. His mouth moved.

"No!" The voice startled her, for it was as strong and loud as she'd ever heard it. "No!" Then he fell back into the seat.

If Leif was taken aback by this, he didn't show it. He rose without a word, bowed to Bjorn, turned, and bowed to Gudrid. His eyes were as expressionless as his face. With nothing more to be said on either side, he left the house.

20.

Although Gudrid had imagined that the interview with Leif could now be used as the vehicle to escape marriage to either of the brothers, she couldn't force herself to hold on to him and cry out. She had to let him go.

She cast about hopelessly. Who in Greenland could help her? The only one who came to mind was Brother Ulf. Something about the look on his face when he first came to Greenland spoke of wisdom. Not at all like Sira Geir, thinking only of his own advancement.

Brother Ulf was in Einarsfjord now. There was only one way she could get to him. She found Tyrkir in the smithy, forging arrowheads.

"You said you might help me one day. The day has come."

Tyrkir looked at her, winking the way he had the day they'd first spoken. "If there is anything a thrall can do to help a lady." He stood up and did a little dance to a tune only he could hear.

"Take me to Einarsfjord."

Tyrkir stopped dancing. "You think I have a ship, to go a-roving?"

"You'll only need a little boat. Take me down Eriksfjord. I'm told there's just a neck of land separating us from Einarsfjord there. Just take me. I'll walk the rest of the way myself. I must see Brother Ulf."

Tyrkir nodded. "It could be done." He hesitated.

"You think your master wouldn't approve. Don't worry. I've got to find a way to stop this marriage. Leif would thank you if you helped me frustrate his brother."

"And how is Brother Ulf going to help with that?"

"I haven't any idea. It's the best I could think of."

Tyrkir rigged a small sail in one of Leif's boats and made as if Gudrid had asked him to take her to Stokaness. The wind was behind them, and the tiny boat bucked over a light chop. They came to ground at the low plain that Sira Geir had said would one day support a cathedral. Gudrid had brought a man's cloak with her, one made from sheepskins. As they came down the slope on the other side of the isthmus to the first farm in Einarsfjord, the people who'd been watching them showed their surprise when she shook out her hair and revealed herself to be a woman. They nevertheless took her to Brother Ulf.

She couldn't get to the point right away. As they sat near the fire in a house on the shore of a small arm of the fjord, their faces in the glow of the lamp, she drew out his story. He had traveled south from Norway to see the wide world, but along the way he'd seen the light of faith and taken baptism. Not one to do things by halves, he'd quickly seen where the essence of the Christian life lay and had joined the Benedictines at Cluny. Then, true to his vow of obedience, he'd bowed to the will of his abbot and made the long journey back to his home country as a missionary.

It had been his good fortune to arrive just as King Olaf was being baptized. He was given the task of taking Geir, one of Olaf's courtiers, south to be made a priest. Geir had fully expected to be sent to Iceland as its first bishop, following Olaf's intended forced conversion of the island. When that project proved less than feasible, the king had seized on Leif's fortuitous arrival to make a point with the recalcitrant Icelanders by planting the new faith at their backsides.

Time and a cup of mead loosened Gudrid's tongue. She told him her story, sparing no details of Ymir, even alluding to what Floki had done to her, feeling that a man might not understand her reluctance to be pushed into marriage with the second son of the Greenland jarl.

"Why does Christ allow these things, or his mother either, if they have power to answer a prayer?"

Ulf smiled. This, together with the tufts of hair encircling his tonsure, brought the beginnings of lightness to her face, until her thoughts came back to her present situation. Then Ulf said, "You'll have to go to someone wiser than me with that question. I don't understand the ways of God any more than you."

This was a startling admission to come from a priest, and it comforted her somewhat. Comforted, but not satisfied. Ulf went on.

"No one should put bounds on the love of God. Do you think that in the end it cannot reach out to everyone, even unbelievers?"

"Do you think it could reach as far as me?"

"Aye. But each one must first accept it and trust in the power of God, and in no other."

"I don't understand."

"The amulet you're wearing. It's Satan's trick on you. You must get rid of it."

"It was my mother's. How can I do what you ask? How can it be what you say it is? It has saved me from evil more than once."

"The Devil is crafty. It may be that he has saved your body in order that he might take your soul." He looked her in the eye. "I'm told your foster mother baptized you."

Gudrid hesitated. "Yes, that's so."

"Your eyes betray you. You wring your hands, your shoulders tilt, everything gives you away."

Gudrid struggled for the words to maintain the subterfuge, but something about this man did not permit the lie to be continued.

"I cannot offer you the saving water of baptism unless you renounce Satan and his works."

She sensed finality in these words, but Ulf smiled and blessed her nevertheless. "I will ask the Virgin to watch over you and protect you, and one day bring you into her fold." Then he stretched out his hand. "Show me the amulet," he said.

Gudrid's face dried up in fear. What was he asking? Would he take it from her by force? His gaze fixed on her, and she had no choice but to do his will. When she had removed the stone from her garment, with the chain still around her neck, he reached out farther toward her, as if to grasp it. She pulled it back.

"You're so afraid to lose it. Yet you should fear more for yourself." He touched her wrist as if to quiet her shaking hand. "I won't take it. Nor will I reveal what I know. But thus"—he touched the stone and then grasped it between his thumb and forefinger—"do these fingers that hold the Lord's Body now crush the Devil and the work he would do upon you."

Brother Ulf's eyes were as on fire, and they pierced Gudrid's, so that she could no longer bear it. He seemed so confident in his power, the first man who, knowing what it was, had not feared to take the amulet to his bare flesh. Even Bjorn, when he'd dared her to drop it into his cupped and outstretched hands, had done so as a matter of courage, knowing full well what the consequences would be if she had done it. She left him then and quickly made her way down to the shore, where Tyrkir was waiting. It occurred to her that once Ulf had fixed his look upon her, she'd entirely forgotten Thorstein.

The cold air changed that. She must press on. The sibyl was the only one with power enough. This would be as dangerous as being in the water with a walrus or on the same ice with a polar bear, but she could see no other possibility now.

"Could we get to Herjolfsnes from here?" she asked Tyrkir.

Tyrkir, who had already planted his feet in the direction of Eriksfjord, showed his surprise.

"It's a long way, around through the skerries. You go by ship, or a big, stout boat at least."

"Not everyone has such a vessel."

"In that case, you go by way of Vatnahverfi, the Lake District. It's a wild but beautiful place. No one whom God has put on this shore should pass through life without seeing it." She could see him bringing the place back to memory. "Then you go over the pass to Hrafnsfjord. If you have kin there or someone owes you a favor, you might get a small boat to take you to the south side, where you can cross over to Siglufjord. It's shorter than Hrafnsfjord, and you come out at the head. You go around to the south side and out to the mouth. A pony helps, if you can borrow one. Then you need someone to take you round the headland to Alptafjord, where the south side is passable up to the end. A valley goes inland and over to Ketilsfjord. Again, you need ferrying to the south side, and it's a long journey out, almost to the mouth. From there it's not far to Herjolfsnes.

"You sound like you've been that way."

"I did it once for Leif, when two of his ships were out trading and he needed the other for some business in Vestribygd."

"How long did it take?"

"The good part of a summer. Why do you ask?"

"Because you're going to go with me."

Tyrkir looked at her as if she were mad. He held out his hand as if to guide her gently back to sanity or, if that were not possible, at least to keep her from hurting herself.

"Come, it's getting late. We'll have to stay the night here. Tomorrow we'll go back to Eriksfjord."

But the morrow saw them skimming down Einarsfjord in a borrowed boat rowed by borrowed thralls, Tyrkir shaking his head and muttering something about what Leif would do to him when he got back to Brattahlid. Gudrid did her best to reassure him.

If she had thought of Greenland as bleak and uninviting, the Lake District of Vatnahverfi did much to soften those feelings. Salmon leaped in the streams running down from the lakes. The meadows ran yellow rivers of long-stemmed buttercups, dotted with islands of wild pinks. Willow thickets abounded, so much that the travelers often had to cast about for a way through. Small groves of birch thrived in the sheltered places. Birds abounded—red-necked phalaropes, redpolls, snow buntings, longspurs. Weasels scurried among the rocks, and a fox poked along a lakeshore in his after-dinner mood. A white-tailed eagle hovered over peaks of rock and ice. The mountains, which in themselves appeared forbidding, here set off and intensified the beauty below.

They were four days getting to Hrafnsfjord, staying at farms each night, except for one night when they were out in the cold. Tyrkir lent her his cloak, but she could see him shivering and demanded that they huddle together for warmth. He reminded her of Orm, the way he held her. It emboldened her to ask a question.

"You've told me about Leif. What do you know about Freydis?"

"Freydis . . ." He took time to compose his answer. "She bides her time as long as she sees things going her way in the end. She knows how to use people, rewarding those who do her will, punishing those who don't. I don't know how she does it, a woman. But I'd offend her even less willingly than I would earn Leif's anger."

Gudrid was moved to defend Freydis, taking Tyrkir's reaction as what a man would say about Freydis' unusual behavior. But something in Tyrkir's expression held her back, and they said nothing more that night.

The next twenty days saw Tyrkir work his magic, the journey a succession of boat rides and pony treks interspersed here and there with a stretch of walking. Gudrid became increasingly impressed with Tyrkir's leverage as Leif's foster father, a thrall in name only. They crossed the final neck of land, a bleak valley with bare cliffs rising over a lichen-covered plain, and they were in Ketilsfjord.

At the head of the fjord, bare monoliths speared the sky, the wild glens between threatening an outrush of trolls. Then, as they made their way seaward, the landscape gentled, overflowing with birch. Their progress slowed—here Leif's name carried less authority. It was slog, slog, down the shoreline, day after day, begging a night's shelter at each farm. Each day they inquired of the sibyl, knowing that it was one of her sources of strength that she might show up unexpected and unannounced at any time.

The uncertainty began to wear on Gudrid. By now, she was conscious of how ill conceived and hopeless this expedition was. She became irritable, snapping at Tyrkir, treating him in the basest manner, all the while knowing how ungrateful and unworthy she was. It was in one of the last farmsteads in Ketilsfjord before the sea—where she'd demanded they lay over the day, alternating between self-recriminations and bouts of petty whining—that the sibyl walked through the door, preceded by three men and an old woman even flimsier-looking than she was.

Gudrid knew immediately who it was, even in the gloom of the lampglow, the fire already dying down for the night. Life surged back into her. She rose up and moved quickly to the door to face the seeress.

The sibyl also knew whom she was facing.

"We meet again." The sibyl's voice was as she remembered, on the surface thin but commanding in its deeper resonance. Gudrid could not speak. She reached into her garment and pulled out the amulet, holding it out for the sibyl to touch.

"You've come a long way," the seeress said.

"It's often some trouble to correct an error. I should have stayed with you."

"You offer me this stone now."

"Yes." Gudrid was slow in her answer.

The sibyl smiled. Then her face cracked open and she began to laugh, a slow, mirthful laugh at first, then higher-pitched and penetrating, like the cry of a loon. The men who'd come with her closed in to support her, while the crone made strange circular motions and little jerks of the hand around her face. Gudrid could only wait for this demonstration to die down. The sibyl's face gradually took on a composed, even rational look.

"Girl," she said, "it's impossible. You set the wheel of fate in motion, and it rolls faster every day. How could a frail old woman like me stand in its way? You do not wish to marry Thorstein? The rolling stone comes your way now. See if you can stop it. I cannot. All Greenland is set for this marriage. You ask me, a woman, to stop it?"

"It is said you are the most powerful woman in Greenland."

The sibyl made a sweep of her hand, a gesture of modesty. "Tales are exaggerated to make them more interesting. You think I possess the missing rune? What could I do against Erik?"

"You have your spirits."

"I do. They have spoken. Your fate is determined."

Again she laughed raving. "You'll find the rune before you learn the secret!"

Abruptly she spun away from Gudrid and from the proffered stone, neither being of any further interest to her. She turned to the master of the house to negotiate business of the kind that Gudrid had observed in Herjolfsnes. Another woman sang the conjuring song. Gudrid took small comfort that the sibyl seemed off her form, complaining of a paucity of spirits and making only a few ambiguous prophecies. She and her troop left in the morning.

Two days later a ship appeared in the mouth of Ketilsfjord. It stopped at the first farm and, after a hurried inquiry, made straight for the place where Gudrid lay. Thorstein had come to take her home.

A picture of the wedding flashed through her mind, the line of people wending their way from the house, along the sloping meadow, to the church that Leif had built for his mother in spite of Erik's disapproval.

Their only concession to Erik was to pick a site over the hill, out of sight of Brattahlid. As soon as the sod had sufficiently thawed, the cutting began. A circular dike was constructed around the church. Within the dike, the sod side walls went up to breast height. Leif donated some of his best staves to form the gable ends and wooden posts to support the roof. A low table at one end, a cross, and benches down the sides—these were the only furnishings. A dozen people were all the building could hold comfortably—twenty if they jammed in. On Midsummer's Eve, Brother Ulf sprinkled holy water over the grass on the roof and Sira Geir said the first mass. Erik rode up the hillside and burnt a lamb to Thor.

There'd been one last commotion when she'd seen that Sira Geir was to marry them and she'd demanded Brother Ulf. It was such a small thing, and she'd lowered herself so much in everyone's eyes, but even that small boon was denied her. Sira Geir led the way, followed by Thorstein and Gudrid. Leif and his mother came next, for Erik still refused to set foot in the church. Then came Bjorn, helped along and half carried by a slave, and Freydis, and the most important men from all the fjords in Greenland. Inside, the sunlight coming in through the cross-shaped opening cut into the wall behind the little altar gave a feeling of space and lightness that surprised and awed Gudrid each time she experienced it; how different it was from the dark houses lit by dim fires and smoking lamps.

The Latin words of the ceremony were strange, and stranger still the unknown runes in the book that Sira Geir held. The priest hesitated as if to draw from Gudrid something she did not wish to give. Thorstein stood beside her in his bulk, growing ever more impatient.

At length the priest sprinkled them with water, and it seemed that they were married.

Afterward, at the wedding celebration, Freydis took her aside. "There was no help for it, I know, but marriage to my brother is not what I would have wished for my friend."

"I know," said Gudrid. "You've said as much before. You have freedoms I don't. In the end, marriage to Thorstein may be one of the less troublesome fates."

"Don't speak of fate until you're on your deathbed," Freydis countered. "And as for what is possible, you must make possible what you desire."

"I don't know what you're talking about."

"Use your wit. Plot. Plan. And that little fox pelt between your legs is the only weapon you have now. You had better learn how to use it."

Freydis had never seemed more self-assured, as though she were holding some power in reserve. Gudrid could not look straight at her, afraid as she was of what the green eyes might call up in her and afraid, too, that what Tyrkir had told her might be true.

In Erik's house the feast went on.

Erik had borrowed a freeholder's house for his son's wedding bower. He'd had it cleaned and decorated for the occasion and a large fire laid in a newly built hearth. Gudrid waited for Thorstein, warming herself near the flames of driftwood. She was angry and afraid that all around her had conspired against her to this end. How different would this be from the day on the shore in Iceland when Ymir had come to rape her, except that now the law was on the side of the rapist? It was true she'd given her assent, but what did that mean when no choice was offered?

Nevertheless, she prepared to give herself to him. Maybe if she undressed now it would be over with more quickly. At least the fire was hot. She undid her brooches and removed her outer garment, displaying the white linen shift that Halldis had woven for her many years before. She'd hoped for its use on a happier occasion. She pulled up her shift and felt her smooth thighs. She imagined Einar stroking them, nuzzling his face in the soft flesh. She lifted the shift over her head and undid the strings of her hose and her linen undergown, so that everything fell away.

She took her breasts in her hands sadly, wondering at their round-ness, the redness of the nipples hiding among the loose strands of her golden hair. She touched her belly, her mound of soft brown fur, almost relinquishing them, as if they were not a part of her anymore. She looked at her hands and saw in them the effects of her journey to the sibyl: already old age had left the beginnings of its mark.

Noises came from the door. She slipped under the great sheepskin coverlet, felt her warmth penetrate the soft fleece above and below.

Thorstein walked in. A low greeting passed between them; neither had anything else to say. Thorstein dropped his cloak by the door, then came over by the fire.

He flung his boots into the darkness and pulled off his trousers and tunic. Standing in his woolen underbreeches, he looked down with a smile of pleasure. Then that last garment was off. His penis was distended already, large and firm. He lifted the coverlet and heaved his body in beside her. His hands were cold, and his body also, except for the circle of warmth that was expanding around his excited groin. He stirred, drawing her closer to him, and she smelled the man-smell and the rank breath. She felt his mouth on her mouth, his hand reaching to her thighs. Then his strong arms encircled her, the muscles of his chest squeezing her breasts, and she felt a small but sharp pain. The amulet! She still had it on, and it was pressing against them both. She had not intended this, whatever she thought of Thorstein. She twisted her body to make a space between it and Thorstein's chest, even though this forced her to take his full weight on one breast. She struggled quietly to encircle it with her hand, then worked it off to the side, breaking the chain at last and hiding it under the bedclothes. Thorstein was unaware of all this in the force of his passion.

His penis worked its way into her, as he bit into the soft place where her shoulder joined her neck. The pain there was hot, with the feeling that her life was running into his hungry mouth, and masked whatever pain she'd expected from his entering her. He was all eager-ness and harsh rhythm of muscle and bone, then a final throbbing thrust, and then repose.

She lay awake a long time, looking at the fire, sensing Thorstein's sleeping form next to her. A night bird flapped its wings and took off from the roof of the house. It must have been there the whole time, she thought, and somehow the thought, combined with the smoke that swirled through the little room, brought drowsiness at last. Somewhere in the back of her mind a little girl jumped into the water and swam out boldly into the mist of dreams.

21.

For two weeks Thorstein rutted Gudrid like a ram on a favorite ewe, until she was so sore the tears ran, and even sour butter didn't ease the pain of his coupling with her.

When the day came for her to join him aboard ship for the journey to Vestribygd, everyone gathered on the shore to see them off. She looked at her cousins from Stokaness awkwardly, not having been able to confide in them very much. For the Greenlanders, this was a festive occasion; she had to hide her feelings from them. Thjodhild knew, of course, but the look on her face told only of her satisfaction, with nothing of fellow feeling in it.

Only Freydis seemed a friend. They embraced for a long time, Gudrid not caring what others might think. The longing she had felt before was dried up, along with all other longings. The fear that the longing had bred was dried up also, in the face of the greater fear now, of going away alone, in the power of a man she could not love.

"I'll be there when you need me," Freydis whispered. A moment later she was gone.

Erik stepped closer. "You see how it is with my family. Honor my son." He looked toward Thorstein, who was leaning against the bow of his beached ship. His head jerked as though a thought had just come to him. "You've got no wedding gift from me. I'd like you to think well of me. Take what you want."

This was a generous offer. She was touched by the gesture from this rough man, showing his age and beset by an ungrateful elder son. She knew what she wanted.

"Let Nika come with me. As my maidservant."

Erik nodded. Nika ran to Gudrid, eyes gleaming with pride and happiness, unable to speak. She gathered folds of wool from around Gudrid's ankles and kissed the hem.

Brother Ulf came to see them off. He said a mass, reading the strange words from his book, and he preached a sermon on the power of the Devil that Gudrid knew was meant for her. He did not give out the host, and she knew this was because he did not want to have to refuse it to her. She breathed silent thanks to him; in her uncertainty about religion she was not sure she would have wished to take it. At least in Vestribygd this would not be an issue, since neither of the two priests would be going there.

The ship's company was not large. Eight men and four women wished to return to farms in Vestribygd but lacked ships of their own. The men were an adequate crew to handle the middling-sized vessel on a short coasting voyage; their service was their payment for passage.

Thorstein commanded the sail to be raised, hauling on the line himself when it snagged. The sail, woven of wool here in Greenland and reinforced by a network of leather strips, flapped ponderously in the breeze until a gust caught it and it popped taut. The ship jumped forward like a startled hare.

Vestribygd, the Western Settlement, lay three hundred miles up the coast. Thorstein owned the biggest farm there, in Lysufjord, in equal shares with another man also called Thorstein, but nicknamed Svart because of his dark complexion.

They reached the foot of Eriksfjord and turned to the northwest, beating around the looming height of the island called Hvarf. Two days later, under an ice-blue sky, they turned into a bay that was filled with flat, barren islands and led to a fjord with mountains on both sides, cliffs sheer above the water. Several hours' sailing brought them to a divide. They steered into the southerly arm, and here the country become more inviting. The hills were round and green. Sheep grazed on the hillsides. Willow clumps huddled in the hollows. To the south a sparkling river splashed into the bay.

At the head of the fjord, up the slope far enough to command a view, was the long house, longer than any she'd seen in Greenland or

Iceland. It was built of stone and turf, with a roof of thatch, like Brattahlid, but the door was in the middle instead of nearer one end, as was customary.

A dozen people lined the bank; there could be no mistaking the one called Svart. Thorstein had warned her never to mention his dark skin and hair in his presence. Many people thought he had the blood of slaves in him. "Maybe he does," Thorstein had said. "All the more reason to stay clear of it."

The stem of the ship struck land, to shouts of greeting. Thorstein jumped from the ship. He embraced Svart and shook him as though to see that all of his limbs were securely attached to his body. His frame was sturdy and muscular; aside from his dusky face and black hair, he might have been Thorstein's twin. Thorstein took the hands of a stout woman with very large breasts. This had to be Svart's wife, whose build had earned her the sobriquet "Ship-Bosom."

Her name was Sigrid. She called to Gudrid to come down from the ship. The greeting was friendly enough, but her face remained straight, with only the hint of a smile, even that requiring obvious effort. While climbing down the ladder, Gudrid noticed Thorstein talking to a thin, bony-faced, expressionless man. His lips lay limp on his mouth, without color, like two dead worms. A chill ran through her body.

The door of the house led into a small earth-floored vestibule, which was empty except for some skyr tubs stacked in the back, a heap of reindeer antlers, and some old leather harnesses. It opened left and right to half houses as nearly identical as could be managed with stone and turf. Svart's family occupied the left side; the right was Thorstein's.

Sigrid invited Gudrid into her house. Nika came along, and Sigrid's twin boys, fair-faced towheads three or four years old, ran ahead. Gudrid asked quickly, before the others came in, "Who is that man?" Her voice was almost a whisper.

Sigrid knew who she meant. "His name is Gard. He manages the farm." She patted Gudrid's arm. "Don't be put off. You'll get used to him. We really couldn't do without him, you'll find that out."

Sigrid's skin was rough, and her shoulders moved like those of an ox. She had the same mother as Freydis; she was born some years

before Erik cuckolded her father. Though her face had by no means
lost all of its youthfulness, it had nothing in common with that of
Freydis, who bore so clearly the stamp of Erik's paternity, and it
showed the effects of hardship and forbearance. Perhaps that is why,
Gudrid thought, she'd spoken well of the overseer: apparently he'd
brought them a measure of prosperity.

A certain abundance, perhaps, but without the orderliness she'd
thought should go with it. Not that she'd expect a fastidious palace
like those of Mikklagard, as were told of in stories, how the Byzan-
tines laughed at the Norse traders and considered them unclean. The
thought struck her as incongruous. Halldis unclean? In her father's
ship? Smelling of sea salt beneath the tall towers? It was not to be
thought of. Only a certain degree of tidiness was meant to be kept on
an earth fed by decay.

For all that, this place fell as far short of proper trim as the per-
fumed men of the East went beyond it. Dung belonged on the fields,
not rotting in the byres in the high summer, crawling with insects.
The privy was dug lazily, shallow, and too near the house, so that
even the fjord seemed to smell of it. And everyone seemed to have
lice.

The house was marginally better than the farm. Enough slave
women appeared to be about, but they moved slowly, responding to
Sigrid not with impertinence but with a seeming inability to go any
faster. Had they been recently captured, that might serve to explain,
but they spoke Norse well enough and their faces lacked the bewilderment that usually accompanied those for whom slavery was a new
experience. When Gard walked in, however, the thralls' demeanor
sharpened. Gudrid's mind attended to him also; it took no great talent
for observation to notice the strips of metal dangling from his belt.
She looked quickly at Sigrid, noticing for the first time that nothing
but scissors hung from her brooches. She ran to confront Thorstein.

"The keys! Where are our keys?"

"Gard carries the keys here. Svart and I hold everything in common. We agreed the overseer would hold the keys."

She resented this more than anything else he'd said or done to her.
"Is it not the custom for the housewife to wear the keys on her

body? Perhaps you judge me incapable. If you do, you should have said so to my father before he gave me to you."

It was no small point. Taking the keys from a wife was like relieving a man of his sword.

Thorstein was treating her like a child in this matter of the keys. That Thorstein, who'd never had anything intelligent to say to her, should behave toward her this way reddened her cheeks doubly, with embarrassment as well as anger. She bit her lip until it hurt and then walked away.

"It's always been that way," Sigrid explained about the keys. "No, it's never bothered me."

Thorstein's house had not felt a straightening hand in more than a year. It had benefited only from the natural cleansing of disuse. Some kind of feast had apparently been held here in the last days of its occupation. Old dry bones lay strewn about, picked clean by whatever vermin had nested here in the interim. Nika found a broom and began to whisk cobwebs from the roof timbers. Gudrid sank onto a stool, not bothering to wipe away a thick coating of dust. Thorstein and Svart came in, followed by Sigrid and Gard, with mugs of a hot tea made from a native plant, the one with long oval leaves and white flowers that grew in the bogs.

Gard looked Gudrid over carefully. She forced herself to stare back at his tangled hair and unkempt beard, visibly lousy even in dim light. When his eyes turned to Nika, she felt even more uncomfortable.

A few words were spoken of hunting and fishing. The economy of Vestribygd was very different from that of Eriksfjord. There, seals and fish were a sideline, pursued to eke out the staples of wool, mutton, and cheese. Here, things were reversed. Sheep were kept, and even cows, but when hard times came it was always the sea that saw them through.

They drank in silence. The others showed no feeling of tension among them; they seemed to accept the lack of conversation as normal. Only Gudrid was uncomfortable in the quiet, marked out by the creak of a roofbeam, a scratching of something off in the dimness. She finished her tea and went out to the afternoon sun.

The fjord glistened blue in the bright light. Around to the south the great stream roared broadly down from the hills. Inland, pink and blue flowers spread across the slopes, up to where a long lake stretched into a mountain cleft. A young family, she was told, made their home there. She resolved to visit them.

Gudrid and Nika walked up the slope in the direction of the lake. As the perspective of the fjord deepened, the snow of the peaks was reflected in its blue waters, which, for once, were nearly calm. A few icebergs lingered beneath sheltered cliffs.

They reached the pass about midday, the fjord stretching to the horizon. On the other side was the lake, long and narrow, like another fjord. The farm gave it warmth, reaching to it like a child's hands spread in front of a hearth.

Suddenly her heart ached, for Orm and Halldis, for Hakon, Sigunna, and Arnora, and, though it only emphasized her desolation now, for Freydis. Then Bjorn came to mind. Was he still alive? She'd felt a change in him after he was stricken, and more and more she became convinced that something lay beneath the coldness he'd always showed to her, something his rough nature did not account for.

They walked down to the house at the nearest point of the lake. No one was about, so she rapped on the door. When that brought no response, she pushed it open and called out. A low moan greeted them, then the halting shuffling of a woman tending a man and three children too sick to stand. The stench of vomit was in the air. The thin woman's red eyes and welted face showed that she herself had not gone unscathed.

Gudrid introduced herself. The woman whispered, "I am Hrodny. This is my husband."

The man rolled over and groaned again. Hrodny bent over him, then raised herself up, not knowing what to do with these unexpected guests.

While Gudrid stood uncertainly, Nika busied herself. Even in an unfamiliar house she knew what needed setting right, what pot needed stirring, where water might be drawn. This did not cure the sick ones, but they seemed to rest easier.

The worst was over, Hrodny assured her, though to Gudrid the youngest appeared far gone. Hrodny raised her voice suddenly, praising the gods for their mercy. Gudrid crossed herself. She took surprise at her own action, having done it before only rarely and only in the presence of one of the priests. Hrodny gaped openly at the gesture until she thought to hide her befuddlement.

They drank warm tea and talked until it was too late to go home. Gudrid was glad to have found a friend, even though Hrodny's talk was full of disturbing allusions and indirections about life in Vestribygd, which Gudrid could not induce her to clarify.

Gudrid was afraid of what Thorstein might do when she returned the next morning, but he gave no sign of having noticed she'd been gone. She thought this nearly as bad as a beating and put it down in the little book of grudges she had begun to inscribe in her memory. She closed the book, but not too tightly. The day hardly went by that was not the occasion for some new inscription on its pages.

22.

"A nuisance, these people," Svart said the next morning when Gudrid brought up the subject of Hrodny's family. "We never have anything to do with them." Gudrid looked to Sigrid for some rebuttal, but the woman's face remained flat.

This was the day Thorstein and Svart were to go off hunting. They'd planned to stay in the Vestribygd fjords with the small boat and six oars, two cronies from the second farm down the shore and two of the more trustworthy thralls rounding out the crew, but word of Thorstein's arrival had brought a dozen men in, ready to go to Nordrsetur. The season was late for this, but the summer seemed to be holding, and it was too good an opportunity to pass up.

Nordrsetur was the name of the northern hunting grounds that stretched up the west coast of Greenland as far as anyone had gone and across the wide strait to the Western Barrens, all gray and white, with no habitable fjords but where the waters were even more prolific. Erik himself had first sighted the loom of the Barrens from the top of a high mountain on the Greenland side and had sailed across to explore it. They would go there now to kill seals and catch fish, and perhaps bring back a load of walrus ivory to trade with some Norway merchant.

After they left, Gudrid tried earnestly to make friends with Sigrid, doing what she could to penetrate the stolid exterior. Sigrid came forward as far as her nature would permit, even explaining the finer points of sex from the married woman's point of view, how to gain respite by prolonging the menstrual period, how to squeeze out a man's semen quickly, and how seal fat was much superior to sour butter for keeping the vagina supple and free of pain. When Gudrid expressed her distress over the frequency and coldheartedness of Thorstein's attentions, Sigrid's answer was, "Be glad he wants you. Do what you must to please him. When he tires of you, your life will grow hard." Sigrid apparently practiced this philosophy; Svart looked satisfied with her, though she was no great beauty. As for Gard, Sigrid would only repeat that although she didn't like him any more than Gudrid did, they needed him.

"He knows thralls," said Sigrid. "He was one once himself. We gave him freedom, and he gets a portion of the increase of our farm. In return, he keeps them in line."

"Don't you have any kinfolk," Gudrid asked, "who might want to come and live here? There's enough room." The spaciousness of the house in relation to the small number of inhabitants struck a visitor immediately.

"Some used to live here," Sigrid answered. "They went away."

Gard made his move soon after this. Gudrid had kept Nika nearby at night, sleeping just off the dais, near the rough board bed where she and Thorstein slept. Now, Gard said, Nika would have to sleep in one of the thrall houses, small structures in which the slaves were locked up at night. There were four of them, one for females and three for males.

Gudrid protested vigorously. "I don't think you understand," Gard said almost condescendingly, "how difficult it is to keep this farm under control. I have to play one thrall against another, know how to use rewards and punishments. This girl may belong to you, but it would upset the whole system to give her such special privilege."

"I don't care," said Gudrid. "I'm mistress of this house, and Nika sleeps with me."

"You really don't understand," said Gard, a false pity in his voice. "Maybe Thorstein never told you. I run things here."

With that he took Nika by the wrist, digging his thumbnail into the soft flesh, and dragged her off. Gudrid could do nothing but hope for a hearing when Thorstein returned.

The next day Nika came in tears and told her about Gard's system. Male thralls he wished to reward were taken aside at night and given access to the females. The girls were so used to this that they didn't bother putting up a fight. If any did, it only earned them a whipping. If they pleased the men, they would be given their own little rewards, a trinket perhaps or a day of rest.

The system worked. And Gard himself had taken Nika.

Gudrid ran at him, but he only stood as though not noticing her ineffectual blows. "Don't try me, lady. You think Thorstein will take your side when he comes back? I think he'll say enough of you, and then I'll have you for myself."

Gudrid gave him a hard look. She hated his little laugh, almost a giggle. She walked behind a byre, pulling out her amulet as she went.

"What good are you to me" she asked of it, "with your secret Arnora kept hidden, and now my worst fear always comes to pass? I should throw you away." She knew she couldn't, though, even as she said it.

One thing she could do. She lent it to Nika. "If he takes you again, make sure this touches him. Push it into his bare skin firmly as many times as you can." She explained to Nika what this would do.

Gard did use Nika often, as he had taken a liking to her small, lithe body, the breasts hardly bigger than a boy's. Nika pretended the amulet was harmless and made as if playing a game with Gard. Gard went along with it, as it seemed to make Nika more pliable. Nika, in spite of what was being done to her, took some satisfaction in her secret knowledge.

If Gudrid and Nika expected Gard to keel up dead immediately, however, they were to be disappointed. The color of his cheeks became almost rosy, and he was first to the shore when Thorstein's ship returned. The hunt had been successful beyond prediction. Atop the skins and the casks of salt meat and fish, a polar bear snarled and chewed at the bars of a driftwood cage. The bear lurched from side to side, attempting to topple the prison, which remained upright only by virtue of several stout chains. Wafting from it was a stench unlike that found on any man, woman, or cow. Its stink was nauseating, as though it were itself rotten and not just surfeited on rotting meat. No matter. This shortcoming would not at all reduce the weight of silver or gold a king might pay to have such a beast for his amusement.

Thorstein's reaction to what had gone on in his absence was exactly what Gard had predicted. It was not that he rejected Gudrid's plea; he simply did not understand it.

Gudrid remembered what Freydis said, and tried to reach her husband in bed. She thrust her breasts out and turned her head, exposing her white neck to him, and gave out little moans, and she ground her belly into his in a way she knew he liked. She squeezed him as Sigrid had taught her, but slacked off a little, prolonging his heat. While fondling his nipples, she begged him, "Let . . . my Nika . . . sleep here."

Thorstein ejaculated, then rolled away. "Talk to Gard," he said over his shoulder, even as he was falling asleep.

Another night, she took the other tack, stiffening and making him force his way into her. He seemed to like that even better, pitting his strength against her weakness. In the morning she hurt, every bone of her.

So matters held as winter closed in. The female thralls were allowed a little fire in their byre, the males none. This made the man-slaves even more eager for Gard's favor, to be warm as well as to have a girl. After a time Gard tired of Nika. Now she was given at random, along with the others.

In the early morning, before dawn, the girls would turn to each other for comfort.

As for the bear, somehow they managed to skid it, cage and all, off the ship and down to the shore. It was a young male, about half grown. It stared out vindictively, raking its paws when anyone came near. Sometimes Gudrid could quiet it with soft words, but only for a moment. The next instant it would again be hurling itself against the bars.

They'd kept it fed on the ship, but now there didn't seem to be enough meat in Vestribygd to keep it satisfied. Its ribs began to show, and it bellowed its hunger loudly, especially at night. As winter approached and they had less and less to feed it, Svart and Thorstein considered whether they should kill it. Such discussions always ended with a reckoning of what they could get for the animal, an amount of treasure that grew with each telling until it exceeded the declining weight of the bear.

They built a house around it, right there by the shore, just big enough for the cage and a space at one end for the keeper to stay out of reach of the claws. They built the walls thick, with a stout door, in case the bear should break out of the cage.

Early one morning Gard came into the house. Gudrid was awake, and she saw that his hands were red with blood.

"Killing sheep so early?" Gudrid said softly.

"Hrrmf."

"What was that you said?" Gudrid asked.

"I killed him."

Killed? Who? But she knew. "It was our neighbor, Hrodny's man, wasn't it."

"The same one."

Gudrid was stunned. "Why? Did he attack you?"

"He was taking ptarmigan without my leave."

Gudrid stood up. She grasped at her nightshift to make sure she was covered. Fury washed over her, ebbing to disbelief, then crashing again. Then came futility, the sense that she was a weak woman and could do nothing to avenge this iniquity. "You killed that unfortunate man, hardly off his sickbed, who's lost his favorite child, the little girl? You call this courage, man? You, with the cock of a horse that you suck yourself to sleep with after you've fucked my Nika! Hel take you! Go fuck the carrion lady!" She flew at him, nails spread like claws, willing herself to scratch out his eyes. He reached out with his arm, almost lazily, knocking her to the floor with a blow to the breastbone.

He was smiling. "Check yourself, woman. I killed him in accord with the law. He had his sword in his hand."

Gudrid sat up, struggling to get her wind. "You know he was in no condition to fight. He nearly died of the sickness."

"He was in good enough shape to kill our birds," said Thorstein, who by now was awake.

She looked at him. He'd seen what happened, and not only was he ignoring what Gard had done but he was taking his part.

"There's no game up by the lake," Gudrid said, a wave of despondence washing over her. "He *had* to come down here."

"He should have asked us first." Gard snickered. "Not that it would have done him any good."

"Nika and I were there yesterday," Gudrid said. "I gave him permission to hunt or to come for anything else he needed. I had no idea it would come to this." Her eyes filled up, though she would have given much to prevent Gard from seeing her wet cheeks.

Gard stood over her. His too familiar man-smell drifted down. Had it been especially foul, it might have cheered her somewhat to sense an accord between his outer aspect and his evil nature, but lousy as he was, it was as good a scent as she'd ever smelled on a man. This only spilled more anger over. She rose and stepped back onto the dais, leaned forward, and spit in his face. She spat again and again, until her saliva ran down his nose, white and viscous like semen. Gard stood impassively, hands on hips; then he glanced toward Thorstein, who by now was awake and naked on his feet. His body rippled; he was wild, like the white bear, a mass of surging flesh and grotesque genitals. He steadied himself, then slapped her in the face, again and again, until blood ran onto her nightshift. She tried to pull away but was frozen in bewilderment and terror. Only when Thorstein paused to catch his breath did she escape to the far end of the house. Sated for now, Thorstein did not follow.

She did not know where to turn after this. In a way, Thorstein's response did not surprise her, but it made unbreachable the barrier between them. She had not loved him, but until now she had accepted him, had come with him to the end of the earth, and she had held out hope that one day the feeling between them might grow more tender. She'd known of women who had come to love their husbands, and men their wives, after years of shared life had tested them and allowed them to show themselves to one another. Halldis had suggested as much, though in her heart Gudrid always kept the conviction that Orm and Halldis had loved from the start.

It had not entered her mind before to leave Thorstein, but it did now. A woman could dissolve a marriage as well as a man. Law and common usage were clear on that. Acceptable grounds, however, were few.

Impotence was one. But Thorstein? Hardly.

Another was a husband's wearing of effeminate clothing. This she dismissed as quickly as the first. Thorstein's attire was drab and functional and strictly masculine.

A wife might also end a marriage if her husband aided her kinfolk's enemies. A clear case existed if the husband assisted the slayer of the wife's brother. This was no help either. Bjorn had no enemies in Greenland, and Gudrid had no brothers.

When Gard left, Thorstein dragged her to his bed, stopping her mouth with his hand when she tried again to complain of Gard's crimes. He took her rampantly, twisting her arms in his urgency. Never had his sex been so raw, so like rape. Thorstein was no longer driven by lust for pleasure but, like Ymir, by another kind of lust—for power over a creature without defense.

When the ordeal was over, she tried to guess what Freydis would have done, but she knew that Freydis would never have let herself into this situation. This thought made her feel even less capable. Why could she not be strong and resourceful like Leif's sister? More and more she blamed herself for the chances she'd rejected—Einar, the sibyl—and for her failure of nerve when, unable to feign love for Leif, she'd seen her plan to thwart both brothers come to nothing.

The final blow, as the cold set in, was that, in spite of all her efforts to keep herself clean, washing her clothing herself, combing her hair each day with a fine-tooth comb, even soaking her menstrual rags in a separate barrel from the others, the lice were on her. The others seemed used to this, but she would never be. She and Nika groomed each other daily, but it was a losing battle, living close among infested people.

As winter bore on, her will to resist was stressed to breaking, and she saw herself becoming more and more like the slave girls. At night, Thorstein would drive into her, galling her in his clench. Or else he would bring a slave girl into the house, and Gudrid would lie alone, listening to his grunts of satisfaction. She gathered all her remaining strength to kindle and nurture the fire that still blazed up within her, burning for deliverance.

23.

Gudrid resolved to go up to the lake to see what could be done for Hrodny and the children. She was watched now, on Gard's initiative and at Thorstein's order. Also, it was still winter outside, though the worst of the cold and snow were past.

She'd want Nika with her. This complicated matters. Even if she could contrive a way to slip off herself, doing so with a thrall would be nearly impossible. Too many eyes were watching, masters' heavy eyes and slaves' eyes trained to engage in the basest sort of behavior in return for a meager reward.

Even as the project faded in plausibility, its scope broadened in her mind. Why stop at some humble works of mercy? Why not escape? Someone might take her in, perhaps with a pretext for breaking off her marriage. She'd need Hrodny's help. Whether any of this could be done, particularly in this season, she did not know.

One thing she did know. It had to be tried. Her mind fixed on Nika and how to manage getting both of them loose at the same time. Only facts intervened. Escape by day was impossible, and Nika was locked up at night.

What if Nika got sick? Not just mildly ill, able to be left alone in a corner and then punished for laxness when she got better, but violently, disgustingly, running-at-both-ends sick? She'd have to be thrown out of the slaves' quarters. She'd be dumped into Gudrid's care then to be nursed back to health. With any luck at all and a dropped hint of contagion, they'd both be relegated to an outbuilding. Gudrid's heart nearly burst at the cleverness of the plan.

That night she mixed the potion and set it in the embers to boil down to a paste. The next day she explained to Nika what would

happen. The following night an angry Gard thrust the pale and stinking girl into the house. Gudrid affirmed the seriousness of the affliction.

Thorstein began to thrust at Nika with the pole of his halberd,
pushing her back out the door. "Drown her. We won't have some
southern plague here."

Gudrid hadn't prepared for this. Could she have so underestimated
his cruelty? What could she do? She hesitated a moment, ideas running wildly through her mind. Then, without knowing what would
come next, she went to Nika and embraced her, kissed her. She
scraped some of the phlegm and vomit from Nika's face and clothing,
and ate it.

"Whatever Nika's got, now I've got it too," she said. "If you want
to drown us both you can, but it will win you ill fame. Give us the
smithy. I'll bring her back to health if I can, or else I'll die with her."

Thorstein gave her a look of disgust, as if asking the gods "What
can you expect from a woman?" Gard's eyes were like swords em-
bedded in blocks of ice, blade up. He allowed that they might go to
the bear house, sharing Thorstein's amusement at the suggestion, but
Sigrid and Svart came in then, and in the end it was decided that they
would go to the smithy. Gudrid snatched up a makeshift bedroll
from sheepskins lying nearby, gathered her cloak and leggings, and
led Nika into the night.

They found the smithy in the moonlight and pushed the door
open. It was cold and dark. It occurred to Gudrid that Nika might be
in trouble, weakened as she was, even though she suffered no real
plague. Given flint, steel, and some dry tinder, Gudrid might have
made fire, but she had none. She huddled with Nika, ignoring the
foul smells that came from the girl's clothing. They would have been
like that all night had Sigrid not come. She would not stay; she left as
soon as the flames had caught, her eyes as wide as her mouth. Gudrid
longed to be able to reassure her, but she dared not.

The next day Sigrid called to them through the door. Gudrid told
her that Nika might live, and asked for meat and water and fuel for
the fire, and some warmer clothing. For Nika, recovering now and
excited at the thought of getting away with Gudrid, it was all she
could do to keep quiet.

On the third night they opened the door and crept away from the farm. They were adequately provisioned. Gudrid had fashioned greatcloaks from the sheepskins, and they'd saved a large piece of seal blubber wrapped in its skin. A gibbous moon was up.

They reached the house by the lake just before dawn. The door was cracked open; the inside was cold and dark. This was a severe disappointment to those expecting a greeting, a place to warm themselves, and a proper meal. In spite of the real danger this put them in, it was nothing compared with what they felt when they stumbled onto the corpses of Hrodny and the two boys, frozen where they sat, in the high seats. Nika screamed in fright, bumping her head several times in her frantic effort to get out of the house. Gudrid was scarcely more composed in her retreat.

They waited in the cold for sunrise, then reentered the house, using the faint light filtering in to assure themselves that what they'd found in the night was not just an imagining. The boys wore their finest summer tunics, their skin blue under the light cloth. Hrodny wore rough wadmal, one layer only. Their dress and their resigned faces made it clear they'd died of their own will, in protest against the injustice done to their husband and father. It was a mystery to Gudrid what they'd hoped to accomplish by this. Was there no limit to what grief and desperation could drive some to?

She took only a moment to mourn the dead. The living had problems of their own right now. The bodies would keep. There was no question of burial until the ground thawed.

Corpses or no, she'd have to make fire here or there'd be five dead bodies instead of three. She opened wide the door to let in as much light as possible, then searched the house for dry tinder. She'd brought Sigrid's flints along, and as it would happen, finding something only when it isn't needed, she found flints and steel enough to get ten fires going all at once. Her search for tinder was less successful, and she resorted finally to cutting linen from the bodies of the two boys. The fire was no less warm for that.

More to the immediate point, this darkened her hope of gaining freedom, but she would not let it die. They could not linger the night here, with ghosts about, so they lost no time in gathering what they could best use for a journey: some dried mutton and, for each, a knife, an extra wool wrap, warmer mittens and leggings, and fur boots.

They set out, not knowing the way to anything, only that somewhere to the north was another fjord where people made their homes. The day was bright. The morning sun glinted from the ice and rock as they made their way up a valley toward what looked like a pass. It was so high they had to tilt their heads back to see it, its whiteness like a frozen river.

The going was difficult. Only Nika's chatting voice—which alternated maddeningly from the Norse back to her southern tongue just as she was getting to the point of a tale—cheered Gudrid until she understood that Nika's courage was engendered by the girl's faith in an older, trusted companion, a faith Gudrid could not call up in herself.

Progress was slow. Where the snow had a crust, they slid back; where it didn't, they sank in deep. With no path or knowledge of the way, they blundered often into cul-de-sacs, which forced them to retrace ground painfully won.

In early afternoon the sky clouded over and a cold wind began to blow from the east. A light snowfall gradually worsened, and soon it was obvious they could make no further headway, either forward or back. Gudrid led Nika to the lee of a cliff, where the snow was thick, and with their knives they cut a hole in the crust. Then they scooped out a space in which to hide.

The snow continued into the night. The two huddled in their cave, one or the other going out to clear new snow from the opening so that they could breathe.

In the morning Gudrid saw that one of Nika's mittens was torn and that her fingers were curled in on themselves, hard and white. She scooped up a handful of snow to rub onto the frostbit hand; then she stopped. It's what everyone did, but it didn't seem right, to treat cold with yet more cold.

She tried to force herself, to will her hand to obey tradition. She was conscious of the stone on her chest, as much a part of her as the breasts it nestled between, yet like them alien, too, stuck onto her. It seemed to radiate warning like a small star. Gudrid suddenly felt close to its secret, almost able to see it. She sensed that the secret was not the kind she had thought, not some grand elucidation of mystical powers but something very simple, though no less powerful for that. Yet, as quickly as the feeling came, it left, and the secret remained hidden. She knew only that she must now do what made sense to her, and not what someone had once told her.

She took the sleeping girl's hand and put it between her thighs. The cold went quickly in, and she held Nika close until the girl woke, pulling back her hand and screaming in pain. That was a good sign, confirmed by the pinkish color returning to the fingers.

The snow had stopped, but the air had grown much colder overnight. They climbed upward on the new snow, gaining the pass about noon. A long valley lay on the other side, with another lake in the distance. It was too far away to see any farm, but the shore was gentle enough that it might be inhabited.

"Nika," Gudrid said, "I don't know what's going to happen to us now, but I want you to know that I wish you were my sister." She hugged Nika and kissed her until Nika began to cry, long blubbering sobs. Gudrid stood up, took Nika by the hand, and led her down.

They reached the lake as the last glimmers of light left the mountaintops. No farm was in sight; it meant another night in the open. They dug a trench in the snow under an overhanging rock and settled into it. They sat facing one another, each one's feet on the other's belly, their cloaks about them, their hands in their boots. Nika told stories of the bright land she remembered, how the sun was so hot at midday that it drove them under the olive trees, the sea blue as the sky and full of mermaids, and how everyone had laughed at a sailor who spoke of a place so cold the water turned to stone . . .

At first light they ventured onto the frozen lake. The walking was not hard, but the wind found them, and they knew they must find a human hearth before dark. Noon came, their progress to be pitied against the expanse of ice, and then the inexorable passage of the hazy sun, filtered through ice crystals in the air until the afternoon cleared and the mountains stretched shadows over them.

Then they saw it, though they might have gone by, set as it was at the end of a narrow bay. Smoke came from the roof. They ran to the door.

The house was full of people—children, babies, men and women, young and old. At least it seemed so until Gudrid reflected that this was normal for a farm, that she'd become used to the emptiness of the house on Lysufjord. The housewife gave them hot broth, some mutton, and a little hard bread. Then came the questions: Where did they come from, and why?

Gudrid had to think quickly. Her first impulse was to make up new identities for herself and Nika—was it possible she'd given no thought to this during the long nights in the snow?—but she recognized the dilemma immediately. If she picked names she'd heard spoken, of young women from some far fjord, distant enough that she might hope these people hadn't seen them in years, she'd get tripped up in details of their lives she had no way of knowing. If she chose fictitious names, she'd have to weave a story—recent arrivals in Vestribygd, perhaps, come to live with kinfolk on this or that fjord—and she'd still have to explain how they'd come to be here.

Some prevarication would, however, be necessary. By law she still belonged to Thorstein, and she would not risk everything now on whether these folk, whose names she did not yet know, would flout convention on her behalf.

"I am Gudrid, Bjorn Vifilsson's daughter," she began, "wife to Thorstein Eriksson of Lysufjord. This is my maid, Nika. A sickness came to our house. The thralls overcame their master and killed everyone except us two." She drew in a long breath before giving out the explanation. "We'd gone to the privy when we heard the shouting. We had no choice but to run into the night."

"You ran all the way here." The man's voice conveyed his incredulity. "You were well clothed for a trip to the outhouse. Provisioned, too, I see."

"First we went to Hrodny"—she searched her mind vainly for the husband's name—"Hrodny who lives on the next lake south of here. It's not that far . . ." Why was it that the truthful part seemed the hardest to put across?

The man nodded in recognition. Gudrid went on. "This plague, or whatever it was, struck harder there. They were all dead, the children too. We took what we needed and went on, and so we are here." She forced a smile.

The man appeared to accept this. He led her to his high seat, introducing his wife and householders—cousins mostly, though two small families, having suffered ill luck and heavily in debt in Iceland, had attached themselves to him for the voyage to Greenland and were now working to repay him.

She knew her stay here could only be temporary. A guest could impose on a host only so long, and moreover, come spring, the truth of how things were in Lysufjord must come out.

She held a slim hope she might find someone she'd be willing to trust, who might convince the man of this house to let her stay. They treated her well enough, and Nika too, giving them beds as warm as their own, sharing their food, and helping them to rid themselves of lice, rubbing them down and washing their hair with a mixture of ashes and bog mire. For all this, she had not yet found the nerve to tell the whole of her story to any of them.

And when the ice began to melt in the lake, Gudrid climbed the fells to see how the land lay. Everything was a jumble of mountains and ice, with a thin strip of green emerging along the lakeshore.

She took Nika exploring along the shore one bright day and found that the lake let out into a great tumbling stream, bounded on both sides by willows.

This must lead somewhere, Gudrid thought. Soon we must follow. They'd find more farms, farther from Thorstein and Gard, and perhaps at one they would be able to hide a long, long time.

When their welcome began to wear, Gudrid made known her intention to leave. To her surprise, this sparked a new solicitousness in her hosts. Little things, like offering her the last piece of mutton in the pot, moving her bedding several places nearer the fire, a pair of brooches for Nika, a new comb.

They'd overstayed long, now, but each time she was ready to leave, something stood in the way. The weather was unsettled. The ground was too soggy underfoot. The stream was too high to cross. And also, the refrain went, what were a young widow and a girl doing traveling by themselves? A group would be going down to the fjord soon. They'd help her find passage to her kin in Eriksfjord.

In spite of her misgiving, Gudrid was persuaded to stay. The place was comfortable and warm, and this was the first decent treatment she'd had in a long time. She felt easy enough now with two or three of the women at least to consider confiding her true situation. Only indecision held her back, over which would be most likely to plead her cause and which most able to argue it well. Tomorrow she would decide. Today she would sit by the shore and comb Nika's hair. She hadn't found any nits in days now. Soon she would be able to relax her diligent searching. Soon she'd be able to relax everything and live in a place where she and Nika could be free.

She woke from this reverie to look out onto the bay. A boat was approaching. Poised above the steering oar was the last face in the world Gudrid wanted to see.

Gard had come for them. The chief of the house delivered them personally into his hands. Gudrid did her best to walk with dignity and to comfort Nika, whose body shook uncontrollably. The first thing Gard did on getting back to Lysufjord was to whip Nika on the back and on the thighs, so that the blood welled out from torn skin, and then he cut her face so that no man would ever call her beautiful.

Gudrid expected a whipping from Thorstein, but he ignored her, indicating only a place in the corner where she might sleep while he cavorted in bed with Agatha, the thrall who knew best what a man liked. Gudrid did what she could to salve Nika's welts, but could do nothing to ease her own conscience for having brought her to this.

"We'll see about selling the girl, though I doubt she'll bring much now. It will be better here then with you." These were the only words Thorstein spoke to her for eleven days, until he again noticed her light skin and the soft shapes of her breasts under her woolens, which she had taken to wearing even to sleep, and he dragged her back to his bed.

His breath smothered her even as he pressed into her. Out of bed, the face of Gard hovered over all her days. The future loomed like an open icefield in the arctic night.

24.

Freydis' ship appeared in the fjord one day in the spring after the ice had broken up. Gudrid ran down the hill in surprise. She couldn't hide her excitement. This was like a bright sunrise after many days of rain.

When they were alone she embraced Freydis, shivering like a half-drowned child, until Freydis had to laugh at her shaking. Gudrid started to laugh also, but stopped abruptly when Freydis' eyes caught hers. The yearning, half-forgotten in Freydis' absence, threatened once again. Gudrid let go and spoke in a low voice. "If anyone ever needed a friend, I do now. How did you know I wanted you so much to come?"

"There are more ways of knowing than seeing or hearing," said Freydis, "as you well know. I guess things have gone more poorly than I imagined."

Gudrid stood in silence, taking in again the red hair, the androgynous face, the green eyes at once deep and penetrating. Then she told her about Nika and the killing of their neighbor, and of how she found Hrodny and her children.

"And what had the overseer to say for himself?"

"He laughed a laugh that I hear in the night, when I awake in terror from dreams. He said, 'Now our farm will be that much larger, if we will take it.'"

Freydis thought for a moment. "Gard's presence is no comfort, then?"

"I would kill him if I could."

Freydis looked directly into Gudrid's eyes. "The young girls in Iceland don't seem to be very well educated, if you're any example."

"What do you mean?" The remark stung.

"You don't seem very enterprising. It isn't hard to kill a man."

Gudrid said nothing, but she knew her face was betraying her interest.

Thorstein came in then with Freydis' husband and several of the crew. A young girl was with them. She sat down next to Freydis. By her dress and bearing, it appeared she must be Freydis' maidservant, yet she had an air of forwardness that hovered just beneath her deference. Her features were reminiscent of Freydis' own, except for the color of her hair, which was that of newly dried hay. Gudrid immediately felt jealous of the girl. Ashamed of the feeling, she tried to speak lightly, asking her name. "Inga," the girl replied with a confident face, as if she had no need to say more.

They all sat down. Talk was of the winter. Freydis' husband spoke of Brattahlid, of Thjodhild and Erik still at loggerheads over religion. Some Greenlanders had begun to think of going to Vinland, the warm, green land that lay to the southwest. Leif's sailors had spoken of it in awe. It was not just an island; it went on forever. The man who made himself lord of it would eclipse the memory of all the kings of Europe. This bothered Erik even more. "We're small in numbers here," he quoted Erik. "We can't afford to split ourselves up. If we try, we'll all fail." Nevertheless, a refrain had begun to be heard in the Greenland fjords. "Vinland is better than Greenland, better than Iceland—better than Norway, for that matter. We should go there." For now, Erik had the last word. "Without Greenland, Vinland will die. You'll be too far away for traders to go. You can't live without trade. Go for wood and grapes, but stay here for the winter."

Little was said in return of the winter in Vestribygd.

Gard stomped in. "It's said someone here likes little girls," Freydis said. "And thinks it manly to murder the sick."

Gard stared at her. "The she-wolf feeds on carrion, and spews it from her belly for her toothless mate."

Freydis' husband looked at Gard angrily but did not challenge him. Gudrid expected Freydis to say something, but she didn't, either. After this the conversation between Thorstein and Freydis was forced, and Freydis made an excuse to go to sleep early. Thorstein had offered his guests sleeping room in the house. Freydis now picked up her bedroll and went down to the ship. Her husband followed, his face betraying that he was not looking forward to another night with no roof over his head.

The next day Thorstein went to the smithy and found Gard dead. His mouth, a rictus carved by fear and frozen by death, showed that he had seen his fate coming. His spine was arched backward. His right eye was pierced by an arrow.

The house was in an uproar, but no one could offer any clue. The arrow had come from the house by the lake. Some said it was the dead man's spirit that had avenged its slayer. Others noted, however, that Gard had left several of the man's hunting arrows in the smithy after the killing, so that anyone could have used one of them.

Suspicion ran immediately to the thralls, and several were tortured. Three confessed almost immediately, and the two others, under greater duress. Their stories, however, were inconsistent, and although Thorstein would have killed one or two of them as an example to the others, Svart argued against such profligacy.

Svart made no secret of his mistrust of Freydis' crew, but Freydis herself vouched for every one of them, and Thorstein would not accuse his sister without evidence. Gudrid took care not to give Freydis away by any sign or gesture. For several days Freydis confined her dealings with Gudrid to perfunctory courtesy. Then she invited her for a walk.

"You wished Gard dead," said Freydis, "and so he is. How much more, then, must you wish the same for Thorstein."

A part of Gudrid was shocked by this, but another part had seen it coming. Still, it was too much against nature for her to acknowledge it immediately.

"He deserves an evil fate, does he not?" said Freydis. Freydis raised her arms, pretending to take aim at a low-flying gull. She released the feigned arrow.

"Are you suggesting something?"

"A woman can alter her fate, satisfy a desire."

"You would kill Thorstein the same way you killed Gard?" She tried to say this cooly, even putting in a tone of disapproval, but there was no hiding the hope in it.

Freydis laughed, her face opening up in mirth at the suggestion. "You'd put me to work, is that it? Gard was easy enough. He could hardly have expected death to come the way it did, until the last moment, when it was too late. Now . . ." She sighed.

"I'm told you were taught sorcery when you were a child," Freydis continued. "I'm surprised you haven't done more with it."

177

"What?"

Freydis' face turned angry. "Don't play dumb with me! Do I have to show you everything? You poor, innocent, put-upon, *Christian* creature! If a man had done to me a tenth part of what Thorstein's done to you, I'd have put him in his grave a long time ago!"

"Easy to say," said Gudrid. "Hard to do."

"Not so hard if that pretty face of yours has anything behind it. A man can die in many ways. Poisons, for example. Toadstools. Deadly herbs and berries. Caustic. Quicksilver. Excess of drink. Or try something else. A knife while asleep or during sex. An arrow. The sword. The spear. The halberd. A walrus. Fright of spirits. A falling rock. A landslide. Avalanche. Falling from a cliff. Falling into a crevasse. Burning in one's house. Burning in a neighbor's house."

"Wait!" In spite of herself, Gudrid found herself wanting to laugh at the multitude of deaths—most quite implausible in her mind—that spilled from Freydis' mouth like curds from an overturned crock. Freydis took hold of Gudrid's chin and shook it gently, so that now Gudrid did laugh—for the first time, it came to her, since Thorstein had taken her from Tyrkir in Ketilsfjord. Freydis laughed too, and for a moment Gudrid forgot all else in the fireglow of friendship renewed.

Freydis was not done with her litany. "Buried alive. Drowned. Frozen. Struck by a falling beam. Pestilence. The bellyache. The limb-rot. The king's evil. Starvation. Shipwreck. Lost at sea. Lost in the wilderness. Chained to a rock. Chained to an eagle's nest. Ordeal of the snake. The blood eagle."

"An impressive list," said Gudrid, "although there are no snakes in Greenland."

"Conjure one up," said Freydis. "I thought you were the great seeress!" She punctuated the irony with a light jab of her finger, and softened it with a smile.

"All right, I will," said Gudrid. "You can stick the horn in his mouth and I'll put the snake in. Nika can hold the torch to the end."

They both thought this was hilarious.

"And we'll watch the wiggle-worm crawl down the bugger's throat!"

Gudrid had to bring in a note of practicality. "Who do we get to hold him down while we give him this medicine?"

At this, Freydis sank to the ground, having completely lost control of her laughter.

"Seriously," said Gudrid, "I suppose I'm just to pick one of these deaths and wish it so. Or should I come at him one morning with an axe?"

"Not necessarily. Look around. Pick the method that suits you."

Gudrid could only look blank, and she accepted Freydis' scowl as her due. Sometimes memory dulled, and thinking Gard the principal author of the crimes she'd experienced, she'd almost been able to forgive Thorstein. But she had only to look at Nika for her hate to flame up anew. She imagined herself raping him with a knife, the space between his ribs a hymen, his heart a cunt. Her fantasy went beyond, to dancing blood-red in the moonlight, her hair dull-soggy with his life.

"He deserves what Gard got," she said. "Only I can't say yet I'm able to kill. I do remember more of Arnora's teaching than you think. Come."

They went to the back of a byre in which Nika was feeding three hares. "We snared them. No poison I know grows here, so I'm trying every strange plant I can find, one by one. So far, nothing has done more than make them sick a little, except these in the corner, all so bitter they wouldn't eat them, nor would they disguise well in a man's food either."

Freydis smiled a little. "This is good. You'll hit on something. Follow it up with action when you do." She leaned closer. "Widowhood has much to recommend it." Then, offhandedly, "I'll be leaving soon."

"No!" Gudrid said, showing her distress before she could catch herself. However afraid she was of her feelings for this woman, she couldn't bear to have her leave. Now the girl Inga came running out to join them, and Freydis ran her fingers through the thrall's hair. Gudrid resented this and felt her own hair, which Nika just that morning had so painstakingly combed out. Freydis had decided that Gudrid would never go through with killing Thorstein, and was rejecting her because of it. It wasn't fair!

She imagined the babies left alone to die in the mountains. This is how she felt herself to be, abandoned, as she had been by everyone who had ever befriended her. She knew these were the emotions of a mewling child, but she couldn't put them away, though they lowered her so much in her own estimation.

Fight! She'd fight the feeling, forget Orm, forget Sigunna, forget Hakon, who must have felt as she did now, the day he leaped from the cliff.

Forget Freydis.

No! The green eyes were too strong, boring into her even as their owner tousled Inga's hair. She returned Freydis' stare, for Freydis was staring. Freydis knew, not only knew but invited, teased, compelled, even while she played with her thrall. Gudrid longed to embrace Freydis, to find in her soft arms what she'd done without too long. But something else stopped her. Fear. Fear like the fear of jumping to safety from an ice floe across a narrow span of water, the fear that kills when, in a moment, the fissure has widened too much, and Gudrid is doomed to remain alone, cold.

Still, if she couldn't take Freydis' soft love, she might borrow something of her skill. So what that Freydis sneered at her queasy stomach?

"Why is it necessary to kill Thorstein?" Gudrid asked. "Couldn't you help me find a way to leave him?"

Freydis' smile recalled Arnora's sometimes, when Gudrid had said something especially stupid. "What accusation could you bring against the son of Erik? That he couldn't get stiff between the legs? Who would believe it? Thorstein's got more bastards than the King of Norway. You didn't know?" Freydis was going too far. Gudrid's fists tightened, the nails biting into the palms.

"His man killed a man."

"And the man he killed was your brother, I suppose."

"He could have been my cousin."

Freydis' smile became almost maternal. "Don't you think the first thing I did when you told me about Hrodny was to look into her husband's genealogy? You think I wouldn't like, more than anything, to get you free of Thorstein?" Gudrid fought the dark feelings. She sensed Inga's hateful eye. She felt Freydis watching her, so in control, so sure of things, so confident that time was her ally. Freydis spoke again, the emotion washed out of her voice. "The man isn't your kin, not even a third or fourth cousin. You could never carry through the lie. If there's one thing we Norse are meticulous about, it's our ancestry."

Gudrid could only nod agreement.

"So if you want to get rid of Thorstein, there's only one way. Kill him. I'll help you afterward in any way I can, but I won't do it for you."

Freydis went off with Inga, leaving Gudrid to ponder her once beautiful hair, nit-ridden again after her return to Lysufjord. For this affliction alone she would have rejoiced, had Thorstein not returned from Nordrsetur. To lay her own hand to it, however, seemed beyond her.

Freydis hadn't said when she was going, but one drizzly day she and her husband walked down to the shore with their crew and were gone as quickly as they had come. The wrenching of it recalled Einar's leave-taking, except then she'd been able to proclaim her love and she'd had Orm to console her. She bid Freydis goodbye with just a touch of the hand, then ran up the hill to watch the ship shrink to nothing in the rain.

25.

A mouse gnawed under the bed, one of the many they took for granted, even when they'd have to pluck a tiny drowned body from a milk pail or a skyr tub. Gudrid half slept, half dreamt beside Thorstein's bulk. How easy it should be to kill him now. He mocked her, sleeping like this, emphasizing her inadequacy with his dormant flesh.

The gnawing stopped, but then there it was again, like the gnawing eyes of the slaves, plotting revolt. Nika had told her, though she might have guessed it from their churlish behavior and sloppy performance. Svart and Thorstein sensed it too and took what precautions they could, keeping some slaves locked up each day as hostage against the good behavior of the others.

Nika warned Gudrid also that if the slaves seized the farm, they would make no distinction between the wanton master and the unwilling mistress. Nika risked her life to tell Gudrid this.

With Freydis and her crew gone, the balance of numbers was in favor of the thralls, with no more of Gard's guile to tip it back. Svart tried his best to continue Gard's system and perhaps thought he was succeeding. As for Thorstein, to be afraid of what thralls might do was beyond the scope of his imagination.

Gudrid's experiments in the byre yielded nothing. As long as she had only been testing herbs, she did not have to face squarely the fact that she was thinking of killing her husband. Now, as she began to consider other plausible schemes, the enormity of it weighed on her. She thought of seducing Svart, then screaming rape. Estimating Svart's and Thorstein's relative strengths and guessing how they might handle swords, she concluded that this had a less than even chance of achieving the desired result, and anyway, she wasn't willing to shame Sigrid. She considered getting Thorstein drunk, then drowning him in a tub. Unfortunately, there wasn't enough drink in the house to render an ordinary man helpless, let alone her husband. Perhaps if she knew when the thralls would attack, she and Nika could get out of harm's way. No, the other slaves didn't trust Nika, seeing how she loved Gudrid.

Maybe she could still learn to shoot. Hrodny's husband had left more than one bow in his house. No, it would take too long, and too many watched her.

The amulet lay heavy on her breastbone, and the chain gouged her neck. She spoke to it softly. "I'll take your help if you'll give it." She expected it to respond somehow, but it remained inert. Then an unfamiliar feeling touched her—that she might believe in herself as much as in it. She didn't recognize this at first, and it hovered next to quenching, but it moved her to add, "If not, I'll do the best I can."

Svart's face grew more worried with each passing day. He even asked Gudrid to speak to Thorstein, to make him more aware of the danger. Gudrid would have been glad enough to provoke more danger, were she and Nika not caught up in it. She noticed the thralls laughing at Svart behind his back; she knew Svart saw it too. For safety Svart's family moved in with Thorstein and Gudrid. Svart offered to let Nika sleep in the house with Gudrid, but Gudrid knew it might be her death if the thralls should break loose in the night.

Thorstein and Svart went about with halberd and sword. The thralls seemed to know that one man experienced in war and armed with a good weapon could be the equal of several undisciplined, poorly armed men. This enabled even Gudrid to relax a little. After a while, things settled back to something like their old routine. Svart spoke of going back to his own house at night. Thorstein slept comfortably.

They struck in the early morning, on a day when Thorstein was late rising, after Svart unlocked two of the slave houses. Armed with hoes and adzes that they had hidden, they might have killed Svart had they been swift enough, but disorganized as they were, Svart was able to scatter them with his swinging sword and make his escape down the fjord in a boat. Since the farm had only the one boat, the thralls could only shout curses from the bank.

Sigrid heard the whoops and shouts, and came running to see what was happening. The thralls killed her with no more thought than they would have given to a rat. Sigrid's children came running after their mother. Two of the thralls snatched them up. Gudrid came to the doorway just in time to see the thralls, halfway down the hill, grinning broadly while slitting the boys' throats.

Gudrid stifled a shriek. She ran inside and slapped Thorstein's naked back to wake him up. She peered out to see the thralls running up toward the house. Thorstein appeared, clothed in nothing but his sword. Gudrid ran down the sidehill at a broad angle to the thralls' approach. Thorstein swung his blade at the dozen slaves and they stopped momentarily, just out of reach. Then they began to surround him like wolves around a stag, backing him against the wall of the house. Gudrid, glancing back, thought he might occupy them long enough for her to get over the next hill, but with a swipe, a shout, and a lunge Thorstein broke through the circle and ran after her. The thralls came behind, screaming.

Thorstein caught up with her by the shore, near the bear house. He threw back the outside bolt, pushed open the door, and ran inside. Gudrid jumped in too, even as Thorstein was hurling it back against the jamb.

Several bodies hit the door, and it took all of Thorstein's strength to hold it shut.

"Let them come in!" Gudrid shouted. "You can kill them one by one."

Thorstein ignored her. He cast about desperately, seizing on a loose piece of driftwood, which he pushed up against the door. Each time the thralls hit the door, it rebounded a little, enabling Thorstein to jam the log a little tighter against it.

The bumping of bodies stopped; everything was quiet for a while. Then the door bounced to a louder thump, the crash of a driftwood stump. Even the ram proved futile, however, and after a while the thralls gave it up.

Now Gudrid had time to experience at close quarters the smell of the bear, its hair turned dun-color from wallowing in its own feces. It had stunk for so long that even the walls had absorbed the smell, so that now the odor came equally from all directions. The animal looked at them with cold, small eyes that spewed a ghostly venom, like steam from a geyser. Its paws scratched out at them, forcing them to the far end of the room. Gudrid tried the soothing words that, however briefly, had pacified the animal before. Now, not having eaten in many days, it perceived only that before it, just out of reach, stood two warm, living bodies, full of blood and hunger-stopping offal.

Thorstein's eyes gazed at her also, exactly like the bear's eyes.

Gudrid moved closer to the cage, fixing her sight on the bear, ignoring the paws that could have reached her. She stood now by the door of the cage, watching it, hearing Thorstein's breathing behind her. The bear shitted then, this new exudation adding its own higher-pitched aroma to the loud, low tones of stench that surrounded them.

Still she held the bear's gaze. She had always been afraid of it, but now she felt a kinship with its fury and its implacable hunger. She ran her finger between her breasts, feeling the hard lump suspended there. Suddenly she remembered. The wedding night! Thorstein grinding the amulet into her with his own flesh! "I'll trust in you now," she whispered to it. With a deft reach she threw aside the bar of the cage, letting the rude door fall open, with nothing but air now between her and the bear.

At first the animal did not grasp the significance of this change in the patterns that fell upon its eyes, but then it moved slowly, first putting its head out, then its great hump, then its paunch. It gave a little cough.

Mouth full of flies and bits of rotten flesh, its breath surrounded Gudrid. She felt her consciousness slipping away, yet she forced herself to stand stone-still. The bear brushed past her. Thorstein growled in terror. He jumped to free the door, pulling with all his might on the driftwood, but it only budged a little, and before he could give a second heave, the bear was on him.

The jaws clamped on his shoulder, sending red jets spurting through the open spaces between the bear's white teeth and the pink skin of its mouth. Thorstein howled like a thrall under the lash. The claws raked his belly, pulling away strips of skin, then clods of flesh. Thorstein groped for his sword, not knowing that the bear was standing on it. He beat madly at the animal's nose. When his intestines came out, he screamed louder, for just an instant, until a liquid gurgling sound came from his throat. A mixture of blood and vomit gushed from his mouth.

The bear laid the maimed body down, almost tenderly, and after a toss of its matted red head, lolling its tongue and flashing its dog-teeth, it began to dine on the innards. Thorstein's head rolled back and forth and his arms twitched, whether through conscious effort or in dumb response to the bear's proddings, the only witness could not know.

When the bear finished the contents of Thorstein's abdomen and pelvic cavity, it worked its way upward, breaking the ribs to devour the lungs and the heart. Thorstein's eyes, which had glimmered with pain, now glazed over, and Gudrid knew that he was dead. The bear cracked the skull like a nut, the dry crunch followed a moment later by a liquid ooze. It lapped up the brains, spitting out pieces of bone.

The beast's forequarters were drenched in blood. Gudrid had to think it was gorged at last, but now it reared as much as it could in the confined space, scraping its nose on the roof. Ignoring what remained of her husband, it thrust its still-hungry nose toward her. Only an eyeblink away from clawed death, she jumped into the cage, slammed the door, and slid over the bar.

The bear seemed to know she was out of reach. Turning back to the remains on the floor, it consumed the legs at its leisure, picking clean first one thighbone and then the other, working its way finally to the calves and feet. Then it sat on its haunches and scratched itself, staring longingly at what it took to be the second course of its dinner. Gudrid stepped about dazedly, hardly comprehending what had just happened, only hoping for a solid island in the sea of bear dung. Then, finding none, she leaned against the far corner of the cage and stared back at the bear. Her pulse and breathing gradually slowed.

The light had been dim even at midday, coming in through cracks in the doorframe and one small hole near the roof, but now night was falling, and only the ghost of the bear was visible, sitting on its rump, licking its lips.

For the first time since the attack she thought of Nika. Had the thralls killed her? Where were they now?

The bear's grunts became less frequent, and she could hear the animal shuffling about, searching for a bed. After a time, everything was quiet.

Now Gudrid had a great thought. The amulet's secret. She was surprised that it was so simple, but what else could it be? What greater messenger than this bear could be sent to reveal it to her? It was this: For every power, there is a greater power to set against it; one has only to find the way. The bear had taught her that. The knowledge brought her to the peak of alertness, and she understood that now was the time for her to escape.

She unbarred the cage and stepped to the outside door. She reached out her hand. She felt fur. The bear was sleeping against the bar! As gently as she could, she tried to move a paw away from it. More fur. The bear's whole body was draped across the piece of driftwood. Desperation now began to seep in around the numbness. She pulled on the bar, even tried a tentative jump on it. The stench was overwhelming. She must get out!

Finally she tried pushing on the bear's body, until with a gruff cough the bear awoke and Gudrid sensed searching claws inches from her face. She jumped back into the cage. She could only stand ankle-deep in excrement, skirts gathered to her knees, and hope for rescue.

26.

Gudrid lay limply beside the mast, seasick for the first time in her life. Nika held her head over a bailing bucket. Perhaps it was the memory of the two days she'd waited, standing, then leaning against the far wall of the cage, and then, thirsty and exhausted, sliding down into the soup of dung and rancid hay that formed the only bed available to her.

Adding to her ill ease was the rolling of the ship, broadside to the waves. Svart felt obliged to report to Erik, and Gudrid had no desire to remain in Vestribygd, so she supposed she ought to feel grateful to him. Still, among the few who were willing to go along, there were no experienced sailors, so that what might have been an easy dash, one that some essayed in boats, became a miserable passage.

Nor could she turn toward the future to quiet a nervous stomach. She imagined Erik's reaction when he learned what had happened to his son. Up to now, no one had blamed her, but some would soon begin to ask questions. For now, she could only attempt to quash these fears by reminding herself of her new standing as a widow.

A widow! She'd always thought of widows as old, like Aud the Deep-Minded, claiming land in Iceland and parceling it out to her followers just as any man of rank would have done. The idea that she might now gain wealth and freedom and still have youth to go with it had yet to settle itself firmly into her head. Her right to inherit Lysufjord was clouded by the lack of issue from the marriage, but she had the dowry from her father (meager enough, given his straitened circumstances) and Thorstein's morning gift (in this, if in nothing else, he had been generous). Not that young widows were all that unusual, she reflected. It's just that she never expected to be one herself.

Stokaness edged into her mind also. She didn't know whether she'd find her father alive or dead, but in either case, she'd have to face his chief men, who would surely stand in the way of her inheritance. Floki, the unspeakable, from whom only Orm had saved her. Knut, the inscrutable, who'd never been bested in matters of guile. Asgrim, the unpredictable, slow of wit perhaps but quick to act when the mood struck him.

Then there was Freydis. They'd meet again, and again she'd peer into those green eyes that promised so much, demanding perhaps yet more.

The closer they approached Eriksfjord, the more its master commanded her thoughts. She felt no guilt about Thorstein; he deserved his fate. She did feel unsure of her ability to maintain the fiction that the bear had broken loose on its own at the very time she and Thorstein had taken refuge in its dungeon, and in the face of facts: the cage remained intact, and the bar to the door was not broken. It must therefore have been slid back by a human hand. Erik was not stupid. If he did not think to pursue this line, Leif would.

Such thoughts were enough to bring up green bile from any woman's gut.

The short space of a winter had brought many changes to Brattahlid. Thjodhild's church, which had seemed so raw and out of place last autumn, now blended into the landscape, as though it had been there a thousand years. Erik had constructed a new storehouse. But it was in the people that the most change was evident. Age had worked visibly on all: the children growing, the grown ones' faces beginning to wrinkle (what must the others see in her face?), the elders more halting and slow. Thjodhild especially seemed older. When Gudrid had first seen her, she could imagine Erik still lusting for her on a winter's evening. Now her shoulders had taken on a definite stoop, her breasts drooping down onto a protruding belly. Bjorn was confined to his bed now, and no one thought he would live through the winter.

The big news had been brought only weeks before by a trader from Iceland. King Olaf Tryggvason of Norway was dead. Erik was elated. He burned a ram to Thor in thanksgiving.

Of less importance to the world than the death of a king, but of more to Gudrid, was the other piece of information—that a rich Orkney trader named Einar had married a woman in Iceland and had settled down there.

Gudrid met Leif the day after her return. He was pacing worriedly back and forth across Erik's dais, with Thjodhild sitting nearby. No one else was in the house.

He provoked a strange feeling in her. The instant after she saw him, but before she recognized him, she felt the subtle attraction for the lanky body clothed in fine silk, the stony features, the long golden hair.

The next moment, seeing who it was, she was again repelled, without knowing why. The only altercation they'd ever had was that day on the hill when they were children. He'd have forgotten that, and in any case, it was not enough to explain what ran through her now.

"Is that you, Father?" Leif said anxiously; then, looking, "Oh, it's Gudrid." He extended sympathy along with his hand, formally, perfunctorily. She gave the expected response, then passed on down the house. Leif paid her no further notice, but continued to Thjodhild, "How do we know that what the trader says is true? He may be lying."

"What reason would he have to lie?" responded Thjodhild. "He's a Christian himself, and so are all his crew. The story of the battle, the taking of the Long Serpent, and of Tryggvason leaping from the ship into the water at the end in full armor—this is too detailed to be made up."

"Erik may have bribed him to lie."

"He told the story before he saw Erik."

"We must discredit him then. Maybe some of his men are open to bribes."

"They have a very good trade," Thjodhild said firmly and with a touch of exasperation. "And Erik has been entertaining them liberally."

"With my goods!" Leif cut in.

"Why are you panicking?" Thjodhild asked him, almost in a whisper. "Most of the women are Christian now and some of the men too. This is not going to be changed by the death of a king, however great he was."

Erik entered. He was dressed in working clothes, and his shoes were covered with mud. His nostrils flared in anger.

"You're plotting against me again! I should give everything I have to that bastard boy who that woman in Alptafjord says is mine, and I guess he could be! She worships me, the way your mother worshipped me back when you were got"—here he turned to Thjodhild —"or were you screwing with the thralls even then? Thorstein's the only son I was sure of. Thor did me justice for letting you have that rotting byre you call a church." As he said this Erik paced about with a limp, showing the pain in his knees and hips.

He continued. "I've been speaking with Ari Sigurdsson of Isafjord. He told me all about you."

Leif turned abruptly and stared at Thjodhild.

"And what has he told you, husband?" she asked.

"Don't you call me husband, woman, until you'll be my wife! Ari told me how Leif plans to make Greenland all Christian and then demand I be baptized. You're a fool, Leif. Why stir up all this trouble? All this will come to you. You may not have long to wait. I'm getting to be an old man." The limp was more obvious now.

Thjodhild smiled. "Either Ari has lied, which I doubt, or you misread his words. Leif is no plotter. I'd never be part of such a scheme. You yourself have said how foolish it would be. You are the leading man of Greenland. You brought us here. You have nothing to worry about."

"Your words do not soothe me," Erik said. "But the death of Olaf does. The priests will go back to Norway soon."

"Sira Geir will stay."

"So he can go on dipping his tusk into your mead cup!"

Thjodhild stood up. "You're a stubborn man, Erik. All the world is becoming Christian because they recognize the One True God as the only source of power in this world. The gods are dead, Erik. No, they never lived. I've done what I've done for your sake. Give up your old dead gods!"

"No! Even if I'm the last one alive, I'll call Thor's name."

"Then you will surely be damned," Leif said. "That, however, is your affair. As for me, there is only one more thing I have to say. You have been using up my goods entertaining this trader and celebrating King Olaf's defeat when we do not even know whether this is the truth. For my part, I cannot believe it. As for here and now, I intend to remove my goods to Freydis' farm. She will not waste my substance."

"Take your substance! I hope some skald will make a saga on your stinginess. A good one. One who knows the storytelling business."

Leif brushed past Erik and stalked out the door, bumping his head on the lintel. Those within earshot were treated to a rich mixture of Christian and heathen oaths.

Thjodhild walked over to Gudrid and spoke in a whisper.

"Fortune has smiled on you. You know that, I hope. You have a second chance now to get the husband you should have had the first time."

This shocked Gudrid, visibly, she knew, though she tried to hide it. Could the mother be matchmaking so soon after the death of the son? Did she suspect nothing? The need for circumspection was never more obvious.

"I value your counsel. I only wonder that you speak of such things so soon."

"You could use an alliance like this. You're on soft ground, you know."

So Thjodhild was pursuing this, not through ignorance, but in spite of what she surmised.

"I need friends, I know," Gudrid replied softly. "Shall I look to you for guidance?"

Thjodhild smiled and put her hand on Gudrid's shoulder in an unaccustomed way. Gudrid fought the urge to pull back.

"Trust me."

Gudrid could not, for all that she tried, discern a reason why Thjodhild should be so eager, in a way that bordered on unseemliness, to foster once again a marriage that, she must know, her favorite son did not especially desire. Nor could she understand why, all through the conversation, Thjodhild's eyes had avoided hers, fixing instead on the space between her breasts.

191

The latter question, at least, was answered presently. Thjodhild came right out with it.

"When we were pagan we could accept this, a woman calling herself a Christian and wearing that stone. A Christian world cannot. The day is coming when you must decide what you are. Get rid of it! Or give it to me. Let me do what you can't."

Her eyes gleamed in anticipation. Her outreached fingers twitched.

"No!" Gudrid said, though the look on Thjodhild's face frightened her more than did Leif's.

The days that followed were strange ones for Gudrid. Once word of what had happened had circulated and all who wished had come to have a look at her, it seemed that was the end of it. She knew it wasn't, though, from Erik's order to her not to cross over to Stokaness.

Freydis' presence would have been a comfort, and it vexed Gudrid that she stayed away.

The inquest was held in Erik's house. Erik sat on his high seat, his face even more drawn than Gudrid had expected. Leif stood beside him, the picture of the loyal son and heir. The leading men from surrounding fjords had been called in. Now they stood uneasily facing Gudrid on the opposite platform, Svart with her, and the others from Vestribygd.

It was not a trial, since there had as yet been no accusation. It was a formal proceeding, nevertheless, and everyone present behaved as if they were in a court. Gudrid sat motionless, hardly breathing, lest a betrayal of her apprehension convince those assembled that she was a murderer.

Erik asked the questions. He called on Svart first.

"I raised the hue and cry," Svart said, "after I escaped from the thralls." He said the last three words in a hushed, embarrassed tone, knowing what others must think of a man who would run from his slaves. He did not mention Sigrid or the boys. "I came back with these others here, and we chased after them, caught them, killed them." He looked around, searching for at least some approval as a man who would destroy his own property in the interest of preserving the social order.

"We found the girl there"—he pointed to Nika—"in a slave house, huddled under blankets. We thought she had nothing to do with the uprising, so we let her live.

"Then we searched the farm. At the last we came to the bear house"—he needed to explain about this—"and found Gudrid. She called out to us just as we were about to force open the door. We would have had some fun if she hadn't." He forced himself to laugh, his hope evident that others would join in, but the stony faces remained set, he couldn't get it started.

"What did you do?" Erik asked.

"We had to kill the bear. We speared it through holes in the roof. We took Gudrid out. She told us Thorstein was in there. Otherwise we wouldn't have known it, except we knew the bear got hold of something to be so bloody all over."

Several women crossed themselves. Gudrid noticed Thjodhild whispering to Sira Geir. The priest was nodding vigorously.

Someone nudged Gudrid, and she saw that Erik was addressing her, demanding her account of what happened. Gudrid felt cornered, between truth and denial. Her only idea was to play the frightened woman, answer incomprehensibly. It went against her nature, but what else was there?

"I hardly know what happened," she said, shaking her head and letting her knees shake. "I only know there were slaves on the outside, trying to get in, and this . . . animal . . . and then . . . and then I was inside the cage." This did not satisfy. Then she thought of her amulet. She drew it out. "Perhaps this saved me. I don't know."

That stopped the questioning. Heads nodded vigorously, knowingly, the men nearest her stepping away a little in fear of it, without even knowing they were doing so.

Now Erik's expression changed, from the tautness of mistrust and anger to the slack jaw of worry. "It won't do," he said, "for this to be told abroad. When outlanders come here, say Thorstein died of a sickness." He gave lavish gifts to all, taking what remained in Leif's storehouse as well as from his own, and for once Leif did not complain, seeing that this affected his own reputation as well as his father's. Erik paid a young poet ten marks of silver to compose a saga about Thorstein with the approved ending.

Erik asked that whatever was left of Thorstein be brought back to Eriksfjord. Thjodhild agreed and said, moreover, that because he had been baptized, he should be buried in consecrated ground. Svart went out abruptly, returning some time later with a small parcel of sealskin tied with strips of walrus hide. Without a word, he handed it to Sira Geir.

27.

The cowherds at the high end of the field were the first to see the ship. The wind was blowing down the fjord, so the sails were down. The oars pulsed rhythmically against the water. Now the others, hearing the shouts, climbed up the hillside and watched.

Fully a week had passed. Gudrid was free to go to her father now, but something held her back. He was still alive, they said, and might not last long. What, then, was keeping her on Erik's ground, within Thjodhild's reach?

When it became clear that the ship was going to put in at Brattahlid, she ran to Erik's house to put on her best wool wrap, the one with the blue border, which she fastened with the gold brooches Einar had given her in Iceland. She sensed something. Halfway out the door she turned back for her ermine-trimmed shawl. Approaching the beached ship at a dignified gait, she saw that this was no ordinary trading mission. The ship swarmed with people, women and children as well as men, perhaps as many as had come with her father.

The others seemed to know who this was, so she asked. "It's the trader, the one who brought the news about King Olaf. He's got settlers with him, after land. From the looks of things, they didn't find any."

Her attention was drawn to a man leaning over the bow. Even at this distance his face fixed itself in her imagination. His bright blue eyes were shaded by prominent brows, and they seemed full of curiosity, like children peering from favorite hiding places at newly arrived visitors. His high cheekbones pointed toward his eyes also, adding to their power. His nose was broad but not flat, and his firm mouth, though smiling between a bushy mustache and a close-trimmed beard, had just a hint of sadness in it. His blond hair, parted in the middle, was close-trimmed also, falling only to the base of his neck. His tunic was gathered to his slim waist by a belt encrusted with gold, and the hilt and scabbard of his sword, which he now removed and ceremoniously handed to an important-looking man standing next to him, were laced with silver. He had a haughty air about him, as though the need to mingle with these rustic Green-landers were one of the burdens of a trader's life. She wondered whether he would care to sully his tunic on their rude furniture. Beneath that tunic, she knew—and she did not know how she knew this—moved a body quick and strong, on land, as was the dolphin in the water.

In age he would be about twenty-five.

She stood on her toes, the better to see him, and she felt her body moisten like soft grass in the morning dew. Everything that had happened to her since she first met Einar receded before this feeling, and it was as if she were standing again in Orm's doorway. Except she was a woman now, not a budding girl. She was astonished that the feeling could come back to her, and so strongly, after Thorstein —she'd thought herself finished with men forever—but there it was. She resisted it, knew no good could come of it. She struggled to avert her face, to run, somehow to stem the tide within her, which she could no more control than the rising of the sea, but it was no use.

A fleeting thought of Freydis broke the ice-calm certainty of this new feeling. Freydis herself, however, remained as elusive as the memory, down the fjord at her husband's farm.

The man who was the object of her fixation spoke, of parts of the ship, then something about the cargo. It was an imperative, but it was delivered not staccato, as was usual with captains, but with a sonorous resonance, as though his tongue were the shuttle of a loom weaving a tale. She'd never heard the inflections and aspirations of the Norse tongue spoken so harmoniously. The voice penetrated her, not in one place, like a knife, but from all directions, like afternoon sun reflected from day-warmed cliffs.

Several men responded to his order. Seeing it attended to, he jumped to the ground. Erik stood at the head of the group on the shore.

"Jarl Erik," the man said, stretching forth his hand, and then Erik said with a wry smile, "Torfin!"

Then, more quietly, so that those on the ship might not hear, he added, "Thor throws you back on me as burdened as when you left. Some trader you are. You couldn't even unload the women?" Both men chuckled at this.

Gudrid pushed her way through the crowd. She moved to gain Erik's attention, giving out a little cough, and when that had no effect, she bumped into him. At last he noticed her.

"This is Gudrid, my daughter-in-law."

Torfin looked at her. He was still smiling, but if she had any effect on him, he didn't show it. "Your son is a fortunate man," he replied to Erik.

"He was. He's dead now."

Torfin looked back at Gudrid with more evident appreciation. He forced a frown as he turned again to Erik. Gudrid's blood ran to her cheeks.

"I regret that. I have no wish to intrude upon a lady's sorrow or a father's. I wish we'd come at a better time."

"It can't be helped," Erik said. "It's the will of the gods."

Torfin winced. "I hope you take no offense that most of us are . . ."

"Christian," Erik sighed. "I know. I see the crosses on your belt. I even see the marks where the Thor's hammers were taken off."

"Don't you know all Iceland has converted? The Althing decided it last year."

Erik's face went flat. "My days are numbered, and so are those of Odinn and Thor. Even the fog has Fenrir's spit in it. He lunges at his chain."

During this conversation Thjodhild had come up silently behind Erik. Now she spoke. "Your words are well spoken, for once. The gods are broken. From Norway to Mikklagard the power of Christ is showing itself and driving everything before it. These priests whom you scorn carry this power in their hands. It can be used by those who have the will."

A shadow passed over Torfin's face. "The power of God is not a thing to be used. I have seen it work its way among men."

Gudrid looked anxiously up at the ship. Women's faces peered down. Was one of these Torfin's wife?

"Come up to my house," Erik said, taking in with his glance two or three of the men who had joined Torfin. "You come too, Gudrid. Help me get our guests laughing again." Then, to his steward, "Find some thralls to set up their tents. Get them some meat."

"What will you do now?" Erik asked his guests when they had eaten their fill of skyr and seal meat and tasted the single crust of bread and cup of ale, which were all Erik could provide of these scarce commodities.

"I'm a trader. I'll do all right. Snorri here is the colonist," Torfin replied. He looked to the stout older man beside him. "His people have gold to pay for land, but we find that ships and land are the things most valued here, and people are reluctant to sell either."

"That's true, I'm afraid," said Erik.

"I came to deliver these colonists," said Torfin. "I also have goods to trade. But maybe you'll have to come home with me, eh, Snorri?" Torfin managed the right expression, reassuring and friendly, but conscious that his own prospects were brighter than those of his companion.

Torfin looked back to Erik. If the two men's behavior meant anything at all, a solid friendship was forming between them. Perhaps it was the similarity of Torfin's name to that of Thorstein. She could see no other way that Torfin resembled Thorstein, or Erik either. "Jarl Erik," said Torfin, raising his hands in a formal gesture, "I'd like you to go on board my ship and take what you want as a gift."

"You're a generous man, Torfin. For my part, I ask you all to stay with me the winter."

"All of us?" Snorri said in surprise.

The winter! Gudrid thought. Her pulse sped at the thought of the possibilities this would offer.

"It'll give you time to get a fair price for your goods," said Erik. "And maybe I *can* find someone with land to sell."

"You've outdone me," Torfin said in a low voice.

Erik looked at each of them. "I know what you're thinking.

Where will forty people stay? If your men will join mine, we can put up one more house before the cold sets in. We have plenty of sod, stones too. Wood's the only scarce thing."

"And ale," a voice behind Gudrid whispered. It was one of Erik's householders. He was right. Greenland held a lot of thirsty men.

They sat in silence. Gudrid's eyes ran to Torfin, her lips moist and warm, and he was returning her look!

She yearned to impress him with her intelligence as well as her beauty. What could she say? For a while she sat dumbly. Then it came to her. She spoke out boldly.

"I would like to suggest a solution to your problem, Snorri." She faced the older man, but took Torfin in with the sweep of her eye.

They all looked toward her.

"Good land is scarce in Greenland now because no one wants to give up what he has. And yet it would be a disappointment to have to take these people back to Iceland. There's another place, called Vinland. Both Leif and the man from Herjolfsnes say there's plenty of good land there, and timber too. Seems to me this would be a good place for you to make a home, Snorri. And Torfin, you'd have an empty ship to load up with wood to trade back here in Greenland!"

The words were hardly out of her mouth when she understood her blunder. How stupid could she be? She looks at a man, knows she wants him, and the first thing she does is to send him away!

She closed her eyes and held her breath, hoping her remarks would pass without serious consideration. They didn't. Torfin and Snorri seized on the idea at once. She excused herself clumsily, but they were already so absorbed in planning the voyage that neither one saw her go.

Freydis came up at last from Gardar. Gudrid ran to greet her, though she'd not been able to quell all the resentment she'd felt before.

"You've taken your time coming," Gudrid said, knowing how harsh this sounded but not able to hold herself back.

Freydis looked straight at Gudrid. "I thought you might miss me." Her voice grew softer, as though she were talking to someone else and wished Gudrid not to hear. "This time I think I've made a bad mistake."

Then the darkness passed from Freydis' face. She regained her tall composure, smiling and smoothing her red hair.

"I knew you could do it," she said, "whatever I might have said to goad you. I had no idea you would do it so spectacularly." The sheen of Freydis' eyes conveyed sincere, and new, respect.

"It's time we went for a walk," Freydis continued briskly, "like we used to do." Gudrid listened quietly as Freydis' voice led her down to the shore and then behind the hill, the same hill where Freydis had displayed her prowess with the bow. Freydis talked easily of whatever came into her head—seals, ships, Thjodhild, winter, giving birth, Sira Geir, masturbation, thralls' eyes, arrow-making, love.

By the time she reached this last subject, they were behind the hill. Gudrid's whole body was burning with a strange fever. Her breasts itched beneath heavy wool. She willed herself not to scratch. Freydis took Gudrid's arms in her hands and held her.

"I need you. I loved you the first time I saw you."

Gudrid felt the woman's warm lips on her mouth, her arms trembling as she held Gudrid close, stroking her hair with trembling hands. The desire she'd felt in Torfin's presence welled up here too, but softer, a resplendent moon of passion compared with Torfin's rising sun. Still, Freydis was weaving witchery on her, and she knew she would not so easily be released from this woman's spell. Now she yearned to strip bare, to feel Freydis move on her, to take Freydis and be taken by her. Freydis' shaking stopped now. Her hands moved with assurance, as though assuming possession of what was already hers. All Gudrid had to do was let it happen. The copse was only a few steps away, out of the wind . . .

For a moment she could not move, as though she were in a waking dream. She willed the dream to remain, but this only made it more fragile, less real. Her mind ran like a hare before the fox. It fled from the possibility of such a thing, such a love. It was not done! Then she had to admit that it was done, was heard of, if only as the adumbration of one's darkest secret. Arnora had spoken once of a woman in Haukadale whom she'd loved, but until now Gudrid had not guessed that this is what she'd meant.

Torfin's image woke her from the dream.

She imagined the boys and men she'd known. Suddenly she knew that the only ones who'd ever truly loved her were dead, and moreover, even when alive would not, could not, ever have taken her to bed. Orm. Hakon. She remembered Tyrkir, the night in the open in Vatnahverfi.

Hakon's face flashed before her, so fair, so trusting. He was like Balder, the god loved by all, in whose presence no blood had ever been shed, no lie or taunt ever spoken. Balder, the god killed by treachery, whose death foreshadowed the deaths of all the gods.

What reason had she to think that Torfin, who most certainly could take her to bed if he wanted to, would, like Balder, justify the promise of his smile? What reason to think he would be any better than Thorstein? She must rid herself of the lust for him, which threatened to overwhelm the gentler feeling she had for this woman standing before her. Freydis was here, after all, offering herself, and what had Torfin done but cast a cold eye?

She imagined Freydis taking her, in a little nest in the willow thicket. Freydis would have this prepared, with her foresight. She dreamed of Freydis' soft mouth again on hers, she looking straight into the green eyes, unblinking, unafraid. Her mind felt Freydis' warm hands on her, describing the shape of her body, telling her need. She would know Freydis intimately; they would search for each other, each giving herself over to the other's darkness.

She moaned deliciously. This was no fantasy. She was on the soft ground with Freydis, as warm as if they were before a fire, and Freydis was showing her the secrets of her body. They were not naked; it did not warm enough in Greenland for that, even in a most protected place like this. But they were naked to one another. Gudrid released herself to Freydis' slow, knowing hands, and she allowed Freydis to teach her also, how best to return the sweetness that was pouring over her like a spilled cup of mead . . .

The loud crack was followed by the whoosh of a branch and a heavy thump. Freydis jumped up instantly, her garments falling back over her loins. By the time she had pulled her bow from its hiding place and fitted an arrow into the drawstring, a figure had risen from the heap of leaves and twigs. He'd been sitting in the tree, watching them, and it was Mord!

Gudrid willed the arrow to find its mark. Mord was up and running now, but he would not get away. He would not know, until the iron bit his back, that revenge was hunting him down. She warmed to the thought that the spells she'd been weaving against him, the poor remnant of her knowledge, had actually taken hold.

Mord churned his feet madly, climbing a little slope, raising his body above the undergrowth, so that the dull red of his tunic made a sharp contrast to the green surround.

"Now!" Gudrid breathed.

Then a bright fear passed through her, and without knowing why, she lunged at Freydis' hand, so that the arrow thwack-thwacked harmlessly to ground, and Mord was gone.

"Why . . . ?" Freydis' expression was disbelief, turning rapidly to anger.

Gudrid herself had not known why. Now she did. "If Mord had been killed by an arrow, that would have linked you and me to Gard's death, and that to Thorstein's. These were no ordinary killings, Freydis. They were secret murders, unacknowledged, what men consider the most reprehensible of crimes. We'd both be drowned for them or made to suffer some worse death."

Freydis' anger turned to thoughtfulness and then open gratitude. "I've underestimated you, my love, in many ways."

They had to leave quickly then, Freydis to find a new place to hide her bow and arrows, Gudrid to circle round behind Brattahlid, to come from a different way, in case Mord chose to share his knowledge.

28.

That afternoon the fog lifted for the first time in many days, and the sun reflected brightly from the ice and the water. Gudrid noticed a small knot of men moving slowly up the hill beyond Erik's house. At first it seemed nothing remarkable, but then she heard the thrall's voice, plaintive, wailing, and curiosity proved stronger than reserve.

The slave was bound hand and foot, and they were dragging him upslope. His face bore the abandoned look of despair until he saw her. Then the eyes straightened and the mouth pleaded with her for succor. Some of the men looked at her tensely, making it clear she wasn't wanted there. She stepped off a little to one side. No one made further attempt to remove her.

They now approached the destination, a high post that formed the corner of one of the cow pens. The ground at the foot of the post bore a dark stain. Quickly they bound the thrall to it, above and below, then stood aside and waited.

The small image of a man, unmistakably Leif, emerged from the house and grew larger as he approached with a purposeful stride. He saw Gudrid standing on the hillside. At first he waved her away, but then he changed his mind. "Let her stay." The flint in his voice left no doubt concerning his intentions. It startled her because it was so different from his usual style, cunning and smooth.

He laid his tunic to one side and took up the thong. Before a thought could pass through her mind, he began the flogging, a tentative stroke or two, and then with a will.

The thrall made no attempt to be brave, but howled at the first bite of leather into his back. Again and again the thong hit, and again the man screamed into the clear air. A little smile came across Leif's face, almost a serene look, until at last, after many strokes, the whipped man ceased to cry out. Still Leif continued, the veins standing out from his arms and the skin moving up and down across his ribs, until fatigue finally slowed him. Wiping the sweat from his face and body with his tunic, he departed as rapidly as he had come.

The men cut the thrall loose and hauled him a short distance to a shallow grave. Some spark of life still seemed to glow in the man's face, but it did not matter. They threw him into the hole and covered him over with the thin Greenland earth.

She sensed that a man was behind her only in the instant his hand touched her shoulder. She jumped in fright and anger, and then, seeing it was Torfin and that he was laughing, she began to laugh herself, though she resented his taking such liberty with her. Still, she welcomed this attention.

"I've noticed you out here," he said, "the last two evenings, looking down the fjord. It's beautiful, isn't it?"

"I never thought of Greenland as beautiful. I've often wished I never saw the place."

"It's true these people must be hard to live with."

"You like Erik well enough."

"He's a bit rustic for my taste, but a good man nevertheless."

"Perhaps you like Leif better."

"I don't like him at all. He picked up a pretense of culture at Tryggvason's court, but he's really quite provincial. He didn't know, for example, when I spoke to him, that Prince Vladimir has been baptized at Kiev. He'd never heard of Boleslav Chrobry, who's uniting all of Poland, or King Stephen, who's doing the same in Hungary. For all his enthusiasm for the Faith, I doubt he'd know a Nestorian from a Monophysite!"

She didn't know what to say. She didn't know about any of these things either and took small comfort that he wouldn't expect her to. She picked up on an earlier remark of his.

"You think this fjord is beautiful, though I suppose it can't compare with what you've seen elsewhere."

"Oh no!" He held her shoulders in his hands. "I never try to let one place surpass another in my mind, and you shouldn't either. Never begrudge your eyes. There's enough of the ugly to deny them what pleasure they may find. I hope, then, lady, you won't think it unseemly if I feast my eyes on you."

She was warmed by this talk, but put off a little also. Who was this man of the sea who flaunted his urbanity, and what would a trader know about beauty?

Stokaness occupied more of her thoughts than ever before. Watching the evening sun playing with the crags, she told Freydis what she'd seen Leif do and how that made it necessary for her to cross over at once. Leif's action had brought home to her more strongly than ever that he was a man to fear. The thrall's offense could not have been great, for her not to have heard about it. The Stokanessers, being newcomers, had more to fear than most. For the first time Gudrid sensed the responsibility inherent in her lineage.

Freydis didn't see the logic of this and implored Gudrid to come home with her instead. Gudrid took Freydis' hand, but then she rose and stood a little way off, and in a voice that sounded strange even to herself, she made clear that her mind was made up.

She tried to explain this sudden urge to Freydis. Had Freydis herself not extolled the advantages of widowhood? Soon she would be mistress of Stokaness, with as much right to rule as if she were a man. Fate must have designs on her, to have denied Bjorn sons. Floki would stand in her way, for sure, with his sniggering son Mord at his back, and Knut would also. Even old Asgrim, loyal though he might be to Bjorn, would be loath to be governed by a woman.

Her father's father's memory crept up to her awareness. Aud the Deep-Minded was talking to her. She must sit at her father's side, and in his place when he died. She must do honor to Aud's memory and take the staff of rule, as Aud did. She must not shrink back, not for anything or anyone.

None of these motives, however, explained the feeling of urgency. Only the scene with Leif and the thrall did that.

The next day Freydis came upon Gudrid while she was walking among the sheep in the meadow, inspecting the lambs.

"We leave for our farm tomorrow," Freydis said. "I'll miss you."

Gudrid said nothing, but continued to look at the lamb she was holding.

"I see you think you can do without me. I think you're afraid of me." Her voice had a tense little laugh in it. "Can't you see that I would never do you the least harm?"

Gudrid rose to face Freydis. It wasn't Freydis she was afraid of, but if that's what her friend thought, she would have to let it be. "Can you blame me for being afraid? You know more than how to shoot a bow."

"You're hardly a simpleton yourself, you know, though you pretend your knowledge goes only as far as the distaff." The voice was even tenser now. Her hands jerked. She forced a smile. "All the same,

I wish you well. You'll need some good luck when you go to Stoka-ness."

"You think so."

"The land is yours, Gudrid. You're Bjorn's only trueborn off-spring. It's the law. But the Stokanessers are a disputatious lot, and you a woman on top of it." She took a deep breath. Her lips parted.

"One more thing. Thjodhild will be trouble. She's ambitious, and she goads Leif on to challenge his father."

"Why?"

"If Leif becomes chief before his time because of Thjodhild, she'll rule him. If he waits for Erik to die, he'll rule her."

Freydis made as if to take Gudrid's hands, but Gudrid was afraid that if she touched Freydis, she would lose her resolve to go to Stokaness. She clutched the lamb as an excuse to avoid contact. Freydis scowled darkly, but then her face went flat. She turned and walked away slowly and disappeared behind a byre.

29.

On the second Sabbath after her return to Brattahlid, while it was still morning and the Christians had just come home from Thjodhild's church, Gudrid saw her father's boat being rowed across the fjord in the glinting sunlight. She strained her eyes to see who might be coming, but it was not until Floki stepped onto the land that she became aware once again how much this man was cast in Bjorn's image. He was kin to her, but on her mother's side, so the resemblance was even more remarkable. Even in age this man was not far separated from Bjorn.

She'd expected a boatload of thralls to answer her summons, per-haps with a younger cousin or two to drive them. The one who came was the one she least expected, the one she least desired. She knew why she quivered in fear of him. Early memories could not be quenched easily.

"It's time you came over to sit in our midst." So began this Floki, and Gudrid acknowledged the words of greeting with a reply that was meant to sound gracious. Still, it struck her as inappropriate that he should assume such a fatherly attitude toward her, especially since Bjorn wasn't dead yet—or was he? She would have to be careful.

"I must warn you of certain things," Floki went on, "and especially of certain people. Knut and Asgrim have set themselves up on the high seats of the North Farm and the East Farm. They still worship the heathen gods. I've been baptized, and I'm planning to build a church on the slope between the farms so that everyone will have a place to honor the Christ."

"And who has taken the high seat at the West Farm, Floki?" It was said he'd taken to calling it Flokisstead.

"I am the closest of kin to you of any who now live on Stokaness."

"My father has died, then?"

"No. He's alive, barely. You'll do well to place yourself under my protection."

"You think I need protection."

"I can assure you there are some who don't wish you well."

"I'm grateful for your concern," said Gudrid guardedly. "But I can't believe I've anything to fear from the people of Stokaness."

Floki did not reply to this, but reentered the boat and held out his hand to assist her. She hesitated. Why should she go with this man?

In spite of her better judgment, the voice within drove her forward. She stepped aboard.

With a word to the thralls, in a tone that seemed to her like nothing so much as the screech of a carrion bird, Floki ordered the boat pushed off. As they approached the other side, she could see they were not heading for the farm in which her father lived, the original one he'd built before he was stricken, but up the shoreline to the southwest.

"Why aren't we going in to my father's hall?"

"The North Farm?"

"First House. The only home I ever knew on Stokaness. I intend to live there."

"There's no landing," said Floki. "We'll go up to the West Farm.

It's much better there. You'll see. The North Farm was built in a hurry, to beat the winter. It's not the place for you."

Anger rose in Gudrid's throat like foam in a Frisian bottle, and fear was the stopper. Was he abducting her? "Put in by the shore there," she said sharply. "If you're afraid to land, I'll swim the rest of the way."

Floki scowled, but did as she demanded. The boat struck land and she jumped. Then, quickly, the boat was out on the fjord again.

Gudrid looked up toward the long house that, though she had lived there less than a year, seemed like an ancestral home. She'd been glad to hear that it was now occupied by Asgrim Eilifsson; of her father's henchmen he was the only one she would even consider trusting.

Now she saw that her appearance, unheralded and with neither baggage nor retinue, would hardly command respect, even among those willing to recognize her just claim.

The first sounds she heard were the tinkling of cowbells and the calling of a young boy. He appeared from around the nearest byre, leading three cows down the grassy slope. He saw her and stood still for a moment, then ran to the house calling something she couldn't make out. Soon a man and several women appeared, the man walking down the slope ahead of the crowd. When Gudrid saw that it was Asgrim himself, she hurried up to greet him.

If Floki reminded Gudrid of her father, Asgrim reminded her of Erik, though his beard was much lighter in hue and he did not have Erik's paunch. He held out his hands.

Inside the house, Gudrid felt she had made the right choice. She noted dust on the high seat and felt grateful that Asgrim at least had the decency not to occupy it in sight of her dying father. The thought drew her mind to Bjorn's silent presence. Her eyes sought him out. Even in the dimness of the small morning fire, she could see him on the crude board bed that was the best Greenland could offer a landowner. His hand rested on a woolen blanket, the veins about to burst from the skin. His beard had been cut short. What was left of it was flecked with spit blood and bits of dried food; the rest must have been removed the easier to keep him clean. The ridges of his windpipe made his neck look like that of a dead chicken. She hesitated, but feeling Asgrim's eyes on her, she willed herself to move forward. She looked into Bjorn's eyes, the only part of his body that retained the taut alertness that had so awed her ever since she was a girl.

She stood for some time as motionless as he was. The others were close behind her; she heard the stifled coughs, the shifting feet.

Bjorn's hand moved slightly, then his cracked lips parted, struggling for speech. It came in a whisper so low she had to put her ear to his face. It took him a long time to utter each word.

He said something that sounded like "Orm rands," but then he must have seen her questioning face, her upturned palms. With manifest effort he repeated more clearly, "Horn Strands."

"Did you say 'Horn Strands,' Father?"

Knowing she understood stimulated him to say more. "Listen, daughter. Do all you can for Erik, against Leif's treachery. Repay the debt of honor I owe."

Gudrid was not sure she had heard him correctly.

"What do you mean, Father? Why Horn Strands? Of all places in Iceland, it is the bleakest, north-facing shore. Why do you speak of treason? Leif is at odds with his father, but isn't that the way of fathers and sons? Has Leif struck at Erik? Is there something I don't know that happened while I was gone? And what is this debt of honor you speak of? It seems to me Erik owes you. You saved his life, didn't you? What if he did give you land? I don't think all Greenland is worth one good Iceland farm! Does Erik think he can pay for his life so easily? Why do you think he has more than paid for it? Answer me!"

She realized now that she was screaming into her father's ear. He did not respond. Lowering her voice, she pleaded, one more time, "Answer me. Please, Father."

Bjorn's form lay still, the eyes closed. Only the shallow breathing showed that life still retained an uncertain hold. Gudrid allowed herself to be pulled away.

Asgrim's words did not reassure Gudrid about her future life. They were full of complaint about Floki, of disputes about grazing rights, and of the latest point of contention, which was that Floki had denied Asgrim the right to gather eggs in the cliffs and mountains that rose up behind the farms and had threatened force to prevent this.

"And what of Knut? Where does he stand in this?"

"He's the smart one, he. One day he supports Floki; the next he seems to take my part. I think he's not sure whether to share the spoils with whoever has the better of it or to aid the one who seems the weaker, and so put him in his debt. He keeps his own counsel, and is friend to no man."

"Are these eggs a scarce item that you and Floki must fight over them?"

"Oh no. The folk of Eriksfjord have never seen such an abundance of birds and eggs."

"Then why . . . ?"

"You don't know much about men, you have to ask."

She ignored this. "And you, Asgrim. Will you honor me as mistress of this place?"

Asgrim had to look up at her, for he had seated himself on a stool and Gudrid had remained standing. He rectified the imbalance at once.

"Your father never showed his mind about this. To be ruled by a woman . . ."

"Aud ruled a greater estate than this. Asa ruled Norway!"

"What you say may be so, Gudrid. Erik gave Bjorn this land, but Bjorn has never given you his blessing. I believe you are his only lawful child. Others may help themselves by doubting it. Even so, it's not settled who's to rule us when Bjorn goes to the spirits."

"It's perfectly clear what you're suggesting." Gudrid turned to face those who had gathered around. "Bjorn has no heir but me. I have no brothers. I am a widow. The law is not open to interpretation. I am to inherit. I am to rule."

An amused smile floated above Asgrim's beard. "Unless Bjorn recognizes your right, that you are trueborn of him, neither I nor anyone else will recognize it. You have a place to live here, nothing more."

Asgrim was playing with her, she knew, depending on Bjorn's inability to say much of anything. She saw now that he was not the beef-brained man she'd always made him out to be. She wrung her hands, hesitating.

Slowly she moved to Bjorn's bedside. "Father. Listen." She took care not to shout this time. "I am your only child. Things were never easy between us. There's no help for that. We're out of time now. Tell them I am trueborn, that I am your lawful heir."

All was quiet. It seemed that Bjorn was trying to say something but could not.

"Tell them, Father. I, your heir. To rule them exactly as you have done." She lowered her voice almost to a whisper. "Don't let them say I am a bastard!"

Bjorn lay motionless. Gudrid stood still. Then an impulse came on her. She knelt before him and kissed his hand.

She felt the tremor in the hand even as she released it. Slowly, it rose, suspended now a short span above the bedcover. The sinews of Bjorn's shoulder, flaccid and stringy through age and disuse, struggled to life, and the whole limb rose, the hand groping toward her. She thought perhaps he was in a delirium, meaning to strike her, as he nearly had in Iceland the one time she challenged him. Then the spread fingers coalesced, and the hand came to a stop on her head.

The gesture could not be misconstrued. The hand rested, lightly, almost caressingly, with a feeling she had longed for but never received from him before. The face lost its gaunt hollowness and once more took on the brightness she had always so admired in him. Now she no longer needed to fear this face, and in the fading of the fear she saw that the mouth had curved upward into a smile.

Only for a moment. Too quickly the hand fell, the limp fingers cold again, even as they grazed her face in their fall. His face went limp also, so that some whispered, "He's gone," or "His spirit is in the room now." Gudrid knew better. His chest still moved a little, and a bit of hair stuck to his lip swayed back and forth beneath his nose.

She pulled the sheepskin up to cover him and replaced the slack arm that hung over the bedside. Then she rose and strode to the dais. With meaningful ostentation she blew at the dust that covered the high seat, sending up a little cloud, and sat down.

Reluctantly Asgrim led his wife before Gudrid.

"We will serve you as we served your father, Asgrim Eilifsson and Hildigunn Ketilsdattir and all of this household." Hildigunn nodded her assent to this.

"For this I am thankful," said Gudrid, doing her best to sound regal.

"You should know," said Asgrim, "that it will not go this way with Floki and Knut. They never cared much for Bjorn's authority and will care even less for yours."

"I know," said Gudrid. "Nevertheless, if I am to govern at all, it must be over all the land that Erik gave my father. This matter of the eggs is as good a place to begin as any." Gudrid tried to imagine Aud in her high seat, dealing with such a problem arising among the proud men around her. Excitement and trepidation made her aware of everything before her, every line on every face, every axe chip in every roofpost, every flicker of the fire. She tried to appear at ease, as if she had been deciding these issues for years.

"It is essential that this dispute be settled in peace; I suspect much lies underneath it. Let us not forget that we are still strangers in this strange land, with only Erik's goodwill toward my father for support. My father's soul is straining at its bonds, and I think it may not be long before Erik's does the same. We must not let Leif find us quarrelling."

"What is there to settle?" said Asgrim. "Floki has no right to keep us from the fells. You can't allow this. Bjorn wouldn't. We're going tomorrow as well armed as we can be. Let him try to stop us!"

Gudrid gripped the arms of her seat. "Now I am going to test the faith you just pledged to me. You will not go up to the fells, not tomorrow or the next day or the day after that, not until I give the order. And you will see that the rest of this household does likewise."

Asgrim scowled, and Hildigunn too, but he agreed to obey her command. Gudrid asked for a man and a horse to take her to Floki.

Floki rose from the high seat of the West Farm to greet Gudrid as she entered, then quickly sat down again and bade her sit opposite him. He made no deferential move either in word or in deed. She felt at a loss to know how to behave. To sit would only confirm the right he claimed here and would at best leave her with a token title to this third of her land. He had no right to the high seat now that she was here. She could challenge him, but he would certainly remain where he was, a grievous loss of standing for her. She saw nothing else to do but to stay on her feet, at some distance from him, at an angle to his face. She struggled to find appropriate words.

"It's not for you, Floki, to welcome me to my own house. You've kept the high seat warm, and it looks as though you mean to keep it warm awhile longer. But this I say to you that you may listen with both of your ears: My father did not divide the land, nor did he give any of it to you. We all are here by Erik's gift, and for us to split up, one from another, would not be wise. Now I must say to you that all of the lands, the pastures and the fells and the summer pastures, are yours to use in common with the others, but title to these lands is mine. As for the eggs, you are in no way to hinder Asgrim or his householders from gathering them, even though he must pass close by here to reach the paths to the bird cliffs. This I command."

She had made up this speech as she went along, not knowing from one sentence to the next what she would say. Now that she was finished, she watched Floki for sign of a reaction. At first he sat in his seat without a word. Then, from somewhere deep within his belly, the laughter started, silent at first, then loud guffaws that filled the hall. Immediately others—and by now nearly everyone who lived with Floki had come in—joined the merriment. She steeled herself to this, but one voice, laughing a little louder, a little more raucously, than the rest, like a young raven, nearly caused her to lose control. This was Mord. She glanced at him, then looked away. That he should have lived all this time instead of Hakon—she could spit in the face of God for this. It was all she could do to refrain from kicking or scratching at him. To have stooped to such behavior would have cost her dearly in respect, and she knew this was what Mord wanted. Still, it would almost have been worth it. To her, it was plain that further words could not have any desired effect, but would only show the fear and turmoil that she felt, so she turned without taking leave and went outside.

She strove to ignore the eyes that followed her out past the byres and barns and over the hill pastures that separated the farms of Floki and Asgrim.

30.

The household of Asgrim Eilifsson were determined to avenge the treatment that Floki had dealt Gudrid. He had seven able-bodied men, all ready to take up arms. For three days they waited, at Asgrim's behest, for Gudrid to think the matter through, but this was as much time as they could hold themselves in check, and she knew it. She called them together.

"It's time now for us to establish our rights," she said, to impatient murmurs of agreement. "Today we will go to the fells and see whether anyone stands in our way. I don't want any bloodshed yet, if we can help it. Those people are my cousins, the same as you. We ought to be able to live together. We did in Iceland. My father took only those he thought had no grievances against one another. I'm amazed that in so short a time so much anger has sprung up." She sensed she was losing them. "Listen to me now! If Floki and his men bar our way, we will turn east, as though we were going all along to visit Knut. If there must be fighting, it will be on another day. Do you all agree to this?"

"By Odinn, we swear," said Asgrim, and by this he reminded her that for all the loyalty he had shown her, she was the only one here who professed the new faith.

They went out then, in the early morning before sunrise, up the grassy pasture toward the steep hillsides. From a distance they seemed nearly vertical, so that the idea of climbing them must be a mad dream. They appeared utterly devoid of life; the profusion of birds of which Asgrim spoke must only be an imagining. They walked in shadow over the short grass, carrying wool sacks half filled with seaweed, which would cushion the eggs against breakage. The sun was not yet up over the ice-browed cliffs; its rays grazed overhead to light the fjord and the opposite shore and to paint the few clouds a brilliant red.

Soon they began to see texture in the cliffs, shallow declivities where water from melting ice rushed out in the spring, and far overhead the slow turbulence of myriad dots. Above the sound of the breeze, faintly at first, then louder, their one continuous collective cry gradually resolved to individual birdcalls.

The only place at which a good climb could begin was directly behind Floki's farm. As they approached, they kept their weapons covered with cloth to keep them from clanging. They saw no one, only plumes of smoke rising from the thatch roof.

They crept behind the byres, keeping as much architecture between them and the main house as possible. There'd be no animals left in byre this late in the season, but the horses hobbled behind the outbuildings were coughing and whinnying, and the cows were crying to be milked. Floki's homefield boar, said to be the largest in Greenland, was running along the turf fence, grunting loudly.

They must have drunk the last of their ale last night, Gudrid thought, and she could almost smell the odor of the midnight copulation that would have followed such a bout.

They stole up the slope leading to the bird cliffs. It was as steep as any she had ever been on, with few toeholds, but she insisted on going forward in spite of Asgrim's offer to stop. He was wheezing a bit himself and would have liked a face-saving way to rest, but she was not going to give it to him. After a while, though, solid rock gave way to loose scree, and her clothing got too much in the way. She found a narrow ledge and watched as the men spread out over the cliffs and scooped up eggs, and the sun finally splashed her with its glory. Their movements stirred up the clouds of birds, but after the men had passed, the birds would settle stupidly into their former patterns of activity as though nothing important had been taken from them.

It was barely midmorning when the sacks were full, and it was time to start down.

Floki's farm lay directly below, the line between sun and shadow slicing it like a swordcut. Their own house shimmered in the distance. The other farm was out of sight behind a promontory that projected from the main line of cliffs. The fjord sparkled blue. Far on the other side lay the houses and barns of Brattahlid.

Floki's house commanded their attention. A line of armed men was issuing from it like wasps from a nest. They ran to be first to the opening in the cliff.

The two groups met just as Gudrid reached level ground. Asgrim would have made her stand behind him, but she evaded his grasp and now was standing between the rows of men and swords. Her knees shook at the sight of so much sharp metal. Instinctively she felt for her amulet, but this did not quiet the shaking at all. Until this moment she'd believed unreservedly in its power, the only question being whether that power came from gods or devils. Now she was conscious of doubt, that her faith in it was dimming like a lamp nearly out of oil. She felt alone.

"We are going to my cousin Knut," Gudrid said, hoping to appear brave at least, if not confident. Asgrim and his men began a sideways movement toward the east. Floki matched it. Gudrid saw that they could not escape this way, because the outthrust of rock that hid Knut's house would soon force them either to stop or to challenge Floki.

"You did not have my leave," Floki said. "We will bar your way until you acknowledge yourselves to be in the wrong."

A fight was clearly in the offing. Swords were in the air. Only Gudrid's presence seemed to hold them off, but that would not deter them for long.

"For my father's sake, I say to you, let us pass."

"We hold Bjorn in high esteem," said Floki. "It's a bad fate he had no son."

Anger flushed through her cheeks, threatening to overwhelm her judgment. "My father's father came to Iceland in a woman's ship."

Floki laughed. "If you would compare yourself to Aud, see how you get out of this." He carried a heavy two-handed broadsword, one she would have had to strain to lift. He held it in one hand, his forearm bulging as he moved it back and forth like a piece of straw. His face bore an expression of contempt.

She must decide now. She could let the anger flow, that sprang not only from his insolence now but from that other time, when she had been small and even more exposed. She remembered his hands between her child-legs, his tongue in her mouth.

Or she could keep it stoppered up. Asgrim's small army was overmatched both in strength and numbers. Though the childhood memories flooded onto her now, of the many times Floki had abused her, she knew that Floki was not the greatest danger. Leif was. She saw that when she saw Leif's eyes the day he killed the thrall. She prepared herself to accept this new humiliation.

She knelt down before Floki. "I beg you, hold back before you deal death to the Icelanders of Stokaness. I predict that the time will come when you will need the friendship of Asgrim and the others."

Even Asgrim and his men now backed away from her as if she had done something contemptible, and Floki sneered. "Go," he said, "visit your cousin Knut, and see how he receives the Viking's daughter!"

Knut, indeed, was somewhat unsettled by the news of Gudrid's disgrace, his huge hand stroking his beard, and although he had held aloof from her and her claims, he now did not hesitate to give her some advice.

"You are Bjorn's only child, I recognize that, and by law our rightful mistress. But I'm afraid you will have ill luck in hauling the winds of ambition in your small sail. Floki would rule Stokaness. So would I, though I am perhaps less willing to see my cousins die for it. Asgrim is content with his lot—so much the worse for him. You and Asgrim should throw in with me. Together we'll force Floki to submit. I'll rule better than Asgrim, as I think even he will agree, while Floki is a greedy fool. I'll find a good man for you to marry, worthy of your birth, either here or in Iceland, as you prefer, and I'll see you have a good dowry, in addition to the silver you have now from your father and from Erik's son. You can convince Asgrim to come along. If you do, you'll find me generous." He measured his pause with the tapping of his foot. "The alternative will be very bloody for us all."

Gudrid was stunned, not only by Knut's speech, which he had clearly thought through beforehand, but also by her own reaction to it. Before now, she had supposed her right to Stokaness to be a burden, something she might give up if only she could do so honorably. Torfin's face came back to her, as vivid as the time she first saw him. Knut's offer to sponsor her marriage could promote a match with him. Why didn't she jump at it? Was it possible she feared more than she knew? Or was it simply an unwillingness to be so easily taken advantage of?

"I'm grateful for your kind offer," she said, suppressing any hint of irony from her voice, "but Stokaness will be mine by right of inheritance. You'd have me wrong my father even before he is in his grave."

"I see no wrong," said Knut, "in your seeing to the proper governance of the land. You seem to set great store by peace and sneer at the warlike ways of men. Yet I see that you yourself are not entirely free of the sense of honor that leads men to fight."

His words are true, she admitted to herself. But aloud she could say only, "I claim your loyalty, Knut, unworthy though you think I am."

Although Knut did not agree to this, she remained with him for some days. Asgrim returned home immediately. Then she went back to Asgrim.

Gudrid's dedication to Stokaness did not sit well with Freydis. Repeatedly she offered to take Gudrid home with her, but this only increased Gudrid's resistance. Freydis, visibly frustrated and at a loss for the first time in Gudrid's experience, finally desisted. But not beyond recall.

"This is not the end. You love me. You've said as much yourself."

Gudrid nodded. She allowed Freydis to embrace her.

"Yes, I do love you. But I can't come with you. I can't be your . . . woman."

Torfin came also. In contrast to Freydis, he maintained a reserve that maddened her. She tried enticing him with a mouth-parted smile, face upturned, standing in that breasts-forward, hip-turned way she knew men liked. He responded just enough to fill her with desire, but not enough to give her confidence. She couldn't understand this. She'd always had to hold herself stiffly when men looked at her, lest they think she was encouraging them. Was it possible that Torfin was one of those men who did not like women?

Some weeks later, toward midsummer, a thrall came from Knut's household.

"Kol and Unn have asked you to come, Gudrid," the slave announced. "It's said you know something of the healing arts." She recalled her friendship with Unn on Bjorn's ship, and Kol, her betrothed, up the mast.

"Is it the child?"

"Yes. Helga, the little one. She has a high fever."

Gudrid mounted the spare pony the slave had brought, and they crossed the hilly pastureland. It was well toward evening, and she drew her shawl tightly around her against the cold wind that came off the fjord. She hoped that her appearance astride the little horse, her garments drawn up to her knees, would not arouse laughter when she again came in sight of free men, but that was not something that she could worry much about now. She also deliberated whether she should show anger that a slave had been sent to fetch her, although she felt none in her heart. So little did she know of men's ways of honoring and insulting each other, subtly and directly, that she did not know how to respond. But soon enough she came within view of Knut's long house and barns, and she gave herself over to thoughts of the child and what she might do to help her.

Unn came out to meet Gudrid, with a smile on her face but a worried look in her eye, and Gudrid could read the fear in her heart easily enough. Kol held open the door, and Knut stood inside to greet her formally.

"I accept your welcome, Knut," Gudrid said, "but I must have none of your ale. Show me the child."

The tiny girl lay near the far end of the long room. Gudrid carried her nearer the center of the house, by the fire, where she could see better. The body was hot and limp. Could anything living weigh so little? The face was red and moist. Unn's concern was well placed.

"Bring more of those wet linens, and keep the child as cool as you can," she said, and this was quickly done. She opened her small pouch of herbs, some of which she still retained from the days of her childhood.

Night came. By now most of the men had retired from the long house and had taken refuge in barn or byre, leaving Gudrid and Unn and the other women. The child's face had lost its redness and now was pale and dry. Gudrid tried various herbal broths, but the little girl would not drink these. The child began to gasp noisily. Unn, who had remained silent until now, wept uncontrollably, as though her daughter were already dead.

Gudrid searched within her garments until she found her stone. In spite of the doubt that had seeped into her mind, the thought of losing it still incited the same fear it always had. She struggled in desperation, her desire to cure the girl set against her equally contending thoughts and feelings about the amulet. Then, with resolve, she withdrew it, pulled the chain over her head, and placed it around Helga's neck. "Nothing else I have can save you, little one. Take this now. If it brings you back to health, you may keep it." She begged the Virgin to forgive her for clinging in a new way to the pagan charm. But the child was dying, and she would seek help where she could.

Helga stirred a little, and the white dryness of her face seemed to soften. Gudrid convinced herself that a hint of a smile had appeared on the child's face, so that she now felt free to go outside and breathe the fresh cold air blowing across the fjord. She was hungry and thirsty, too, and she gratefully accepted Knut's offer of a half loaf of bread and some ale. She sat on a stone, watching the morning light turn the water of the fjord from black to gray, to blue. She had just finished the food when Kol came out. It required no skill to read his face.

"I see that the child has died," Gudrid said softly. Now Kol knelt before her, seeking some solace, and seeing how she reached out her hands to him, he buried his face in her lap and gave himself over to silent, convulsive grief. Gudrid smoothed his tangled hair, and they remained there for a while, until a footstep caused Kol to rise instantly and compose himself. It was Knut. Kol said only, "How goes it with Unn?" and without waiting for an answer hurried back into the house. Knut would have followed, but Gudrid took his hand and told him to wait.

Unn and Kol emerged toward noon with Knut's wife. Kol was carrying Helga's body, and Unn held the amulet in her hand. Gudrid went down to meet them. She was turning over in her mind how to console them when Unn stepped forward.

"I am returning this charm to its rightful owner. It may be that its power is fixed on you, not to be given away. All the same, you were willing to part with it in order to save my daughter. For this we thank you, and for this we will always remain loyal to you, in whatever you may command." Unn now knelt before Gudrid and took her hand to kiss it.

Knut rose from where he was sitting, but not in time to prevent Kol from emulating his wife's gesture. "You are my rightful mistress," he said, "and I will obey you, though it cost me my life."

Knut's wife, too, knelt before Gudrid and swore her fealty. Knut reached them then, a look of mixed frustration and anger on his face. Until now, everything he had done to further his cause had been cloaked in subtlety and reasoned self-interest. Now the question was put squarely, and to refuse a gesture of allegiance would mean open rebellion. No longer could he count on his own household, and it was an unknown whether Erik across the fjord would raise his hand to support Gudrid's claim. He had no more room to maneuver, and his face showed that he knew it. Though he could not bring himself to kneel, he bowed low. "You will find me as loyal as Asgrim," he said to her. Then he strode away around the corner of a barn, and a while later sharp sounds came back, the rending of wood and the splitting of stones, and after that Knut was seen striding, dark-faced, up toward the fells.

31.

Gudrid had never imagined what it would be like to be looked up to, respected, *obeyed.* Her movements from farm to farm took on the character of royal progresses: women would wave gaily to her, while two or three men would hold her horse and lift her up to the sidesaddle, and then, preceded by a young man, she would go, out over the windy, high-grass hills, gazing slowly left and right as if ascertaining that all was still well in her domain, everything in its place, even to the smallest lichen-covered stone. Then her eye would take in the mountains and the fjord, and her ears would almost hear the whispers, not the previous murmurs of disapproval but hints of praise for her care, for wisdom rare in one so young, and for her beauty, this last seen by most as bounty from the gods (or from God, depending on the speaker), and she was conscious of the sidelong looks men gave her, replacing the frank stares she'd accepted as natural before.

The scene with Kol and Unn had become woven into everyone's mind like a great tapestry, though Gudrid herself could only with effort recall it—Kol carrying the child, holding the head up, the feet dangling in a way that made her seem to be waking from sleep, and Unn holding the amulet cupped in her hand, the chain stretched from one arm to the other. The return of the amulet had been more than a restoration of property. It had in some mysterious way conferred on her the badge of headship, and in an equally mysterious way everyone, even Floki, had been forced to recognize it.

For Gudrid the summer was a long one, but she had no time to enjoy it. Now that the people of Stokaness had accepted her leadership, she worked hard to show that she deserved their trust. She struck them all with her energy in solving the many problems, from the almost daily disputes over issues as inconsequential as whose horse should have the stall nearest the byre door or whether one woman might use the spindle that another had set down. Sometimes she would laugh to herself over their triviality, but mostly they wore her down with their frequency and seeming urgency. Strangely, she was less unsettled by the more serious matters—sickness among the cattle or among the children, a controversy between the Stokanessers and the people of Dyrenes. Though much might hinge on her decision, she took satisfaction when it proved to have been the right one. Some began calling her their Little Aud.

The decision that pained her most was trading her father's ship for livestock. It was especially hard in that Leif had taken his brother's ship, even though Erik would have given it to her, Leif's winning argument being, "What does a woman need with two ships?" That he himself owned three in no way entered the reckoning. In the end she knew she had made the right choice. Not only were they well supplied with hardy Greenland cattle, but the colonists at Stokaness began to look on their land as home, now that their line of retreat to Iceland was cut off.

Most satisfying, however, was the peace she had now with her father. He was almost like a baby, helpless as he was, but still she could imagine the effort and the pain it must have cost him to raise his hand to bless her, and that one gesture had washed away all the anger and hurt she had carried with her through her growing years. She tended him herself whenever she could, smiling to him and seeing the faint trace of a smile on his lips, his feeble squeeze on her hand. Still, the questions remained, *Why could he not have loved me when he was alive?* and *What was it that he could not tell me?*

The next day a boat came over from Brattahlid. Somehow she knew that the figure guiding the steering oar would be Torfin. She waited to greet him.

When they entered the house, Torfin went to Bjorn's bed and stood before it.

"Hail, Chieftain," he said. His tone was deferential and sincere. Gudrid wondered whether Torfin expected him to rise and take a horn of ale with him.

Bjorn did not move, but his face brightened a little, so that Gudrid knew he had heard.

They seated themselves, Gudrid in the high seat, Torfin opposite. Nika brought out the mead, lowering her head to hide her scarred cheeks. Gudrid, curious about the purpose of his visit, sat on the edge of her chair.

Torfin leaned back. "We owe you thanks for your story of Vinland and for your suggestion that we go there. I came here as a trader, but it is now my intention to go to Vinland as well."

Gudrid nodded. "I know," she said softly.

"No," he said. "I don't mean just to trade. To stay."

Gudrid could no longer maintain her smile. Despite that she hardly knew him, and knew his heart not at all, she still hoped to have time to test whether she might win him, that he might share with her the good land that Stokaness had become. She knew it was a forlorn hope, to tie a trader down to such a backwater as this must seem to him. Now even this slim chance had gone, and by her own mouth.

Torfin seemed not to notice Gudrid's disappointment. He continued slowly, in the deliberate, formal way of a man whose words carried import. "Snorri has asked me to lead the expedition. We have a fine ship, strong men, good women. Even the children are eager. We have animals, male and female, and goods for use or trade. I lack only one thing. I have no wife."

Gudrid's eyes quickened.

"Now I must tell you that I've spoken to Erik about you. He said he would consent to a match between you and me, if you're willing." He held up his hand. "I don't expect an answer right now. I've been very sudden in this. There's time for you to consider my proposal. We can't leave until the spring.

"It's not an easy life I offer you. We'll be making our homes in a new land, with none but ourselves to turn to in difficulty or danger. I can see you're an accomplished woman, with courage, and so I have emboldened myself to think you might accept my offer."

Gudrid felt as if her soul had been hurled high from a precipice. A moment before, she had despaired of her heart's desire; now it was presented to her for the taking. But Stokaness, too, was her heart's desire. Often she had wearied of Stokaness, of the demands of the people who now depended on her to maintain amity among them. Yet how could she leave them? They were almost her children. Some were devoted to her, like Kol and Unn, and Asgrim and Hildigunn here. Others met her eye with sullen, closed faces, but they all needed her and they all now recognized her right. And if they recognized her right, she must acknowledge her duty.

A vision of the new land spread itself before her. She was standing there with Torfin, their children playing nearby. She would be queen of that land. Their children would have children one day too. A great line would spring from her body. Her memory would live long after Aud's had been forgotten. Suddenly she understood what men were talking about when they spoke of fame as the thing that lived on after one died. The dream faded, and again Torfin was standing before her.

She recalled Brother Ulf's sermon about the Devil. It had all been so easy—the appearance of Freydis to save her from Gard, which led so quickly to the saving from Erik's second son. And the Stokanessers had accepted her all too easily, she thought now, though on that day when Floki had humiliated her, it had not seemed so. And did Satan bring the sickness to the child Helga so that now she, Gudrid, might be tempted?

If this was Satan's design, she would not yield to it. Hard though it must be for her, her duty lay here, and somehow she must summon the will to turn this man away. Unconsciously she felt among the folds of her clothing for the pendant, and finding it, she quickly relinquished it. She set such great store by it, to the peril of the salvation of her soul, yet when her life came to crisis, it was of no help to her. It was a poor joke, she thought, and could mean only one thing. She did not know the secret after all.

Be that as it may, she must say no to Torfin, of this she was sure.

Torfin now rose to go, and Gudrid rose also. She tried to avoid his eye, but she could not help being caught in his glance. She held out her hands in a gesture of leave-taking, and he took them. Such strong hands, she thought, yet how easily he holds mine. She longed to throw herself into his arms, but she remembered the demands of her station. She must maintain her dignity until she could find within herself the will to refuse him. She turned over the words in her mind, but she could not manage a definite no just now. She pieced together a noncommittal speech. She parted her lips to give voice, but her voice was no longer under her control.

"I am yours, Torfin, whenever you want me."

32.

Now Gudrid must suffer the pain of the winter, living among the people she would betray. True enough, they had not recriminated against her, even after she could no longer hide that she would be going away with Torfin. But this only made her feel worse.

Occasionally Torfin would come across from Brattahlid, over the tricky ice, he and several others dragging a boat to negotiate the stretches of open water. Gudrid brightened at his coming, but soon even he would notice the dark shadow on her mind.

One day, when Torfin had left, Hildigunn took her aside. "It's no secret you were ill treated at Lysufjord, and I can see how strong and fine a man this Torfin is." She fought tears. "I am grateful to you, lady, for the peace you have brought, for I know how it would have gone with my husband and Floki. I know we can all live together now, and be strong together besides, so that those who would use us wrongly may not . . ." She could hold back emotion no longer, but knelt before Gudrid and held her knee. Gudrid was taken by this opening of Hildigunn's heart, but she was puzzled by the older woman's last words.

"Who would harm us, Hildigunn?"

"We must pray for Erik's health. His goodwill is not shared by his son."

"I don't understand," Gudrid said.

"Leif— Oh, I don't know how it has come on him, this spirit. Don't go, Gudrid. Don't go!"

Gudrid felt sympathy at first, but then it came into her mind that Hildigunn was playing unfairly on her feeling of shame. Was she not lawfully betrothed? Didn't she belong with Torfin? And weren't Asgrim, Floki, and Knut reconciled enough now to look after Stokaness while she was gone?

She stood in anger. "How dare you say such things to me! It is right for a woman to give herself to a man and go where he goes! Did you cling to your parents in Iceland when Asgrim sailed here? Am I a slave? Do I need your permission to go?"

She pushed Hildigunn away roughly and stomped outside, without even her shawl against the cold. She went behind the corner of a byre, where no one could see, and wept bitterly.

And so, in a winter as cold as her heart, she returned with Torfin to Erik's farm. Though it eased her mind not to have to bear the looks of the people she was abandoning, it did not ease her sense of honor. Nevertheless, she had chosen her fate, and she would not shrink before it.

Torfin showed that he understood her anguish. A hand on her shoulder, a stroking of her hair, did far more than the most passionate of kisses to ease her burden. Nevertheless, he could not lift it entirely, even on the best of days.

Now that she was at Brattahlid, she waited for the opportunity to find Erik alone. This was difficult in winter, close as everyone was, Snorri's people adding to the crush. The Yule came, with plenty of ale for once, brewed from Torfin's grain, then the deep-cold months. She did not manage it until almost the equinox, on one warming day when Erik decided to walk up the snow-covered hill to do homage to Thor. Halfway up, he turned and called to Gudrid.

"My footsteps are long for a lady to follow! Why are you coming here?"

"I've no desire to go up to Thor! I need to talk with you!" The wind blew her hair sideways, and she wondered whether her voice had been lost in it. Erik let her catch up with him.

"What do you know about Horn Strands? My father . . ."

Erik cracked a smile, though laughter eluded him in this wind, which came in gusts that nearly blew him over. He had to shout to be heard now, even face to face.

"Bjorn would remember! The best friend a man ever had! It's where my father built his house in Iceland when he brought me there! Not a good place, but nothing better was for us then!"

"What did Bjorn have to do with it? Did he know you when you lived there?" The wind picked up.

"Only when I was getting clear of it! He brought Thjodhild up! After the wedding! I'd meant to move to her farm right away! Then I got into a fight! Killed a neighbor's thrall! Bjorn found out his owner was coming to kill me! With more men than I could count on! He helped me get away! Then he brought Thjodhild! Winter came early! He had to stay with us!"

Erik gasped each word. Gudrid strained to hear. Then the wind slackened a little. "It warms an old man to think he'd remember that winter . . ."

Gudrid was frozen to the bone. She turned and ran down the hill. Entering the door, she bumped into Leif. It was as though he were waiting for her.

"I have not had the opportunity to congratulate you," he said. "Torfin is a good man." His smile seemed genuine, though Gudrid did not trust it.

"I have been meaning to speak with you," he said, "about Stoka-

ness. Although now, I suppose, it will make no difference to you."
He stood over her, not in a menacing way, but she was very uncomfortable nonetheless. She wished Erik were here.

"Your father won't live much longer, I expect. Nor will mine."
Gudrid started at this brazenly expressed expectation. Leif held up his hand. "I just wanted to make sure you understood. When they're both gone, I'll be taking Stokaness back."

Gudrid sucked in her breath. "You can't do that! Erik gave it to my father."

"My view is that he lent it. The point, in any case, is moot. With you away in Vinland, there's no one to inherit. The land reverts to me."

"Nonsense," said Gudrid. "Many a landowner has been away for years without losing possession. My high seat will keep."

Leif smiled more broadly.

"What do you propose?" she demanded. "To take it by force? Where will the people go?"

"Iceland. Norway. Vinland, if they can find it. It makes no difference."

"They have no ship."

"They don't have to go. I'll take rents."

"Rents! The land is my father's. It will be mine. We owe Erik allegiance for the land, and you when the time comes. Nothing more."

"When Erik dies, I will say what you owe."

Gudrid looked at him, stunned. She had no answer just now. Only a question.

"Why are you telling me this? I could make trouble now. Why didn't you just let me go with Torfin and then do whatever it is you have in mind?"

Leif's smile became openly malicious. "Perhaps because of something you once said to me, when we were both small."

Gudrid recalled it: "There'll be a day when you'll kiss my feet and admit that you're my slave, and you'll beg me for the smallest drop of mercy."

Leif patted her on the head. He knew she had remembered. Thorstein at his worst had never been like this. She wished she could lay Leif alongside his brother.

Some days later she was able to seek out Brother Ulf, who was on one of his rare visits to Brattahlid. She could have gone to Sira Geir, but he was very close to Leif, and she had never seen him as more than the worldly man he was. Though she believed that the power of God might flow through him, she doubted he had any wisdom to impart. She'd had to spin a web of excuses to stay away from Sira Geir's masses and to leave before the communion rite on those occasions when she'd found no way out of going. She would not suffer humiliation at his hands. Torfin had begun to question her about this, but so far she'd been able to put him off by telling him that Sira Geir had wished the Devil on her.

Ulf was different. With him she had to exert an effort of imagination to suppose he could effect the magic that brought the Christ to this far shore, but when she listened to his words, she knew he held a far greater power to work magic on a soul. She forced herself to speak.

"It's not only that I want to marry Torfin, and live with him and give myself to him. I want to go to Vinland too. A greatness lies asleep in that land. It's what I saw in my mother's sister's eyes when I was a child, when she foresaw Leif's voyage. I will be its queen, the mother of its children."

The lines on Ulf's face deepened as she said these things, though she doubted that Ulf himself was aware of it. His sad look almost made her wish to take them back. Now that they were out, she would let them be as they were, and she felt her face harden as the silence between them grew.

Ulf finally spoke. "You dream great dreams, Gudrid. I would have said that this is the Devil's mischief, but that is not for me to know. One thing I can tell you: dreams carry within them the seeds of their own disappointment."

"Did you learn this at the monastery?" She made no attempt to hide her indignation. "Did they teach you this?"

"No. It's not something I'd thought much on until now."

"Nor had I," said Gudrid, "thought much on dreams. But I see something now, and I will have it if I can."

She backed away from him then. As soon as she was out of his sight, she ran along the shore and over the little hill that separated the church from Erik's house, and though she knew he had spoken out of concern for her soul, she was relieved when she finally passed over the rise. Below, she saw Torfin inspecting the shed containing his ship. She ran to him and threw herself into his embrace. She felt the questioning in his mind as she trembled like a frightened bird. But Torfin had something else on his mind.

"You'll have to get rid of the amulet," he said.

She stepped back from him. She hadn't considered what his whole-hearted embracing of Christianity might mean. What right did he have to demand this? At the very least, he should have made this condition clear the day he asked her to marry him.

"No," she said quietly. "I can never do that."

"Get rid of it, Gudrid," he said. His voice was friendly, but it was also firm. "It's a spell the Devil has over you."

An anger was burbling up now, as though he had poured red-hot lava into the caldron of her heart. How little she knew him. "You talk like Brother Ulf. Devil, Devil, Devil." She was sure of nothing now. "How do you know there is a Devil? Have you ever seen him?"

"Have you ever seen Mikklagard? Gudrid, no one doubts the existence of the Devil. Not even the Arabs. Our Faith is not something some philosophers dreamed up. I've heard enough of those. Every drunken merchant thinks he is one. No, Gudrid, it's the Truth, it's the way things are."

"If you're afraid of it," Gudrid said, "I'll keep it in a little bag, to make sure it never touches you."

"I'm more afraid for you, Gudrid. Your soul is in danger."

She let out a nervous, incredulous laugh. "You really believe it's evil, don't you?"

"It would be foolish not to be wary."

"I can't do it, Torfin. It was my mother's."

"Then I can't marry you. I'll have to find another wife."

"Just like that? One woman as good as another?"

"No, not as good. No one else could be half what you are. I know that. You women think you're the only ones who see without their eyes. Whatever you do, I'll never forget you. But unless you throw that thing away, I can't live with you."

"I'll think about it." Her voice betrayed the irony of denial.

"Do that." His tone matched hers. Then he softened. "Oh, Gudrid. I'd do anything to have you. Except . . . except have the Devil for an uncle. I'll help you with it if you can't do it yourself. Tomorrow we'll talk again. Granted, my lady?" He kissed her and left.

She resented having to plan a subterfuge, but there was no help for it. She would not give up the stone, nor would she walk away from Torfin. She'd hide the amulet where he wouldn't see it. When she went out and needed its protection, she'd use a special inner pocket that she'd sew in each of her linens, low at the side, in the hem. It would be all right.

Torfin, Snorri, and Gudrid sat in Erik's house, talking of the voyage to Vinland. Snorri stated their main problem. "We don't know how to get there. Leif won't tell us, and the man we sent to talk to Bjarni Herjolfsson came back with gibberish." Gudrid recalled her conversation with Bjarni in Durkel's house just before the Little Sybil had come in.

"We don't even know the height of the polestar there," Torfin added. "Leif wouldn't tell me."

Snorri turned to Gudrid. "Didn't Tyrkir tell you that on the longest day of the year, they had as much darkness as in his native Rhineland?"

"That's exactly how I heard it," she confirmed.

"This is important information," said Snorri. "It tells us how far south we have to go, almost as well as the polestar itself."

They were so engrossed in their conversation that they did not notice that Erik had come in. His cough alerted them. He waved them back into their seats, then sank onto a stool himself.

"Take my advice," he said. "Go north first, past Vestribygd, to a mountain we call Hrafnsgnipa. Then head out to sea for a day, until you come to the other side. Another mountain there. Then go south along the coast, to Bear Island. That's as far as I've ever gone. After that, you're on your own. It's a roundabout way to go to Vinland, but the safest. Unless I miss my guess, it won't be far to the last of the lands that Bjarni saw when he was blown into the Western Sea. If you follow the coast, you must come to Vinland sooner or later."

Erik was a man of few words, and when he said this much, he was worth listening to.

The door opened and Freydis walked in. She surveyed the room, and though she tried to hide it, Gudrid saw the look of pain on her face when her gaze fell upon her and Torfin, Torfin's hand on her hip.

Freydis did not wait for an invitation to speak.

"Some of us Greenlanders have heard about this Vinland colony. I have a ship. Thirty people are going with me and my husband. We can go by ourselves if we have to, but it seems to me it'd make more sense for us to go together."

Gudrid dropped her cup, still nearly full. Nika swept it away and brought a cloth for Gudrid to dry herself. The ale trickled over the edge of Erik's dais and onto the earthen floor by the fire. Torfin stood up quickly and faced Freydis. Gudrid attempted to get his attention by tugging on his sleeve, trying not to be too obvious. She had to let him know that Freydis should not come with them. She was afraid of her feelings for Freydis, now that she had committed herself to Torfin. She also had not forgotten Tyrkir's words on the heath in Vatnahverfi. She pulled harder, but he continued to converse with Erik's red-haired daughter. Finally she thrust herself between them. "No," she said to Torfin in a hoarse whisper.

Torfin heard, but he went ahead anyway. He looked at Freydis over Gudrid's shoulder. "It will be good luck to have Erik's kin along." He turned to Snorri. "How about it?" Snorri nodded. Gudrid sank back down onto her seat, shooting Torfin a look of frustration.

Freydis continued. "There are two traders, Finnbogi and Helgi. They're at my farm, just come from Iceland. They want to go to Vinland too, and they've got room for some Greenlanders. They seem all right to me."

Erik scowled, and even Torfin was taken aback by this new addition to the expedition, led by people he did not know. Snorri said he knew them, that they came from good family, and he was much in favor of enlarging the group. After some talk, Torfin gave in.

She came upon Thjodhild unexpectedly. The disemboweled raven lay before Erik's wife, and though Thjodhild's first impulse had been to throw her mantle over it, she held back, for Gudrid had already seen. The unanswered question passed between them. Gudrid turned in haste and ran down the hill. Only after she reached the house did she recognize the girl who had been with Thjodhild. It was Freydis' maid, Inga.

She waited for him in the sauna. Nika had prepared a fire to warm it, but had withheld the water from the hot stones. The contrast to the cold church where Gudrid and Torfin had been joined in marriage made her feel even warmer now.

This was what she'd wanted, she had to remind herself of that. She recalled as much as she could of the day she'd first seen Torfin, and she held in her mind the hope that his reality would equal the image in her mind. Still, the heaviness in her womb remained, as though she were about to give birth to a stone.

He entered, and seeing her standing by the fire clad only in her undergown, he quickly closed the door. She turned toward him and smiled. She took his outer cloak—how cold it was—and put it down on a bench.

Instinctively she felt between her breasts. Remembering, she glanced sideways, assuring herself that the amulet was hidden safely in a crack in the wall. Again she felt the annoyance at what she'd had to stoop to, to keep her inheritance. She did her best to put it down.

He touched her. She jumped back, jolted by his cold hands.

"You'll have to warm those in the fire if you want anything to do with me," she said, laughing, and he, laughing too, complied. She let the thin smock float to the ground. She exulted that her form so held his eye. Slowly, as though not wishing to wake from a dream, he slid off his tunic and trousers, and the two of them stood facing each other, naked.

He explored her body with an appreciation born of rich experience. She stood straight and tall, thrusting her breasts forward to his hands. He kissed her softly, and then more fervently, on her lips and on her cheeks and on the small part of her neck, pulling her down with him onto the soft bedding.

A VIKING'S DAUGHTER

He stroked the curve of her spine. She moved to share with him the heat of her belly. He kissed her feet, the tender flesh behind her knees, her thighs, her soft, secret flesh, and intoxicated by the warmth he spawned in her, she spread her hands over the taut curve of his buttocks, molding her lips to the form of his hardness. So they lingered on each other. Then she drew up again to kiss his mouth.

She lay on her back, stretching herself to his soft stroking. He raised himself up to enter her. She had feared this moment, dreading that it would bring back memories of those other times when she had been used, but this was different. She exulted that she could still love a man. Defiantly she opened her thighs to take him in.

The oscillations of his body were deliberate at first. The shaft that joined them seemed not only his but something they shared between them. A feeling she had never felt before welled up within her: she wrapped her thighs around him, clasping, twisting, squeezing, and the sound she heard, which she'd thought was the moaning of the wind, was her own bridled spirit breaking free. They moved as one together, she looking at him in the firelight, enjoying the flexing of sinew under the taut flesh and soft golden hairs. She rolled back her head and let the heat spread outward until her whole body was glowing with it. She smiled at his urgency, plunging in the surf of his desire. She yearned to open herself even more, to let him dive deep within her, moving with him, feeling her own body and his, where they joined, crying out, Almost!—the burning almost bursting her open. And then his seed did burst, leaving her, almost.

They lay together for a while, he stroking her hair, she running her fingers over his face. He rose to throw some driftwood on the fire. Her eyes followed him and came to rest on the crevice where the amulet lay.

He returned to their bed and pulled the cover over them. She lay back and felt his fingers stroking her belly, her arms, and, lightly, her breasts. She still burned, and she tried moving on him, but he kissed her more and more sleepily. Soon she was alone with her burning. A long time later she cast herself loose from consciousness, drifting like a cut branch of heather, tossed on a turbulent fjord.

33.

The three ships coursed down the fjord, the wind from the mountains filling the sails, and a chill wind it was, even for Greenland at the beginning of Lambs Fold Time.

Freydis' ship ran ahead. Nine-and-twenty Greenland adventurers were with them, all younger sons who remembered the wealth that Leif had brought. Other than Freydis and Inga, not a woman was among them. Gudrid had thought this unwise, but she could not get Torfin to intervene.

The traders from Iceland came behind in their large, new ship, half again as long as Freydis' vessel. It carried a mixed lot. The crew numbered the usual twelve to fifteen men, but as they were not on a charter, with colonists and cattle to contend with, they allowed themselves the luxury of five women. Gudrid had seen these sailors' women peering over the sides. They seemed at once very young and very old. She had wondered that any woman would choose such a life, when she found out they were not slaves.

"They're orphans," the bearlike Finnbogi had said tersely, while playfully pummelling his little half brother Helgi, whom he could have tossed about like a ball. "From the north of England. It was either this or a nunnery."

One young man had attached himself to these traders—Gudrid did not know how—but she wished mightily that they hadn't taken him on. Mord Flokisson. God has sent him along to remind me of what I would rather forget, she thought. Mord would punish her for her sin of abandonment, she was sure.

They set the course that Erik had suggested—north, then west, then south. Roundabout, but as safe as an ocean voyage could be, since it gave them a known jumping-off point as close to Vinland as possible and since it put off the time when they must sail out of sight of land.

Gudrid went to Torfin at the steering oar. Preparing for the voyage, he'd been full of anxious concern, but that was gone now, replaced by the smiling posture of a man who's glad to get back to sea.

"Vinland." He said the word slowly, savoring it like the wine that grew there. He was as excited as she was. But to him it was just one more new place to add to the many he'd already experienced. He said he was going to stay, but was that possible? The look on his face told her more than words could. He was a wanderer, a lover of beyond the horizon. Could he ever love just one place or just one woman?

They reached the bend in the fjord. Torfin pulled the steering oar. Men on the port side hauled on the heavy rope that held the lower corner of the sail in place, while others to starboard let out slack. The yard slowly swung around, and the red-and-white-striped sail settled into its new position. The bull bellowed. The wind eddied, bringing aft the smell of fresh manure. The ship lunged forward, spray splashing over the stempost onto the animals.

Thirteen women were on the ship. The thirty men were about evenly divided between colonists and crew, between those who had come to Greenland for land and those who sought wealth through trade. So many men without women—it concerned Gudrid, as it did Torfin. There were three children, all boys not yet past their third year.

Gudrid felt constrained to this close accounting because of her position as wife of the expedition's leader. It would not do to ignore anyone or not to know their relative rank and importance. She genuinely tried to gauge personalities, to determine likes and dislikes. Such knowledge might one day help her to head off a feud.

When her mind stopped she'd think of a cousin in Stokaness, and then she would feel the pain of regret.

She did, however, have reason to smile. There is a forty-seventh passenger on this ship, she reminded herself, and she felt the moving life within her. Her mind raced into the future: A new land, a good land, land that reaches back no one knows how far from the shore. A land for my children.

For three days the ships made their way along the Greenland coast and beyond the mouths of the Vestribygd fjords. She was not sorry to see them go by. Then, early on the fourth day, the great peak of Hrafnsgnipa showed itself off the starboard bow.

There was a quick conference aboard Torfin's ship. Freydis sought Gudrid's glance, but Gudrid would not risk being drawn once again into those turbulent pools.

They sailed away from the land, close hauled, separating themselves so that none would steal another's wind. In less time than it took the sun to make its lazy swing around the horizon, the mountains of the Western Barrens appeared over the waves.

Course was changed again. Now they were southwesterly, into the face of the wind, and endlessly the ships tacked, sliding back and forth in relation to each other, in a graceful dance. After a day and a half the ships anchored once again in the lee of a large island whose mountain rose steeply from the shore.

"Bear Island," a crewman said in response to a question, gesturing toward the white bears on the hillside and the shore.

Again the leaders congregated on Torfin's ship. This time Freydis caught Gudrid's eye, but neither spoke.

"The sun is low against the wilderness shore," Torfin said. "You may sleep for the few hours he hides. Then we're away."

They were not to see the sun again, not that day, not for many days. The wind shifted to the northeast, and low clouds sculled overhead, obscuring the top of Bear Island.

The ships headed into open water. The waves were mounting higher by the hour. After a time, the ships became separated.

Early on the third day Gudrid awakened to a muffled cry. "Oars!" A curse. Shouts. Pounding feet.

Directly in front of them was a cliff so close that it seemed they must smash into it in a moment and so high that its upper reaches were lost in the clouds.

The oars came clattering down from their storage rack head-high at the mast. As the rowers raced for their positions, others lowered the sail, while everyone did his best to avoid the yard as it crashed to the deck. Torfin ran to the steering oar. He and the helmsman pushed hard. The ship began a tight turn on the strength of its own momentum.

For many hours the men rowed, and the ship began slowly to leave the cliff astern. At last Torfin judged that they were sufficiently far from the rocks to claw their way offshore. With one last effort, the crew raised the sail, tightened the stays, and set the sheets.

The storm died, and the ragged heavens opened to let shafts of sunlight reach down to the still-active water and the cliffs beyond. Their full height could be seen now. Forty ships laid end to end would not have reached from the water to the brink.

Everyone scanned the horizon for the other ships. Just before sunset they caught a glimpse of one far to the north, when both ships happened to catch the top of a swell at the same time.

They waited through the night, keeping their offing by moonlight. When dawn came, the sea was much calmer, and as the sun cleared the water they saw one, then two, sails! Cries of jubilation went up, becoming shouts of greeting as the ships closed on each other.

As they coasted southward the cliffs increased in height, rising unfathomable distances straight out of the water. Around noon of the next day they passed the greatest cliff of all, which formed a point as the land bore off to the southwest.

Then they were in a bay full of islands, and the sight of waves breaking over reefs and hurried soundings of shoal water forced the flotilla out to sea, where they maintained their southerly course. When next they closed with the shore, it was low and heavily wooded.

Then came an incredibly long sand beach. No one had ever seen anything like it. For hour after hour of sailing it went on, so that "Wonderful Strand" seemed the only appropriate name. Punctuating this shore was a promontory with a broad-backed hump of a hill that looked like an upturned ship. They called it Kjalarness—"Keel Point."

Just at the end of the Wonderful Strand was a large and attractive bay that opened up well into the land. They came ashore there and made camp. They settled in so comfortably that they didn't want to leave. But Torfin looked at it with a trader's eye, not a settler's. The trees were softwoods, no good for shipbuilding, and there were no grapes.

Freydis spoke to Gudrid, her lips an easy smile, and Gudrid could not help but return the look, her swelling abdomen a rampart of safety.

"We'll sail on," Torfin said, ignoring the increasing chorus of grumblers.

They came to the end of the land, where it began to curve to the west and they could see nothing south except an island on the horizon. As they sailed toward it, the ships were caught in currents for which they were totally unprepared, not only because the currents were so strong but because they changed so much from place to place and even from hour to hour.

And so, at last, they had come to Straumfjord, a name that would hang in Gudrid's mind like a petrel over the streaming water that gave the fjord its name. The chiefs climbed to the top of the island in the fjord's mouth. Another dispute brewed atop the plateau, among the cries of the nesting birds.

"This is the end of the earth," said Freydis. "This island, and another to the south, as barren as this. Then nothing, all the way to Africa. We must go back to Wonderful Strand to look for Vinland."

It took all of Torfin's persuasive power to keep the expedition together. Snorri was with him, and Finnbogi went along out of loyalty to the chosen leader. Freydis and her crew had little choice but to go along.

They sailed to the south shore. The coast extended on, and the fjord narrowed somewhat. They put in at a little bay to the south of some islands. They had only intended to stay there a little while to refresh the livestock and the weary travelers. As it happened, they stayed all winter.

34.

The first thing Gudrid did on getting ashore was to find a place to hide her amulet. All through the voyage, she'd worried that Torfin would take it into his head to search for it. Often she'd had to suppress indignation that she had to conceal what was rightfully hers. Now that they were landed, the feeling quieted a little. She credited their safe arrival to its magic, and she was glad that she'd kept it.

She ran up to the little scrub woods that grew under the lee of a low rise. Once in the trees, she looked around for a place where it would be safe and where she would be able to find it again. She found a small cavity in one of the trees, just above eye level, into which she could barely reach her hand, and after feeling around inside she deposited her treasure.

That night she could not sleep. At first light she crept from Torfin's tent and stole up to the wood. Into the hole her hand went, a moment of panic, and then her fingers closed on it. She drew it out, chain and all, and her pulse slowed.

It quickened again when she heard the snapping of the branch, glimpsed the fleeing shadow.

Now she must find a new place for the amulet. She couldn't take it back with her, for fear whoever saw her would alert Torfin. She ran deeper into the woods, stopping in many places to throw off whoever might be behind her. When she finally ran home she hoped she'd be able to find it again.

Torfin felt her cold feet. "I had to take a walk," she said. Torfin gave her a strange look, but smiled when she pointed to her growing middle.

She was determined to find out who had seen her. She instructed Nika to slip into the woods from the far side and wait for her in a clearing they both knew. Then she went up from the near side and changed clothes with Nika. She bound Nika's hair with her scarf, in the manner of married women. Then she hid in a bush.

A figure soon skulked up a little ravine, hiding himself as much as possible from the heavily wrapped woman moving slowly ahead. He passed within a step of Gudrid. It was Mord!

Gudrid stepped out, startling him. A growl came from her throat, her white teeth flashing. Now she let herself go as she had held herself back on Stokaness the day Mord's father had demeaned her. She clamped her jaws onto the flesh of his arm, right through the sleeve of his tunic. His blood warmed her cheeks. Mord howled and began to strike at her with his free hand. Nika heard the commotion and came running back. Mord grabbed her as he jerked free of Gudrid. He put his knife to Nika's throat. Looking at Gudrid, he said, "I want the amulet."

"You wouldn't dare . . ." she said.

"Wouldn't I? She's only a thrall. Anyway, it'd be your word against mine. At worst I'd have to pay twenty or thirty marks of silver for her. And then I'd tell Torfin how you've hid the amulet all this time. You'd likely deny it, for all the good that'd do you. Torfin would order his men to scour the woods, to see who's telling the truth. It'd take them a while maybe, but they'd find it. No one would care much about a slave girl, then."

"That's ridiculous!" Gudrid said. Nika shook in Mord's grasp.

"Shall we try it and see?" Mord said, grinning.

Gudrid had no choice. Nika had been harmed enough already through her miscalculation. She found the stone, dropped it to the ground as he ordered, and watched him pick up its chain with a stick.

The anger rose again, and this time it had animal claws, not to be put down. Torfin had made her hide it, and it was his fault she was losing it.

Later in the day, Torfin asked her if anything was wrong. She could not prevent her body from stiffening at his touch.

Her time came without warning. She lay on a crude bed of hewed branches covered with sheepskins, inside a sod house that had been hastily constructed when winter was closing in and it was at last clear to everyone that there would be no leaving this raw, exposed place before spring.

All that autumn she had felt the new life growing within her, had watched her belly swell to its present ungainly proportion, while the men went about in boats, looking for some evidence of Leif's habitations. When they did not find them, the bickering began, with petty recriminations over who was to blame that they had not found Vinland.

Another pain came, this time stronger and farther down. She bit on a piece of cloth someone had given her. Through eyes wet with tears she saw the women hovering about her, whispering encouragement. She relived her mother's fate, felt the midwife's dirk. Her amulet was gone. She cursed Mord, wished eternal damnation on him. She saw Torfin standing over her and she reached for him, only to find him a phantom. She cursed his fading image in a loud voice, for his lack of

understanding that had forced her to hide it. Nika kept bringing wet
cloths from the brook.

She had known they were short of food, and had tried to make the
men aware of the need to hunt rather than explore. But they were all
so intent on finding Leif's Vinland that they had no time for a
woman's words. Even Torfin had told her to be quiet. So the season
went on. The fish had been so plentiful, and the seabirds so easy to
catch. Now the ice was jammed up to the shore, the ships were hauled
out, and not even a boat could go into the bay for fish or to the
islands for birds. Then, when the ice was thick enough to walk on,
the fishing had become poor, and the birds, at least the ones they
could snare, were gone.

It was an effort of will to keep from saying, "I told you so."

The baby was moving now, and the pains came back, too great
now for silence. She screamed. She howled curses and prayers to gods
and God alike. The women did what they could to comfort her.

Even midwives get tired. One by one the women slipped out,
leaving only Nika. Gudrid settled into a dreamlike state, fantastic
shapes swirling before her eyes, the baby pulling, somewhere, far
away. Nika held her hand, nodding, slipping finally to sleep beside
her mistress.

She couldn't see the face. Only the voice imposed itself on her
impaired consciousness. It was laughing, a female laugh. Her vision
cleared only enough to see the hand dangling the amulet over her.
Then the laugh again, a female laugh just like Mord's nettling laugh.

"You're going to die. If you had this, you'd live, but you don't
have it. So you're going to die. I am going to live, and you are going
to die." The laugh again.

Was this how she would learn the secret of the stone, too late?
That one must not cling? She'd done that, clung to it, and therefore
she'd lost it. She'd clung to life, and now she would have to give that
up also.

She was too weak now to cry out. When finally her feeble movements woke Nika, the visitor was gone.

The tightening fear held the baby back. Shrieking pain, in spasms,
washed over her. She was thirsty, but could not drink. The laughter
still floated above her.

"Cut the baby out!" she shrieked. "Let her live!"

Then came a sound both wonderful and strange—the cry of her own baby—and an overwhelming joy that was too great to be just relief from fear and pain. She would remember seeing her son for the first time, so little, so fragile, and yet so full of life. She would remember taking him to her breast, and she would remember the love that burst within her, a new kind of love that made it seem that nothing else mattered.

They moved her to a clean bed, and now she could settle in, let her baby suck, watch him sleep, sleep herself.

The euphoria was short-lived, as reality closed in again, the cold and wind that none of them had expected to face in a land this far south, the shortage of food, the bad feelings that seemed to be sprouting up everywhere.

The baby's naming day provided some relief. Torfin had withheld even from Gudrid the name he had chosen. Since no priest was available, he would pour the water himself, provisionally. He took the boy on his knee, sprinkled water on the little one's face, and said, "In the name of the Father, and of the Son, and of the Holy Ghost, I baptize you Snorri." Snorri the elder allowed himself an avuncular smile.

The backbiting continued. Freydis was the worst of the gossips. The men seemed to take from a woman what from a man would bring out swords, but was it necessary to fan the flames of unrest? She harped on the fact that Finnbogi happened to be a bastard; that she herself was illegitimate deterred her not at all. Most serious was what she said to Torfin. "It seems to me that Snorri is leading this expedition," she said before others, her smile underlining the ambiguity, whether she had meant the baby or the man.

"Don't listen to her, Torfin," Gudrid said to her husband. "Snorri's counsel is the best you have."

"Except for your own," he said sarcastically. "Perhaps I have named the baby all too well."

Gudrid wished then that she had remained silent. After that she avoided Snorri, even though the thought of being unfaithful with him had never occurred to her. This made her sad, for she genuinely liked his company.

One day Snorri came to Gudrid. "Ever since the baby was born you've avoided me. I'd like to know why."

She told him of Freydis' taunt and of Torfin's suspicious remark. "It's better if we avoid each other, then, at least for a while," he said. After that they would pass quickly by, giving each other only a nod. She was happy at least that he understood.

Winter wore on, and the shortage of food grew more acute as the last of the ships' provisions was used up. There was some grass for the livestock, which gave them a little milk, but what was that little among so many?

The company were divided between those who followed Christ and those who still acknowledged the lordship of the gods. The Christians had been gathering each day, under Torfin's leadership, to pray for help in their need. Each day one of the Greenlanders would compose a new poem, often ribald, taunting them. Finally Gudrid asked him, "What's Thor done for you lately?"

The Greenlander said nothing, but that evening they noticed that he was nowhere about. When he did not return the next day, Torfin organized search parties in each direction from the camp. After three days Torfin and two others found him on top of a cliff. He was lying on the ground, groaning and muttering, his eyes bulging out, his nostrils flaring, his mouth wide open. Occasionally he would beat himself about the thighs and belly.

They knew that this was his way of appealing to Thor, so they said nothing about it, but simply asked him to go home with them.

By the time they reached camp, a commotion had arisen among the people. They sprinted in, fear on their faces, only to have the cause pointed out to them by Freydis. A whale had been seen spouting through a hole in the ice not far from shore. Now the spout was red, for many spears and harpoons had been hurled into the luckless creature. Hemmed in by the ice and shallow water, and held fast by the ropes attached to the harpoons, the beast soon expired.

The Greenlander was jubilant. He danced on the shore and praised Thor. All those who were pagan joined him and gave great shouts of triumph.

Later Gudrid said to him, "That was quite an exhibition you put on. I suppose you think there was some connection between your prayer to Thor and the whale on the beach. I say the whale would have been there, Thor or no Thor."

"And suppose it had come a week earlier," he replied, "while you women were telling your beads. What would you have said then?"

Hauling the whale out was no easy task, but by chopping the ice on the landward side and pulling on the carcass with stout walrus-skin ropes, taken from the ships, they managed to get it up onto the ice. There they flensed it. They hung the meat up on makeshift racks on shore. Soon the smell of roasting whale pervaded the camp, and everyone prepared for a feast. A few of the more pious Christians suggested that they would have nothing to do with a whale of Thor's, but their bellies overrode their convictions and they were among the more voracious diners.

Then, with full stomachs, the leading men gathered around the main fire in what had come to be called Snorri's house. Several women were present, including Gudrid and Freydis. With a shock Gudrid realized that she had gone out of her way to sit next to Freydis, even though other places were available.

Freydis spoke up for going north to the land they'd passed up. Finnbogi argued for sailing south, on the theory that neither land they'd seen so far was Vinland.

"I agree with Finnbogi—we should go south," Gudrid began, but Torfin looked at her oddly and she stopped short. A bitter taste came into her mouth.

Snorri shifted and coughed. He leaned toward Freydis. "I agree with you—we should go north."

A few others spoke briefly in praise of one plan or the other, but no one added anything of substance.

Finally Torfin made known his decision. "We will go south. Spruce wood has its uses, but it's not what we came here for." Freydis shook her head balefully, but said she'd go along.

Snorri winked at Gudrid. Had Torfin really decided to go south merely because Snorri had advocated going north, as the wink suggested?

Then the discussion passed over to details, and Gudrid slipped away, out the door into the night. She hurried over to her own house, where Nika nodded sleepily to her entrance, and the baby was sound asleep beside her. Everyone said he was Torfin's image, but Gudrid saw much of Bjorn in him. She thought of her father expiring in Greenland. She thought of Leif patting her on the head like a dog. A bitch in heat, that's what she'd been, to chase after Torfin when her cousins needed her. She deserved whatever fate was coming to her.

She gazed at the little one for a while, then moved away soundlessly. As she passed again through the doorway, the moonlight struck her in the eye, and there was more than a promise of spring in the air. She felt between her breasts. The loss of the amulet was painful enough. Even more painful was the evil magic this loss was working on her heart. She was losing Torfin before she had ever been able to find him.

35.

Spring came at last to the camp on the stream by the fjord. The ice was largely gone, the ships had been hauled down into the bay, and what was left of the whale had been towed far from shore, to be carried out to sea by the tide. The ships were made ready, and the reluctant animals were herded aboard. The bull bellowed his displeasure, but with eight or ten men on all sides, he had no choice finally but to go where he was goaded.

Gudrid walked through the empty house, pausing at the place where she had given birth. She winced at the memory of the robbery. How could she get revenge on Mord? She picked up the few items of hers that remained and headed for the door. As she did so the soapstone whorl from a spindle she was carrying fell and rolled underneath a platform. She stooped and peered to see whether she could find where it had gone. It was too dark though. Torfin was calling impatiently, so she gave it up and went outside. He was pacing back and forth along the beach, hurrying on the last of the stragglers.

They sailed out into the fjord, the three ships in a line, and coasted southward along an uninteresting shore with nothing but bog and marsh inland to greet the boat crews sent ashore to scout. In the distance the flat horizon gave way to low hills that gradually increased in height.

Several days passed this way, the expedition groping carefully down the coast. The monotony of the bog and scrubland was relieved only by the mountains, which in addition to their steadily increasing height were encroaching nearer the shore, until only a broad plain separated them from the water.

Now the character of the land began to change. Forests supplanted the bogland, and those who went ashore reported ponds teeming with fish. Once they saw an animal that reminded them of a reindeer.

Only one thing was lacking—a place of refuge for the ships—but then even this was granted. Everyone heard the shouts of the returning boat party announcing the harbor, and though its channel was so narrow that they had to be led in by men in the boats, taking soundings, they all exclaimed with wonder at the expanse of blue water, the deep green forests, the lush grass on the foreshore. Many kinds of waterfowl—some they had never seen before—skimmed the water. Fish jumped all around the ships. The wind brought the smell of grass, and the cattle bellowed in anticipation.

They landed on the south shore of the great pond. Torfin, Freydis, and Finnbogi set their men to building houses—wooden houses— using spruce logs hewn in the forest and dragged to the shore. A hunting party did its work well, and soon two of the reindeerlike animals were roasting over open fires.

Gudrid walked among the cattle and sheep smelling the sweet grass and the salt smells from the pond. Freydis walked beside her now, and in her enthusiasm for this place, Gudrid forgot her fear, though she still would not look straight into the green eyes. Nika carried the baby.

"What a wonderful country this is! The lake and the grass, the forests, the fish and the birds and the four-footed beasts—can this be anything other than Paradise?" She hoped that Torfin would like it as much as she did.

"No hardwoods here," said Freydis in a voice that mimicked Torfin's. "Or grapes."

"I know. But I'll win him over. What a fine place to watch this little one grow to manhood!"

Freydis shook her head. "Do you really think Torfin will settle for a farmer's life? It's not only for gold that the trader sails the sea."

"That I wouldn't know. I only hope he'll want to stay."

Two weeks later the Skraelings came. Rowing across the estuary in nine skin boats, they drew opposite the beached ships. They stopped and stared. By this time the colonists were lined up on the shore, weapons at the ready, staring back. Then the natives began to whirl their harpoons around their heads. Attached to the harpoons were inflated bladders that made an eerie noise as they whirled, such as none of the Norse people had ever heard before.

"Maybe it's a sign of peace," said Snorri. "They don't look as if they mean us any harm, and in any event there are more of us than there are of them."

Torfin ordered his men to sheathe their swords. His first mate handed him a white shield. Advancing to the water's edge, he stood facing the natives, saying nothing, holding the shield in front of him.

A voice came from the rear. "I see some skulls worth splitting today." It was Mord. Gudrid gave him an ugly stare. He grinned at her, then slinked back into the crowd of younger crewmen, barely out of adolescence, with whom he was standing.

The natives began to paddle in toward shore. Torfin continued to stand, several paces in front of the others, as they approached. They landed and surrounded him, feeling his clothing, his helmet, the shield.

They were short in stature and dark, and had long tangled black hair. They wore skins about their bodies, and had skin boots with the fur side out.

Gudrid saw that Torfin wished to make them some kind of gift, and she sent Nika hurrying for a bolt of cloth. Coming down to the shore, she cut strips, giving one to each man, indicating by example that they might want to tie the pieces around their heads.

The natives appeared delighted with the gifts. They smiled, danced a little, and uttered a few sounds that she took to be words of thanks. Then they were off, as quickly as they came, out the mouth of the harbor toward open water.

That evening Gudrid took Torfin aside and told him what Mord had said. "The younger ones seem to follow him. You may not be able to control them the next time the dark people come."

"The Skraelings," Torfin said.

"Yes, Torfin, but I don't like the word. It's true they are short, and they make a lot of noise, and maybe it's more than a coincidence that our words for shriveling and for shrieking are so similar. But the name is not meant as a compliment, and will make it easier for the wilder young men to cause trouble if you let them use it."

"What am I supposed to do?" He obviously did not expect a helpful answer.

"I don't know," Gudrid said. "You must find a way to keep the men—especially the younger men—in line when the natives return, as they will sooner or later. If we're going to stay here, we must be on peaceful terms with them. They were few in number today, but they must have kinfolk somewhere."

"No doubt," Torfin agreed, moving away from her as he did so.

"I have an idea!" Gudrid said to his back. Torfin turned around.

"Build a stockade of posts around the houses, running down to the shore where the ships are. Then give an order that on sight of strangers everyone must go inside the wall. Then you go and meet them with men you can depend on not to do something stupid."

"That would be a lot of work," said Torfin. "Many trees to cut, holes to dig. How do you know it'll work?"

"It would keep the young men away from the natives. They would have to disobey you openly in order to get closer."

"What would keep them from hurling spears over the posts?"

"You know the answer to that one without my telling you," Gudrid said, doing her best to hide her exasperation at her husband's obtuseness. "These young men want to prove themselves as warriors. There's no glory in throwing spears over a wall."

Torfin had no further objections, but he did not use her plan. She broached it to Snorri, but he could not think of a way to press it on Torfin without arousing his jealousy.

Through the rest of the summer, everyone was busy at tasks de-
signed to make the place a permanent home. The first houses by the
shore were completed and made wintertight. More houses were
started farther up the slope. A large barn was constructed for the
winter's hay, and a byre for the cattle. The sheep they would leave
out all winter.

Spruce logs were piled up for firewood—what a luxury for the
Greenlanders, who husbanded every scrap of usable wood that
washed upon their shores.

Halibut in abundance were captured in the tidal flats by the simple
expedient of digging a broad hole between the low- and high-tide
marks. The unsuspecting flatfish, isolated at low tide, were easily
speared out and carried back to camp on a litter. Some were eaten
immediately—a finer-tasting fish none of them had ever enjoyed.
Others were salted away for the winter.

A party was sent south in a ship's boat, and while they reported
neither hardwoods nor grapes, they did speak of a vast and inviting
land that would support many people, both in the raising of livestock
and in getting a livelihood from the sea. They had seen no further
sign of inhabitants, though they had not ventured inland beyond the
shoreline.

How soon it was winter again, but what a contrast to the year
before! It was so mild that not only the sheep but even the cattle
could be left out of doors to graze. What little snow there was
quickly melted or blew away. The houses seemed like palaces compared to the sod shelters at Straumfjord camp. Food was abundant,
fish and meat both, and with the rich grass the cattle gave more milk
than they ever had before. There was even a little wild grain, enough
to make a hard, crusty bread and to brew a beer of sorts for the Yule.

Still the dry feeling would come over her, the emptiness of heart
when she felt between her breasts. But if she couldn't entirely forgive
Torfin for his ultimatum concerning the amulet, she could at least
understand that her anger was as much against herself for yielding to
his demand as it was against him for making it.

Baby Snorri was a year old now and beginning to walk. Torfin
would often take him up and dangle him in his great arms, sometimes
upside down by the feet. The baby would laugh excitedly during this

play, and the mother would come over and sit nearby, sharing the father's pleasure.

Then she was almost able to convince herself that things had gone for the best. Perhaps the stone was the work of the Devil. Maybe God sent Mord, in His mysterious way, to help her. Perhaps she should take the good things as they came and not fret too much over trouble. She was mistress of a new land, mother of its first son.

36.

The days had been growing longer for some time, until now they nearly equaled the nights in length. No ice at all had formed in the salt water of the estuary, though its mouth had been closed since the Yule by pack ice that drifted into the great fjord from the north. Now even this was breaking up, with broad expanses of open water appearing near the shore.

Freydis was loitering outside the houses near the pond, where she and her husband and several of his cousins had built their houses. Nika stood beside her, looking out toward the water.

Gudrid rounded the corner of the building on her way to the spring. Seeing Freydis and Nika, she stopped to talk. At that moment Nika pointed out to the place where the harbor opened to the sea.

"Look!" she said.

First in ones and twos, then in greater numbers, the skin boats entered the harbor pond. They were everywhere. Again the natives whirled the bladders around their heads.

The women raised a shout, and the men tumbled out from all the houses, wearing helmets and leather jerkins, swords at the ready.

Torfin strode down the slope toward the water and shouted the order. "Don't touch your weapons unless they attack. If they want to trade, you may offer them whatever goods you have to spare, but don't give them any weapons, no matter how much they offer. Understand?" Heads nodded amid grunts of assent.

The nearest of the Skraelings were now approaching the shoreline, and Torfin ordered an area of the beach kept clear for them to land. Again he carried the white shield in front of him. Gudrid could not say whether any of these were among their former visitors: they all looked so much alike. A few of the natives came on shore and walked up to Torfin. They peered with intense curiosity at everything they saw—the bearded men in their strange clothing, the houses. Some went as far as the nearest ship and ran their hands over its planking.

More of them landed, many with bundles of furs. They laid these down on the ground in front of them, then stood and waited. Torfin ordered tubs of skyr brought out, and he gave samples to what appeared to be the leading men. From the lip smacking that followed, it appeared that this was an item that would find acceptance. By pointing alternately to the furs and to the skyr, Torfin gave them to understand that he desired a trade.

Some of the more inquisitive Skraelings had begun to walk up the slope to where the women were standing, feeling the logs of the houses and the smooth wood and iron of buckets, hoes, a pot on a tripod, a ladder. As the natives dispersed through the settlement, the Norse men grew increasingly nervous. Hands fingered the hilts of swords. One of the natives came up to Gudrid. He raised his fingers toward one of her brooches, his fingers making a slight circular motion in anticipation of stroking its texture. Gudrid, unwilling to tolerate such familiarity, put up her hand to block that of the native. He moved on.

Then, from behind them, came a series of loud snorts, followed by a tumult of bleating and bellowing. It was the bull. It had always been an intractable beast, but somehow the stress of the voyage had driven out the last vestiges of tranquillity from its soul, for now it would charge whatever it didn't approve of, which was just about anything that got in its way. Since it usually kept to itself in a small stand of trees behind the houses, no one had bothered to tether it.

Now the sight of all the strange men was too much for the animal. Grunting, pawing the ground, roaring, it charged first one group of natives, then another. The Skraelings, at first surprised, were now terrified. Running at random and screaming, they sought whatever means of escape they could. Some even tried to enter the houses.

At this, someone shouted the alarm, and Torfin's men responded as if to an onslaught. Rushing to a house where a group of natives was crowding the door, they drew their swords and cut them down from behind. At other places, too, the natives saw the strange men with their weapons, who moments before had been offering them food and accepting their gifts of furs in return, now attacking them with murderous intent. The Skraelings piled into their boats shouting and whooping, and paddled off to the middle of the pond. Then they headed toward the inlet and were soon out of view around the point.

Standing in a loose circle, the colonists assessed the slaughter. That there was no attack was obvious; none of them had been hurt in the least. Seven Skraelings lay dead. The split skulls brought back memories of Sigunna, no matter that the hair now matted with blood was black and unkempt rather than gold and flowing. Gudrid turned away, struggling to keep down her gorge.

The men clustered in groups of four and five, swords in hands, looking around apprehensively. The women huddled among themselves, sharing the fear. The Skraelings would be back, probably in even greater numbers, and when they came, they would have revenge on their minds. To Gudrid, the water and the trees and the fields that before had seemed so friendly, so much a home, now took on a sinister aspect, and it was brought home to her as never before that she was in an alien country.

Then her fear was replaced by anger, at the men for their rashness, at the Icelander who had brought the bull, at Torfin for not accepting her plan for the palisade.

Torfin did order, now, the two main groups of houses to be fortified, the one nearer the shore in the form of an oxbow, with the open end where the ships were beached. The work was no easier now than it would have been before, had Torfin taken Gudrid's advice. She struggled to hold her tongue and for several days succeeded, but then Torfin came to her just as her hand was, for the hundredth time that day, feeling for her missing stone. If he hadn't made her hide it, she wouldn't have lost it and this wouldn't have happened. She could no longer restrain herself.

"I see you've finally seen the wisdom of my suggestion. It's too bad you took so long."

The words were hardly out of her mouth when she regretted them.

Had he hurled angry words back at her, she might not have thought much of the incident, but his look was of genuine chagrin, as though too preoccupied to conjure up a retort. Instead, he merely turned and walked away.

In the days that followed they remained huddled behind their fences, afraid to go out of sight for any purpose. Torfin called the leading men together and gave them his plan.

"We'll use a decoy," he said. "When the Skraelings come back, ten men will go out to the point of land that lies just west of here and the rest of us will hide in the woods. The Skraelings will have to land on this side of the point. There's nothing but bog beyond. When they do, we'll charge out of the woods and drive the bull in front of us. We'll catch them in between. That should give us the victory."

Someone objected that the decoys would be in great danger.

"That's true," said Torfin. "That's why we need the best fighters to go there." In the end he selected thirteen out of nearly thirty who had volunteered. Gudrid noted with satisfaction that Mord, who had spoken so bravely of mayhem on the Skraelings' first visit, had not now volunteered for the hazardous duty, and she gave him what she hoped was a sufficiently withering sneer when she saw him. He sneered back. She was almost certain he had given the first cry that had set off the bloodshed.

After three weeks of watching and waiting, the Skraelings returned, shouting and whooping and swinging the bladders, this time in the opposite direction to that of the time before.

"This must be their war sign," said Torfin, and he sent the volunteers off to their station while the rest of the men posted themselves in the woods.

The Skraelings landed just where Torfin had expected they would, and turned toward the men on the point as though to make short work of them.

Torfin and his men emerged from the woods with their war shields and charged the Skraelings. The natives began to hurl short spears at the attacking men. Torfin and his men raised their shields to ward off the darts, but next they saw something so unexpected that it put them to flight.

Some of the Skraelings had large throwing sticks with which they hurled their harpoons. As the spears with their bladders, the size of sheep's bellies, whizzed overhead, some of them burst with a loud noise.

The warriors fled in panic past the stockades. "They're coming out of the woods!" someone shouted, and this only increased their terror.

Some of the women had come out from the stockades to watch the battle. Seeing their men turn to flee, they ran back inside. Gudrid, as frightened as any of them, nevertheless was awestruck by the sight of the natives and so was the last to turn away. Just as she did, Mord rushed by.

It was not something she considered consciously. The split moment of decision would not have allowed that. She did step forward into Mord's path, and she extended her foot to trip him up. Then she ducked under the lintel as two other women struggled to close the door.

Mord had gotten only to his knees when the Skraelings reached him. A stone axe cleft the back of his head. His body sprawled forward, his sword clanking on the stones.

Now the women peering over the wall noticed to their horror that Freydis too was outside. She had foolishly gone too far, to get a better view of the fighting, and was unable to get back in time.

Gudrid stared helplessly. A cry of anguish strangled itself in her throat as she watched the Skraelings surround her.

Freydis hesitated. She looked around in desperation. Some of the Skraelings were brandishing spears at her, while others reached forward, tugging at her brooches and tearing loose her outer garment.

She raised her arms and let out a howl. The natives stepped back for a moment, but then they closed in again. She dropped off her torn woolen, and this again caused the natives to give her some room. When they closed in again, she pulled her shift over her head.

She could only do this one more time, with her underclothes. As the Skraelings came on again, she noticed Mord's sword on the ground in front of her. She picked it up and began to slap her breasts violently with the flat of the blade, howling wildly all the time.

This was too much for them. They took a long detour around her to catch up with their fellows chasing after the retreating men. When they were out of sight, Freydis ran to the stockade. Gudrid sent Nika to get a robe for her.

She embraced Freydis. Until this moment, she'd not known how she really felt about this woman. She did now. She kissed her on both cheeks and then, without thinking, on the lips. Pulling away a little, she looked long without blinking into Freydis' green eyes. For once, Freydis was the one too surprised to speak.

The whooping of the natives became louder again, and soon they were streaming back past the stockades toward their boats. They paddled offshore just as Torfin's men returned.

Freydis stood forth. "Children! Is this what frightened you?" She walked over to where one of the bladderlike objects had fallen, still attached to its spear. It was a purplish, distended thing, and Freydis punctured it with Mord's sword. The air burst from it with a loud bang. "It is much like you," she said to the warriors. "Full of air, able to make loud noises, but in the end, nothing more than this." She held up the flaccid remains of the object, spat on it, and threw it to the ground.

The men could not withstand this. Embarrassed, they turned away. When the last of them had left, Freydis took Gudrid by the hand.

37·

Gudrid stood on a grassy plain, a soft breeze in her hair, the sky clear and blue. Before her stood a woman, naked and beautiful, her red hair upon her shoulders. Her body was dripping water, as though she had been swimming. Her robe lay beside her.

"Freydis," Gudrid heard herself whisper in a voice that reverberated from icy cliffs in spite of its gentleness. "Is it really you?"

"Yes, it is I," Freydis said. She said no more, only standing before Gudrid.

Only now did Gudrid understand that she, too, was naked, her bare feet feeling the spongy ground. The ground became softer, the grass turning to moss, the moss to an amorphous green surface that could no longer support her weight. She was sinking, to her knees, to her thighs.

"Freydis!" she called. "Freydis! Help!" But Freydis stood before her still, not sinking, her smile the same as it was when she had first appeared. Gudrid was in up to her navel now, and she began to thrash all the more, these movements only drawing her deeper. The green morass was up to her neck, getting thinner all the time, more watery.

Downward she plunged. Freydis was beside her, swimming seal-like through the water, and Gudrid swam too, like a seal. Their movements matched one another's through the green void.

Then they were shooting upward together, toward the light. They broke the surface in a mass of foam, into the *lapis* blue, and as suddenly as she had appeared, Freydis was gone.

Gudrid lay on something soft. Snowclad mountains rose overhead, and waterfalls glistened. From one of the hanging valleys in the distance a lone horn sounded, its notes cascading from one peak to the next, calling out responses until the valley was alive with sound.

Freydis emerged from behind an obstruction, bearing a cup and a yellow flower. She gave the flower to Gudrid and offered her some mead. As Gudrid drank, the flower began to expand. Larger and larger it grew, until it was bigger than the sun. Its petals reached up and around Gudrid, engulfing her. She was swirling in a mass of yellow.

A bee had been in the flower. Now the insect was larger than a house, and its huge eye stared directly at Gudrid. She saw her reflection in each part of the eye, and each reflection was different. Still larger the bee grew, until this eye was all she could see.

"Here, Gudrid. Here!" Freydis' voice called from all around her. "I'm here, come find me." Gudrid was in the eye now, its waxy surface on every side.

She looked out. The bee was flying. Far below were the houses and fjords, all around the mountains. Higher the bee flew, toward the sun. Closer the fiery ball came, until it filled the opening of the eye. Tongues of fire spurted toward her.

Then everything was black. She was hurtling through blackness at unimaginable speed. The bee was gone. This was not what she had expected, this blackness. Was she the only one who knew this secret, that the sun was black inside? Was this the secret of everything, that everything was black inside?

Strangely, she felt no fear, because she was beyond fear. Everything was black; that was the great truth she learned, that behind the fire there was only blackness and cold. She felt her limbs congealing in ice and found that she could no longer move. Her breathing had virtually ceased, and somewhere, as if from a great distance, she heard the slow beating of her heart.

Very softly then, from far away, just as she had heard it once at dawn on a ridge above her father's farm in Snaefellsnes, she heard the song of a single snowbird, the most beautiful she had ever heard. Another snowbird sang, and Gudrid discovered startlingly that it was her own voice calling now. The first bird answered, and Gudrid answered back in birdsong. She saw the other flying toward her, her white feathers brushing her own. Gudrid's feathery wings touched those of the other bird, stroking, caressing, and they were making love. She looked into the other bird's eyes, and they were deep, infinite green eyes. She heard heartbeats, rapid insistent heartbeats. In the midst of this great black nothingness inside the sun, two little birds were making love, and this was the only thing that was left in the world.

The wall came up so fast she hardly saw it before they broke through. Once again Gudrid was lying on the soft fleece. Freydis was in her arms. She saw they were not in the mountains or in the sun but in the sauna, alone.

Gudrid felt Freydis' embrace, and how much it seemed like the times back in Arnarstapi when she had scraped a knee or fallen on a rock and her foster father had gathered her in and held her. Freydis let Gudrid lie back gently in the firelight and stroked her hair, and how like her foster father's stroking it seemed, so long, long ago. But the hand on her breast was as she had once imagined it would be with Einar and was possessed of such subtlety as she had never known. Gudrid felt Freydis' soft lips touch hers, and a racing sea of images washed past—the seal in the pool at Arnarstapi, the teeming lakes of Vatnahverfi, the swaying hay grasses where she and Freydis walked together in the evenings and watched the water birds. Now the warmth of the fire mingled with the warmth of Freydis' hands on her belly, her thighs. She closed her eyes and floated, and again she was a seal swimming in dark green waters. Again they made love, and it was the sweetest, best thing that Gudrid had ever known.

38.

Torfin ordered a muster outside the lower palisade. He recounted the day of the battle, in which two Norsemen had been killed—Mord Flokisson and one of Finnbogi's crew. More important for the future of the colony were the Skraelings who also had been killed.

Torfin spoke. "Fate has not intended this place for us. We will return to Straumfjord." This surprised no one. Everyone was ready to go.

Everyone, that is, except Gudrid. She went up to the woods and beyond, to a place where she could look over the great pond and the beautiful land around it, and imagined what might have been. She looked down on the sauna where she and Freydis had loved. When she was finished, she rubbed her eyes with her cloak and walked back to the stockade.

She took young Snorri from Nika and, sitting down with him, sang a little song:

> *What will you be wanting,*
> *O my little man?*
> *What will you be wanting,*
> *When you are tall?*
> *I'll have a big cornfield,*
> *O Mama, my dear,*
> *Ten barns and I'll fill them,*
> *O Mama.*
>
> *What will you be wanting,*
> *O my little man?*
> *What will you be wanting,*

When you are tall?
I'll have a great byre,
O Mama, my dear,
A hundred cows lowing,
O Mama.

What will you be wanting,
O my little man?
What will you be wanting,
When you are tall?
A thousand strong warriors,
O Mama, my dear,
To eat up the cows
And the corn.

And so, on a bright spring morning when the sunlight glistened on the water and ducks by the hundred splashed down near its center, three ships carefully found their way along the channel, out the harbor entrance, and into the expanse of sea beyond.

All hope of recovering her amulet died with Mord. She'd half expected it to be found hidden in his belongings. It would explain many things, including his ill luck with the Skraelings. But it didn't turn up. It was just possible that he'd left it hidden back at Straumfjord. She'd look for it, but in the expanse of rock and woods and meadow, what chance would she have of finding it, even assuming it was there?

At Straumfjord, Torfin discussed possibilities with Finnbogi and Freydis.

"We'll have the best chance of finding Vinland if we explore separately, then return here. I'll go southeast, down the coast. Finnbogi, you'll go west, along the opposite shore of Straumfjord. It's so big, it may be more of an inland sea than a fjord. Freydis, you'll go north, back to Wonderful Strand . . ."

"Pfah! Blow another fart from your troll ass."

Freydis may not have liked the plan, but she was on very thin ice here. No one could miss the allusion to the Svinafell Troll, who, it was said, used certain men as women every ninth night. Had a man said this, Torfin would certainly have drawn his sword, but Freydis seemed to be able to get away with such things and worse.

It did, however, firm up Torfin's resolve. "You're out of this expedition," he said to her. "Don't follow us. If you do, it will come to a fight between your men and mine." After this there was no further communication between Freydis' people and Torfin's. Freydis, however, remained at Straumfjord.

Torfin was in a hurry to go. He was ready in less than a week, well before midsummer.

They coasted along a rugged land. They were no longer in the fjord, which, though very broad, offered some protection. Here it was open sea all the way to Norway.

After three days the cliffs subsided, and in one tiny fjord they found some birch trees.

Then land appeared on the port side also, and they were sailing into a deep bay. There were magnificent forests on both sides, broad-leafed trees with dark trunks lining the water, and though they were not sure what kind of trees they would be, they knew they were in a lumberman's heaven.

Torfin was ecstatic.

The bay terminated in a tidal flat with a small channel running in to a protected anchorage. Torfin sent five men ahead in the boat to explore, and then guided the ship in according to their directions. Except for building one small log house with a wall around it, he lost no time in sending out the men to fell and cut timber.

This land was different from the paradise they'd lost, but was in many ways as inviting. The steep-sided valley was covered with trees far up the mountainsides. Frogs croaked in the pondlets that bordered the creek. "This could be home," Gudrid thought, and she considered what she might do to make Torfin see this.

Torfin ordered the posting of watches at the palisade and at the lumbering sites. All were to sleep inside the wall at night, the women and their husbands in the house, the others in tents. So things went for several days, until one morning when the sun filtered through the leaves, the long-awaited shout was given and repeated through the woods and the men came racing in, carrying their axes and adzes.

The natives emerged from the woods, not stealthily or cautiously but striding into the open. The men were tall, and though they had black hair like the other natives, they resembled them in no other way. Their faces were painted with red earth, and some of the men wore feathers in their hair. They carried their belongings with them on tumplines around their foreheads, and they had their women with them. The presence of the women and their open manner of approaching made their peaceful intentions obvious, and it was equally obvious that they were confident of a kind reception.

Two or three of the tallest men appeared to be the leaders, and Torfin emerged from the stockade with his first and second mates. The women went to the house as Torfin had ordered. Gudrid prayed silently that all would be well. Young Snorri lay sleeping in a cradle that one of the men had made for him.

She knew that something evil was about to happen and that she must take whatever steps she could to prevent it. She should be outside with her husband, to head off the disaster if it were in her power to do so. But what could she do?

An apparition appeared in the doorway. It was one of the native women. She wore a black kirtle that covered her from shoulder to hip, but left her thighs exposed. Her straight black hair fell down over her shoulders and framed a dark face with liquid eyes. Gudrid stood very slowly, not wishing to scare the woman away, not to lose this loveliness that had come out of the dark side of the earth. She had never seen a comelier woman, even in Iceland.

Gudrid beckoned to her with outstretched hands. "My name is Gudrid," she said. "What is your name?"

The woman looked as if she wanted to come in, but she hesitated. "My . . . name . . . is . . . Gudrid?" she repeated, forming the sounds of the unfamiliar Norse language as best she could. Then she said something in her own tongue.

That was choked off by shouts and screaming. The woman vanished. Gudrid rushed out to the wall just in time to see the last of the natives fleeing into the woods.

The men stood about, flapping their arms aimlessly. In their midst, one of the natives was lying on the ground, gashed and oozing red.

Gudrid raced out the gate and bent over the dead man. Then, red with anger, she faced Torfin.

"What in God's name have you done?"

Torfin replied more evenly than she expected. "We were trading. Everything was going well. You saw the beautiful furs they had. We offered them pots, spoons, but all they wanted was this red cloth." He fingered the scrap that the dead man still clutched in his hand. "When we ran low, we started cutting the strips in thirds and quarters. They gave as much for each piece as they had before for a whole cloth. In the end, we were cutting strips no wider than my thumb and it was still the same.

"When we finally ran out of cloth, we started with trinkets and beads. They wouldn't take that stuff. All they wanted then were our axes. One of them wouldn't take no for an answer. When he grabbed at it someone killed him."

He took a deep breath and looked at his wife sadly.

"That's what happened."

Gudrid could no longer restrain herself. "You call yourself a man?" she screamed. "Is this what the great leader does, lets some fool spoil everything? You couldn't control them even with a palisade! Do I have to show you everything?"

Even at the height of this bluster, she knew she was going too far. Torfin had been as prudent as anyone could have been. She wanted to hold him close, to tell him she understood his disappointment as well as hers. But she could not.

She went back to the house, no longer trying to maintain even the appearance of calm, and buried her face in Nika's shoulder. Torfin came to see and walked away with a disgusted look on his face. The other women took this all in, and Gudrid felt the heat of their eyes on the back of her neck.

There could be no thought of staying. Again they had killed, and again they must expect revenge. As fast as they could, they loaded the wood onto the ship and returned to Straumfjord. Finnbogi and Helgi were back, having explored a worthless coast full of biting insects. Freydis, having remained at Straumfjord all this time, for once seemed undecided what to do. Inga followed her about, her face too much a scowl for such a favored thrall. Although Torfin remained hostile to Freydis, he made no attempt to conceal from her the wealth that lay down the coast and was free with the sailing directions. He spoke of the inhabitants as though they had come heavily armed, in numbers, and with destruction on their minds. The last thread of Gudrid's dream was gone.

39.

She stood in the thin rain, howling grief. Could she have been so negligent, and was Mord's spirit avenging itself so cruelly? She'd been out of the house for barely the time one needs to go to the privy and had left the house empty except for Torfin and their son. When she returned, no one was in the house, except young Snorri on the earthen floor. Gudrid's eyes fastened on the child and on what he was playing with. It was as if God Himself had struck her when she saw it was the amulet. She raced to snatch it away, knowing she was too late.

Then a sound reached her ear, and she turned to see a fleeing shadow. She ran to the door. It was no ghost she saw running down the path. It was Inga!

Gudrid called out, and Torfin, having gone out for just a moment, raced after the fleeing form and soon caught up with her. He dragged her back to the house and pushed her inside, where Gudrid stood still, holding the amulet in her hand. Inga knelt, shivering, while Torfin faced Gudrid, demanding to know what was going on. When he saw the amulet, his mouth became firm, his eyes fixed.

Gudrid told how she'd found young Snorri with it, and that she'd seen Inga fleeing the house. Torfin began to throttle Inga and would have killed her except for Gudrid's pull on his arm. Gudrid demanded of Inga, "Why did she make you do this?"

That Freydis hated Torfin she had no doubt. Was he not an ever-present reminder that she could never have Gudrid truly for her own?

She had never imagined, however, that Freydis would seek to harm her husband by plotting evil against her child.

At this moment Freydis walked in, responding to Inga's wails. Her immediate comprehension of the tableau—Gudrid holding the amulet, Inga imploring for her life, and Torfin red with rage—only fixed her guilt in Gudrid's eyes.

Had Torfin not restrained her, Gudrid would have torn Freydis' eyes out.

Freydis, however, shook Inga. "Tell the truth about this." She lowered her voice, almost to a whisper. "But beware of me. I can do to you what Leif did to your father."

Was it possible that the poor thrall Leif killed was Inga's father and that Freydis had done nothing to save him?

A long time passed before Inga could open her mouth. She kneeled silently, breathing slowly, looking half upward from time to time as if in expectation of the deathblow. At length, she did speak. Her voice came in a gasp, but the name was unmistakable.

"Thjodhild."

"What?" Several voices said this.

"I paid Mord to get the amulet for me. For Thjodhild. With Thjodhild's money."

Listening to Inga speak these words, Gudrid knew that it was she, and not Mord, who had dangled the amulet above her during her labor.

"Then why did you lay it on this child?"

Freydis looked at Inga, and it was obvious that Inga feared Freydis more than Torfin. She said nothing.

Torfin considered what to do next. Then, abruptly, he kicked Inga from the house and faced Freydis. "I could have her tortured, but what good would it do? She's your thrall. You're responsible for this. I'd kill you right now if it wouldn't spill more blood than yours." Despite this disclaimer, his hand went to the hilt of his sword. Freydis backed out as fast as she could.

He turned to Gudrid. "You defied me, wife, and now our son has the Devil's curse on him. I don't think a woman ever betrayed her husband the way you have."

Gudrid took the boy into her arms. She gazed in sorrow on this doomed little one. Snorri looked back at her, tugging at the brooch above her breast, telling her he wished to nurse. He needed several tries to get her attention, and then she responded slowly, as in a dream.

"I couldn't give up the amulet, nor can I now. If you had let me wear it, this would never have happened. If you need someone to blame, blame yourself. As for me, I will no longer skulk in the shadows but will carry it with me once again. Take it away, if you dare!"

Torfin's grief showed through his anger. "No. I'm still afraid of the Devil. I won't touch the stone, though I'm surprised your pride is stronger than your love for your own child."

Torfin did not speak of the matter to Gudrid again, and to all appearances the couple were back on good terms. But he no longer took her, except when he had drunk too much from the small store of pale beer, and then roughly, as she imagined he would a ship woman after a storm.

This meant the end, also, of love between Gudrid and Freydis. Gudrid didn't believe Freydis' protestations of innocence. Inga was Freydis' thrall, not Thjodhild's. If Inga were working for Thjodhild, she would hardly have relinquished possession of the amulet. Gudrid hated Inga now for what she'd done to her child, and remembering Freydis tousling Inga's hair, she closed her mind on Freydis also.

The affair of the amulet confirmed a decision that Torfin had already made. There would be no living with Skraelings, not because of any ferocity on their part, but because of the Norsemen's lack of discipline. Their only success would lie in the wood they carried back to Greenland, and for a trader this would be enough. The next morning, when the wind was fair, Torfin and Gudrid sailed for Greenland.

They were five days at sea now, and although the weather had been clear and the breeze fresh and from a favorable direction, they had lost sight of any land three nights before. Now they were alone on the wide sea, heading directly for Greenland.

Such a course could be dangerous, should storm or fog envelop them. Wasn't this the reason for Torfin's cautious approach on the outward voyage? He didn't care now. He was a different man, driven by the single intent to put the episode behind him and salvage what gain from it he could.

The lookout shouted down.

"Land! Dead ahead, and off to starboard."

They closed swiftly with the coast. From its appearance and orientation, from a dead-reckoning estimate of their progress, and from the height of the Pole Star, this had to be Greenland. As they began to recognize specific headlands and islands, the sailors spoke their astonishment: Torfin had put them smack in the mouth of Eriksfjord.

Though there was no way that word of a ship's arrival could travel up the fjord faster than the ship itself—certainly not if the wind was a following one and the ship was making good speed—somehow the people of Brattahlid always seemed ready to receive visitors. This time was no different. Gudrid gulped when she saw Leif in front of the crowd, in the very place that Erik had stood on that day when Bjorn first brought her here. The rest of the crowd was a sea, but in its midst came a glimpse that made her shudder. Then it was gone.

Torfin brought the ship in precisely, gliding to a stop just as it touched the shore. He was dressed for the occasion, wearing the same golden belt and sword he had on the day she first saw him. She recalled her reactions then and compared them with her present feelings.

Leif had left nothing to chance in his own attire, his best silks, in red and gold, gold chains and ermine trim. He advanced up the gangplank to clasp Torfin's hand.

"Welcome to Brattahlid," he said. "I see you all came back." He was gloating over the colony's failure, and Torfin was suppressing a scowl. "But what is this I see? Very fine timber! The trip has not been a total loss then." By this time, Gudrid had joined Torfin, with Snorri wriggling in her arms.

"And I see you have not been totally idle either, Torfin," Leif said as he tickled the boy's chin.

"Where is your father?" Torfin asked abruptly.

"The Redbeard is not well. He lies abed. It is sad. 'Cattle die, and kinsmen die—' "

" 'And we ourselves must die,' " Torfin finished the line.

"Precisely," said Leif in a manner more to be expected in the palace of a king than on the mossy shore of a Greenland fjord. "But come. I am lacking in hospitality toward my guests after their arduous journey."

Torfin and Gudrid followed Leif up the hill while Torfin's lieutenants made the ship secure.

As they entered the long house, Gudrid sensed a strange smell. It was not peat smoke or burnt mutton. It was not fresh-tanned leather or wet wool. These were familiar and pleasant smells. This was strange and rancid. The odor grew stronger as they approached the center of the house, where Erik lay in his bed behind the dais. Then she knew. It was the smell of death.

Erik smiled when he saw Torfin and Gudrid, the smile of one who has received succor after a long siege.

"It's good to see you, though the sight of you here speaks of bad luck in Vinland. I begged Thor to help you, even though you do him no honor. He owes me a favor or two. I have no more use for favors."

He began a siege of coughing, into a tattered cloth. Gudrid was startled by the laboring and violence of his exhalations, and although he did his best to conceal it, when he removed the rag from his lips she saw that there was blood amid the spittle.

"I'm in good hands," Erik continued after his coughing subsided. "A wife who plays with a poxed priest and a vulture of a son who hovers, waiting for the old bird to die."

"You say wrongly, Father," Leif said. "Surely you will recover and be as fit as ever. Maybe you will even lead a voyage to Vinland. You will surely fare better than these—"

"Enough, Leif! But tell me, Torfin, of my daughter. She at least is good seed, planted in sweet ground, not in the fetid turf that spawned this . . ." He glowered at Leif, and Leif glowered back.

Neither Gudrid nor Torfin spoke, not wishing to become involved in this family quarrel. Finally, after Leif had stepped back a pace and Erik had sunk back onto the bed, Torfin did begin.

"Freydis was well when we left her. That's the only good news. The Skraelings—"

"Bloody Thor! How many sacrifices have I given you? You let my loyal son die, and then my friend across the fjord, and now . . ."

He started another coughing fit. Gudrid held in her sorrow at this confirmation of her father's death.

Between coughs Erik said, "I am in a pit of vipers!"

"Like Ragnar Lodbrok," sneered Leif.

"Like Ragnar," said Erik. "At least his sons were steady, as that Northumbrian king learned when they pulled his lungs out of his back!"

"It is not seemly to speak of such things before guests," said Leif. "And such exertion of your humors is not good for you either."

Erik's face was bloodred now, and Gudrid feared he might have a seizure. She placed her hand on his shoulder and gently eased him back. She felt him slowly relax; then, with a suddenness that astonished her, he was asleep, snoring loudly.

"He's not well," said Torfin. "How long has he been like this?"

"He took sick at the Yule," said Leif. "The winter saw him only worsen. He hardly rises from bed now, except for the privy. Sometimes not even for that. He is fortunate though. He has a devoted thrall. A man who has treated his slaves well reaps the harvest at a time like this."

"Do you think he'll live?" asked Torfin.

"You saw him. Who knows? He does not seem to have gotten any worse since the thaw. I doubt he will last another winter." Then Leif changed the subject.

"Your return was a sad ending for the colonists. But not for a trader. I trust you are doing well."

"I do as well as life and God allow."

Leif turned to Gudrid. "The land in Stokaness, which my father lent to your father—"

"He didn't lend the land; he gave it."

"Gave it, lent it, it is all the same. Bjorn, your father, was to have it as long as he remained upon it, and his issue likewise. But you are going away."

"I've just returned."

"This is true, but you'll be going all the same. Take my word for it. When you do, the land returns to me. In the meantime, I have appointed an overseer to collect the rents so that the tenants do not grow lax. I think you may know the man."

Gudrid stiffened. "It is my intention to give the land to the people who live on it. The land is mine by right of inheritance."

Torfin broke in. "The land is yours, but you do not have the right to sell or to give it away. Only I can do that."

"As a widow I could do what I wished with my property," said Gudrid. "You may think that by marrying you I gave up that right. We'll see. I'll find a way."

"We'll discuss this later," said Torfin. Then, turning to Leif, he said, "The land is Gudrid's. Erik gave it to her father. He will confirm this."

Torfin looked again at the sleeping form, scowled, and turned to go. Gudrid followed, casting a backward glance at Leif as she did so.

"Wait!" Leif said. "Where do you plan to stay?"

"Some out-fjord. You don't have to worry about us."

This was the first she heard of this. She'd assumed they'd be going to Stokaness. She'd steeled herself to it, welcomed the opportunity to beg forgiveness. If she didn't do it now, she never would.

"I'd think that Gudrid would wish to be with the people of Stokaness, for whom she has shown such concern."

Torfin stood close to Leif. "That would be her wish. I don't want her to get too attached to the place. We're going back to Iceland. I wouldn't stay on this wretched rock of yours for anything. Make no mistake, however: Stokaness is hers, if there's any law in Greenland at all. She will sell it to the farmers. Then we'll go."

Now Gudrid feared the worst for the Stokanessers, especially after Leif's speech. She remembered Arnora's warning: Fail to learn the secret, suffer the fate you fear most. She feared more for them than for herself, and perversely, it seemed that very fear may be hastening their doom. She wanted to go there now, no matter how she might be received, but it was clear that Torfin would not allow it.

They emerged from Erik's house. Blinking in the sunlight, she saw him, and there could be no doubt that this was the man Leif selected to harry the people she abandoned. How he came to this shore she did not know, but it had to be the Devil's work, for this was the man who had leered over her, just as he was doing now, and then tried to rape her. It was Ymir Hrolfsson.

40.

She expected Ymir to speak hard words, but he did not. He said her name, by his tone making clear he knew who she was, but he acted as if he had completely forgotten his crime. She was even beginning to doubt that this was the same Ymir, though the resemblance to the image in her memory was too close, even allowing for the passage of years.

Leif resolved the doubt, referring to Hrolf as Ymir's father and mentioning Froda in ways that were not required by any business at hand so that Gudrid would know for sure who he had selected to carry out his design.

On the ship, Torfin and the elder Snorri were engaged in a lively discussion.

"We ought to go back to Iceland right now, while we still can," Snorri was saying. "Things could get very difficult here."

"No," Torfin replied. "We're too heavily laden. I took a chance coming from Vinland because I knew how much these Greenlanders need good wood. It should pry loose a lot of gold and silver from their tight little fists."

"Better you should give the wood away than have us all die for it. Something very ugly is going on."

"We'll be leaving soon. I'll only make one trading run. Then we'll go."

"Find us a place to stay, then. I don't want to be anywhere near Brattahlid when Erik dies."

Torfin agreed to this. He sailed around into Einarsfjord and entered negotiations with several farmers, finally settling on three farms reasonably close together on the south coast where the streams from Vatnahverfi run down to salt water.

To Gudrid he said, "I'll leave it to you whether to come with me or stay here."

She saw this as his way of testing her, whether she wished to reconcile herself with him or not.

"I will come with you, even though it's not the voyage we planned when we were wed."

He looked at her strangely, not knowing her meaning. She did not know her meaning herself.

Torfin began his trading in Eriksfjord so that he could keep an eye on Erik and see how he was doing. "If Erik's going to last a while, we'll be safe. If he's going to die soon, I want to know about it. We can expect little comfort from Leif. You once refused his offer of marriage, I'm told, and he wants your land. He'd like to get rid of me too. He senses I'm not in awe of him the way these Greenlanders are."

They covered the entire fjord, from Dyrenes to Brattahlid, but Torfin would not visit Stokaness. Gudrid was of two minds whether to press him. She knew she ought to visit her kin there, and if she had any pretension of ownership, it was a matter of protocol. Still, she was far from eager to face them, and it was all too easy to use Torfin's resistance as an excuse.

Torfin disposed of about a fourth of his wood. He was not pleased with the trade. The Greenlanders talked poor, claiming to have no silver or gold. Not only that, but the past year's hunting had been a disaster. "There's not much to be gotten here. If we'd known, we could have gone up to Nordrsetur and brought back enough to buy all your wood." Torfin asked them to do the best they could.

"We either trust them or take a paltry return for our work," he said to Gudrid. "I know they won't get much in these waters that's worth taking home. A few sealskins maybe. I don't like it. I may have to go up to Vestribygd. Maybe we'll have to stay the winter."

"No!" Gudrid half swallowed this, but for once Torfin held her arm in understood agreement.

By the time they came back to Brattahlid, another trader had arrived, a Christian Dane from York. He brought iron pots from Dublin, silks from the East, and honey from the south of England for the brewing of mead. Torfin cursed his luck. Competition.

"At least he didn't bring wood," Torfin said. "But I'll have to get out to the other fjords right away now if I'm to make any good deals at all."

In the dim long house, Erik was close to death. Gudrid could not tell whether he recognized her amid his pain and delirium.

The poor thrall who attended Erik did his best to remove the blood and the liquid feces that issued from opposite ends of the diseased body, but it was a losing battle, and Gudrid had to fight through her revulsion at the hopelessness and the stench to see the man who had moved so nimbly not many years before. Torfin stood by the bedside, showing neither emotion nor awareness of the squalor of Erik's dying.

Thjodhild had been standing in a corner, though Gudrid had not noticed her. Now she strode forward. She has aged greatly, Gudrid thought. Can it happen so fast? She wondered how much of an inroad the same slow dying had made upon her.

"Beware the fires of hell!" Gudrid started at the suddenness of Thjodhild's ejaculation. "Bones! Crushing of bones! Worms will creep into your eyes and devour your brains, and then you will be made whole and eaten again and again. Accept the cross, lest you be lost forever!"

Erik did not appear to notice this sermon. Torfin turned to Leif with raised eyebrows, and even Leif was compelled to make some response.

"My mother has been going on like this for some time. It is the priest. She is inseparable from him. There is nothing I can do."

"You could cleave his bloody forehead with an axe."

"You would like me to do that, wouldn't you. Destroy the very thing that will make my power secure. But you do well to return to Iceland. There is no future for you here."

Erik turned his head and spit up more blood. A gurgle came from under the filthy robe that covered him, and again the fecal odor. Now he began to cough, a choking wet cough that seemed as if it would never end. Erik's head rolled back and he drew a deep, gagging breath. Slowly, very slowly, he let the breath go and with it life, like the fading embers that filled the room with smoke.

Gudrid knelt before the bed of Erik's that was now his bier. Even as she did so, something inside her shrank back in wonder that she could grieve over a man she once had blamed for her first bitter loss.

Then she pulled out her amulet. "As you are something for man to fear in life, so may you be a help to man's spirit on its journey." She touched it to Erik's forehead, then stood, holding it in her hand pensively.

Thjodhild stared at it wide-eyed. Her hands groped uneasily forward. Gudrid stared, fascinated, then with a quick jerk slipped it back inside her woolens.

"Inga," Thjodhild whispered in a hoarse voice. "You failed me. Or did she kill you? Is that why you didn't come back?"

Suddenly Gudrid knew how much she had wronged Freydis. Inga really had been doing Thjodhild's work. She remembered the scene at Straumfjord, with Freydis standing over the girl. She should have seen the jealousy on Inga's face. Inga had, after all, had Freydis to herself before her mistress fell in love with Gudrid. Gudrid had ignored Inga because she was a thrall. She shouldn't have.

Would she ever see Freydis again?

All this time Leif stood easily, as though nothing unusual was happening. Now he ordered a henchman to see to the removal of Erik's body.

As they were leaving, Leif took Torfin aside once again.

"The land in Stokaness. My father erred even in lending it to Bjorn. Let me be plain. I can take it back anytime I want, but I see some value in observing a meticulous scrupulousness in regard to the law. If you will agree not to make trouble, I will smooth the way for you as long as you choose to remain here. Resist, and I will have it anyway, but you will not prosper in the meantime."

"I will need time to consider your generous offer," Torfin said. "There may be more honest men in Greenland than you think, with enough courage to support the law even against their chief." He paused for breath. "You couldn't do this in Iceland."

Torfin soon found out what Leif meant. No one would trade with him, though good, straight lumber was what the Greenlanders needed most. He related this to Gudrid and explained to her with forced patience, much as a father might explain to a dull child, the folly of her attachment to Stokaness. He also admitted his own stupidity in expecting gain from it.

"We have no choice but to give in to Leif's demands. He'll take what he wants anyway. We'll go to his house tomorrow."

"You'd take from me the one way I have of recovering my honor. As I am your wife, this will bring dishonor on you too."

Torfin, however, did not follow her argument. That night he needed a woman, and she repeated the technique she had used on Thorstein when he sent Nika to sleep with the thralls. Torfin felt her stiffness and rolled away unsatisfied. Gudrid felt angry, sad, guilty, sweaty, and mean. She wanted to reach out to him, but she also wanted to put an axe through his head. Now he was asleep, snoring, and he did not mention it in the morning.

As summer wore into autumn, Gudrid remained in Einarsfjord as Torfin, now able to trade, sailed throughout the Eastern Settlement. Trading in the out-fjords was as dismal as it had been in Eriksfjord, even with Leif's approval. So Torfin decided to go up to Vestribygd, even though this would require them to winter over. At least he would find the high-value items—the falcons, the walrus ivory, and the skins of white bears.

Gudrid was left to herself, which would have suited her except for what she must hear of the land dues that Ymir exacted from Stokaness. Boatload after boatload of livestock, leather, wool, and hay were ferried across to Brattahlid, until the tenants were left with a meager remnant of the wealth they had so carefully husbanded. She could see that a cruel winter was in store for them, for Leif had gone too far. If only Torfin had stood up to Leif, she thought, the outcome might have been different. Stokaness could have been defended, she told herself. Torfin's Icelanders, together with the people at Stokaness, could have enforced their will. But this would have required Torfin to commit himself to a protracted stay in Greenland. He would not rebel and then leave the Stokanessers to their fate.

Torfin returned just before ice-in.

"I've had to give an awful lot of credit," he said to her. "But I only traded with those I thought I could trust. I know it's a gamble, but I got my price. We'll be wealthy by midsummer. Enough to buy a good farm in Iceland and maybe a chieftainship too."

His euphoria carried over to her, and for once they put differences aside and took each other obliviously. Afterward she felt remorseful that she could so easily forget the people who were suffering because of the choice she had made, and was sad to think how much still stood between this man and her.

The ice set in on the fjord, the snow fell, and the cold came, the awful cold that freezes not just the skin but to the joints and the center of the brain. There was no Yule feast at Stokaness. Word found its way to Einarsfjord that soon they must kill what remained of their cattle and sheep. Gudrid appealed to her husband.

"You come to me, wife, to ask for help, and I will give it. Go to the storehouses and say what you want. My men will sledge it to Stokaness."

It was done. Mutton, seal, beef, bread, eggs, and two kegs of ale and one of mead were loaded and dragged away.

Gudrid tried to show her gratitude. She stood before him, head downcast, and fingered her brooches. For a moment it seemed that he would reach out for her, but then he turned and walked away.

"Torfin," she began, but he walked past the fire and kicked at the smoldering peat. He gestured to the far end of the house and a thrall brought a horn of mead. He gazed into it dejectedly. Then he hurled it against the wall, sending the sweet liquid splashing onto the floor.

Gudrid slept in the dairy, next to a little fire a thrall built for her. She yearned for his warmth, as she had known it when her heart was filled with hope.

41.

Freydis appeared suddenly in the spring, in the doorway while Gudrid sat, singing to her son sleeping in his small bedplace. The appearance shocked Gudrid, reminding her at once of the native woman who had stood in the doorway that brief moment when it seemed the spark she struck might yet set fire in the new land.

Freydis was looking at her strangely, but this was to be expected, considering what they had last said to each other at Straumfjord. The surprise was that Freydis had come at all.

Gudrid threw herself into Freydis' startled embrace. Freydis was more than willing to forget Straumfjord when Gudrid told her about Inga and Thjodhild. As Gudrid said, it was Thjodhild who sent men against her on the fell her first day in Brattahlid, and Freydis who saved her life.

Gudrid told Freydis about the plight of the Stokanessers.

"I may be able to help," said Freydis. "I have some influence over my brother."

Gudrid's eyes lit up. "Do you mean it? Is it possible you might be able to change his mind?"

"I can try. After all, this notion of renting land is dangerous. Nowhere in Greenland, or Iceland either, has it been done this way. The land-takers always distributed parts of their claims to their kinfolk and followers. All that was expected in return was loyalty."

"It's different in southern lands," Gudrid said. "People are bound to the land there. They have to pay heavy taxes."

Little Snorri sat up and rubbed his eyes. Gudrid sent him outside, where he soon was scattering the chickens in the yard. A big pecking rooster ran at him, and he came hurrying back. Nika came out of the house and took him in tow.

Gudrid looked down toward the water and saw that the ship drawn up on the shore was not the one that Freydis had before but the larger and newer one that Finnbogi had sailed in.

Freydis sensed the question in Gudrid's eyes. "We traded ships with the brothers," she said. "They decided to stay another year."

Gudrid could not think of a reason why they would trade their ship for Freydis' less valuable one or why they would wish to remain at Straumfjord such a long time. Freydis offered no further explanation, and Gudrid did not press the matter.

"Where's your husband?" asked Freydis.

"Out trading," Gudrid replied, though in truth he was apart from her in so many other ways. She felt a need to talk to Freydis about her troubles, but in spite of everything she did not want to be disloyal to him.

Freydis' husband came round the corner and greeted Gudrid formally. His was a gray personality, remaining always in the background. Though no weakling physically, he reminded her of a mouse, and he acted even more like a furtive rodent now, avoiding Gudrid's eye, scurrying off on some chore.

That summer was brighter and warmer than any that was remembered in Greenland. The sheep thrived, the cattle thrived, and the seals and seabirds were fat and plentiful. The Greenlanders felt prosperous too, because of an unprecedented influx of trade goods brought from Iceland and Europe by several traders and by the two ships returned from Vinland with their cargoes of wood. Lambs Fold Time was a golden time, with laughing children chasing the lambs, and the young men and women looking forward to the warm time out from under the eyes of their elders. It would not be the same at Stokaness, Gudrid knew, and yet she could not ask Torfin to take her there.

Gudrid and Freydis were firmly renewed in friendship and secret love. Freydis' farm lay on the isthmus between Eriksfjord and Einarsfjord, so it was an easy matter for her to be rowed across to Gudrid when Torfin sailed off on business. Sometimes they would speak of Stokaness, and Freydis again promised to intercede with her brother on behalf of the people there.

This was a special day. The sky was clear, and the air was warming rapidly. Freydis came shortly after sunrise and proposed that they spend the whole day exploring the rocky hills below Vatnahverfi. The morning sun glinted down on the fjords and the green shores, the stray icebergs and the rocky heights. A whale spouted far out toward the skerries.

They came to a shallow concavity in a south-facing cliff. A carpet of green moss lay about, and the heat of the sun, focused and concentrated by the shape of the rock, made it seem that the place was heated by a fire. Gudrid remembered when she and Einar had come to a place much like this.

For a while they sat in silence. Then Freydis asked a question. "Gudrid, you don't look happy. Is something the matter?"

Gudrid had already told Freydis of her disappointment at the failure of the colony, at the foolish desire of the men to fight rather than make peace with the natives, of her longing to speak to the native woman who had come to her door, of her desire to help the Stokanessers, of her profound feelings about the death of Erik. But she had said nothing of Torfin or of their drifting apart because of the amulet and she not knowing what to do. Now she could hold back no longer, and Freydis encouraged her with her eyes.

"There are so many things I could say."

The images flashed by, of her first seeing Torfin on his ship, of his taking little Snorri on his knee, of his going forth among the Skraelings and allowing them to touch him, and of his mastery of the ship. She told also of his unwillingness to listen to her ideas, when they might have changed everything for the better, and she told of his preoccupation with trade over everything else.

"Why do you stay here, Gudrid?" she said. "I once asked you to come live with me. I ask you again. Let Torfin go back to Iceland with his gold. I will protect you. I am Leif's sister after all. Torfin can do nothing. And Gudrid, I will set things right with your cousins and get Leif to send Ymir away."

Gudrid would have agreed right then, but something held her back. Something about Freydis' strange look when she'd first come back to Greenland. Something even more about her husband's surreptitious scurrying.

Freydis showed her how to make love in the outdoors in Greenland. Even with the sun shining and no wind, it was still briskly cool, but with the swarm of people down below, it was hard to be alone.

Freydis unpinned her brooches from the straps of her outer wrap and laid it aside. Gudrid did the same. Then they both placed their shawls, shifts, and underclothing on the ground. Freydis showed how to fold their rectangular woolens together like a blanket and wrap themselves in it. Then they lay on the shifts.

Gudrid warmed again to the feel of Freydis' soft body. She rolled back a little, so that Freydis was half on top of her, and she opened her thighs to let her lover put her own thigh between them. She relaxed into the feeling, opened to the muscular rhythm of the smooth knowing leg, playfully brushing a nipple with the back of her hand. Freydis drew the warmth from her body as a shepherd draws music from a set of pipes.

Then Gudrid began to feel an unevenness in the ledge, and she wanted to ease her own thigh up to give the same pleasure to Freydis, but in the process of shifting her body one of the wraps slipped a little. Freydis pulled it back, but then another corner was loose. Gudrid caught at that, but pulled the two pieces apart, opening a gap in the middle. Freydis was laughing now, tugging her way, and then Gudrid, too, was laughing, and they were all elbows and knees and the wind was coming up, and they both stood up, laughing and naked as plucked ptarmigans. They were covered with goose bumps.

Gudrid took Freydis' face in her hands and kissed it. "I love you," she said. "I never want you to go away from me again."

Freydis smiled, but she was the one stooping to get her shift. Only now did the heat within Gudrid subside, and she went in a rush to pull her own shift down over her loins.

They sat with their backs to the cliff and nuzzled, blanketed together by their woolens and shawls, which now they thought to pin together with their brooches, and Gudrid remembered the time she'd kissed Hakon the same way, in the fog, the day after Sigunna was killed. She held Freydis close, as she had held Hakon, and feeling more safe than she ever had since leaving Sigunna's breast, she and Freydis let their hands and fingers have their sweet way.

Afterward she sat with Freydis, watching the afternoon sun course over the fjord, the eagles and cormorants flying over the crags. Neither said much, but both knew at the same moment when it was time to go.

The evening meal was already being served when they returned. As they entered the house, Gudrid saw Nika with a strange, fearful look on her face.

"Mistress Gudrid, I have been looking for you all day. I must speak with you." Then, seeing Freydis approach, she dropped her voice to a whisper. "Alone."

42.

Gudrid could not believe the story Nika told her. "Someone has lied to you," she said firmly. "How could Freydis be guilty of such crimes, when she's been such a friend to me?"

"I'm only a thrall, Mistress Gudrid," Nika said, "and only a young girl. But thralls talk to each other. Maybe I know some things you don't."

Gudrid did not know what to think. She didn't want to believe Nika's story, but it explained a great deal—the absence of the traders, Freydis' possession of their ship, and her husband's skulking behavior, evasive even by his standards. Could Freydis really be responsible for wholesale murders, not of people who richly deserved death but of innocents? Could the thralls be mistaken? What would Freydis do now to her? If this were true, Gudrid knew she could never have anything more to do with her.

Gudrid resolved to play for time, hoping somehow to find either corroboration or counterevidence. She would put a distance between Freydis and herself, but would not confront her with Nika's revelation. Freydis, however, pressed Gudrid to walk with her and at every turning followed the path that led upward to the place of the moss and warm sunshine. The day was the twin of the one that had gone before, and Gudrid knew that once they reached that spot Freydis would want to make love.

Could Freydis be working magic on her? Who but a witch could change her face so completely from axe-wielder to soft lover?

"I've been told of what took place at Straumfjord," Gudrid said abruptly.

Freydis fixed Gudrid with a blank stare. "The thralls?" she said.
"Yes."

"And what have they told you?" Freydis said, regaining her composure. Gudrid noted the quick progression from shock to concern, to studied nonchalance. That in itself told her more about Freydis than she had ever learned in the years she had known her.

"They told how you plotted to arouse enmity between your people and Finnbogi's. How you used the women who were with them to stir up the embers because they would not share them with your men."

"It's true they would not," Freydis said.

"They would not because they were men of honor. Those women were not slaves; they came of their own choosing. Each of them agreed to give herself to any man in the crew of that ship, but they did not agree to give themselves to others. Finnbogi could have forced them to satisfy your men, but he wouldn't, because he believed that an agreement once made should be kept, even one with five orphan girls. He paid for his honor with his life."

Freydis gave out a little sneer. "What else did your slave girl tell you?"

"That the bad feeling continued through the winter and that at every turn, you did what you could to make it worse when you might have healed the wounds. Finnbogi's crew built new shelters up in the woods to get away from you and were prepared to wait out the winter there.

"One morning early, as spring was approaching, you slipped out of your husband's bed and went outside. The sun was up when you returned, and you stormed in the door shouting rape. Then you hurled insults at your husband, calling him a weakling incapable of avenging a woman's honor."

"And then?" Freydis said, almost as one who was hearing an exciting story for the first time.

"Then he led the Greenland men into the woods. The attack did not take long—the Icelanders were asleep.

"What happened next is what surprised me most," Gudrid continued. "After the bloody deed was done, your men pulled the five women out into the clearing in front of their house. You ordered them to kill the women! God damn you! How could you do such a thing?" Gudrid felt herself losing the control she had struggled so hard to maintain. "And still they would not do it! So you took the axe yourself and one by one you split their skulls."

Gudrid withdrew a small distance away from Freydis, sat on a rock, and buried her face in her hands. The thought that Freydis might magically produce an axe and spill her own brains occurred to her, but at the moment she did not care.

Freydis walked over to Gudrid. "You're not pleased by this bit of news, I see."

"You don't even deny it?"

"No, it's all the way you told it. I'm surprised at the accuracy of it actually, after three tellings. There are one or two points where you got it slightly wrong, but . . ."

Gudrid looked up at Freydis. "I cannot believe that you take this so lightly. Have you no sense of shame?"

"Shame? Why should I feel shame? I've played by the same rules men play by, the ones they use to get power and wealth and that strange thing they call honor. And I've won. I have wealth. I have a fine ship. I rule my house. And I have you."

Gudrid stood up and backed away. "What about your brother? What will he do when he finds out about this?"

"He'll do nothing at all. He already knows. I told him. I rule Leif, even as I rule my little husband."

"Leif? How?"

"When we were growing up, I could see what he was destined for. It was not only that he's Erik's elder son. Erik made no secret of his love for Thorstein. No, it's because Leif has the capacity to manage affairs: he has energy, he has confidence, and he attends to details. The same as I do. But he lacks imagination and foresight. These I provide."

"So now you are the ruler of Greenland," Gudrid said. "Then maybe there is still hope, although I don't know what to think of you. You did promise to help the people of Stokaness. Though you have committed murders, I have never known you to break a promise. Will you keep this one?"

"Of course I will," Freydis said, "and you will help me remember, when I have need of you. Come, my little snowbird, we haven't much farther to go till we reach our nest."

Gudrid stepped back abruptly. "You think you can use me the way you use everyone else?"

"Of course. You're no different. Everyone has eyelets and hooks that can be used to turn and tie them. Stokaness is your great hook, and I have the rope to hold it fast. So let's get on with it. I have need of you. Now."

Gudrid felt the blood rushing to her face. She wanted to scream at Freydis, to hit her, to kill her. She thought with regret of what this might mean for her cousins at Stokaness, but not even for them could she give herself now.

"No, Freydis, you are wrong. I will have no more of you. Not today, not ever."

Not waiting for a response, she hurried down the path, feeling the heat of Freydis' eyes boring into her back.

43.

Torfin returned to Einarsfjord shortly before midsummer. To forestall gossip, she told him that Freydis had visited and that they had fallen out. She held in reserve her knowledge of what Freydis had done in Vinland, in case Torfin should ask for a reason, but to her relief, he did not seem to care.

"I spoke with Leif," Torfin said. "He's having a midsummer feast. We're to be his honored guests."

"You're a poor joker, Torfin," Gudrid said. "I'd imagine we're the last people on earth that Leif would want across from him."

"I wouldn't disagree with you," he replied. "Nevertheless, it's true."

"I can't be part of his merriment. Tell him I'm ill."

"You haven't been sick a day since I met you. You have the constitution of an ox."

"I'll think of some other excuse, then. I can't go. Not after what he's done."

"You have to go. As long as we're in Greenland, we're in his power. We don't dare offend him. And while we're there, you'll keep your tongue in your mouth."

Gudrid felt her face redden, exactly as it had during her last interview with Freydis, but she couldn't think of anything reasonable to say. By his lights, Torfin was right. The thing to do was to keep Leif mollified until they could collect on their debts and then get out.

Torfin brought the ship around to Eriksfjord with Gudrid, young Snorri, and Nika. The elder Snorri and his colonists stayed where they were.

On the appointed day Gudrid and Torfin dressed in their finest. Gudrid wore the gold brooches that Einar had given her. She'd never seen any larger or more finely wrought in Iceland or Greenland.

When they went on shore the ale and mead were already flowing, and the guests spilled out of the main house into the side buildings and down to the shore. This is no ordinary party, Gudrid thought, but she could not think of a reason for Leif's largesse.

They entered the house that once had been Erik's and looked around for Leif, in order to give the customary greeting of guest to host. At the moment, he was nowhere to be seen. A group of men near the fire were engaged in the telling of ribald jokes, and their laughter, together with that of some of the women who stood about in various poses of feigned disinterest, helped to raise the degree of noise even above what was usual at feasts like this. A man and a woman to their left were having a domestic quarrel. Gudrid found herself straining to catch the details of their sex life, which was the subject of their argument. A beef bone whizzed past her ear. In the haze, off to one side, she caught sight of Ymir.

Freydis was talking with some people Gudrid knew only vaguely, but when she saw Gudrid, she came over, smiled, and held out her hands. Gudrid returned the gesture but not the smile, and after a few words Freydis moved on.

Then Leif appeared, and he soon was leading Torfin and Gudrid to their places of honor. Thjodhild was seated next to Leif, and Gudrid saw even more clearly the rapid inroads of age on Leif's mother. Perhaps it is not age only, she thought as memories of Thjodhild's rantings during Erik's last sickness passed through her mind. The meaning of Thjodhild's presence at the high seat was not lost on Gudrid. Leif had yet to become betrothed. He would still be under Freydis' influence, then.

After a decent interval Torfin rose, and Leif followed shortly, leaving Gudrid alone with Thjodhild. Gudrid tried to think of something she might say to her, but she could only stare, fascinated, at the twitch of her eye. Thjodhild stared back at Gudrid's breast, at precisely the place where the amulet lay hidden. Then Freydis sat down next to Gudrid in the seat Torfin had just vacated, and Gudrid was almost grateful for the intrusion of another, whoever that might be.

"Soon those red lips of yours will be as brown and cracked as hers," Freydis said. "And your eyes as wrinkled." Gudrid was sure that Thjodhild could hear what Freydis was saying. "And those beautiful breasts will become as distended and misshapen as Thjodhild's."

Gudrid could not let this go on. "And so they shall. Do you imagine that you will escape the pursuit of time?"

"By no means, my pretty one. But I know how to make the best of the time that is given me. That is the only thing that has been given. Everything else I take."

"You must have some sense of honor," Gudrid said. "Even men do. You did promise to help the Stokanessers, and when you made the promise, you did not attach any condition."

"Promises! What's a promise? A noise in the wind. To be kept when advisable, to be broken when expedient!"

"You will not help, then."

"Of course I will. But you must help me." Gudrid turned aside from her glance.

"Once I thought you were my friend. Now I see that to you I am just a thing, to be used and discarded."

"What makes you think you are better than the others? You are no different from them."

"I know. That's why I'm afraid of you. But not so afraid that I will be your slave."

"You'd reconsider if you knew what's in store for you. But to return to your question—yes, I will get old too. That's why I must get my power now. What's more useless than an old woman? The old men have power, and so they are revered, their white beards looked up to as signs of wisdom. Old women are scorned, spat upon, though their dugs are no more wrinkled than those of the men. Have you ever seen an old man naked? It's not a pretty sight."

Freydis accepted a horn of ale from a thrall. "The old queens were not derided. Asa of Norway. Ethelflaed of Mercia. Maeve of Connacht. Theodora of Mikklagard. Zenobia of Palmyra. And Aud the Deep-Minded, who was queen in Ireland before she brought your grandfather to Iceland. They were revered beyond the men because they were so rare. They were buried in ships, or in great mounds. That's what I want—a ship's burial! Freydis the Bastard, cruel but wise! And to that end, I must see that no one would thwart my will, or if they do, they pay the price."

"The Stokanessers have not thwarted you. Why revenge yourself on them?"

"Not them, Gudrid. You."

Then Freydis relaxed her stern tone and adopted a brighter expression, and Gudrid was left in a quandary whether Freydis was playing with her or really meant to carry out her threat. Freydis went on about inconsequential, mildly funny happenings in Greenland and on the Vinland voyage. By this time Torfin had returned and was standing beside, then in front of, Freydis with growing impatience. Finally he spoke.

"I'd like to have my seat, sister-in-law."

"Ah, my dear Torfin, do not be so impatient. We perhaps should have a small discussion of who this seat belongs to."

"What do you mean, Freydis? Gudrid and I were invited by your brother as guests of honor."

"As I recall, the invitation went specifically to Gudrid."

"What difference does it make? She's my wife." Then Torfin lost the remainder of his reserve. "Get out of my chair, woman, or do I have to throw you out?"

"Rein in your temper, Torfin." Freydis spoke in a louder tone. "I have as much right to be called this woman's husband as you. Which of us knows her pretty body better?"

Torfin stood mute. Some of the others around began to take notice of the conversation, and the surrounding din softened to a buzz.

"For example, Torfin, you who have explored the great ocean. How well have you explored Gudrid's round belly? When is the last time your fingers put into the warm cove of her cunt, your lips tasted the sweet juice of her love? Mine have been there since!

"And I can tell you, O Sea Rover, that from the tips of her soft hairs to the crook of her knee, her thighs are perfect, without spot or blemish!"

Torfin's expression became increasingly grave during Freydis' speech, his face redder. By now nearly everyone in the hall was listening to this. The only sound was that of whispers, of those only lately come to attention being filled in on details by those who earlier had caught the drift.

Torfin stood still only for a moment longer. Then he took Gudrid by the arm, nearly flinging her from the chair, and dragged her to the end of the hall. There he let loose his anger.

Gudrid faced him, fire in her eyes. The full import of Freydis' treachery was only now beginning to sink in, as well as the shrewdness with which Freydis had predicted the reaction of this man who was her husband.

People crowded around them, Leif and Freydis in the foreground. She struggled to find the proper words to answer her husband.

"I would rather you had been spared this embarrassment to your honor, but you are the father of any hurt that has come to you. You took my amulet from me, made me skulk into the woods to hide it . . ."

Even now she wanted to reach out to him. She knew the blame was not entirely on his side. Was this amulet really that important? It came to her that aside from his peremptory order to rid herself of it, she could not think of any other cause for complaint. He had a far heavier recrimination to lodge against her. Nevertheless, she could not bring herself to yield.

"I acknowledge before you all that Freydis was my lover. Her love was sweet and it was good. I regret none of it. Therefore I ask no forgiveness, either of God or of man!"

She stared at her husband, then at Leif and the other men. She gazed defiantly at them all.

After that she went silently with Torfin down to the ship, where he stormed from stem to stern, stopping only to glare in Gudrid's direction. At last, the force of his emotion spent, he sat down beside her.

"You'll have to leave Greenland right away. The Dane was planning to go in a month or two. He didn't get much for his goods, because he wouldn't wait to be paid. I'm sure that a piece or two of gold will get him to leave sooner. There's a convent now in Iceland. He will take you there."

"And you'll come for me?"

"When my anger cools."

"What of our son?"

"I will find a woman here who will raise him properly."

"You're a hard man, Torfin, harder than I ever thought possible."

Gudrid rose then and left the ship. She walked alone along the shore until the figure of Nika came running to join her. She fell at Gudrid's feet, tears flowing freely from her eyes.

"Mistress Gudrid, I . . ."

Gudrid reached out to touch her. "Rise, Nika. I may have no other power left in this world, but this power I still do have. By these words I free you. She removed a gold brooch and exchanged it for one of leather that Nika wore. Then she exchanged the ones on the other side. After that they walked in silence, past the church of Thjodhild, where the priest stood outside, and on farther still, until the sun went out of sight past the stone mountain.

44.

When Gudrid awoke, the moon was shining on the peaks and sparkling drops of light were splashing up from the ripples on the fjord. Only a few of Torfin's company were sleeping on board the ship. Gudrid rose silently and wrapped herself in warm wool and moved toward the wooden plank that led to shore.

No one was about except for one of Leif's henchmen. He looked her way but made no move to prevent her going along the shore toward the church of Thjodhild.

Thjodhild! She saw now how much Thjodhild must be involved in everything that afflicted her. She coveted the amulet. Was it only for the amulet that she sent thralls to the fells and Inga to Vinland?

Gudrid had almost reached the church when instinct made her dive beneath a boulder resting against the slope of the hill. Just in time too. Two forms were making their way up the path. Thjodhild and Inga treaded softly past to the door and in. Gudrid heard nothing except muddled voices, then a scream, then quiet. The impulse to run was strong. The stone hung askew against a breast. She must enter the church and face Thjodhild, just as she faced Freydis.

Though she'd seen them once before, in the wild, she was not prepared, in the dim light of a lamp, to see Thjodhild the Christian dressed in seeress' garb, with Inga beside her, spreading the raven's entrails on a Christian altar. They both heard the door as she came in and, whispering "The priest!", they brushed aside the dead bird and turned to face the intruder.

Their faces froze when they saw Gudrid. For a moment no one spoke. Then Gudrid did.

"You come late to pray, Mother-in-Law. Or were you only here to sweep the crumbs from the altar?"

Thjodhild did not reply.

"What do you want from me?"

"You know what it is, daughter. You're no fool."

"It's hardly a thing a Christian should lust after."

"You've held onto it yourself at great cost."

"It was my mother's . . ."

Thjodhild broke into a harsh laugh. Inga stared at Gudrid. There was hate in her eye.

The two of them approached Gudrid menacingly, from different angles.

"Give me the stone," said Thjodhild.

"Do it," said Inga. The girl's wiry arms were bare, and Gudrid could see the power in them.

"What can you give me in return?"

Thjodhild seemed ready to break again into the fearful laugh, but instead, she smiled.

"What do you want?"

"Your son's friendship for the Stokanessers. And that the Icelander called Ymir should be sent away."

Thjodhild smiled, a sickening gap-toothed smile. "What you ask is impossible. Haven't you seen the warriors come up to Brattahlid? The ships?"

Gudrid was too consumed by her own pain of heart to have noticed much of anything, but now she did see in her mind, five, six ships beached alongside Torfin's, and two more in the fjord.

"Some Stokanessers killed one of Leif's thralls. I can do nothing for you now, though I know how much you would like to help them for your honor's sake."

"What do you know of honor?"

"More than you can imagine, daughter. But I will have your magic!"

Thjodhild lunged forward, grasping for Gudrid's arm, while Inga sprang to the side and grabbed her other arm. She sank to the floor, the rough stones grinding into her back, with Thjodhild and Inga on top of her. Hands groped around her neck.

She lashed out with elbows and jaws. Her spine warped. The bodies slammed down on her, the one old and noxious, the other young and warm in the heat of the fight. Her teeth sank into flesh, and one of her arms was loose.

Loose but not free. Pinned as she was, she could not pull back enough to deliver a hard blow. They were smothering her.

She jerked. It took all the strength she had, and Inga bounced up only a little, but it was enough. Gudrid shot her fist into Inga's breast, sending the girl reeling backward, screaming. Then she rose with the weight of Thjodhild hanging on, and rammed the woman's head against a doorpost. Thjodhild slumped off as Inga rebounded in a fury. Gudrid managed a foot to Thjodhild's face the instant before Inga's body hit her, throwing her again to the floor.

Inga was even stronger than she looked. She had Gudrid down, arms pinned to the floor, and then one hand went to Gudrid's throat. Gudrid wrenched the freed arm forward just in time to keep the clutching fingers short of their target, but she was tiring. Inga showed no sign of weakening. Thjodhild moaned and rolled over.

The thought that Thjodhild might revive and come to Inga's aid gave Gudrid a brief burst of energy and will. She pushed Inga up and over onto her back. They fought like this, clawing, slugging, ripping loose pieces of each other's clothing. The sweat on their bodies glistened in the lamplight. Inga's strength had no end, and it was only Gudrid's own need to prevail that enabled her jaws to find Inga's nipple and bite it off.

Gudrid ran for the door. She could have escaped, but she paused to see that she still had the amulet. Inga caught from behind what little remained of her shift, the force of the grasp ripping it free. Gudrid again tried to run, but Inga's arms encircled her neck. Gudrid writhed to get free, but Inga's naked thighs clung to her loins as the fingers pressed into the sockets of her eyes. Nauseous with pain, she felt herself going down, down. She was on her knees, retching. She clawed desperately at the evil tendrils clinging to her face. Her last reservoir of strength was in her legs. She thrust herself upward, unbalancing Inga, and hurled their combined weight against the wall, twisting at the moment of impact to smash the back of Inga's skull onto a protruding stone.

The weight dropped from her, and she ran into the open. She didn't feel the sweaty chill until she reached the ships. As silently as she could, she tiptoed up Torfin's gangplank. She held her hand between her breasts, enclosing the amulet.

Torfin had begun the night ashore, but now he was sitting on the port gunwale amidships.

"Do you always run around naked at night, or is this something new?"

She expected him to resume his angry tirade, and she would have to stand there shivering until he was through. He didn't though. Apparently this bizarre event meant little to him, compared with what had gone before.

"You thought you could sneak off unnoticed," he said calmly. "You may think I'm not very careful, not even posting a guard, but that's just to throw Leif off. I don't want to alert him. I know what's going on. You've been out in the moonlight, playing with the Devil."

"Two devils. They tried to kill me."

"God protects His own. But you have your amulet, I see."

"Leif wants more than rents from the people of Stokaness. He'll kill them if they don't submit. You know this, don't you."

"Yes."

"And you said nothing to me about it."

"What could I say? It's not as though it won't cost us anything. We're going to have to get out of here before I can collect most of what the Greenlanders owe me."

"We?"

"Yes. I thought the Dane was a smart man. He's staying on to settle small accounts. It's the Greenlanders who will settle with him. We will go before any blood is shed. Once begun, the slaughter will not be limited to Stokaness."

"When do you plan to leave?"

"Two more nights should be safe. No more. I've sent a messenger to Einarsfjord, to tell Snorri's people to cross over the isthmus and be ready for me to pick them up. I'm pressing my debtors as hard as I dare. Most of them are here, as you can see. Not a word of this to anyone, understand? Leif must not know I'm getting ready to leave. I put some of my goods there on the bank, to make him think I'll be here a while."

"How can you leave my cousins to die? I know them well enough. They won't give in anymore. They're a stiff-necked lot."

"It runs in the family."

"It's true they are my kin."

"They're not mine."

Torfin slouched down into the ship, pulled his cape around his head, and fell to sleep.

In the morning it seemed as though all of Greenland had settled on Eriksfjord. The clatter of arms was heard aboard the ships. Men sat on the shore burnishing their helmets.

All of Torfin's men were in and around the ship, making furtive preparations for their escape. Some of the crew were visibly frightened, and several had the temerity to urge even greater haste, but Torfin always ended such conversations by peering down the fjord. One large landowner had gained his particular trust and was in debt to Torfin the weight of a calf in silver. "Everyone else in Greenland is here," Torfin would say. "He'll come too."

As for their son, Torfin had taken him away from her, and the child now lay sleeping in another woman's arms. She resented that her own child had suffered this disruption with so little complaint.

What can I do? she thought. They're outnumbered over there. I've had only false friends, and no one to turn to now. I can't blame my husband for wanting to go. The others are right. Torfin's greed holds him here too long as it is.

She looked slowly about the encampment with desperate sad eyes, at the ships and boats on the shore, the tents, the animals, the people. How somber the gathering before a fight, even one like this, in which those on this shore had little to fear.

Suddenly she knew what she must do.

45.

She would wait for the moon to follow the sun over the mountaintops. So far everything had gone according to plan, and she would take no unneeded risks now.

The most important thing was to find a grappling hook with its rope of hide attached. This had taken some time—she must not arouse interest by appearing to be searching for something. During the day she sat in the jumble of goods amidships, first in one place, then another, while mending a cape. Her eyes cast over all the ship's gear, down into the crevices, until they found the hook buried amid a pile of sailcloth. She had despaired of ever getting it free, but with one hand she did, while smoothing the cape on her lap. Now it lay beside her, against the mast.

She couldn't get down the gangplank again without being followed. Torfin had told her that. So it would all be up to Nika.

The moon was well down now, and she considered it dark enough to creep about. One of the crewmen went to the stern to relieve his bowels. He seemed a long time at it, but when he had finally finished and returned to his bedplace, she took comfort that no one would think much of her own going aft. She shivered nevertheless as she made her way, her hands going over the knots in the rope.

The water slapped against the side of the ship. She threw the rope over the side and jammed the hook onto the gunwale. How foolish, she thought, this stealthy flight. How even more foolish, where she was going. She peered forward to catch a moment when the lookouts might both be looking in another direction.

She climbed over the side as quickly and as noiselessly as she could and let herself down, knot by knot. Her fingers ached when her foot finally touched the steering oar, just above the point where it entered the water. She felt it move when she settled part of her weight onto it, and the ship shifted and groaned slightly.

Where was the boat? She looked around in the darkness, but could not see it. Nika had never failed her before! There was no way she could climb back up the rope. She could give up the game and call for help. She could swim . . .

A liquid murmuring came to her ears and a dim shape hove in sight around the stern. In the boat was Nika, huddled down, paddling slowly with part of an oar. She let the boat drift toward the ship, then silently paddled close enough for Gudrid to step in. Then they drifted again until they'd made enough distance that they dared try to row.

It looked so easy when the men did it. Why was it so much trouble now, Nika on one side, Gudrid on the other, and no one to steer? They'd planned to drift to the little cove beyond the hill, where Nika would get out. Then Gudrid would go over to Stoka-ness. Nika, however, kept turning the boat offshore.

"Nika," Gudrid whispered. "Stop!"

"Mistress Gudrid, I won't leave you. You can't make me. I'm free now. I will go where you go. I don't care what happens." She held Gudrid's sleeve for a moment, then went back to rowing. Gudrid's impulse was to argue with her, but then she thought better.

"My sister," she said, and she held Nika close in the dark.

They managed a sinuous course across the fjord, and now, as the eastern sky began to lighten, they saw the houses of Stokaness.

The boat struck shore, but no one seemed to be up. Then a lookout hailed them, and several men came out of the house. There were rough words at first, but when they saw that only two women were in the boat, they relaxed and led them to the house.

Gudrid felt more afraid to face these people now than she did of anything that might happen later. Nika held her hand as they entered the house. Always before, it had been she who led Nika through difficulty. Now she kept close to Nika, grateful for the comfort of a friend.

Asgrim's face showed his surprise, but he took Gudrid's hands as if she were returning from a short visit. There was an awkwardness: Asgrim was struggling within about whether to show Gudrid to the high seat. She ended the hesitation by selecting a vacant space near the end of the platform. Someone brought bedding.

In the morning Gudrid looked about the farm. There were a few animals in the courtyard, and it did not take an experienced eye to see that only the worst had been left to them. Rheumy-eyed sheep lifted their heads at Gudrid's approach. Three or four cows grazed listlessly.

Inside the house there was a barren feeling, as though many things were lacking, small things that one ordinarily would not notice but that were obvious now by their absence.

Knut and Floki and many from their households came over when they heard that Gudrid was there. They greeted her as Asgrim had done, correctly but without enthusiasm. They questioned her concerning the preparations on the other shore and inquired of Torfin's intentions. Then they came to the point.

"Why are you here?"

She considered how to answer. Their grievance against her was real. Had she not left them, Leif might not have gone as far as he did. The chief men of Greenland might have restrained him for their own sakes, if not for the sake of custom. She had, it was true, caused aid to come their way when they were in need, but even one as young as she knew well that charity often evoked not loyalty, or even gratitude, but resentment. If there was a gulf between them and her, however, words would not close it. She chose the simple answer.

"I have come to share your fate."

Floki's look made it clear he did not believe her. Knut eyed her closely, considering, tapping his foot. Asgrim's worried look did not change. They stood like that for some time. Gudrid stood too, her head bowed a little, but not too much, ready to accept whatever judgment they might make.

Then Hildigunn came to her, and Unn, and then Kol and several others. Unn embraced her. A baby girl not two winters old tugged at the folds of Unn's dress and of Gudrid's also, and Gudrid reached down to lift her up. This child looked so much like the other, Helga, that Gudrid had tried to save.

By now most of them had shown her their goodwill. Smiles returned to faces that for a long time had known nothing but worry. Even Floki gave his shoulders a little shrug.

The lightness around her was for the moment only. Their situation closed in upon them again. Even a woman untrained in fighting could see how inadequate their preparations were. Yet she could think of nothing better, and she did her best to encourage them.

Knut made everything explicit. "We are so few. We have sought a parley with Leif, but he sends the henchman Ymir, who only wants our blood."

"Would it be possible to escape over the fell?"

"To where? To an arm of the sea or to more mountains? Or to Freydis' estate? We'd expect her to stand by her brother."

"What else is there, then? Surely you don't intend to let them come and . . ."

To this they were silent.

Night came. The moon dappled the fjord. Lookouts stood on the hillock facing the water. Gudrid watched with them. The moon set. First light hovered over the eastern crests. Now one could see the far shore. A small shape appeared on the water and grew larger. It was a ship. Word was passed, and everyone came out with their weapons, expecting more sails. Gudrid resolved that before the attackers touched shore, she would pass her amulet to the child of Unn and Kol, secretly if need be.

No other ships appeared, however, and the Stokanessers watched as the sail came close enough to be recognized. It was Torfin's! Now Gudrid went down to the shore and watched as her husband leaped from the bow, waded ashore, and strode up the bank. He approached Gudrid clothed in helmet and coat of mail, with a shield on his arm, but the expression on his face as he removed his helmet was not what she expected. It was soft and smiling, and she saw the cast of eye that bespoke only admiration. He took her hands in his, and as he did this, he knelt before her and kissed them. Rising, he spoke.

"True wife, you've showed what you are made of. I ask you to forgive a foolish man." He reached for her, to take her in his arms.

She yearned to press herself into his embrace. How could she not acknowledge his noble act, something he'd done in spite of her having brought him to a humiliation as great as her own? Yet she could not forget the angry words that had passed between them. The best she could do was to smile and take his hands, and for the moment it seemed enough.

Now all attention turned to the men who were coming down from the beached ship. Gudrid greeted the crewmen who had chosen to come with her husband. She thought of one other.

"Where is our son?" she asked Torfin.

This was answered by a cry from the ship. She ran down to the shore, reaching up her arms as the boy was handed down. She kissed and hugged and cooed, and did not blame him for his insouciance through the days of their separation. Nor, for this brief moment, did she give any thought to the fate that awaited him now.

Torfin's men soon passed on their enthusiasm, and the feeling went around for a while that now they had a chance in a fight. Sobriety returned when Torfin's men saw how few the Stokanessers were, and some even cast dark glances at their leader.

Gudrid thought of those who had, in some way, touched or been touched by the amulet as she searched for an answer. Arnora's thrall. Hakon. Ymir. Gard. Thorstein. They were dead now, except the one on whom she most wished death. Then there were the women. One wanted her. One wanted her stone. No vision came, only vague shadows.

At this moment a shout came from the fjord. A boat had come near. It was one of Leif's henchmen.

"Noble Torfin. Leif calls to you as a friend. He would like to speak with you, to correct you as gently as he can, to call you away from this foolish venture."

"I will not speak with the unspeakable," Torfin began, and grasping a spear, he rose to go down to the shore. Gudrid stopped him.

"You must do as he wants. Don't ask me why. I can't explain yet, but something tells me we must speak with Leif. I do know that you must demand one condition. Thjodhild and Freydis must both come with him."

46.

The day broke with promise. The sun rose precisely between two crags and spread its light underneath the cloud bank that was slowly moving in from the west. But clouds soon covered the sky and lowered, so that rain now appeared imminent.

Torfin and Kol pushed the boat into the water. Knut came out of the house and strode down the slope, striving to appear confident but betraying his nervousness by the way he fingered the hilt of his sword. He was joined by three others. The six of them stood in the boat, looking up toward Gudrid. Now, afraid they might decide to leave her behind, she ran down to the shore.

She still wondered why Leif had asked for the parley. True, his word had come as a haughty demand, yet with so much force available to him, why should he have broken the silence other than by the cry of battle? She answered her own question. With Torfin's men in Stokaness, he had ever the slightest fear that others might join against him, and this he wished to forestall by overawing her husband.

The parley was to be held at the only place that would expose neither side to treachery, a small headland open to the view of both Stokaness and Brattahlid. Across the fjord a second boat departed from the shore, with four rowers and several figures seated in front.

Each side was to bring six armed men, no more. Six men and two women were visible, but the Stokanessers watched closely to make sure others were not crouched low.

The headland was rocky and lifeless except for green and orange lichen tucked into the crevices. The wind had picked up too, so that now as she stepped ashore, it was all Gudrid could do to hold her cape against her body.

As the other boat approached, they all strained to see who Leif had brought with him. The unkempt hair of Thjodhild could be recognized halfway across the water, and Freydis' red hair. Leif would not have neglected to include Ymir in his party. The others were good swordsmen, no doubt, but otherwise not important. The boat came within hailing distance, but no words were spoken. The oars slapped the water. The water ran from them like blood from a ladle.

Leif stood up as the boat touched shore, and he stretched out his hand in the manner of a king. Torfin and Knut went forward to greet him, but they did not take his hand. Leif wasted no time with polite phrases.

"You have not pleased me, Torfin, by going over without my leave. Perhaps you think you can come and go in Greenland as you wish, regardless of my displeasure."

"I came only for what is mine," Torfin replied, "but if I stay a while, what concern is that of yours? Other folk sail on these fjords without asking your permission."

"Of late they do not go to Stokaness." Ymir said this, and Gudrid jumped at the voice. Ymir stepped toward her, looking her up and down. The face was older than she had remembered, but the sneer was the same. "Some men still do go," he said as though correcting himself. "It's said easy women are there, to be had for the price of a chicken."

Gudrid flashed hot and was about to respond to the insult, but Torfin had already stepped forward, sword drawn. He faced Ymir, but spoke in a sideling way to Leif.

"This man's words demand retribution. By your honor and mine, I claim the right of combat, here and now."

Leif seemed taken aback by this sudden turn of events. Ymir smiled as he drew his sword. Gudrid could only stand and compare the two men who stood ready to fight. Ymir she had always remembered as a giant, yet he was only somewhat taller than Torfin. As for girth and sinew, here it appeared they were well matched. What was it then about Ymir that made him seem so unnaturally large? At once she knew. His arms—Ymir's arms were longer than those of any other man she had ever seen.

He swung his sword in front of him to the full extent of his reach. Torfin jumped back, surprised by the broad arc that Ymir's steel could command. He brought his own sword into play quickly. Metal rang against metal. Out of the corner of her eye, Gudrid could see Leif move nimbly out of the way when the fighters came close to him. It was clear he knew who would win.

Though Torfin was outreached, Ymir's victory did not come easily, and a hint of worry now came into Leif's placid face. Swords clanged, incessant and loud, while now and again one man gained a momentary advantage and the other was forced back. Ymir thrusted, and Torfin parried the stroke aside. Ymir slashed, and Torfin jumped to avoid the tip of the blade. But the brows of the Stokanessers furrowed, and their faces fell as Torfin was forced more and more to defend, with little chance himself to attack. Soon he must tire.

Ymir's sword nicked Torfin's sleeve twice, but no blood flowed. Then Torfin put together a series of thrusts that would have put many a man into his grave, but Ymir was strong enough to bring his sword down each time. On the last of these parries, Ymir's steel came around in a wider arc than usual, and Torfin's arm was torn and bloody. His sword clattered to the stone.

Torfin retrieved it before Ymir could deliver the deathblow, but he stood there, bleeding slowly, the sword drooping awkwardly from the hand that was not meant to hold it. A calm gloat spread across Ymir's face, sickeningly sweet like spoiled honey. He stood with his sword now, running his finger lightly over the edge. Then he spoke to Gudrid.

"You think, woman, that the stone you wear may save you from me, the way it did that other time. You're going to wish it didn't have the power. You're going to be my ship woman. I will have you when I want you, as long as you are pleasing to me."

Gudrid shuddered, but the fear for herself was overpowered immediately by a stronger emotion. As Ymir turned back to finish Torfin off, she looked at the man she called husband and knew that she truly loved him. How much she yearned to throw herself into his arms, to beg his forgiveness as he had begged hers. She was filled with regret that she had not accepted his gesture with the grace it had deserved.

Torfin stood on the blood-spattered rock, his face covered with bewilderment. His left hand moved the sword slowly, unsurely. Ymir moved his sword in quick loops, much as a butcher might circle his knife before cutting the life out of a sheep.

His smile was the same as long ago, when Gudrid was the one he was assailing.

Then Torfin's sword came to life. He leaped sideways as Ymir's blade came around, and then he brought his own sword up as quickly and as truly as if his accustomed hand were wielding it. The tip caught Ymir's groin. The rapist's face showed his surprise, but he was not quick enough to avoid Torfin's next thrust. Ymir looked down dumbly as his gut spouted red.

He stood for a moment, gazing at the wound. Then he began to sink, his knees buckling, his sword slipping from his hand. The face hit the ground, the head bounced, the body lay still. Knut picked up the sword, which had fallen in front of him. Gudrid took her scarf from her head and bound up Torfin's wound. He responded to her ministration in a new way, and Gudrid could feel the unspoken message of one who loves.

Leif's voice broke the thought.

"Do not think this changes anything. He was a henchman of mine, nothing more. I have others. I came here to speak with you because it is not my wish to do injury to one such as you, of illustrious family. Nor to this lady, who was my brother's wife.

"Now, let my terms be known to you, and generous they are! First, I ask no recompense for the killing of Ymir, either in gold or in goods. Second, you are free to leave Greenland with your ship and goods and as many of the people of Stokaness as you can or will carry. Third, any you leave behind will become my thralls, for me to use as I will, either in Greenland or to be sold beyond the sea."

When Leif had finished, he stood back, pleased with himself, obviously expecting these terms to be accepted. Even Gudrid wondered what the men would do. They could not take everyone back to Iceland, not with a shipload of colonists waiting on the isthmus, but wouldn't it be better to save some than for all to die? Brave as Torfin's men and the men of Stokaness might be, there were not enough of them. They had no choice.

Such reckoning did not consider the nature of a man like Torfin.

He paused, seeming to consider, but she knew what his answer would be. He would not back away.

The drizzle had stopped, but now it started again, and Gudrid felt colder than she ever had before, even in the middle of winter, even when she and Nika were caught in the snowstorm, fleeing from Thorstein. Freydis' face showed nothing of her feelings in this matter. Thjodhild had been staring at Gudrid the whole time.

She searched for some solace in faith, and the face of Brother Ulf moved through her memory. "No one should put bounds on the love of God," he'd said, and his life showed he believed it. Later he'd said something more mysterious: "Dreams carry within them the seeds of their own disappointment." She still didn't understand this Faith that spoke of God's love and yet placed so little value on this earth that God had created. Then Ulf faded, and she saw instead Sira Geir, and she knew that he represented most what would come in place of the old religion. For how many years, she did not know, the land would be trod by the boots of such priests, turning holy words to the service of tyranny.

The gray clouds of the two beliefs roiled confusion in her mind. Then, at the darkest instant, a bright rift opened, of blue enlightenment.

It was the missing rune. The old religion had covered it with magic. The new one buried it under articles of faith. It was there, nevertheless, for the one who could find it, and Gudrid now had it firmly in her grasp.

It was the rune of reason.

She'd had it all the time, and didn't know it. Reason had led her to Thjodhild as the one whose curse had set her father against her, and she'd been right in her logic. Now she must use that same logic to solve the darker mysteries still before her.

So many riddles, jammed together like logs in a stream, and so little time to think. Nothing came to her at first, but then she had a little intuition. The questions involving Bjorn were the most paradoxical. There might be a reason for Thjodhild's curse and for her promoting the marriage with her elder son. But why would Bjorn oppose her marrying Leif if he'd had no objection to Thorstein? Even he admitted that Leif was the better man. Why did Bjorn, who valued honor above everything, feel dishonor in Erik's presence? And what was Bjorn trying to say about Horn Strands?

She didn't know.

Then the words of the sibyl came to her: "You will marry as well as you might in Greenland." The seeress had been wrong in this at least.

Or had she?

"What will you do if we refuse your terms?" Gudrid said to Leif.

"My answer is the same as Tryggvason's: Death to those who defy me."

Gudrid drew herself up to full height.

"You would kill your own sister?"

Leif showed his surprise. "What do you mean? I have nothing against Freydis."

"Freydis is not your sister. I am your sister."

Leif lost his composed look for an instant but regained it so fast Gudrid doubted anyone saw it except her. Then he laughed. "It would appear that Erik has ranged farther afield than I thought."

"Not Erik. Thjodhild."

Gudrid looked straight at Thjodhild when she said this, and Thjodhild screamed a scream such as one hears from birch groves on spring-moon nights.

"How do you say this?" said Leif.

"Bjorn Vifilsson was your father, just as he was mine."

"What proof do you have?"

"Your face is proof enough. You're the very image of my father, just as Thorstein was of Erik. Do you think that Erik didn't know, or that he favored Thorstein for no reason?"

Leif spat, then trod the spittle into the moss. "That is no proof."

"Before my father died," Gudrid continued, "he spoke of Horn Strands. Everyone knows that. Do you know where that is?"

"Of course I know. It's where Erik came with his father from Norway and where he stayed with my mother the winter their wedding ale was drunk, before they moved down to my mother's farm in Haukadale."

"Who stayed there with Erik and Thjodhild?"

Thjodhild spoke now in a shouting scream. "No! Don't say it!"

Leif laughed. "This is still no proof. Erik entertained many over the years. Are we to suppose they all cuckolded him?"

"Remember this, then—the sibyl at Durkel's farm when I first came to Greenland with my father. She said that I would marry as well as I might in Greenland. I married Thorstein, not you."

For a moment Leif said nothing. Then, "It's good for me I didn't marry you, seeing the fate you led my brother to."

Gudrid did not reply, but withdrew the amulet from within her garments and held it out before Thjodhild. Thjodhild's hand began to shake.

"Bjorn wouldn't let me marry Leif," Gudrid said, "even though his only thought was to do honor to Erik. The reason is that he knew we were brother and sister."

"That can't be," Leif said. "My mother was in as good a position to know as Bjorn, and she wanted me to marry you even more than Bjorn wanted you to marry my brother!"

"Exactly. She wanted to make sure this would never come to light. If I had married you, it would have sealed Bjorn's lips forever. She didn't trust his honor. She is the one who can tell the truth in this."

Thjodhild's face was even more agitated than before, but she said nothing.

Thjodhild's silence was the last barrier to their salvation. Gudrid wished with all her heart that Thjodhild would speak. She felt for the amulet. If only she knew its secret!

The missing rune. She would apply it here. The amulet had killed men. Arnora had demonstrated its power with a poor thrall. Hakon had touched it and died. So had Gard. Thorstein touched it and the bear had gone after him and not her. Even Ymir, finally, had met his end.

But any connection between the stone and these deaths was worked out in the darkness of magic. When had she actually seen this power working? Only when men feared it. When Leif had run from it. When Erik had left off his questioning about Thorstein's death, satisfied with its explanation. And when Gudrid, trusting its power, had stood motionless as the bear went for her terror-crazed husband.

She remembered Brother Ulf, squeezing it with his fingers as though it were the Devil. Ulf still lived. And so did Snorri, her small son.

She remembered her insight in the bear cage: For every power there is a greater power to set against it. That was true if one could find that power and use it. But that was only part of it. There was something else, something that now was within her reach.

Then she saw it.

The stone had power only over those who believed in it. That was its secret. And knowing that, Gudrid now knew what to do with it. She faced Thjodhild.

"This amulet has rested on my shoulders long enough. It has grown heavy. I would give it to one who is truthful. Will you name Leif's father here and before the free men of Greenland?"

Thjodhild maintained her silence.

"If I must return to Stokaness with the truth unspoken, I will drop this amulet to the bottom of the fjord, where neither you nor anyone else will ever find it. I do not wish to be a ship woman, Leif's any more than Ymir's, and would prefer death to such a life." Thjodhild's hand reached out toward the stone, but Gudrid pulled it back. Leif's mother almost shriveled, as though seared by some supernatural fire, and Gudrid knew the woman was beaten.

"It is as you have said. It was not your father's doing. I enticed him. I was wedded to Erik against my will, and I would have kept him from my bed even then if I could have. I do not repent of what I did."

"And that is why you cursed my mother, out of jealousy. When she died of me, Bjorn would not marry again, afraid that the curse would fall on the new wife as well. He was a man of honor! If I had only known."

She thought of all the times her father had faced Leif, knowing him to be his son.

Leif was unmoved. "Let these women prate on. What concern is it of mine? The only thing that matters is those ships and men across the fjord!"

"It means only this," said Gudrid. "Now we must bow to the will of Freydis. She is Erik's only living offspring. Freydis, you'll have your ship's burial! It will be yours by right of birth."

Knut showed that he knew what was happening. He went to Freydis and knelt before her, as to a queen. Gudrid noted with satisfaction the look of pleasure on Freydis' face.

Gudrid spoke to Leif. "The people of Stokaness and the Icelanders and Freydis' friends and kin will not be so easy to master. You also would do well to bend your knee."

Leif was red with anger, and he glared at Freydis. But he spoke to the Stokanessers.

"You know that none of this is true. You know me for my magnanimity. It has always been my purpose to confirm in you the ownership of the lands at Stokaness, and your heirs also, until God takes us all."

Knut looked at Gudrid with admiration in his eyes. Torfin took her hands in his, and she kissed him.

"You will speak these words before the chieftains," Gudrid said to Leif. "Send your men across while you wait here, and let the leading landholders return in the boat. Repeat your promise in their hearing. Then we will believe you are a true son of Erik. If you are not willing to do this, we will throw in with Freydis."

The darkness passed over Leif's face like a storm cloud, and then it was gone. Standing between Thjodhild and Freydis, he was hemmed in. Thjodhild's lust for the amulet, Freydis' will to power, these would force him to submit to her demand. Gudrid recalled the scene, so many years ago, on the slopes of Snaefellsjokul, when she'd said to Leif, "There'll be a day when you'll kiss my feet and admit that you're my slave, and you'll beg me for the smallest drop of mercy." It hadn't gone exactly like that, but it was close enough. She allowed herself a thin smile.

Leif stood mast-straight. He faced Gudrid. "It shall be done," he said.

Epilogue

The ship moved away slowly from the shore as the crew hoisted the sail and the people of Stokaness raised a great cheer. Leif and Freydis and Thjodhild were across the fjord, and Gudrid was happy that, for certain now, she would not see any of them again. Thjodhild, she knew, had the amulet beneath her robe, and what good it might bring her she was happy to leave behind.

Leif's position at the head of the Greenlanders was again secure. The Stokanessers would not tell what they knew, as long as Leif remained bound to the bargain he had sealed by public oath. Nor would Thjodhild, who would have no reason to hurt her son or aid her husband's bastard. Nor would the four remaining henchmen Leif had brought to the parley. If he could not find that many loyal men, what kind of a leader was he? Freydis' eyes, which had grown bright at the prospect of power, had hardened along with the rest of her face, but at the last, when the parley had ended and Freydis was stepping into Leif's boat, she shot Gudrid a look of grudging recognition.

Gudrid picked out one special face among the crowd on shore. Brother Ulf. He'd come to see her off, and when she'd told him she no longer had the amulet, he'd offered her baptism. Despite her ambivalence concerning all things sacred, she'd known that in a world become Christian it would have been foolish to refuse. After he'd poured the water, with just the two of them together, he'd held her a brief moment, and the look in his eyes told her that for all his prayers and his tonsure, he was very much a man.

Young Snorri tottered on the rolling deck, watching the crowd recede. Gudrid led him over to his father, who shouted an order to the men forward, and then he lifted up his son and showed him how to handle a steering oar.

About the Author

John Andrews is a physicist doing research on energy conservation at Brookhaven National Laboratory on Long Island. He holds degrees from MIT and Notre Dame, has done postdoctoral research in particle physics at Yale, and is a licensed professional engineer. He lives with his wife and daughter in Sag Harbor, New York. *A Viking's Daughter* is his first novel.

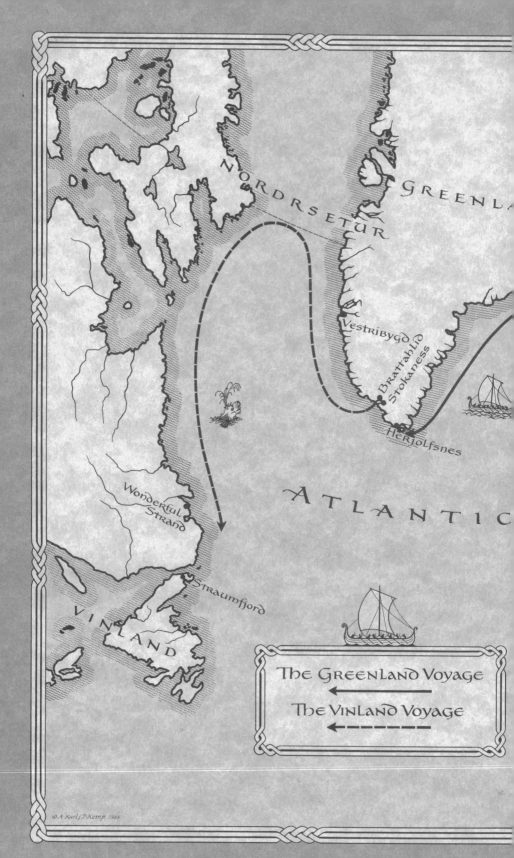